WinterWind

A Novel

Louise Adrienne Lajoie

Copyright © 2004 by Louise Adrienne Lajoie

ISBN 0-7414-1823-1

Published by:

PUBLISHING.COM

519 West Lancaster Avenue
Haverford, PA 19041-1413
Info@buybooksontheweb.com
www.buybooksontheweb.com
Toll-free (877) BUY BOOK
Local Phone (610) 520-2500
Fax (610) 519-0261

Printed in the United States of America

Printed on Recycled Paper

Published March 2004

Prologue

Baie de Saint-Jacques
P.Q., Canada

The year: 1887

The great bronze bell of the Church of Saint John-the-Baptist rang in unison with the chimes of the "Sanctus" on the altar.

The Reverend Jean-Philippe Bérard, a visiting prelate from Sherbrooke, was singing the eight o'clock Mass. Seated among the faithful attending this morning were most of the members of his immediate family.

It was obvious at a glance that Father Jean did not feel like a visitor to this altar. Too much of his youth had been spent here in the North country. These people were a part of him and no amount of time or separation would ever change that.

By anyone's measure, Bérard was a striking man: his broad, angular frame stretched more than six feet in height, and the finely chiseled nose and cheekbones lent him a genteel but authoritative air.

As he descended from the altar to the Communion rail, Father Jean caught sight of his parents, Michèl and Emilie Bérard. Kneeling alongside them were three of his sisters, two of whom were cloaked in the raiment of the religiously committed.

Life had dealt harshly with his loved ones at times; there was no denying that. It was reflected in the set of their jaws as they awaited the Host they would receive from his hands. They were indeed a hardy and courageous people and he felt a special respect for them.

The briefest of glances in his mother's direction betrayed her flagging spirits. This was not in keeping with Emilie's usually warm and cheerful nature. She appeared pinched and drawn, the ever deepening lines in her face giving testimony to the hardships she had endured for all of them.

Jean-Philippe cherished his mother and had always felt committed to protect her—a duty that fell naturally upon his shoulders as her firstborn and only son. He seemed to sense this responsibility even more keenly now that his mother was approaching her sixty-fourth year. At the very least she deserved peace of mind and contentment, and he strongly resented anything preventing it. The events of the last three days had certainly done that; they'd crept into the marrow that bound them together, and torn his family apart. It would be a long time before Jean-Philippe Bérard would be able to forget that.

Moving closer to where they knelt, Father Jean once again experienced the strong surge of emotion that never failed to rush up inside him whenever he served the Eucharist to his family. It was no less intense this time, despite the adverse circumstances surrounding this visit to Le Baie.

* * *

Earlier in the week, Father Jean had traveled to Montreal from his seminary in Sherbrooke. He'd met there with the rest of his family to bid farewell to Melinda, the youngest of his four sisters. She, her husband Joseph, and their infant son Philippe were leaving Quebec for the United States of America, a pilgrimage that Father Jean had prayed never would be undertaken.

His twin sisters, Soeur Marie-Agathe and Soeur Marie-Adèle, had gained permission to make the trip from their nunnery at Courrèges, a remote little village five miles west of Le Baie. An unusual concession, seldom ever granted. This was the first time these nuns had journeyed so far from their motherhouse since the taking of their novitiate veils. It made for a nervous stomach for Sister Marie-Agathe, the frailer and less adventurous of the two. During the sixty-mile journey into the city, she'd sat with Sister Marie-Adèle, a bit apart from the rest of the family, observing periods of silence as the train brought them nearer to their destination.

Marie-Élise, the eldest of the girls and Father Jean's favorite sister, sat next to Melinda and the baby, wanting to feel the nearness of them until the very last moment. She relieved Melinda of the child from time to time, carrying him across the aisle now and again to Emilie's arms for a soothing, grandmotherly caress.

At some point Marie-Élise had taken over the nurturing of the family. Neither she nor her mother knew exactly when it had happened ... only that it had. Actually it had begun some years before when, following their marriage, Marie-Élise and Daniel decided to make their home with her parents.

* * *

Coming east from Sherbrooke to join them, Father Jean kept mulling over the sequence of events that had brought the Bérard family to the horns of this dilemma. He found them as frustrating and as difficult to understand now as he had in the very beginning. Opening his breviary, he chose instead to read his offices rather than ponder any longer over a situation he would never comprehend.

Slowing its pace, the train passed row upon row of large, unsightly apartment dwellings as it made its final approach into the terminal. Looking out, his mind still preoccupied and his eyes having seen this scene from the window too many times to give it recognition, Father Jean vowed once again to put aside the ill feelings that had plagued him ever since hearing of Melinda and Joseph's intentions to leave Canada. He wanted their final hours together as a family to be unsullied by rancor—especially for the sake of his parents. The loss of their daughter and grandchild was enough of a burden for them to deal with. Reaffirming this vow, Father Jean left the train and hired a taxi to take him to their hotel.

On the following morning as the pre-dawn darkness hid the tears in their eyes, their final farewells proved as he'd feared: a heart-wrenching severing of strong family ties, and certainly more so for some than for others. Clinging to each other's hands, his parents watched as the train to Boston moved steadily away, hissing loudly, and belching clouds of heavy black smoke. They'd turned away, each of them carrying inside the emptiness and finality of personal loss.

They'd gone back to the terminal, to the hard uncomfortable benches, where they'd waited for nearly two hours before Father Jean escorted them to the train that would return them to Le Baie.

* * *

Marie-Élise strode beside her brother, her arm linked through his, a watchful eye on her parents and the nuns who walked a few yards ahead of them. Her voice, usually so calm and self-assured, wavered slightly when she spoke.

"I'm concerned, Jean," she confessed, her grip on his arm tightening.

"Don't be," he reassured her, "Melinda is young, she'll survive all of this."

"It isn't Melinda who worries me, it's Mama. Look at her, Jean, she's so tired. Papa told me this morning that she'd spent the night sitting in a chair saying her rosary beads." Marie-Élise raised a hand to her mouth and bit down on her middle fingernail, a nervous habit from childhood that returned in times of stress. "I hate to say this, Jean, but I'm afraid our parents are no longer fit enough to travel."

Jean's eyes followed the figures of his parents ahead of them as they made their way through the crowded waiting room. Suddenly he felt a stabbing dart of conscience. Why hadn't he noticed that they'd grown so frail?

Michèl, whose back had always been so straight and strong, was now stooped and misshapen, with an aging palsy shaking his once powerful and facile hands. And Emilie, his dear mother: work-worn and inches shorter than she had been as an energetic slip of a thing who'd easily handled the work of two women. The ravages of time had sculpted them into a bent and crooked man whose step sometimes faltered embarrassingly, and a fragile, forgetful old woman who could no longer cry.

If only they could've remained as they had been, proud and courageous, eager to meet the challenges of life. If only the milky grayness of old age had not crept so insidiously into their gentle eyes. ... The priest looked away. Taking his sister's hand into his, he gave it a reassuring squeeze. "This has been hard on them. Give them time."

Marie-Élise grimaced. "I tried to convince them not to come here, Jean. I knew it would be difficult. But nothing I said would deter them!" The last was spoken almost churlishly, her head swaying dejectedly from side to side.

"Don't blame yourself, Marie-Élise," the priest chided gently. "They had to be here. Otherwise it wouldn't have seemed real to them. You do understand that, don't you?"

"I don't know," she answered, her tone still somber and totally out of character.

"Écoute, ma petite," he said in his firm academician's voice.

Marie-Élise stopped walking abruptly and cut him off. "I'm sorry, I shouldn't be bothering you with my worries."

"Of course you should! Of what use am I if I can't share your burdens from time to time?"

Her great, dark eyes swam with tears and a second bout of morning sickness threatened to engulf her.

Impulsively, Father Jean blurted out, "I'll see Mama and Papa back to Le Baie with you."

"But what about your students at l'Académie?"

"They'll have to manage without me," he replied a bit archly. His tone moderated, he added, "Not to worry, dear. I'll telegraph Monsignor. He'll see to everything in Sherbrooke."

Approaching the platform, they were suddenly caught up in a rush of people. Father Jean looked ahead to see the nuns and his parents safely mounting the steps to the car. Reaching out, he took hold of Marie-Élise's arm securely, as one might hold onto a child. She turned to him. Droplets clung to her lashes. Never had he seen her look so vulnerable.

In that momentary meeting of their eyes, Father Jean was instantly given to believe that despite her denial and whatever concern she had for her parents' well-being, this display of emotion had far more to do with Melinda's leaving for America than Marie-Élise would admit. It was a wrenching loss, for in so many ways she had been more mother to Melinda than sister—a bond never easily broken.

So rather than returning straightaway to his seminary as he might have preferred to do, Father Jean boarded the train to Baie de Saint-Jacques, seeing them all safely home to "Les Érables" (The Maples), the family homestead where he'd been born more than thirty-five years ago.

It was sometimes hard for Father Jean to believe that so much time had passed since that too tall, too thin youth of fifteen had obediently, and without question, left the comfort and security of his parents' home to study under the guidance of the Dominican Fathers in Sherbrooke. Six years later in the great Cathedral of the Sacred Heart, Jean-Philippe Bérard embraced his priesthood. Through those many years, he'd continued to return to Le Baie, giving his support to his loved ones when needed. ... And in times of personal stress, to feel the firmness of the native soil beneath his feet again.

* * *

The Mass was ending. Turning toward the congregation, Father Bérard sang out the "Ite Missa Est." Then, after offering his final blessing, he followed the altar boys into the sacristy.

While removing his vestments, Father Jean mentally prepared himself to take leave of his family. His time with them had come to an end. Much as he might wish to, he could no longer tarry here. His duties at l'Académie had gone too long unattended.

Leaving from the side entrance of the vestry, he found

them gathered together, close to the massive west wall of the church, sheltering themselves from the chilling wind of the late October day.

Alongside the rectory Pastor Lucier's carriage awaited. The sacristan, perched high atop the driver's seat, hoped that Father's farewells would be brief. The road to Saint-Denis and the nearest railway station, was long and he could smell snow in the wind.

While buttoning his overcoat, the tall cleric strode to his mother and put his arms around her. Emilie raised herself onto her tiptoes to receive his kiss.

"Au revoir, Mama ... à bientôt." Jean tried to keep his voice cheerful, but as she drew away, her deep-set eyes misted—the first display of emotion Emilie had allowed herself since returning from Montreal. Jean quickly moved on, pretending not to have noticed.

He turned his attention to his twin sisters who, in the black garb of the Order of Saint Ursula, stood shivering in their inadequate dress. He seldom saw them anymore. Since the taking of their final vows, they'd virtually remained cloistered within their convent walls.

Despite loving them dearly, Jean had never felt a kinship to them as he had to Marie-Élise and Melinda. Even as children, the twins had unwittingly set themselves apart from their siblings by virtue of their closeness to each other.

Feeling slightly ill at ease, he embraced them on both cheeks in the European custom that still lingered in Quebec.

"Take care of yourselves," he told them, adding: "You shouldn't go out in this weather without your shawls on."

They smiled benignly, their thin, pale faces half hidden by the stiffly starched wimples that pressed against their jowls.

"It was very nice to see you again, Father. Have a pleasant journey to Sherbrooke." Sister Marie-Adèle, the self-appointed spokesperson for the two, stepped back allowing him passage in front of her.

He took a few steps, then hesitated. He took Sister Marie-Agathe's hand into his. Feeling a sudden surge of emotion, he kissed her cheek again. "Bless you," he said.

She said meekly, "Thank you, Father."

Looking into her listless eyes, he wondered if she was ill. Moving past her, Father Jean quickly shook the hand of Marie-Élise's stalwart young husband. "Let me know if I'm needed, Daniel."

"To be sure, Father," he answered. Reaching out, Jean firmly grasped the shoulder of his boyhood friend.

"Take care, Papa," Jean said, releasing his father's hand.

"I will, Father, I will." Michèl's pride shone like a beacon of light from his craggy, weather-beaten features. His eyes followed his son's every movement as he walked to where Marie-Élise stood waiting next to the carriage, holding her two-year-old daughter, Dominique, by the hand. Jean leaned and kissed his sister's forehead.

"Everything all right?"

"Of course, Jean. I feel such an idiot, really." Her smooth, round cheeks took on a healthy blush. She touched his arm, caressing it gently. "Promise me you won't worry about us, Jean."

He chuckled, assuring her that he wouldn't. He no longer wondered after all this time why she was the singular member of his family who never addressed him as "Father."

"I said some things I shouldn't have yesterday. My fragile condition, no doubt. Forgive me?"

His mouth relaxed into a warm smile. Once again, as she so often had done before, she'd succeeded in making him feel a little more comfortable about leaving.

Stooping, the priest kissed the toddler and ran his finger over the velvety arch of her nose before climbing into the carriage.

Once inside, he signaled the driver to leave, and as the handsome pair of bays crossed the flag-paved square of Place de la Sainte Église, he turned and looked back at his family through the small oval-shaped window in the rear of the carriage. All at once, an almost palpable melancholy swept over him, as in unison they lifted their hands to wave him farewell.

Leaning back into the velour cushions, Jean sighed audibly. He'd dreaded facing this weekend, for he had known what a terrible void Melinda's leaving would bring into their lives. Not the least of which would be the absence of the child, Philippe, his namesake. He'd been born at Les Érables, in Melinda and Joseph's bedroom, and his grandmother had grown to love him almost beyond reason. She'd helped care for him from the time of his birth, and she'd almost come to feel as if he were her own. His loss would indeed leave a gaping hole in Emilie Bérard's life.

Jean tried to sleep, to keep from remembering such unpleasantries, but his mind would give him no rest. Images came rushing forth to plague him, nagging at him like a festering tooth.

Dear, sweet Melinda ... would that I could have spared you this.

* * *

For Jean, it had begun in Sherbrooke, on the day that he'd returned to Saint Charles Seminary from the Dominican Retreat House outside Ottawa. He was delighted to be back. The fasting and long hours of prayer and meditation had taken their usual toll of him. The strict denial of creature comforts for a month's time had seemed interminable—a necessary purging of his weak and pampered body, to be sure, but he had long ago admitted to himself that going on retreat was the one part of his priesthood that he did not truly cherish.

After settling once again in his quarters, Jean changed into his cassock. Then, opening the windows on the shady side of the building, he let whatever bit of breeze there was flow through his airless rooms. Sherbrooke was always so humid in August; he'd never quite understood why.

Leaving the door ajar, he walked briskly down the two flights of stairs, his long, slender legs fairly flying as he made for the common rooms, hoping to find the companionship of some of his fellow priests. He was starved for some good conversation, and eager to catch up on the news of the house.

As he passed the small office at the foot of the stairs, Jean stuck his head inside. "Good afternoon, Brother Albert!"

The young man inside straightened, his attention immediately drawn from the ledger over which he'd been bent. "Father Bérard! Is that you? Welcome home, sir! It's good to have you back."

"Thank you. It's good to be back, I assure you." Jean's pale blue eyes, the color of a hazy midsummer sky, glimmered as he spoke, adding extra emphasis to his words.

"Would you care to take your mail along with you, Father?" Turning, Brother Albert reached for a pile of letters and magazines he'd set aside on a table.

"My goodness, that's quite a bundle," Jean said with a chuckle. Tucking it up under his arm, he bade good-day to Brother Albert and continued his pursuit for companionship.

Entering the library, he was surprised to find the room empty. The residence, he now noted, was unusually quiet for late afternoon. Everyone was obviously at work in their classrooms, preparing for the start of the fall semester. Seating himself in a large winged chair next to the windows, Father Jean removed the rubber band from around the packet of mail, deciding to go through it while waiting for his confrères to return for refectory.

Apart from the usual letters from his family in Le Baie, there was little of anything personal. A postcard from a student traveling with his parents in Europe, some notices from the chancellery in Montreal, and one other letter whose handwriting he did not immediately recognize. Curious as to its content, he quickly tore open the envelope and discovered that it was from Joseph Durand, his sister Melinda's husband.

He unfolded the letter. A deep frown creased Father Jean's brow. Never before had he received a letter from Joseph, despite having known him most of his life and Joseph's long association with the Bérard family.

Five years previous, soon after Michèl's health failed, Joseph had been hired on full time at Les Érables. He knew the place both backward and forward, having worked there since he was a youth picking produce and packing it for shipment to Montreal.

Joseph had grown up on a neighboring farm, a rundown place less than half a mile down the road from Les Érables. He'd lived there with his parents and five brothers, until his marriage to Melinda. The Durands were a rag-tag bunch for the most part, except for Joseph, who was an honest, conscientious worker, and highly thought of by the Bérard family. But Jean had never been able to share their lofty feelings about him, and to this day he could still remember the searing pain with which he'd received the news of Melinda's betrothal to him two years ago.

Joseph's letter began without any of the usual amenities:

I wish to inform you that Melinda and I have made the decision to leave Quebec, to live and work in the United States for an undetermined period of time. Our reasons for leaving Le Baie are entirely economic. There is money to be made in America for those who have the courage go there.

I am now, and shall always be, indebted to your family for all that they've done for me over the many years that I have known them, but we cannot continue to depend on them forever. I hope one day to own my own land and to build a good life for Melinda and our children, just as your father has done for his.

We know of no way of accomplishing this end, other than following the course we have chosen.

Father Jean wiped his brow with the back of his hand and wondered, *What sort of nonsense is this?* He felt his heart racing as he went on to the next page.

I would like to request the favor of any information you might have regarding the city of Riverton, in the state of Massachusetts. It is my understanding that a number of Do-

minicans from Saint Charles have been sent there to assist in establishing parishes for the many French-Canadians already living there.

He went on to add that his half-brother, Victor, and his wife, Claire, would also be undertaking this journey, and that they planned to leave before the onset of winter.

Jean put the letter down on the table next to his chair. Getting up, he opened the French doors and walked out into the gardens.

The air was cooler under the giant elms that surrounded the seminary complex. It felt soothing against his hot, moist face. Seating himself on the wrought iron settee, Jean stared down into the lush, perfectly groomed grass.

What in God's name was Durand thinking of? Why on earth would he want to move his wife and infant son to some godforsaken place for the sake of his pride and a few extra dollars? From what Jean had heard and read in the newspapers, life was harsh in the New England mill cities. They were overrun with immigrant families, especially the Irish who were fleeing war and famine in their own country. Housing was poor, and scarce, and men lined up for hours seeking whatever kind of work was available in the cotton textile mills. Melinda was only twenty years old. She'd led a sheltered, unsophisticated life, protected and coddled in the bosom of her family. What did she know of the dangers of such places? NO!! He could not envision such a life for his sister, not even for a few years. His family had lived on Bérard soil and been sustained by it for over a century. Why was it suddenly being found wanting?

He wrote Joseph, not addressing himself to the information requested of him, but proffering instead a stern admonition in which he described the perils that could befall the young couple should they continue to pursue such a foolhardy course.

In two weeks' time, he received another letter from Baie de Saint-Jacques. Not from Joseph, as he might have expected, but from Melinda.

I fear, dear brother, that your good counsel has fallen on deaf ears, but I sincerely thank you for the effort. I have for some time now given up any hope of changing Joseph's mind. He is truly obsessed with leaving Canada, and becomes more so with every day that passes. He is bolstered and encouraged at every turn by his brother, Victor, whom we can thank for sowing the seeds of this folly. If for no other reason than for my sake and the sake of my child, I beg you to reconsider and help us to relocate with the least amount of pain and confusion.

Ever lovingly,

M

* * *

A sudden lurching of the carriage returned Father's thoughts to the present.

Sitting upright, he slid his finger around the inside of his collar. Despite the cold, he was sweating. God willing, the day would come when he could remember all this without feeling rancor in his heart.

Looking from the window at the dormant fields that lay beyond the road he traveled, he once again determined to put the past behind him. Melinda and Joseph were gone, and he would no longer dwell on something over which he had no control. Settling himself once again into the cushions, he closed his eyes. The journey to the railhead at Saint Denis would take one hour. He would try to make better use of the time.

* * *

They'd waited next to the church and watched until Father Jean's carriage turned into the road to Saint Denis. Now, Michèl Bérard sat in the buggy next to his wife as their old mare picked her way down the cobbled streets of the village and along the brown ribbon of road that led past the farms of their neighbors. He tried to think of something pleasant to say, something amusing that would make Milie laugh. But Michèl was not a clever man and all endearing words seemed to stick in his throat.

Reaching down, he pulled the carriage rug over Milie's knees, onto her lap. The cold drizzle that had begun earlier that morning now threatened to become a full-blown rain. He hoped they would reach home before then.

Michèl broke the silence that had been with them since leaving the village. "We'll have snow by nightfall, Milie."

"Good—I love the snow. It's a beautiful sight. It's this rain I can't bear."

In that utterance lay an anguish that Emilie had lived with for fifty-three years. An anguish born on a cloud-shrouded morning when she was a child of eleven. A morning when thunder rumbled overhead and flashes of lightning illuminated the heavens with eerie, incandescent light.

She'd stood next to her father, beside the simple coffin that bore her mother's remains, while a brown ooze slowly rose above the soles of her new high-buttoned shoes. She'd listened as the downpour struck its staccato rhythm on the lid of the homemade box, forming pools of murky liquid that slid down the sides of it into a gaping hole beneath. The memory of it had long since been relegated to those labyrinths of the mind where such painful remembrances inevitably must go, but to this day even the warmest, gentlest rain sent a cold chill darting to Milie's core.

Michèl hurried, urging his old animal on with gentle, timeworn words. Soon they reached the hilltop where they could see the meadows and, beyond them, the Saint Lawrence River. Mist rose from the earth and the bare branches of the trees looked etched against infinity.

It was hard for Michèl to understand why anyone would want to leave this place. To his way of thinking, the beauty and serenity to be found here far outweighed the money to be made in the cities of Canada or the United States. But so many of their young men and women were leaving, falling prey to the seductive call of the burgeoning textile industry of Southern New England.

Leaving everything behind, they began anew, deserting the old ways that had for centuries sustained their forebears. Well ... Michèl was old and sick now, and his life almost at its end ... perhaps the vigor of youth might have permitted him to see things differently.

Turning the buggy into the lane that bordered the orchard, Michèl drove past the barn to the white clapboard farmhouse beyond. As he stood helping Emilie down, he could hear the voices of Marie-Élise and Daniel as they rode homeward in the open dray with Dominique and the Sisters. They were laughing, hurrying, racing the rain.

The comforting heat of the cookstove greeted Michèl and Emilie as they entered the large, open kitchen.

Reaching for an apron that hung from a hook next to the sink, Emilie wrapped the ties securely around her. Turning, she found Michèl raising the lid from a pot of simmering lamb that Marie-Élise had set to stewing before leaving for Mass. Michèl was about to starve from the long Communion fast since midnight.

"Will we be eating dinner soon, Milie?"

"We'll be eating at noon—as usual." Her last two words held an edge of irritation not normally heard in her voice. Emilie's annoyance with her husband's tedious, predictable question was quicker to display itself this morning than it would have been on most any other Sunday. Pushing Michèl aside, she placed the coffeepot over one of the burners. Emilie spoke sweetly to him now, regretting her inappropriate display of temper. "Marie-Élise made brioche last night. Why don't you have one while you wait for your breakfast?"

Michèl was distracted from the urgings of his stomach by the arrival of Daniel and the three women.

Marie-Élise, her cheeks glowing from the brisk ride, hurried to put on an apron. In an instant she was alongside Emilie, preparing a hearty breakfast for the nuns to enjoy, before Daniel returned them to their convent in Courrèges.

"Sit down, please, everything is ready. Dominique, bring Pépère your bib. He'll put it on for you." Emilie walked to the table carrying the steaming pot of coffee in one hand and a platter of basted eggs in the other. She served her twins quickly, hoping that the hot food would take the blue-white pallor from their lips.

"It was ever so kind of Reverend Mother to have allowed you to be with us in Montreal," Emilie remarked as she filled her daughters' cups. "It meant so much to Melinda to have you there. Please thank Reverend Mother for all of us."

"Of course, Mama," Sister Marie-Adèle agreed.

"Here, have more sugar," Emilie urged Sister Marie-Agathe. "It's good for what ails you, dear." They were so thin, her darlings. At times she felt that the meager meals they partook of inside their walls were not enough to sustain the health of a hummingbird. Passing behind her chair with the bacon, Emilie leaned and covered Sister Marie-Agathe's hand with hers, reassuring herself that she was indeed warming up.

Emilie missed her twins ever since they'd taken their vows. But she did not resent the restrictions placed upon them by their order. Such was the life of those who chose to be in the service of Christ. They were a source of great pride to her and to Michèl, as was their son Jean-Philippe.

But Melinda's leaving was different! She thought of that as a kind of betrayal—not on Melinda's part, mind you, but on Joseph's. Michèl and she had entrusted their daughter to him, and he had, in her eyes, failed them.

There were times when she'd been tempted to encourage Melinda to disobey Joseph's wishes, to remain at home in Le Baie without him if need be. But when Michèl put his foot down, she swiftly abandoned the idea.

"Then you speak to Joseph, Michèl," she'd urged him. "Offer him something—anything—that will make him change his mind about leaving."

The following morning shortly after sunrise, Michèl went out to the barn where Joseph was preparing the draft horse for a day of work in the fields. But even as he spoke, Michèl knew it was useless. The man had made up his mind. It was as simple as that.

"It's Joseph's decision to make as he sees fit," Michèl explained to his wife later in the day. "The matter is closed. Stay out of it, Milie."

She'd done as he'd asked, but there were moments in the last few days when she'd wished that she hadn't.

Finishing her coffee, Sister Marie-Adèle rose from her place at the table.

"You're not leaving so soon?" Emilie rushed to her side. "It's still early. I had hoped you'd have dinner with us today."

"I'm sorry, Mama, we must return to Courrèges before vespers."

Emilie anxiously looked out the window. "But it's raining so hard, you'll catch your death out there."

Opening their large black umbrellas, the nuns went out into the rain that once again fell steadily upon the back of the weary old mare. Shifting her weight from one set of hooves to the other, she patiently stood her ground while Daniel assisted the nuns into the carriage. Dressed in his heavy mackinaw and rawhide casquette, Daniel whistled a tune as he drove through the village, past Place de la Sainte Église, toward Courrèges, blissfully unmindful of the weather.

* * *

"Enough now, Mama."

Marie-Élise's voice startled Emilie as she stood in front of the sink preparing to wash the breakfast dishes.

"Please, go and rest until dinner. I'll see to the work in the kitchen." Marie-Élise smiled, hoping there wouldn't be any argument.

Emilie dried her hands and hung her apron away. She was too tired to argue today, more tired than she'd been in a very long time.

As she climbed the stairs, she paused and looked over at her husband sitting in his chair next to the fire, his unlit pipe clenched between his teeth, his head nodding as he dozed. Michèl had grown old, as well as she. Why couldn't she remember where the years had gone?

The pine floorboards creaked as Emilie made her way down the narrow hallway to the room at the front of the house. Entering, she sat on the edge of her chair and removed her shoes, wincing as she rubbed the large, painful bunions.

Covering her shoulders with a shawl, Emilie sighed as she looked at her familiar surroundings: at her things, and Michèl's; things that usually gave her so much comfort. Why did each crack in the floor, each scratch on the furniture, send her thoughts leaping back in time today?

She again saw a cradle standing next to the fireplace, an infant contentedly sleeping there. So much had changed over the years—so much would never be the same again.

Emilie had come here from Outrec as a bride of twenty-seven, no longer a young woman when she began her life with Michèl at Les Érables.

For many years she'd been torn between accepting the role of wife and mother, or of embracing the veil of the Ursulines. Michèl had waited, and finally won her, and Emilie had never regretted her decision.

But what had happened to all those years? To all the little voices that had been a part of this house since that bright April morning when Jean-Philippe was first laid into her arms?

"We have a son," Michèl had whispered, his voice filled with the singular pride of fatherhood.

Emilie'd wanted only to sleep, to forget the dreadful hours of labor when she'd feared she surely would die. Instead, she'd taken the child to her and as he nursed, she could feel his tiny heart beating.

There were other sons after Jean-Philippe. A year later, Claude was born, and in less than another, Armand. She hadn't thought of them in a long time. Both had died within weeks of their birth and she'd never truly gotten to know them. Nonetheless, it had torn at her heart to see Michèl carrying their small coffins to the dray for burial in the church-yard cemetery.

Ever after, when she had passed her time, she'd prayed for another son. A healthy, vigorous boy who would make her husband proud. But each time she'd given him a daughter, then another, and another.

Michèl adored his girls and never made them feel any-thing but cherished.

"Who is my favorite *petite ange*?" he'd call to them as he walked down the lane from the fields, his body bathed in perspiration, his sinewy forearms scorched by the blazing summer sun.

They would all three run to him from where they sat wait-ing on the steps to the veranda. Gleeful cries of, "C'est moi, Papa! C'est moi," rang out into the summer twilight as in turn, each would be kissed and swung through the air, her pale hair bouncing from her shoulders, her laughter carrying into the house to where Emilie stood preparing the evening meal. A smile would slowly tug at her lips, and she would walk to the window and look out over the half-curtains as they came toward the house. Her life had been good, very good, except for having been denied another son.

Following the birth of the twins, Emilie'd thought herself to be barren, for they'd torn her body to shreds and almost taken her life. For nine years she gave not a thought to bear-ing a child. Then, in her forty-fourth year she found that she had conceived again. A miracle!! A gift from God!

Hope for a son once again welled in Emilie Bérard's heart.

"Tu te trompe, Milie!" Michèl found it hard to believe that after all these years his wife was again with child. "This must be a sign of something else. Perhaps ..."

"I know what you're thinking, and yes, I'm old enough for that to be so, but in my heart I know." She put her hand to her belly. "A woman always knows, Michèl."

All doubt disappeared some weeks later when a flutter deep from within stopped Emilie dead in her tracks.

"I feel life!" she called out, with none but the walls to hear her. She put her hands across her abdomen and waited for it to happen again. It didn't, not until that night as she lay next to Michèl in their bed. She took his hand and put it to her, and she heard him suck in his breath when he felt it.

Melinda was born on the eighth day of December, during a raging snowstorm that prevented the doctor from attending the birth.

Marie-Élise, a girl of twelve, and her twin sisters, two years her junior, cared for their mother all during those nightmarish hours when Michèl went out to fetch the doctor. But snowdrifts of three feet and more diverted his team again and again, and when Emilie's time came Marie-Élise delivered her of yet another daughter.

After a difficult moment when Emilie'd fought back the tears, she'd cradled the infant in her arms.

"She's exquisite, Michèl," she'd declared, looking down at the pink and white face with the tiny heart-shaped mouth.

"How could she be anything else?"

"Thank you. You're very sweet, but this has nothing to do with me, or with you. Mark my words, Michèl, this is no ordinary girl." The tone of Emilie's voice made him turn and look at her, and the expression on her face caused a chill to creep up and down his spine.

Emilie's words proved prophetic. Unlike Marie-Élise, who was full bodied and short of stature, or the twins who were thin as rails by nature, Melinda grew tall and stately, with a regal bearing that made her the envy of her classmates.

Her golden curls did not darken to brown with the passage of the years, nor did her eyes change to the nondescript hazel that predominated in the females of the family. Instead, they remained the forget-me-not blue that had taken her parents' breath away when she was but a few hours old.

Yesterday, in Montreal, in the hazy light of a mid-October dawn, Emilie'd watched from the platform as Melinda, the last of her children, boarded a train, carrying her own infant in her arms.

"Five years, Mama—five years," she'd promised as she hugged her mother one last time.

* * *

Looking from the bedroom window, Emilie noticed that the rain had stopped and snow had begun to fall. Like a veil of lace, it dotted the branches of the twenty-two maple trees Michèl had planted along the road to the orchard the first spring that she'd lived in this house. Suddenly, Emilie felt the tightness of Melinda's arms around her and heard her say: "Five years, Mama—five years."

Why did she know that it would be forever?

Chapter One

Riverton

October, 1887

Melinda pulled her coat together and buttoned it against the chill of the train. She held her sleeping infant closer to her bosom, sharing with him the warmth of her body. All throughout this long lamentable journey she'd taken comfort in his closeness, but in these, the early morning hours after midnight, she longed for the relief that a few moments of standing would bring. Yet she would not rise from her seat while holding the boy, for the movements of the train were precarious, and she risked losing her footing on the slick surface of the floor.

Turning her eyes away from the darkness that lay beyond her window, Melinda looked down at Philippe, cradled securely in his christening shawl. Her heart went out to the innocent babe that she held in her arms. His sleep, at best, had been fitful, lasting fifteen or twenty minutes at most. Not the deep, restful sleep he'd been accustomed to having in the sun-drenched bedroom of his grandparents' farmhouse in Le Baie. Again he stirred and re-awakened, the loud whine of the train's whistle having once more penetrated his flimsy slumber as the locomotive made its way through yet another town. Slowly, Melinda resumed the rhythmical rocking that heretofore had succeeded in lulling him to sleep.

Earlier in the evening after finishing their meal, she'd sat side by side with Joseph, her head tilted close to his. They'd spoken in hushed tones so as not to unduly excite the baby. It was then that Joseph noticed the deep mauve circles etched into the skin under Melinda's eyes.

"There are empty seats in the rear of the car," he whispered, trying once more to persuade her to rest. "Go and sleep for a while. I can see to the boy for an hour or two."

"I don't dare do that while he's so unsettled, Joseph. Besides, he'll be wanting to nurse again before long."

Muttering something about nonsense, Joseph sat upright in his seat, and taut little lines appeared around his mouth.

"Don't be concerned about me, Joseph," Melinda hastened to reassure him. "I'd probably not sleep anyway. Find a quiet place for the night. Philippe and I will be all right."

Rising reluctantly, Joseph stood and looked down at her. "At least put him aside for a while."

"I will, Joseph, I will. The moment he's sleeping soundly enough."

Taking one last glance at them over his shoulder, Joseph walked down the aisle, zigzagging from one side to the other, holding onto the tops of the seats as he went. Finding an empty place, he lowered himself into it. Instantly, the stresses of the day struck him a withering blow. Leaning back, he unbuttoned his collar and waistcoat and settled himself for the night.

Unlike his wife, Joseph appeared comfortable. There were no stays that pinched, or laces that bound, and it troubled him not one iota that he was leaving Canada. To the contrary—he was excited about going to America. For months now, he'd thought of little else. The prospect of a new life there, even for only a few years, was for him an exhilarating new adventure. Never before in all of his twenty-eight years had he left Baie de Saint-Jacques, nor had he wanted to, until Victor approached him with the idea.

At first Joseph had dismissed it as nonsense, another of Victor's crazy schemes. But before long he found himself reading the advertisements that the New England mill agents published each week in the local newspaper.

"Just think about it, Joe—that's all I ask," Victor urged him. "You've nothing to lose but your bondage," he quipped

2

as they scanned the newspapers together in the drafty old kitchen of the Durands' farmhouse. Leaning across the table, Victor lowered his voice. "I know what you're up against over there." He jerked his thumb in the direction of Les Érables. "I know how they've taken advantage of you. You're little more than a lackey in that household, and mark my words, that's all you'll ever be." Victor's face reddened and a pulsating blood vessel protruded from the side of his neck. Swallowing hard, he continued: "America is different, Joe. It's like nothing we've ever known. A man isn't condemned for the sins of his father there."

Victor pushed his chair back and got up from the table. "Vièrge!" he spat out the blasphemous oath. "What need have we of this accursed place!" His arm made an encompassing gesture. "It's offered us nothing but the bitterest gall." Walking to the center of the room, he stood belligerently, his legs apart, his fingers curling into fists. "I'm getting out of Baie de Saint-Jacques if it's the last thing I ever do."

Joseph hadn't fully agreed with Victor's appraisal of the situation, but his brother's words had started him thinking, wondering about his life and his future.

Frankly, he'd not given much thought to it before. He'd lived more or less from one day to the next, harvest to harvest, tilling another man's soil without ever aspiring to anything more. And he'd always felt he'd been dealt with fairly. No one, not even Victor, could make him believe that Michèl Bérard was less than an honorable man. He'd demonstrated that many times over. Had it not been for his trust and generosity, Joseph would likely have trapped or lumberjacked for a living. More importantly, Michèl had given him his daughter Melinda's hand in marriage. How much greater respect could one man show to another.

To this day, Victor stubbornly refused to acknowledge these facts. His vindictiveness toward the Bérards, Michèl in particular, sprang from a longstanding hatred between them. A bitter enmity born years ago on the day that Michèl banished Victor from his property for beating one of his dogs.

Victor had sworn then, to one day have his revenge.

"For God's sake, man,—" The harshness of Victor's voice jolted Joseph back to the present. "Don't go to your grave without ever having been anything more than the Bérard's hired hand."

With this parting shot he had walked from the room, leaving Joseph to evaluate his future.

During the months that followed, as the fields lay dormant under a heavy mantle of snow, Joseph had gone into the village now and again—to the library behind the church school. Returning, he'd carried with him an armful of books about New England and the great industrial revolution that was taking place there. After supper, he'd sat on the other side of the hearth from Michèl, reading about New Bedford and its whaling industry, and about Riverton, a thriving young city where the cotton textile industry flourished like nowhere else in the world. The words wove an exciting tapestry which imprinted itself indelibly in Joseph's mind.

He began to dream—something he had never done before. And as blizzards howled through the eaves that winter, the dream became all that mattered.

With the coming of spring, as he'd walked behind the big draft horse, steering his plow through the half-frozen clay of his father-in-law's fields, Joseph made his decision to leave Canada. He'd finish out the summer and bring in the harvest for Michèl in the fall. Then and only then would he feel it honorable to take his leave of Le Baie.

But not forever, as Victor would have him do. No, he would return to Quebec one day, but only when he could do it with pride, and with something of worth to pass on to his children.

* * *

After banishing all doubt about his decision, Joseph went to Melinda. He'd expected a certain amount of opposition from her, but not nearly to the extent that it was forthcoming.

She was great with child and he urged her to remain calm.

"You can't be serious, Joseph!" she shouted. "Why would you want to do such a thing?"

"There are many reasons, Melinda. But first and foremost, I would do it for your sake, and that of our unborn child. We have no future here in Le Baie. Please, believe in me enough to trust in my decision."

"I'm afraid you don't understand, Joseph. You've never felt about your family as I feel about mine."

"True enough, my sweet, and I wouldn't ask you to leave them forever. In five years' time we'll have saved enough to return here and buy a place of our own."

Melinda argued and cajoled, and several times she came dangerously close to refusing to leave. It was only when she reminded herself that in marrying Joseph Durand, she had sworn to forsake all others—including her family. Only then had she abandoned the fight.

Alas—with the final and most formidable hurdle conquered, Joseph and Victor began shaping their future. And never once during those exhilarating months had it remotely occurred to either of them that Joseph and Melinda might be journeying to America alone. That the unpredictable twists of fate would cheat Victor out of being there with them.

Virtually on the brink of their departure, Victor had come to Les Érables. He'd stood on the veranda on an October morning still locked in the bone-chilling cold of a killing frost.

"I don't know how to tell you this," he'd begun, his voice hoarse with suppressed emotion, his face bleak with disappointment.

Joseph led him inside, into the Bérard's pristine Victorian parlor. "Sit down, Victor." The younger man towered over Joseph, and for a moment he looked as if he might lash out at something. Joseph said, "Tell me what's happened."

A pair of dark smoldering eyes looked back at Joseph. For a moment Victor simply stared unable to utter a sound. For a moment Victor's Then, taking a deep breath, his jaw relaxed and he went on to explain: "It's Claire. She's miscarried."

5

His tone was devoid of feeling, except for the underlying rage barely under control.

"A miscarriage! When?"

"During the night; just before dawn."

"I'm sorry, Victor." Joseph was stunned. He hadn't been told that Claire was with child. "Is Claire all right?"

Having married in June barely four months ago, Victor and she were virtual newlyweds. But the mention of his bride's name now made his eyes narrow into slits. He gave no reply to his brother's question.

"I'll not be leaving with you," he said instead, moving past Joseph toward the door. His hand on the knob, Victor stood riveted to the spot, looking straight ahead into nothingness. "She'll pay for this bit of deception," he muttered under his breath.

As he opened the door, Joseph took hold of his arm and turned him. They were face to face, and what Joseph saw frightened and repulsed him. Pulling his arm free, Victor attempted to leave.

"Wait, for God's sake! You don't know what you're saying!"

Victor stopped. Letting out a stream of pent-up breath, he gathered himself together. "I'm sorry," he apologized, "I didn't mean that." Turning, he walked from the house.

Joseph snatched his jacket from the clothes tree next to the door and followed him out. They walked in silence, past the barn, toward the road that led to the village. Joseph stopped next to the fence that bordered the orchard, watching anxiously as Victor continued on his way alone, his shoulders hunched, his long black hair billowing in the wind.

For a while Melinda hoped that this new development might put an end to the whole thing; but she'd sorely underestimated her husband's determination. Although for a time he'd considered postponing everything, Joseph had rejected the idea. Too much had already been set into motion, and he intuitively felt that waiting might jeopardize their leaving at all.

"Victor's young, he'll have his chance," he'd told

Melinda as their buggy drove past the Durand place on the morning of their departure. "Perhaps this experience will serve to mature him ... teach him a little self-discipline."

Melinda hadn't responded, believing full well that Victor Durand would never be anything other than what he had always been.

* * *

Born out of wedlock to Louis Durand and an Italian woman of dubious reputation, Victor had come into this world in a squalid little room on the edge of Le Baie. He'd lived there with his mother until she'd eventually run off, leaving her bastard offspring in the care of the nuns at the orphanage before he'd reached the second of his birthdays. Learning of this, Louis had gone there and taken the boy back to the farm with him, where his wife Laura grudgingly agreed to raise him.

For the most part, Victor and his brothers were considered an unruly gaggle of ruffians by their neighbors, as well as the local townspeople. They were continually involved in some sort of mischief, and were often brought home by the scruff of their necks. Whippings at school were a commonplace thing, and Louis's belt had raised many a welt across their narrow backsides.

In that respect, Joseph had fared somewhat better than the rest, but Victor had fared far worse. Being the youngest, and a bastard to boot, he fell victim to the brunt of the punishment. It was only after years of unjustly absorbing the whip that he was finally able to defend himself against his half-brothers' false accusations. It stopped entirely on the day of Victor's sixteenth birthday when, with the others looking on, he'd pummeled his eldest brother, Damien, into unconscious oblivion.

Victor had grown from an awkward adolescent into a broad-shouldered young man well over six feet in height. He cast a most imposing shadow in this family of short-statured men. Joseph, the tallest of Laura and Louis's sons, measured slightly under five feet, nine inches in height. And despite his fine hazel eyes and chestnut brown hair, he sometimes felt himself a drab caricature alongside his striking young half-brother. But Joseph and the others envied Victor not one whit. Having been blessed with more than his share of physical beauty had not spared him the "peine forte" he'd suffered at Laura's vengeful hands. To this day, the sound of her voice alone was enough to make Victor cringe.

The inevitable result of this disparaging upbringing was a distrustful, often violent, man in whom there constantly simmered a molten fury. A person in whom there lived but one all-consuming hope. To flee his past and never be reminded of it again.

America had become Victor Durand's Utopia. A place where he could live his life without vilification. And now, this too was being denied him.

Like a painted woman, America had beckoned suggestively, then snatched her favors from his grasp. But the day would come, Victor swore, when he would feast on her.

Chapter Two

A crescent of moon floated in and out of the swiftly moving clouds as the train wound its way south through the pine-shrouded New Hampshire mountains. The passengers slept for the most part, emitting a chorus of sounds that added to Melinda's difficulty in falling asleep. She'd held Philippe all evening long, quieting him so that he not disturb those who rested. She'd shifted him from one arm to the other, bracing herself against the window's edge to relieve the strain. Philippe's puny energies had long since spent themselves, but somehow he'd managed to dredge up enough energy to prolong his fight against sleep. He wiggled and whined and rubbed at his eyes with his fists. He instinctively did whatever was necessary to keep himself awake. Inevitably it all became too much for him, and after a shriek or two he'd closed his eyes.

Stretched out on his mother's lap, the child slept soundly for the first time since boarding the train. His almost translucent eyelids were closed tightly, his breathing was deep and even. Cautiously, Melinda inched her way around. Raising Philippe gently, she laid him on the seat next to hers. For a fretful moment he stretched and squirmed, threatening to re-awaken. She watched intently, not daring to breathe until he'd settled down again, his arms outstretched above his lustrous, dark curls.

Slowly, Melinda rose from her seat and walked back and forth in the aisle, never going very far from where her son lay. It felt good to stretch her legs, to pull her clothing into a more comfortable position.

Rays of dim ocher light shone from the kerosene lamps

that burned at each end of the car. Looking back, she could see Joseph from where she stood. He slept soundly, his mouth slightly agape, his head rolling gently in rhythm with the motion of the train. She stood for ten minutes or more, peeking every now and then over the back of the seat where Philippe slept. After a while, the cold filtering up from the floor penetrated the thin souls of her shoes and she seated herself again.

Melinda's eyes felt scratchy, and burned with the need for sleep. But she wouldn't allow herself even one moment of slumber in which she would leave her child unprotected against the peril of slipping to the floor.

Looking again from the window, she could see streaks of light beginning to define the horizon and soon she was able to make out the dull and dreary landscape.

The New England sky was leaden, the fields and grasses colorless. A cold drizzle oozed from the sky and thin rivulets of water sped across the pane of glass. Another dawn was breaking; this one in some godforsaken place she couldn't so much as give a name to.

It was hard for Melinda to believe that only a day had passed since this train had moved out of the railroad yard in Montreal. Turning, she had looked back at her loved ones, watching as they'd dwindled and disappeared from sight. Heading east, the train passed along the big, sweeping curve behind the apartment houses and crossed the bridge leading out of the city. Even now, as its wheels sped across this strange new land, taking them farther and farther away, she could hear Father Jean's voice, throaty and filled with emotion as he'd said: "Don't let the boy forget us."

Another voice—not the voice of a loved one this time, but the adenoidal twang of the conductor—startled her out of her reverie as he walked through the car calling the upcoming station. Passing Melinda's seat, he pulled a watch from his vest pocket. They were on time. They would arrive at the Riverton station at three o'clock that afternoon. Nodding his approval, the conductor walked on to the next car.

Chapter Three

The streetcar came to an unsteady halt at the corner of Bedfordgate and Tremont streets. Melinda moved through the crush of people toward the exit where Joseph stood waiting to help her descend. A steady drizzle seeped from the overcast sky as it had done for most of the day.

Checking the street signs to be sure of his course, Joseph picked up their valises and began the trek up Tremont Street, a gradual incline as far as the eye could see. Melinda followed him, carrying their child in her arms.

They appeared a weary trio as they started the search for the lodgings Joseph had arranged with a Mr. Charles Mulvaney.

Since leaving the Riverton depot at midafternoon, the temperature had fallen steadily and Melinda's harried body shook with a chill as she hastened to keep pace with her husband. After passing a number of cross streets without any sign of Sladesferry Landing, she began losing ground.

After passing two more, she called out to Joseph, who pressed steadily on ahead. The timber of her voice betrayed her impatience. "How much farther is it?"

Joseph set their bags down on the wet pavement and waited for her to reach him. Opening and closing his hands, he brought the blood surging into his cramped fingers. "I'm as much of a stranger here as you are, Melinda," he informed her. A series of knots appeared at the edge of his jaw. "For your sake, I had hoped that we wouldn't have to climb this entire hill, but it would seem that we must."

Melinda's slender body sagged as he made this dire pronouncement. "I'm sorry, Joseph, I'm not sure I can go on."

Realizing she'd not had the sleep he'd enjoyed, Joseph was quick to alter his attitude. "Wait here. I'll go on ahead."

Digging into his overcoat pocket, Joseph withdrew a rumpled piece of paper sent to him by the proprietor. It read: 77 Sladesferry Landing.

"Damn! It has to be somewhere near here." Picking up his burdens, Joseph pushed on once again.

In the next block a church came into view: a small building constructed of wood rather than stone. Upon first impression, the black shuttered, clapboard building looked more like a meetinghouse or a grange hall than a place of worship. Above its simple doors read the words:

L'ÉGLISE DE SAINT ROCH,
ANNO DOMINI, 1884

Next to it and to the left stood a modest cedar-shingled house that Joseph assumed to be the rectory. For a moment he considered asking for directions, but instead he hurried on as fast as his legs would allow, toward the next corner.

"VOILÀ!" he called back to Melinda. The quest for Sladesferry Landing had ended!

Turning to the right, Joseph hurried down the narrow cobblestone street, his eyes darting from house to house, his vision somewhat inhibited now by the fast approaching darkness. Halfway down the block, the number 77 appeared, nailed above a large, glass-paneled door.

Encouraged by the hope of finally reaching their destination, Melinda walked faster. Once more the child sensed her urgency and whimpered. She pulled the woolen shawl up around him and held him tightly to her bosom, softly humming an old French lullaby: "Un petit berçeau d'or pour mon joli garçon" (A little golden cradle for my pretty boy), and plodding onward toward Sladesferry Landing.

Ahead of her, Joseph had halted before an enormous three-story house. He waited as she turned the corner and approached him, his hand holding onto the heavy metal gate.

Melinda stood on the veranda while Joseph went inside to

claim their key. Despite being wet to the skin and her body covered with gooseflesh, she was ever so grateful to be sheltered and out of the rain. Through the glow of the gas lamp that burned on the street corner, she squinted about at her unfamiliar surroundings.

Outside the gate, along the narrow stone-paved street grew a series of giant trees, their leafless branches silhouetted against the deep pewter sky. Unlike the low-roofed cottages that edged the winding lanes of Baie de Saint-Jacques, Sladesferry Landing was lined with a progression of enormous three-story tenements, less than fifteen feet apart one from the other; three stood in this yard alone, staggered around a rectangle of colorless, dormant grass. Melinda felt strangely insecure, as the last vestiges of daylight sank into the serpentine waters of the Takonnet River to the west. She turned abruptly when she heard the door swing open.

As he emerged from the first floor flat, Melinda heard Joseph say: "Thank you very much, Miss," in his heavily accented English.

Starting toward the door, Melinda stopped again when she heard the voice of a woman reply: "Oh, yer welcome indeed. Just ye be lettin' me know if there's anythin' at all ye'll be needin'."

Another quiver of anxiety ran through Melinda as she failed to understand a single word of the woman's rapid-fire response.

Entering the vestibule, Melinda followed Joseph into the narrow stairwell, her legs rebelling against the incredible climb to the third and uppermost floor. Melinda leaned wearily against the wall as Joseph worked the key into the lock and opened the door. They entered into the dingy, attic-like rooms.

They were greeted by a stale, musty odor as well as the sound of mice scurrying to safety. Closing the door behind them, Joseph drew his thumbnail across a match tip and lighted the gas jets on either side of the entrance, illuminating the place with a dismal, sallow glow.

"Good Lord!" Melinda cried. "It's empty!"

The larger of the two rooms was almost devoid of furnishings. Melinda's eyes were instantly drawn to an enormous stove edged in chipped and rusting chromium, resting against the far wall next to a soapstone sink; two old ladder-back chairs stood in the center of a faded, nondescript carpet. As she stood gaping, Philippe began to fuss.

"See to the boy," Joseph said, nudging her gently.

Melinda made her way across the room and laid Philippe on the counter. His whimpering intensified as she rid him of his soiled linens, and washed his bottom in the icy cold water from the pump. Hushing him softly, she set about appeasing his hunger. Seating herself on one of the chairs, she put him to her breast. For a full two minutes he pulled lustily at her nipple, before falling into an exhausted sleep. When no amount of chin-pinching on his mother's part succeeded in rekindling his interest, Melinda carried him into the bedroom. Looking up, she saw Joseph watching them, wearing a grin that almost closed his eyes.

"I think he's finally given up," he said.

"I hope you're right, Joseph, for everyone's sake."

It was a nicer room than she'd anticipated, disclosing a sturdy-looking bedstead and a large chest of drawers. Spreading out Philippe's christening shawl, Melinda wrapped him snugly, leaving him to sleep in the middle of the bed.

Tiptoeing into the kitchen, Melinda found Joseph unpacking their belongings. Laid over the back of a chair was the afghan her mother had sent along with them. The sight of it caused a lump to harden in Melinda's throat and she suddenly wanted to cry. Taking a deep breath, she swallowed hard and smoothed her flaxen hair into place. Going over to the other valise, she opened it and sorted their clothing.

After finishing what was left of the biscuits and fruit remaining from their journey, Melinda and Joseph sat side by side on the creaky old chairs. Melinda suppressed a yawn, and then another. She'd not slept a wink since leaving Montreal and the whites of her eyes were shot through with red.

14

Rising, Joseph put his hand into hers. "Let's go to bed. We'll finish unpacking in the morning."

Pulling her to her feet he led her into the bedroom. Removing only his waistcoat and shoes, Joseph lay on the bed next to his son.

After undressing, Melinda pulled her nightgown over her head. Kneeling on the bedstep, she lowered her head in prayer. She'd barely begun her deca of "Aves" when she heard the steady droning of her husband's breathing. Opening a quilt she'd found on the shelf in the closet, Melinda spread it over him.

She too fell asleep almost instantly. But she slept unsoundly—awakening often—fearing that she or Joseph would roll onto Philippe and smother him to death. During her fitful periods of slumber she dreampt strange, bizarre dreams that left her wide-eyed and shuddering in the somber light of a bleak New England dawn.

Melinda lay awake for almost an hour, surprised that the baby still slept while firmly pressed against his father's broad, warm back. After a time, a gnawing hunger forced her to rise and go into the kitchen.

Looking around, she discovered a number of things that had gone unnoticed the night before.

First, there were the three small windows that overlooked Sladesferry Landing and beyond it, the gray-green waters of the bay. Turning her gaze inside, her brows arched and her eyes widened as they caught sight of the large cabbage roses that embellished two of the walls. Faded with age and its paste dried to a powder, the ancient paper curled away from the ceiling in large, unsightly bulges.

A new copper kettle gleamed from its place on the hob.

"Fancy that," Melinda said aloud as she filled it and placed it over one of the burners. Lifting a stove lid, she struck a match, igniting the kindling inside.

While waiting for the water to be brought to the boil, Melinda foraged around, searching for the teapot she'd packed somewhere. Finding it and a tin of tea leaves as well, she set them out on the counter.

A search of the cupboard above the sink revealed a stack of assorted dishes and a number of odd cups and saucers. Beneath the sink, a cursory look revealed a leaking pipe dripping rusty water into a basin, and a mouse in rigor, its neck crushed under the arm of a trap.

Melinda's attention was then drawn to a door three feet or so to the right of the bedroom. It looked about the size of a broom closet. Opening it, she stepped back, her eyes unable to believe what they beheld. A water closet! An indoor privy! Never in her wildest dreams had she expected to find such a luxury in this grim, denuded garret. Impulse urged that she awaken Joseph, share with him these glorious tidings; but thinking the better of it, she went inside and closed the door.

While washing up at the sink she heard a rap at the door. Melinda moved toward the bedroom and the protection afforded her in the person of her husband. But before reaching it, there came a second knock, this one louder and more assertive. Gathering every ounce of her courage she went to the door and opened it just a crack.

"Qui est là?" she asked, her voice sounding like that of a frightened ten-year-old.

"Good day te ye, missus," came the hefty response. "May the Lord bless this house, and all who abide here."

Confused and curious, Melinda opened the door a bit more. Standing in the hall was a buxom, red-haired woman. She appeared to be about thirty years of age, and every inch of her smiling face was covered with tiny freckles. Pushing open the door, the woman walked inside.

Melinda hurried to raise her hands to her bosom, attempting to conceal her inappropriate state of dress.

The red-haired lady laughed heartily. "Oof! Be gone with ye, girl. Ain't no need to stand on ceremony." Again laughter pealed from her throat. Coming closer, she peered at Melinda through intense turquoise eyes. "Do ye speak any English at all?"

Melinda shook her head "no."

"The saints preserve us, girl! 'Tis a miracle indeed that ye managed to get here at all." The smile disappeared from her face and she shook her head in dismay. "Ye should at least be learnin' a word or two, afare settin' off bag and baggage, don't ye know."

Walking to one of the chairs, she seated herself, then nodding her head toward the chair next to her, she said: "Sit yerself here, dearie. It must be dead on yer feet ye are, child." She clucked her tongue loudly several times. "I've done me share of travelin' and I know how it is yer feelin' this morning." Reaching across her lap, she patted the back of Melinda's hand. "After twelve days in the steerage, I thought I'd never breathe air unscented by the vile stench of vomit." Her nostrils pinched together in disgust. "And as if that weren't enough for a body to deal with, I couldn't close me eyes for weeks without feelin' the rockin' and tossin' of that vessel." Her eyes moved up into her head until only little crescents of white could be seen. "Aye, it was akin to the Purgatory crossin' over—and for what, I'm after askin' meself? I'm without chick nor child, and only a sick old man to give a bit of carin' to. I wonder sometimes ..." She didn't go on, the thought of it obviously too painful for her to dwell on. "Well now, I didn't come here to be tellin' ye all me affairs." She handed Melinda the brown paper bag she was holding. "Go ahead, dearie, open it."

As Melinda did so, the unmistakable aroma of warm Irish soda bread wafted from inside. "Ummmm!"

The woman smiled, showing delightfully deep dimples symmetrically placed in the middle of each bespeckled cheek. Melinda stared at her, not knowing what to say. Such unexpected kindness had completely taken her aback.

Bracing herself, Melinda spoke her first words of English. "Thank you ... madame ... very ... much."

"Aye—I knew it! Ye were pullin' me leg now, weren't ya? Well, yer welcome indeed. I was pretty sure ye'd be needin' a bit of somethin' afore searchin' out the market. I do me bakin' as near after five as I can. I knew ye were up and about when I heard ye runnin' the water." Lowering her voice, she leaned a bit closer. "There's usually not a sound in this house till well after seven o'clock." She pointed down to the flat below and added, "She's not a bit well, Mrs. O'Leary, and sleepin' is what she does most nowadays." With a surprisingly supple motion, she jumped from the chair and walked to the door. Her hand on the knob, she turned to Melinda again. "Me name is Caitlin ... Caitlin Flanigan. Those as wants to, call me Caitie. I'm charwoman to Mr. Mulvaney, the proprietor of this grand house. He's poorly these days, dear old soul." With the release of a sigh, her over-ample bosom heaved up, then down. "Well then, I'd best get meself back to me chores."

She left, pounding the steps soundly as she made her way down to the first floor flat, leaving Melinda staring after her from the middle of the room.

The following day, the weather having changed for the better, Caitlin Flanigan took Melinda in tow. They sallied forth to make the rounds of the second-hand shops on Bedfordgate.

One needed only the expert eye of the connoisseur to ferret out the treasures that lay hidden under the piles of otherwise useless castoffs. And Caitlin Flanigan possessed that eye. She plunged herself waist deep into barrels of dusty dishes, finding enough matching pieces for Melinda to set her table. Linens, a bit yellowed with age but nonetheless fine, were pulled from stack upon stack, and carefully examined on both sides.

"A bit of soaking will whiten this up good as new," Caitie said as she tucked a tablecloth under her arm. After choosing the very best items, she rounded up the shopkeeper, dickering with him shamelessly, threatening to take her business elsewhere should he dare to deny her her price.

* * *

While they were gone, Joseph stripped away the old wallpaper and lead-polished the cookstove to a previously unknown brilliance. Later on in the week he whitewashed the walls and Melinda hung the "new" curtains. Each day there was an agenda. Each day something was accomplished that drove deeper the reality that this was now home. And little by little Melinda thought less and less about those she'd left behind in Le Baie.

Ultimately, on a cold November morning, Joseph left their cozy attic rooms and walked to the mills in search of work.

Holding Philippe in her lap, Melinda sat on the floor and watched from one of the dormers as her husband's feet left their imprint in the dusting of snow that had fallen overnight. She watched until he'd passed under the streetlamp, striding toward Tremont Street and out of sight.

* * *

As he always did, Joseph walked briskly, having learned early in life that wasted time was lost forever. Turning onto Bedfordgate, the long thoroughfare that crossed the city from east to west, he could see the impressive collection of buildings that were the Union Mills Corporation. He stood for a spell just staring at the granite walls that loomed upward five stories high. With more than a little trepidation, Joseph walked through the gates and entered the main building.

Once inside, he looked for the hiring office. Seeing nothing except row upon row of rattling, clacking looms, he approached a comely young woman who stood working at one of them.

"Office?" he called out above the din.

Turning, she looked at him over her shoulder, her face filled with irritation. "Upstairs," she answered, and turning back to her work, she added, "Greenhorn."

Joseph climbed the stairs to the second floor, then the third, and finally on the fourth he saw a group of men lined up outside a cubicle. He fell into line at the end of the queue. Speaking to no one, he looked around, trying to act as if he belonged there.

It was fascinating to see the skill with which the weavers

handled the shuttles, passing them from one side to the other with unfailing precision. Most of them were young women in their teens or twenties, others mere children of ten or twelve years of age. They appeared oblivious to the ear-splitting noise; nor did they seem to object to the clouds of lint that hung in the air, infiltrating their lungs with every breath they drew.

Joseph's hands grew clammy with nerves as the queue shriveled and he found himself standing at the head of the line.

Inside the cubicle he came face to face with an extremely thin, baldheaded man who sat at a table, his back to a set of large windows.

"What kin I do for ya, buddy?" The man's voice was raspy and unpleasant as his oversized features.

Joseph made haste to answer him. "I look for work ... job, like you call it."

"Well, Kee ... rist! If it ain't another goddamned Cannuck. That's all the hell I've seen in here this mornin', them and those goddamn Portaguese. Pretty soon we won't have nuthin' but foreigners in this bloody town." He stopped talking and looked up at Joseph, the dregs of a sneer still clinging to his lips. "Well, what can ya do, Frenchie?"

"Me ... I do any kind of work. ... Any kind. I learn vite, vite." Joseph snapped his fingers together and stepped a little closer to the table.

The man made a swift backward gesture with his hand. "Take it easy, Buddy, you ain't got no job yet. Just back off here."

Joseph hurried to step back to where he'd been standing. A quiver ran up and down his legs and he felt the hair on them rise. He'd never, not once, entertained the possibility that he might have difficulty finding a job. His mouth went terribly dry.

"Ever do any cardin'?" The man's eyes scrutinized him.

"Cardin'?" The word came out meekly. Joseph had never heard it before. He began twisting his cap in his hands. "No, sir, but—I learn very fast," he repeated, a lot less confidently this time.

"Yeah, well, maybe you do and maybe you don't. And the way you murder the King's English ... well, we might have trouble findin' something for ya. I tell ya, there ain't a helluva lot around here for greenhorns like you, fella."

Joseph's heart sank like a stone. The overseer shuffled some papers around on the table and looked up at him through a cloud of blue-white smoke. "We do have the low gears, though. You ain't gotta have no fancy English for that job." He laughed raucously, his stained, uneven teeth gripping hard onto a cigar butt. "Take it or leave it, fella," he said, pushing himself back onto the hind legs of his chair.

"I take it, I take it!" Joseph replied as quickly as he could, fearing that the overseer might change his mind and go on to the next one in line.

"The job pays seven dollars a week. Put your mark here, and be back prompt at six in the morning."

Joseph approached the desk, and signed his name.

"That's all. Send the next man in on your way out." With another flick of his hand he gestured Joseph toward the door.

An hour after sunrise on the following morning, Joseph stood in front of the horse barns in the rear of the mill yard. Inside, a lanky young man named Liam Steele stood hitching a team of horses to a long flatbed wagon. When he finished, he climbed onto the seat and motioned Joseph to climb up beside him.

Without a word passing between them, they drove out of the mill yard and onto the street that was beginning to fill with horsedrawn traffic. Gawking about unashamedly, Joseph craned his neck for a clearer view.

Overhead and for the full length of Bedfordgate, there hung a confusing maze of electric wires and conduits that powered the Bay State Electric Line, the primary mode of transportation used by the city of Riverton. A noisy, overcrowded trolley clanged its bell shrilly as it moved alongside the low gear, stopping briefly to spew out its cargo of mill workers at the other end of the block.

Halfway down to Maincrossing Road, Joseph noticed a series of row houses. Charrington Mews was a shabby cluster of hovels owned by the Union Mill Corporation, rented to its workers on a weekly basis. The buildings looked out onto a refuse-strewn alley that separated one section of the mews from the other. As Joseph and Liam passed, a large rodent scampered across it, burrowing into a pile of trash lying next to one of the entrances. Repulsed, Joseph looked away, not realizing that inside these bleak and squalid premises, Liam Steele and his family of eight made their home.

Beyond the mews, the façade of the Riverton National Bank building on the corner of Maincrossing Road appeared. It was the newest of several banks in the heart of Riverton's business sector. It dwarfed everything around it except the city hall.

Designed by Franklin Trenton, a famed English architect, the city hall majestically spiraled upward, the black-faced clock in its tower sounding the quarter-hour as Joseph and the Irishman passed.

At Maincrossing Road, Liam Steele veered the cart to the left, past the Emporium and the granite block building. Then steering sharply to the right, he started down Anawan Hill. The wheels of the low gear cart screeched as he pulled hard upon the handbrake, slowing it to a near crawl. Tobey and Fiona picked their way down the steep incline, carefully navigating through the frosty cobblestones, toward Lindsey's Wharf at Stoneheep. They reached the docks of the Riverton Steamship Lines forty minutes after leaving the horse barns.

The *Bristol*, one of the Riverton Line's newest and largest ships, rested at dockside, her cavernous freight deck opened to the longshoremen who were emptying her cargo of cotton shipped down Long Island Sound from New York, where it had come north from the Carolinas.

The Irishman drove past it, maneuvering the low gear alongside a long, low building next to the wharf.

"'Ere ye go, Jody," Liam said as he handed Joseph a pair of heavy metal tongs. "Just ye do as I do."

Joseph followed him inside the warehouse. Opening the tongs, they gripped the bales and one by one they carried them out, hoisting them onto the low gear. They piled bale on top of bale until Joseph thought they could pile no more, but still they did, until the cart was heaped to capacity and beyond. After securing the bales with canvas straps, they re-mounted the wagon and slowly pulled away.

Turning into Anawan Hill, the horses girded themselves for the treacherous ascent, their sinewy rumps bearing down, their shoes kicking up sparks as they slid into and out of the crevasses between the cobbles.

Bobbing their heads up and down, the animals inched their way up the hill, nostrils flaring, and spewing a frothy liquid into the crisp November air. Tobey's head reared and Fee whinnied as the cruel bits dug deeply into their hard, leathery mouths. Mindlessly, they hauled their gargantuan load to the top where Anawan Hill met once again with Maincrossing Road.

Joseph felt his fists open and his fingers uncurl. His breathing returned to normal and the painful knots that had formed in his diaphragm relaxed and left him. He was once again able to sit alongside the Irishman without fear gripping at his heart. Liam moved steadily on ahead, saying nothing, but the small smile that played at the corners of his mouth did not go unnoticed.

Aye, Jody, ye'll do, he said to himself. *Ye'll do just fine and dandy.*

Four runs were made that day. Four assaults on the sheer steep of Anawan Hill, and as they turned into the mill yard for the last time, the gaslights burned on Bedfordgate.

Later that evening, bone-weary and longing for rest, Joseph ever so faithfully recreated the events of his day in his first letter to Victor in Baie de Saint-Jacques.

Chapter Four

There was a tense furtiveness about Victor Durand as he sat at the kitchen table re-reading the letter from his brother in America. His oval-shaped, ebony eyes devoured each word as hungrily now as the first time he'd read them.

Lately, he had believed he would never hear from Joseph and never fulfill his own dream of going to America. He'd planned it all so carefully. How could everything have gone so wrong? His jaw clenched and his eyes became flinty as he rose and walked to the window.

Looking out onto the road that led to the village, Victor could still see the dust rising as the Bérard's carriage passed the farm on that bleak morning six weeks ago. Never would he forget the ache he'd felt inside him as he'd watched it take the last bit of road into the village.

"It's her fault—goddam her!" he said aloud, looking toward the staircase.

Whenever he thought of that day last August, when Claire had come to him with the "news" of her pregnancy, the rage rose again. What a fool he'd been to ever have trusted her! To have believed that she would be different from those who'd betrayed him all his life.

Hindsight was indeed a remarkable thing. Now he could easily see through the soft caressing words whispered on a sultry June night, mere hours after they were wed.

"I want to bear your child, my darling," Claire had said as she pressed herself closer to him. "I've never wanted anything so much in my life." Her lips had been seductively close to his as she lay in Victor's arms, blissfully satiated from their lovemaking.

"For heaven's sake, Claire," he'd retorted, "let's not rush into anything. Let's at least get to know one another a bit before thinking of raising a family."

Disappointment had clouded Claire's lovely eyes, but only momentarily. "Of course, Victor, but we mustn't wait too long. Need I remind you, darling, that I am no longer a girl in my twenties?" She laughed, a little self-consciously.

"Shush," he'd said gently, "no more talk about babies. Tonight I want you to think only of me."

Taking her to him again, his passion forced all further thoughts from his mind. Everything vanished but his need to satisfy the hungering inside him.

In his haste to appease that hunger, Victor Durand failed to learn how little his wife knew about controlling such things. In Claire's mind, conception was the natural result of the coming together of a man and a woman. She was incredibly naïve when it came to matters of the flesh. Despite being ten years her husband's senior, Claire Durand was an innocent; unschooled in the methods used in preventing pregnancy. And had she known, she would not have felt able to avail herself of them. The shrill voice of Catholic conscience would have prevented the taking of such measures. God's will had always been her guideline, and would forever be.

Unlike his wife, Victor coveted no dreams of parenthood. He'd seen firsthand what too many mouths to feed could do to destroy a man. How many times had his father groveled and humiliated himself before losing all self-respect? Too many debts, added to too many crop failures, had in the end turned Louis into a prideless beggar. Were it not for handouts from Michèl Bérard and others like him, he would long ago have lost everything. No—fathering six sons in ten years had done nothing to help Louis Durand succeed in life.

Two months passed without further mention of the subject.

Complacent and trusting that all was safe in Claire's hands, Victor put it out of his mind—until August, when his life was instantly turned inside out.

The tragic sequence of events ensuing from that time to this had served to completely destroy Victor and Claire's relationship.

In a warped sort of way, Victor mourned the loss of what he'd shared with Claire. She had accepted him without undue concern over the social chasm that lay between them. He'd questioned that at first, for Claire Clement was of the gentry born. Under normal circumstances, it was doubtful they would ever have met.

A gifted musician, her father had come to Canada from Paris to teach at the Conservatory in Montreal. Failing health had forced him to leave that post early on in his career.

They'd abandoned the city when Claire was five, for the less stressful country life of Le Baie. For twenty-three years, Charles Antoine Clement had been organist at the Church of Saint John-the-Baptist, and with him had come the genius of Bach, Mozart, Franck, and Saint-Saens. Music deserving of the impressive organ that, piece by piece, had been shipped from France and installed in the choir loft.

Charles Clement and his wife had also operated a small music store on Place de la Sainte Eglise, the beautiful square that, along with the church, formed the focal point of the village.

He and madame succeeded in building a serene and happy life for themselves in this unimposing little village, and by far their greatest joy in life was their daughter Claire, an only child, one who'd come to them in the tenth year of their marriage—long after they'd despaired of ever having a family.

But alas, their later years were tragically unkind to them. With advancing age, a progressively crippling arthritis struck Monsieur Clement, and Claire left her studies at the Conservatory in Montreal to return and help care for her father. Mornings they could be seen walking through the darkened streets, halos of mist still shrouding the gaslamps as they made their way down Rue de l'Aigle Noir, toward the church for the first Mass of the day. Using his canes, Clement forced his swollen legs up the narrow, ill-shapen stairs that led to the choir loft. When seated and with his hands upon the great keyboards, his pain "miraculously" disappeared.

The anxious eyes of Charbonnais, the caretaker, followed him every inch of the way, a deep frown forming as he waited at the ready should his aid be needed to help Monsieur descend. Over the years they'd become as brothers, this humble, uneducated "habitant" and the cultured gentleman from Paris.

"Ça va mieux c'matin?" the caretaker would whisper to Claire as they passed him at the foot of the stairs.

The answer was always: "Come toujours, Monsieur Charbonnais ... come toujours."

Finally there came the bitter winter of Charles Clement's sixty-fifth year when, unable to manage the climb to the loft, he was forced to give up his music and was reduced to sitting in the wheelchair that he'd spurned for the previous three years. This seemed to strike the death knell, for with the coming of spring his pain mercifully ended.

Claire tried, but there was no consoling her mother, and in six months' time she lay beside her husband.

After the funeral, Claire shut herself away inside her home. Except for an aunt, her mother's younger sister, there was no family left to her in Canada.

Months passed before she could think of anything but her loss. Later, when she was able to face the world again, she resumed going to daily Mass, fervently praying for God's help to put her life together again.

The following summer she took to walking for hours along the grassy banks of the river and as the season waned and autumn leaves fell from the trees and rustled past her on some endless, purposeless journey, she decided to follow the urgings of her aunt and move to Montreal.

In October, she gave up the lease to the music store. The house, however, had seen little in the way of maintenance for years, and she could not disgrace her parents' memory by offering it for sale in such a state of disrepair.

"I hadn't realized it was so run-down," she wrote her aunt Gabrielle in the city. "I must hire someone to put it to rights before carrying on with my plans."

She availed herself of the local weekly to make known her need for a handyman, and on a cloudy rainwashed morning, Victor Durand came to her door.

After introducing himself, he explained, "I've come in reply to your notice in the paper."

His voice was deeper and huskier than she'd expected. Something fluttered inside her and she hesitated an instant before replying. "Yes ... well, as you can see, there is much to be done hereabouts. The garden needs to be thoroughly cleared, and the house wants for some painting both inside and out."

Walking around the grounds with her, Victor's eyes scanned every inch of the property. When he failed to make any comment, Claire went on.

"I'd prefer that the outside work be finished by November. Is that at all within reason?"

"It is, providing this weather holds."

His name was not unknown to her. She'd recognized it instantly as belonging to an eccentric family who lived outside the village on a weed-infested farm less than a half-mile down the road from Michèl Bérard's place. She'd heard the gossip that passed among her neighbors, labeling the Durand men as hard drinkers and womanizers who idled away their time in the taverns and bawdy houses that had sprung up around the lumber yard over the years.

Looking into Victor's dark, elongated eyes, she found what she'd heard difficult to believe. She'd also attended school with Joseph, his older brother, and knew him to be a decent, hard-working man. So despite the hearsay and a slightly jittery feeling in the pit of her stomach, Claire found herself unable to refuse him.

"When is it possible for you to begin?"

A smile crept across his face, exposing square, almost perfect teeth. "This moment, if you wish it, madame."

"Tomorrow will be quite soon enough. And incidentally, Mr. Durand, it's mademoiselle, not madame."

She found Victor to be a tireless worker, willing to take on the most menial of tasks. At first they spoke little, but as time went on they began sharing greetings and small talk as they encountered each other in passing. And Victor's sultry good looks did not go unnoticed; Claire often stood watching him, protected from sight behind the Austrian lace curtains that hung in the parlor windows.

Some weeks later Victor knocked at her door, holding a small bouquet of chrysanthemums bunched in his hand. He'd not known that today was her thirty-second birthday and that she'd awakened feeling melancholy and alone.

"Thank you ... they're lovely," she'd said, taking them from him. All of a sudden she felt a stinging under her lids, as unexpected tears sprang to her eyes. She quickly averted them from his gaze.

"I hope I haven't overstepped any boundaries, madame," he apologized, as Claire started back into the house.

"Not at all, it was a lovely gesture." Her voice was calm and in control again. "But please, Victor, try to remember, it's mademoiselle, not madame."

Closing the door behind her, she leaned against it, holding the small bouquet against her bosom. Once again tears stung at her eyes. Never before had she received flowers from an attractive young man. Raising them to her face, she breathed in their pungent fragrance. Deep inside her she felt the filling of an empty place. Shaking off her melancholy mood, she went into the dining room, where strewn on the table were numerous swatches of wall coverings. Turning them this way and that, she went about making her selections.

* * *

Victor came early each morning, sometimes before Claire had risen from her bed. He went about his work diligently, never bothering her in any way, and as the days of winter approached, Claire found herself living for the hours when he would be there.

Victor was not unaware of what was happening, for he had seen the passion deep down in her gentle, amber eyes. He bided his time, and when winter's icy breath blew across the land, he began working indoors.

On days when the weather was too foul for him to walk to his meal at the farm, Claire prepared something for him, coaxing him into a bit of small talk as they sat eating together in the kitchen. That eventually led to his remaining for a chat after his chores were completed for the day. At first for only a moment or two, then longer and longer as the weeks of December passed. They would sit on the mohair sofa and share snippets of themselves with each other. Cautiously at first, but soon more trustingly. And when he'd gone, Claire would realize that she'd done most of the talking. She'd climb the stairs to her bedroom, her face burning with embarrassment. Somehow, this waif-like man/boy cast a Rasputinish spell over her that made her behave in a most uncharacteristic manner. She vowed, then and there, never to do it again. ... But she did.

With time, Victor became more sure of himself, responding by taking her hand into his, and later when he felt that he could, he leaned over and placed a kiss on her forehead. He sat very close to her, listening to the hopes and dreams locked secretly inside her for so long.

It was then that a plan began forming in his mind. Here, in this gentle, vulnerable woman could be a means to an end: his liberation from poverty and the stranglehold it had on his life. He saw in Claire Clement the realization of something that he could otherwise never have hoped for. A chance for a new beginning, a new life in America. It could—it would— become more than a dream if all went as he planned.

* * *

Droplets of perspiration broke out along Joseph Durand's hairline. Another attempt to dissuade his brother Victor from marrying Claire Clement had failed and he was tempted to walk away from the whole situation.

"She's not your kind, Victor. Don't try to fit in where you don't belong."

"Why not, Joe? You did!" Victor regretted the words the

30

moment he'd uttered them. The last thing he wanted to do was to alienate Joseph, for he was the only member of his family who did not treat him like so much filthy vermin. "I'm sorry, Joe," Victor apologized, "that wasn't fair."

"Believe me, Victor, I have only your best interests at heart. I'm simply trying to save you some heartache. Oil never mixes with water—never!"

Victor turned his back to him.

Instantly Joseph realized the futility of his efforts. "What is it you see in this woman, anyway?" Joseph shrugged his shoulders. "She's years past your age, Victor, and plain as a titmouse."

"She isn't, really. Not when you get to know her."

Claire's calm, virginal demeanor had been one of the things that had attracted Victor to her. He'd come to admire her proud, sensitive eyes, and the sleek brown hair pulled back into a plaited chignon. It accentuated her high cheekbones and the long curve of her neck. Unlike any woman he'd known thus far, Claire was well-bred and courteous, and she treated him with respect. There was a purity about her—an innocence that excited Victor.

Within three months of their meeting, he'd proposed marriage, and Claire had accepted, for she could no longer imagine living without him.

"I'd like your blessing, Joe, but I'll do without it if need be."

"You don't love her, Victor. You're using this woman."

"You're right, Joe, I don't love her. Not in the way that you mean. But I care ... very much. She's unlike anyone I've ever known. She loves me, Joe, and I know I can make her happy."

* * *

Their wedding was attended by only a few, and as reluctant as he'd been, Joseph finally agreed to stand at the altar beside his brother. Claire's Aunt Gabrielle, who'd come from Montreal to share in her niece's happiness, stood next

31

to her.

Following the nuptials, the newlyweds made their home in the Clement house on Rue de l'Aigle Noir, and their coming together was of such passion that Claire could not have imagined its power over her.

Victor was an incomparable lover. At times sensitive and patient, other times overwhelming in his great need of her. After one such meeting he lay beside her, stretching languorously, and she looked openly at his naked body. The long muscular thighs, the flat abdomen, the powerful shoulders and arms. She marveled at his perfection, unable to believe that he belonged to her. Reaching up, she undid her hair and pulled it over her shoulders, covering her chest with dark, silky tendrils. Victor stroked and caressed it, and instantly she responded to his touch. His fingers worked through the silken strands to the small nipple lying beneath. He fondled it, first with his fingers. Then his lips found their way there and he pressed them against it softly, opening then closing, tracing its contour with the tip of his tongue. Fingers of fire reached to her very core.

"You're so lovely," Victor whispered, his face pressed against her shoulder.

"When you touch me, I feel that I am. I love you so much, Victor."

He pulled her to him and their lips met again. Something ignited between them and he took her once more, as passionately and as greedily as he had the first time.

In January, winter storms resculpted the landscape, outlining the branches of the hardwoods behind Claire and Victor's house as skillfully as if done by an artist's hand. The men of the village came out of their homes carrying ice axes to carve holes in the frozen river for the winter fishing.

Meanwhile, Victor went ahead with his scheme. He met secretly with the American mill agents who came to Quebec seeking labor for the burgeoning textile industry. Regaling in the illusions painted by their silvery tongues, he set about trying to convince his brother Joseph to go to America with him. A hefty challenge, since Melinda would be giving birth to their first child in June.

At home with Claire, Victor feigned discontent. "For a spirited, ambitious man, living in Baie de Saint-Jacques is like being imprisoned," he complained as he restlessly roamed from room to room, pacing back and forth like a caged animal.

"I know, darling," Claire sympathized sweetly, caressing the curve of his arm. "The winters *are* so dreadfully long. Why don't you fish with the men from the village. It would help pass the time."

"Don't be ridiculous, Claire. These people will never accept me as an equal. I'm a Durand—I might just as well be a leper." Waggling an accusing finger toward the neighboring houses, Victor ended by muttering, "Sometimes I think we'd be better off living out on the farm."

"Please, Victor, give them a chance to know you. If only—"

"YES, IF ONLY," he interrupted. "Words I've often used myself. *If only* I were genteel, and educated, like those snobs you call your friends. Perhaps then they would not have cast you aside for having wed me."

At first Claire was puzzled, then increasingly worried by these moods. But after giving it further thought, she found herself agreeing with her husband. Her friends hadn't called to congratulate them or to bid Victor welcome to the village. And when they'd met on the street, their smiles only thinly veiled their discomfort. After the briefest of exchanges, they'd hurried on their way.

Winter passed with little change in their situation. Claire was sure now that the people she'd known for most of her life would not forgive her having married an "outsider," especially one named Durand.

* * *

Sitting next to the window, Claire looked out as an early spring rain fell on the tender foliage sprouting from the shrubs in front of the house on Rue de l'Aigle Noir. She pulled the curtain further aside when she caught sight of her husband turning into the street. Just watching him walk, tall and straight, his long stride revealing the contour of the muscles in his legs, raised goose bumps on her arms. He'd been to the farm again, as he'd done so often of late. He smiled as he passed the window, and she ran to the door to greet him.

"Hurry, darling," she said as he entered, her voice filled with the excitement of his being there. "Come sit with me on the sofa." She pulled him down close to her. "I've been thinking a great deal about what you said earlier, Victor, and you're right—we don't belong here in Le Baie. Other than working yourself to death on the farm or at the lumber yard, there's no opportunity for you to advance here. You're young, my darling, you should have every chance to prove yourself.

"Montreal is a beautiful city, dearest," she went on, her excitement mounting. "Have you ever been there? We could sell the house and stay with Tante Gabrielle until we're able to find just the right place for ourselves. She would enjoy having us, and I have friends there who—"

"No, Claire, not Montreal."

She frowned and her eyes searched his, an uneasy feeling tugging at her insides. "Then where, Victor? Just tell me where you want to go." She would have crossed the earth and beyond to please him.

"I want to live in the United States."

"The United States?" she repeated, her voice trailing off, her mind trying to grasp what it meant. "But it's so far ..."

"Far? Far from what, Claire? Far from who? You no longer have anyone here, and other than you, there's never been anyone, or anything worth my staying in Le Baie for."

"But your family—"

"The only person who matters a damn to me is Joseph, and I've all but convinced him to leave too," he blurted out. "Darling, I've thought about this all winter long. There's nothing to keep us tied to this place. As long as we're together, we have everything."

34

Claire fell into his arms, murmuring her consent.

* * *

As soon as the weather warmed, they sold the house, and the furnishings went piece by piece at auction. It was hard for Claire to see her parents' treasures being carried away by those who now seemed little more than strangers to her. Men from her father's choir, their wives—women who for years had sat across from her mother at the whist table.

She kept only a few precious mementos: a crate of linens; the Limoges her parents had brought with them from France; and a corrugated box filled with some of her father's music. A few small threads gleaned from the fabric of a lifetime.

When all was sold, Victor was more than pleased. The house and its contents had brought much more than he'd hoped for. Being ignorant of fine art and French antiques, he'd miscalculated their worth in his evaluations. On June 11th as they left for the farm, everything had been accounted for in Victor's ledger. Combined with Claire's sizable inheritance, a handsome sum was deposited into an account in Victor's name.

Claire held onto her husband's arm as they walked from the house for the last time. She didn't look back. She looked straight ahead, toward a new beginning—a new life with the man she loved more than anything on earth.

Later that night, word came from Les Érables that Melinda had given birth to a son.

* * *

Learning to live with Victor's family was more difficult than Claire had anticipated.

His mother, Laura Durand, was distant and taciturn, and sometimes even openly hostile. She seemed in poor health and kept to her room most of the time. Louis, his father, did what little housekeeping was done, and the rest of the family more or less fended for themselves. Claire very quickly assumed the household chores. She did not object, for she was anxious to please and eager to put her hand to a task badly in need of doing. By midsummer she'd scrubbed every room in the house, save Laura's, and polished their hodge-podge of furnishings to an acceptable shine. She finished her project by adding some broadcloth to the curtainless windows of the bedroom she and Victor were occupying.

There were days when the temperature rose above the ninety-degree mark on the rusted thermometer nailed to the jamb of the cellar door. On one such day in mid-August, when Claire had finished doing the laundry and was carrying it outside to hang, she stood in the entryway, her head reeling with dizziness. She quickly put down the heavy basket and leaned against the wall. There were a few tense moments when she thought she might vomit, but the nausea passed as soon as she was able to see clearly again. Breathing deeply, she brushed back the wet strands of hair from her forehead and went outside to the clotheslines.

The following week the same thing occurred, only this time it was as she rose from bed, fully rested from a good night's sleep. Claire decided she'd best see the doctor.

Leaving the farm, she walked down the road toward the village, her eyes on the ground, guiding her past the ruts cut into the hardened clay by the carriage wheels.

In the village Claire hurried across La Place, nodding shyly in the direction of the familiar faces she passed along the way. Reaching the church, she pulled open the door and walked up to the altar of the Madonna, lighting a votive candle before kneeling to pray. She lowered her head, not daring to think about, much less try to put into words, the hope that filled her heart.

Coming out onto the square again, Claire stood for a time next to the fountain. Despite tree-lined streets that offered the protection of their shade, the village was oppressively hot. Claire opened the collar of her blouse and dabbed at her face with a handkerchief.

Going on, she passed in front of a variety of shops, looking for an instant into the window of what had been her father's music store.

Papa, I miss you, she thought.

Walking past the marketplace, Claire turned into Rue Alban where Doctor Savard's shingle hung above the letter slot in the door of his house. She entered into the somber, somewhat funereal, waiting room.

A half-hour later Claire left his rooms, still unable to truly believe what he'd told her. She was carrying Victor's child, and had been for over a month. For a wanton moment, she felt like running through the narrow streets, shouting her joy to anyone within earshot. Instead she walked primly out of the village, stopping only at the apothecary shop for some powders the doctor prescribed. Something to settle her stomach and control the dizzy spells.

Arriving at the farm, she found no one about, but she could hear Louis out in the barn splintering the winter kindling. She wanted to go to him and say: *Rejoice, Father Durand, you'll soon have another precious grandchild! Perhaps a little girl this time, one who'll sit on your knee and bring joy to your old age.*

But Claire knew such tidings would give Louis little cause for celebration, for he had given no notice at all to the birth of Joseph's son, Philippe, in June. Nothing seemed to hold meaning for either of Victor's parents any longer. Claire let go of the unhappy thought, lest it turn her joy to ashes.

Entering the house, she heard no sound. Laura, she presumed, was locked in her bedchamber, the ever present bottle of spirits close at hand. God alone knew how this pathetic woman could bear such a meaningless existence.

Just once, Claire had dared to rap at Laura's door.

Laura had not opened it, but had called out harshly, "Go away! This room is off limits to you."

Claire never ventured there again.

Changing into a wrapper, Claire lay on her bed trying to assimilate the miracle that was taking place inside her. After resting an hour, she dressed and went into the kitchen to prepare the evening meal.

When Victor walked in from the fields with his brothers, Claire went out to the pump to greet him. She stood aside and waited while he washed.

"That's the last of the hay," he said with a sigh as he took the towel from her hands and dried himself. "And thank God for that," he added sullenly.

At dinner, Victor was short and abrasive as he spoke to his brothers. Claire listened with half an ear to the conversation.

Louis, in his usual bellicose mood, cursed the price he would get for his grain. "It's hardly enough to pay for replanting!"

"It's one of our better years, Pa," Damien informed him. "With the hailstorm last August, we lost most of the crop."

"Humph ... a lot of good that does me, if I can't get a decent price."

Victor ate without commenting further. He was bored with his father's outbursts and generally ignored them. He felt it useless to offer an opinion, since Louis would carry on regardless of what anyone else might think.

Claire washed the dishes and set the breakfast oats to soaking. The clock was striking eight by the time she'd finished and walked over to where Victor sat. She took hold of his hand.

"You look tired, dear, why don't we go up early tonight?"

As they withdrew, Claire felt Victor's brothers eyeing their backs, knowing that the lurid remarks would soon follow their departure from the room. She didn't care what they said; nothing could spoil this night for her.

* * *

After she'd sponged him, Victor lay across the bed, stripped down to his underclothes.

"Open the window, Claire. There isn't a breath of air in here," Victor complained, throwing back the quilt and propping himself on the pillows.

"There, is that better?" Claire asked as the breeze sent her hand-stitched curtains billowing into the room. "The thermometer read ninety-three degrees when I came home from the village this afternoon. I don't ever remember it being this hot so late in the summer."

Victor looked up at her briefly. Still in a churlish mood he replied, "It's interesting how people choose to forget things. It's always hot at this time of year." He flapped open the newspaper that lay on the bedside table. "You'd be more apt to remember that if you were out in the fields sweating out your salts to bring in a harvest."

Victor's tone again gave Claire cause to reflect. Living in this house had changed Victor, made him petulant and defensive. She'd not seen this facet of his personality on Rue de l'Aigle Noir. She could hardly wait to be gone from this house and be rid of the stigma attached to this dark, depressive family.

In the short time that Claire had been at the farm, she'd come to realize why the people in town held the Durands in such disdain. She'd also learned to appreciate what a tremendous difference the right set of circumstances could make in shaping a person's life. Considering his background, Victor had been doomed from the first. He would have his chance now; he would have it in America!

"Have you spoken with Joseph recently, Victor?"

He answered without looking up from his paper. "No, he's bringing in Bérard's wheat. We won't see anything of him until just before we leave."

"I visited with Melinda last week. I brought her the christening shawl I crocheted for the baby." Claire smiled and looked at Victor from the corner of her eye.

He remained focused on the *Riverton Herald*, sent to him in the mail by a mill agent.

"Philippe is such an adorable child," Claire went on. "He favors the Durand side of the family. I think he'll have eyes like his father's." She looked Victor's way again and despite the "Unh unh's" he uttered now and again, she knew he wasn't listening.

"Emilie is beside herself with joy. She fusses with the boy

every waking moment. She'll miss him terribly when he's gone." Giving her husband another sidelong glance, Claire girded herself. "I do so wish that my parents could have lived to know of the birth of our child in the spring."

Instantly she had his full attention and the room took on an electrified air.

Claire moved closer to him. "I saw Doctor Savard this afternoon, darling. I'm pregnant." Her eyes glowed and she trembled slightly.

Victor's lips parted but he made no sound.

Leaning closer, Claire repeated, "We're going to have a baby, Victor."

She felt his body stiffen. With a sudden lunge he leapt from the bed.

"Victor, what is it?"

He stood looking down at her, his face contorted with rage. Still he was silent, his breath locked in his throat.

"Victor, you're frightening me! Tell me what's wrong!"

"How dare you ask that question? Just what in HELL do you think is wrong?"

Claire began to speak but he cut her off.

"Shut up! Just shut up! I have to think, and I can't think when you're babbling." He walked to the window and slammed it closed.

Everything inside her cringed at the sharp, violent sound. She sat motionless in the middle of the bed, too terrified to move.

Slowly, almost stealthily, he approached her. "Just when will this wonderful event take place?" His lips, stretched tightly across his teeth, were inches from her face.

She could feel his breath, hot against her cheek. Her voice was thin, expressionless. "Not for a long time."

"WHEN!" he shouted.

"Next March."

He stood beside the bed looking down at her, his right arm raised above his head. For a moment she thought he would strike her. Never had she seen so much unabashed fury. She could almost taste it.

With a quick downward sweep of his hand, Victor gathered up his clothes from the chair and walked toward the door. Stopping, he looked back at her. "Why did you do this when I specifically asked you not to?" Without waiting for an answer, he added: "As I see it, you've ruined everything."

Her pulses pounding, crashing like waves in her ears, Claire explained: "I did what I knew of to do, Victor." She burst into pitiful weeping. "Why can't you be happy about this? It needn't change anything!" Breaking down completely, Claire covered her face in her hands.

"Jesus Christ! You don't know what you're talking about." He turned on his heel and left.

From that moment on, it was never the same between them. Victor spurned their conjugal bed, choosing instead to share an attic room with one of his brothers.

After a number of useless attempts at conciliation, Claire gave it up, withdrawing further and further into herself every day. It appeared she was tainted in her husband's eyes. An unclean woman he could not suffer to be near.

Two weeks passed. Weeks filled with unspeakable tension. Nothing resolved itself; to the contrary, Claire became more and more confused.

What must I do to make him understand? she asked herself. Unable to endure Victor's rejection any longer, Claire made subtle approaches that resulted only in humiliating her more deeply. Hurt and angry, she decided to visit her aunt in Montreal. She left the farm without a word to anyone.

Painfully, she bared her soul to the old woman who was so much like her mother.

"He's very young," Tante Gaby remarked, "give him time. And truly, dear—without any condescension, mind you—Victor does not possess your breeding or your intellect. Very frankly, Claire, I'm a bit appalled at the naïveté displayed on your part. You should have been more informed." Reaching across the mahogany table, she covered Claire's hand with hers. "Albeit unfair, ma chère, a woman is burdened with the responsibility of controlling the consequences of what takes place in the bedchamber. Ignorance is inexcusable for failing in this department. A mortal sin, my dear," she added, clucking her tongue loudly a number of times.

Claire dropped her head and stared down at her hands, her face slowly turning florid.

"There are things one can do, my sweet child."

Unbeknownst to her family, Gabrielle Bonnet, a "maiden lady," had been secretly "kept" for more than twenty years as the pampered paramour of a well-heeled gentleman from Montreal. She knew the ways of the world—all of them.

Claire looked at her, her widespread eyes darkening almost to black. "But how could I have known about such things," she asked, "when I had never before ..." Wiping her brow with her handkerchief, Claire shook off her embarrassment and spoke candidly. "If the truth be known, Tante, I never expected to marry. When I did, I was so enamored of this man, and so bent on pleasing him, I gave no thought to any consequences. Besides, the Church takes a dim view of anyone who engages in such behavior."

Gabrielle nodded her head slowly up and down, her sympathetic eyes gazing steadily at her niece. Gaby understood the conflict churning inside Claire. Oh my—how well she understood. "You'll put things right, my dear. Just have a little patience with him." Words of little comfort, but what more could she say?

"I'm not sure I can do that."

"What choice do you have but to try?"

Claire looked from the window, knowing there was but one answer to that question.

* * *

On Saturday morning she took an early train back to Le Baie. During the journey she planned a course of action. It would seem she had wronged her husband and had failed in her wifely responsibilities. She hated the thought of facing his wrath, but her marriage and the well-being of her child depended on it.

42

She let herself into the house through the kitchen door. Upon entering the kitchen, she saw Victor seated at the table with his brothers Damien and Roger. It was set with plates and cutlery, and in the center of it lay a platter of coarsely sliced bread. Victor held a near-empty bottle of brandy in his hand.

She was surprised to see Laura standing at the stove, stirring a kettle of milky chowder. She gave Claire a stern, disapproving look.

Nothing has changed here, Claire sensed through every pore in her skin. She was an outcast in a family of outcasts. All her resolve withered and vanished, and the icy fingers of fear again wrapped themselves around her heart.

She greeted them and was making her way to the staircase that led to the second floor when Victor rose and walked unsteadily toward her.

"Well, the errant fledgling has returned to the nest," he said when he reached her, the rich clarity of his voice lost in a quagmire of slurring sound. His breath was fetid and he reeked of body odor.

Claire halted immediately and rested her suitcase on the floor. She spoke softly, uncertainly. "Hello, Victor."

As he looked at her, a jeering smile played at his lips.

She sensed a volatile situation in the making and wanting very much to avoid it, she smiled in return. "It's good to see you. I've missed you ... all of you," she added, looking in the direction of his brothers.

The sound of suppressed laughter came from the table where they sat drinking. Pretending not to have heard, Claire turned to her husband who now stood between her and the refuge of the staircase. Feeling frightened and desperately out of control of the situation, she yearned to flee, to be gone forever from this house, from the vulgarities, the ridicule, the contempt that filled their eyes. But like a trapped animal, instinct told her to bide her time, to avoid arousing Victor's ire.

He stepped closer to her and with a swift motion he reached out and pulled her to him. She willed herself to remain calm. After being shunned for weeks, Claire had assumed that Victor had resumed satisfying his sexual appetites in the sordid little rooms above the tavern. Now holding her in a vise-like grip, he pressed himself against her. She could feel his passion mounting. She wondered for a panic-filled instant if he would take her, then and there. Suddenly there wasn't a sound to be heard.

As unemotionally as she could, Claire said, "Please, Victor, let go of me. You're hurting my arms."

The jeering smile reappeared. Lifting one hand, he stroked her neck, gently at first, then his fingers slid down over her shoulder and he cupped his hand over her breast.

"You used to like me to touch you, *Mademoiselle.* He mocked her, and again the sound of snickering reached her ears from across the room.

Instantly, her fear vanished. "STOP IT!" she screamed.

A strength she had never before called upon welled up from somewhere inside her. She twisted her body from side to side, trying to break free of his grasp. The more she tried, the more he restrained her, and the more her outrage grew. He threw back his head and roared with laughter. Reaching up, her nails raked across his cheekbone. Blood trickled from the wound, down his face to his jaw, and he cursed her as his hand struck her face.

"YOU BITCH! YOU MISERABLE BITCH!"

She felt herself lurching backward, tripping over the suitcase behind her. Claire's hands reached out, clawing desperately at the air, searching for something—anything that would prevent her from falling. She heard herself cry out as her body met with the hardness of the floor. She lay in a heap, too stunned to move, her breath coming in irregular gasps.

An eerie quiet filled the room.

Victor came to her, his footsteps echoing through the strained silence. He stooped to lift her into his arms.

"Get away from me!" she managed to say as she moved aside and rose under her own power.

A cramp deep within her made her hesitate just as she reached for the handrail. She waited for it to pass before go-

44

ing on to the top of the stairs. She stopped once again in the hallway before going to her room.

Taking a small towel from the washstand, she lay on the bed and placed it between her thighs. Dazed, her thoughts coming in irrational spurts, she lay motionless as the hours passed and the pains grew stronger.

Sometime during the hours before daylight, she was aware of Victor's coming to her, of his asking if she was all right, but she could no longer answer him.

"I'm sorry," he said, completely sobered now. "I was just trying to teach you a lesson."

His words trailed away, and she heard nothing but her heart beating in her chest.

Victor spoke again, but she could no longer hear him, for by then the hemorrhaging had begun and her pain became a living hell. Just before dawn when she felt that she could bear it no longer, the mass that would have been their child passed from her body.

* * *

Still holding Joseph's letter in his hand, Victor looked out from the window. Six weeks had passed since his eyes had followed the Bérard carriage carrying Melinda and Joseph forward to the fulfillment of their dream. Victor vowed to wait no longer before fulfilling his own. He would tell his wife as much in the morning.

Chapter Five

In the weeks since the loss of her child, Claire's body had healed but the wounds inflicted upon her heart still lay open and bleeding.

She left her room infrequently, and only when necessary. By day she sat in a chair next to the window reading verses from her Bible; by night she slept, bathed in blessed, narcotic nothingness.

Her only visitor was Doctor Savard who called each week to check on her. This morning he'd spent the better part of an hour in Claire's room.

He usually left without any communication with Victor, but after this particular visit Victor stood waiting for him at the foot of the stairs.

As Savard walked past him, Victor followed close on his heels into the vestibule and said, "One moment please, Doctor. I'd like to be informed as to the state of my wife's health."

Savard looked at him through skeptical eyes, his thin lips pressed tightly together. Lifting his overcoat from the hall tree, Savard proceeded to put it on. "Physically, Claire is quite well. Emotionally, she's extremely fragile."

"Is she fit enough to travel?"

Deciding to finally have his say, Savard laid his medical bag down on the floor. Probing Victor's face once again, he allowed his distaste of the man to be clearly witnessed. "I don't think you realize the severity of what your wife has had to deal with, young man. It's traumatic enough for a woman to miscarry a child, under *any* circumstance, but especially so when it was wanted as much as Claire wanted her baby." For the first time his voice sounded indicting. "I can't even offer her the comfort of knowing there will be other children, for there won't be—not ever." Savard looked harried and deeply disturbed by what had transpired here. "If only I'd been called. I might have ..." He buttoned his coat and turned to leave. Hesitating, he exhaled heavily, and his voice took on a more professional tone. "Time, Monsieur Durand. It's the only remedy I have to offer you. I don't have a powder or a potion that will make this go away."

Victor followed him out to his buggy. "I asked you if she was fit enough to travel and you haven't answered my question."

The doctor pulled down on the brim of his hat and climbed inside. "That's a decision I'll leave entirely up to you, sir." Taking up the whip, he flicked it at the horse's flank and drove away.

* * *

After receiving Joseph's letter, a sense of urgency had risen inside Victor. With an energy he'd not felt in many weeks, he began putting everything into readiness. He took down their trunks from the attic and got their papers in order. Claire was fit enough, he reasoned. Had she not been, Savard would have forbidden her traveling outright.

Balancing a tray of tea and biscuits, Victor went upstairs. He knocked at the door to Claire's bedchamber. When she didn't respond, he opened it to find her standing before the washstand, bathing. A pulse began pounding in his groin. It was still there, his diabolical need of her—despite everything that had happened.

"Why didn't you answer? Am I supposed to guess whether you're awake or asleep?"

Putting her towel back on the rod, Claire folded her robe around herself and sat on the edge of the bed. "You needn't have bothered with food, Victor, I'm not hungry."

He put the tray down on the bedside table. "Suit yourself," he replied, walking to the chair next to the fireplace.

Seating himself, he gazed at her from across the room. "There's something we must discuss."

Claire's eyes were closed, her hands clasped tightly together in her lap.

"Are you listening to me?" Victor asked impatiently.

She nodded.

"I spoke with Savard when he was here this morning. Based on whatever he does when he comes here, he's found you fit enough to travel."

Slowly her eyes opened and moved to his face. "Travel?"

"Yes. I've made all the arrangements for our trip to Riverton. I expect you to be ready to leave two weeks from today." When she made no reply, he added: "Did you hear me, Claire?"

Her lips pulled into a weak smile. "What choice have I but to do your bidding, Victor?" Her eyes, when they reached his, were hollow. "Since you've stolen every cent I have in the world, what else am I to do but to follow you like a beaten bitch with her tail between her legs."

"It doesn't have to be like this. The past can be left in the past."

Her hand shook as she raised it and pointed a finger at him. "I will *never* be wife to you again! I would rather die first." She stopped and clasped her hands together again. "Your ill-gotten gains will cost you dearly. I promise you that, Victor."

"They already have," he answered sullenly as he rose and walked to the door. His hand resting on the knob, he turned to her again. "If you hate me so much, why don't you go to your aunt in Montreal?"

"You'd like that, wouldn't you? Never, Victor! Never!" Her voice was "sangfroid" as she placed her curse upon him. "I will remain with you, if only to remind you of what you are—a thief and a murderer."

"IT WAS AN ACCIDENT!" he shouted. "Are you so stupid that you can't understand that?"

"I will be ready two weeks from today. Get out of here, Victor, and leave me alone."

Chapter Six

Victor and Claire's arrival in Riverton was every bit as dismal as Melinda and Joseph's had been two months earlier. It half-rained, half-snowed, and bone-chilling gusts blew in from across the bay.

When it finally arrived, the train from Boston was more than two hours late.

The moment Claire set foot on the platform, it was apparent to Melinda that she was not well. She was appallingly thin, her eyes sunken and outlined with dark shadows. Melinda ran to her and held her tightly.

"Melinda ... dear, dear Melinda ..." Claire's frail body shook with emotion. "You can't know how wonderful it is to see you."

"Oh, but I can!" Melinda looked into the tear-streaked face, she too feeling tears very close at hand. "Come, Claire, come inside where it's warm. You'll catch your death out here."

The excitement of their arrival seemed to dispel Victor's fatigue. He talked animatedly with his brother as he sat next to him on the streetcar. "At last! It's all coming true, Joseph!" Victor threw his arms up in the air, his hands doubling into fists. "I've lived for this moment for so long." His voice faded and he looked away, at the elegant houses that bordered on Maincrossing Road.

"I know what you're feeling, Victor, and I dearly hope you won't be disappointed."

Victor turned and looked his brother in the eye.

Just then the streetcar jerked violently as it made a sharp

turn to the left onto Bedfordgate, its bell jangling shrilly, sounding a warning to the umbrella-sheltered pedestrians that filed across the intersection. Joseph pointed out the city hall, its Gothic beauty unimpaired by the gloom of this most inclement day.

Midway down Bedfordgate, Charrington Mews came into view. With his gaze riveted on the Union Mills ahead, Victor did not notice this eyesore, this haven of so much poverty and sickness. Twin cancers, equally dedicated to the destruction of the human spirit.

"This is wonderful, Joe," Victor declared as the streetcar passed the gates leading into the Union Mills yard.

"I hope it lives up to your expectations," Joseph replied, his tone once again subdued.

"What do you mean?" The question put into Victor's mind earlier was finally posed. "I assumed from your letter that you were happy here."

Joseph thought for a moment. "I am, but there are things to deal with I hadn't given a thought to."

"What things? What are you talking about?"

"Well, I'm a foreigner here. Something I've never been before. People aren't always as tolerant as you'd like them to be. Not knowing the language as well as I might, can be difficult at times. And the work—well, you'll see for yourself."

"Temporary setbacks, Joe. All that will change. Have a little patience, for God's sake. You've only been here two months."

"I'm sure you're right, little brother, but at times, when I think of how hard Melinda fought against this, I feel very—"

"Never be fool enough to let a woman dictate your life, Joe. That's the worst mistake a man can make."

Joseph grinned. Victor hadn't changed. Secretly, Joseph had hoped that a little of Claire's gentility might have rubbed off on him by now.

They rode in silence for a while, Victor turning every now and then to look at Claire, who was seated behind him next to Melinda.

"Claire doesn't look well," Joseph remarked, but before

he could say anything more, Tremont Street was upon them. "This is where we get off. Here, let me help you with one of the bags."

Arriving at home, Melinda led them up the two flights of stairs, wondering, as she watched from the second floor landing, whether or not Claire would manage the climb to the third floor tenement.

"Ça va?" Melinda called down the stairwell.

"Yes ... yes, fine. Just a little out of breath, that's all."

* * *

Melinda left Joseph to see to their coats. Running as fast as she could down the steps again, she knocked at Caitlin's door.

"I'm ever so sorry, Caitie. The train was two hours late, and it took us an age to arrange for someone to deliver their trunks." All this was said quite breathlessly and in an interesting mélange of English, French, and a dash of accomplished sign language.

"Now don't ye be frettin' about a thing. He's a lamb, he is, that darlin' boy. Even 'himself' over there had to chuckle a time or two at all the goins on. It's fast asleep on me bed, he is, and I'll not be wakin' him. So get yerself up to yer family and have a good visit. I'll bring him up when he wakens."

"Oh, thank you, Caitie, thank you." Melinda threw her arms around her and hugged tightly.

"Pshaaw! Be off with ye now," Caitlin remarked impatiently, with a twinkle in her eye and a hint of a smile on her lips.

* * *

"Enfin—nous sommes tous arrivés."

Joseph held up his glass in one hand while the other encircled his brother's shoulder that shook ever so slightly as he toasted their arrival in America. An uncommon display of feeling from one who'd long ago hardened himself against expressing emotion. Reaching up, Victor covered Joseph's hand with his.

Melinda served them a hearty dinner: a spicy pork pie laced with onions and cloves, all bound together in a rich, buttery sauce. With it there was a simple salad, glistening with oil and vinegar.

Claire ate with renewed appetite, and as they finished the last of the wine, Melinda thought she could see some of the glow returning to her cheeks.

While clearing away the plates, Melinda recognized Caitlin's heavy tread. Wiping her hands, she hurried to open the door.

Caitlin entered the room, carrying Philippe in her arms. Her face was splotchy from overexertion. "He's a-heavier than he looks," she observed, puffing a mite breathlessly.

Melinda was about to introduce Caitlin to her family when all of a sudden there was the sound of Claire's voice.

She jumped from her chair, calling out, "PHILIPPE!"

"His wee eyes can barely stay open, ma'am," Caitlin warned. "'Tis his bed he's after needin at this hour."

Claire held out her arms. The child looked at her for a long, suspense-filled moment before leaning forward, eager to be taken into Claire's embrace. Pressing her lips to his cheek, Claire strew little kisses across it and on his satiny forehead as well. Finally unable to hold slumber away any longer, Philippe leaned his head against her chest and closed his eyes.

"Look, the dear little thing is sleeping." Caitlin smiled, looking on maternally. "He must feel a kinship to you, ma'am. He's not at all trustin' at first."

"Perhaps he remembered you, Claire," Melinda teased.

"I'd like to think so. My, but he's grown since I last saw him! And what a beautiful child!" she said, holding him snugly in her arms. "You must be very proud of him, Melinda."

"We are," Melinda admitted as modestly as she could. Then she remembered the loss that Claire and Victor had so

52

recently suffered. "Here, let me put him in his crib."

"Oh please, may I keep him just a little bit longer?" Claire begged of her.

Melinda nodded, but Victor quickly rose from his chair and stood next to his wife.

"Give the child to his mother, Claire. It's time we were leaving."

Without a word she handed Philippe over to Melinda.

"I'd best be off as well," Caitlin said, moving toward the door. "God bless ye all—sleep well."

Caitlin had sensed the tension mount sharply, as had everyone else in the room.

"I'm sorry, Victor," Melinda apologized, "you're tired and we've kept you too long." Looking awkwardly at Joseph, she added, "Show them to Mrs. Connerly's, dear."

Chapter Seven

It wasn't long before Victor came upon the little cottage on Queens Lane across the street from Hutchinson Park. The charming white clapboard house had an intimate view of the pine-shaded picnic grounds to the right and a skating pond to the left. A dozen or more energetic young people were engaged in ice skating, but no one was walking or sitting in the picnic area at this time of year. The tables and benches were empty now, dusty and covered with pine needles, yet Victor could imagine how nice it would be during the summertime.

In addition to other obvious advantages, the house was less than a ten-minute walk to his brother's place; close, yet far enough away to ensure everyone a modicum of privacy.

Calling next door as directed by the sign attached to the gate, Victor found the landlord and made arrangements to lease it beginning the first of the year.

On returning to the rooming house, he found Claire lying on the daybed next to the window, where she had been sleeping since their arrival here. Walking to it, he stood alongside her and told her what he'd done.

"Given your present state of mind, I doubted you'd be interested in seeing the place beforehand, so I went ahead and signed the papers."

She lay motionless, her only movement the blinking of her eyes.

"We'll need furniture and the usual housekeeping paraphernalia. I expect you to take care of that," he said rather archly, adding, "Perhaps Melinda will help you."

"There's no need to bother Melinda. I'm quite capable of furnishing a house by myself."

"As you wish, so long as it's ready when the time comes."

On Monday morning of the following week, Claire went to the cottage. She walked through the empty rooms, the hollow sound of her footsteps echoing after her. Small puffs of powdery dust billowed and swirled in a ray of winter sunlight as she moved about making a cursory inspection. She liked the house and its location. She was surprised that Victor would choose such a place. It wasn't luxurious, but definitely a cut above a goodly number of others in the neighborhood. The living room afforded an expansive view of the park from the chintz-covered seat in the bay window. It boasted two quite roomy bedrooms, with a bathroom conveniently placed between them. Inside, at the far end of this extravagant little room, perched on four rather lifelike clawed feet, was a gleaming porcelain bathtub. A long, rectangular stained glass window stretched across the wall above it, portraying two intertwined scarlet roses.

She was quite taken by the bedroom at the rear of the house, for come spring she would see the lilacs blooming along the fence from there. It was the smaller of the two rooms, but it would easily accommodate a comfortable chair to read in, and with its location at the end of the hall it would afford her the seclusion that she desperately wanted. With everything firmly pictured in her mind, she made for the Emporium on Maincrossing Road.

At first she found the shopping a tedious bore. Perhaps she had lived too long with the threadbare belongings of Laura Durand and had lost all taste for anything other than the utilitarian. Or even more likely, she was hindered by the thought of once again sharing a home with Victor.

But as time went on she began appreciating again the beauty of a handcrafted Sheraton secretary and the rich luster of Honduran mahogany. Gradually, the shopping offended her less.

She purchased a charming gateleg table that so resembled one that she'd treasured on Rue de l'Aigle Noir, as well as a dainty Queen Anne's chair for the desk, its seat covered in a pastel petit-point. She ran her fingers along its back, fondling the smoothness of the grain, and for some unfathomable, insane reason, she began to hope again.

They moved into the cottage soon after the holidays and not long after that, Victor decided to go to the Union Mill office and hire on for work.

Unlike Joseph's, Victor's English was excellent, for day in and day out he'd worked on his vocabulary during his final weeks in Le Baie, and with the practice he had talking to Wainwright, the bilingual barkeep at Le Baie's infamous Taverne des Bonne Soirées, he'd made considerable progress. Being thusly equipped, he had no intention of leaving himself vulnerable to, and at the mercy of, the corporation people, as Joseph had done. He could afford to wait, and would, indefinitely if necessary, until a proper situation was offered him. His brother Joseph labored for a pittance, at a dangerous job that was beneath his dignity.

Never again would he, Victor Durand, lower himself to that level. But as fortune would have it, he had only to present himself for the interview, and with a minimal amount of deception and the mettle with which to present it, he was offered what was deemed the most prestigious position other than that of overseer. Loom fixer—a job that many more qualified than he would have given their eye teeth for.

On his way home to the cottage, Victor stopped at the house on Sladesferry Landing to share the good news with Joseph. The longer Victor went on with his story, the greater grew Joseph's disbelief.

"How can you take on a job you know nothing about?"

"What is there to know?" Victor responded with his usual arrogance. "It takes no genius to put a loom together, or to take it apart for that matter. I can read, therefore I can do the job." He slapped his instruction book against his thigh. "I'll manage just fine. You wait and see."

January, 1888

By mid-month the mercury in the thermometer outside the door of 77 Sladesferry Landing plunged beneath the zero mark, and the dormer windows of the attic apartment glittered white with frost. Breathing against the pane, Melinda rubbed away the icy glaze and looked out at the gathering tempest.

The street below was eerily deserted except for the heavy flakes of wet snow splattering against the cobblestones. Shaking her head disconsolately, Melinda walked across the room and emptied another scuttle of coal into the stove.

Since the New Year, bitter cold had held a frigid grip upon the city, and much of Joseph's paycheck was being swallowed up by the sooty giant that sat in the corner of the kitchen. Most weeks, there was little left over after paying the rent and the grocer; naught but a smidgen to put aside toward their dreams of tomorrow. By the end of February, even that paltry nest egg had quickly gone to putting another quarter ton of coal into the bin in the cellar. Melinda trimmed her budget (along with her waistline) as she attempted to stretch the contents of Joseph's envelope to cover their necessities.

It was a truly rude awakening for one so previously "bien soignée." Never before had she had to do without. Emilie's larder had always been filled to capacity, and although she'd heard her parents speak of hard times, they'd long since passed that by the time she'd come along. Now there were days when her soup was very thin indeed, and she'd had to bite her tongue to keep from repeating that they'd made the biggest mistake of their lives in leaving Le Baie. Other than to incite an argument, it would have served no purpose.

Claire's frequent visits brightened Melinda's days considerably. Bound to the house as she was, they brought a ray of sunshine into an otherwise dismal day. Claire brought with her the expensive fruits and buttery biscuits that Philippe loved so well, the luxuries they could no longer afford to provide him.

"You're too good to him, Claire. It wouldn't hurt him a bit to go without for a while," Melinda reminded her, gently pinching the marbled flesh of her son's thigh.

"Nonsense. Why should he, when it gives me so much pleasure to provide them?"

"You're sure it's all right?"

"Of course it is. Victor allows me enough to permit this bit of extravagance."

Melinda looked into the face of this woman she was coming to love as a sister.

"Thank you, Claire," she said softly, reaching out to take hold of her hand.

As February and March wore on, with only brief respites from the elements, Melinda found herself looking more and more often from the window, hoping to see Claire's familiar figure turning the corner onto Sladesferry Landing.

She came one blustery morning, her paisley shawl drawn tightly around her head and shoulders. "Is there no end to this?" she queried as she shook the snow from her clothing before entering the room. "I do declare, it's getting worse instead of better."

With an impish grin pulling at her lips, Melinda hurried to respond. "Well then, Madame Durand, perhaps we should winter at the North Pole next year. I understand it's infinitely warmer there."

The two collapsed into gales of laughter, enjoying Melinda's little joke to the fullest.

But alas, the laughter dwindled away and they sat staring at each other for a long, meaningful moment.

The smile gone from her lips, Claire asked, "You hate it here, don't you, Melinda?"

"I don't think 'hate' is the appropriate word. I guess ..." Melinda stopped, deciding to avoid raking up old resentments. "It won't be forever, Claire, and since you've arrived, everything is ever so much better. I'm not nearly as lonely anymore."

Claire sat in the rocker, cuddling Philippe as Melinda

went about finishing her chores. He was teething and feverish, and she gently rubbed his swollen gums with her forefinger. Soon his whining subsided and he lay quietly looking up at her. In a twinkling, his beautiful dark eyes closed and he slept.

"I see you've worked your magic on him again," Melinda said, walking over to them. Lifting the child from Claire's arms, she stopped when she noticed an angry bruise on Claire's forearm. "What on earth have you done to yourself? Here, let me look at that."

Claire hurried to pull her sleeve into place. "It's nothing, really. Just a bump. I'm so clumsy around the house, not at all like you, Melinda. It'll be gone in a day or two."

"Are you sure? I have some liniment on the shelf. I could—"

"No, please don't bother. I've taken care of all that."

"All right, but do be more careful, dear. That's a nasty wound you've given yourself." Melinda continued to search her face uncertainly.

"I will, I promise." Rising from the chair, Claire prepared to leave.

"Going so soon?" Melinda asked, obviously disappointed.

"Yes. I've a lot of errands to run, and I mustn't wear out my welcome. I'll stop by in the morning. Mr. Whitehead said there might be some bananas tomorrow." As she walked past her, Claire pressed her cheek against Melinda's.

"Be careful," Melinda warned, "the walking must be treacherous this morning."

On the following day at around the usual time, Melinda looked for Claire, but morning as well as afternoon brought no sign of her. When a second day passed as well, Melinda became anxious, and mentioned it to Joseph as they sat to supper that evening.

"She's a grown woman, Melinda. She can take care of herself," he scolded without raising his eyes from his plate. "Don't go meddling where you have no business."

Taken somewhat aback by his rebuff, Melinda took a moment to think, before replying. "I may have to *make* it my business, Joseph. If Claire is ill and I can be of help to her, I shall be. She's been a good friend to me and to our son."

"She has a husband. She doesn't need you nursemaiding her like a child."

Again his insensitive remark made her bristle, and her face reddened with irritation. This wasn't like Joseph. She sensed that he was warning, rather than reproaching her. She let the incident pass without further comment. Fixing her eyes once more on her plate, she went on with her meal, deciding to visit the cottage first thing in the morning.

* * *

The day was awash with sunlight, the back of the bitter cold spell having finally been broken. Streams of water gushed from the rooftops onto the slush-covered cobble-stones. Melinda gathered up her skirts, carefully side-stepping the puddles as she walked down Queens Lane toward the cottage. With every step she took, apprehension mounted and a quiver of nerves rippled up her spine like a scaly snake.

Please let everything be all right, she prayed.

From a block away she could see that the shades were drawn in the windows of the cottage and the milk delivery still stood on the porch.

Opening the gate, she mounted the steps. She lifted her hand and knocked gently. There was no answer, and she knocked again. As she stood waiting she noticed the slightest bit of movement in the living room curtain.

She called out, "CLAIRE! Open the door—please! I shan't leave here until you do! Please, dear, open the door."

She heard the key turn in the lock and in a moment Claire's voice came from behind the half-opened door.

"I'm sorry, Melinda. I've been quite ill. I'm really not up to a visit just yet." She stood hidden in the shadows.

"What's wrong, Claire? I've been worried about you."

"It's just the grippe. Nothing to be concerned about. I'm past the worst of it now."

"Well, at least let me take in your milk."

"No, DON'T—this could be contagious. I'm afraid you might catch something."

But it was too late. Melinda had pushed open the door and a band of yellow sunshine streaked across Claire's battered face. Melinda drew in her breath and stifled a cry. She hurried to close the door.

"God in heaven, what's happened here!" She could barely speak.

Claire's left eye was red, purple and blue, and almost completely shut. Her upper lip, puffed up to twice its size, twisted grotesquely, its thin membranes stretched almost to the breaking point. Another bruise swelled and disfigured the right side of her jaw.

"Please, Melinda, don't look at me," she begged in a meek, pathetic voice. "I'm so ashamed." Her tremulous hands rose to cover her face.

"Ashamed? Why on earth should you be ashamed?"

"That you should see me like this."

Melinda put her arm around Claire's shoulders and led her to the sofa. They sat side by side, neither saying anything for a time.

Melinda broke the silence. "Did Victor do this to you, Claire?"

She began to weep, nodding her head slowly.

"MY GOD ! WHY? Why would he do such a thing?"

Claire wiped her tears on the sleeve of her robe. "He'd been drinking. He didn't know what he was doing. He's like an animal when he's drunk. A Jekyll and Hyde, really."

"This is an outrage! Has he ever done this before?"

"No ... never," Claire lied.

Melinda suddenly remembered the bruise on her forearm. "Tell me the truth, Claire. This must never happen again."

"It won't," she said all too quickly.

Melinda handed her a handkerchief and she blew her nose. "It was mostly my fault, Melinda. Ever since losing the baby, I haven't been able to be a proper wife to Victor. He got angry and tried to force me. I fought him. That's how it happened. He won't do it again. He promised he wouldn't."

"And you believed him?"

"Yes. I did."

Melinda rose and paced the floor. "I'm afraid to leave you alone in this house with him." She stopped, her fingers rising to her temples, desperately attempting to clear her mind, to think of some solution. "Please Claire, let me take you home with me."

"No. I'll be all right. And I don't want Victor to know you were here. It will just make things worse for me." She looked beseechingly at Melinda. "Please don't say anything to Joseph about this. Promise me!"

They stared at each other.

"PROMISE ME!" she insisted.

"All right, I won't. But I'll be back tomorrow."

Melinda left the house and walked down the street knowing she should have done something more.

* * *

She kept her promise and uttered not a single word of what she'd seen at the cottage to anyone. Everything in her wanted to cry out against Victor, against the brutality that he had inflicted on Claire. But she remained true to her word. With time, and reassurances from Claire that no further violence had taken place, she gradually began accepting Claire's explanation: a regrettable, domestic outburst—nothing more.

Yet Melinda felt compelled to walk to Queens Lane each day to reassure herself that everything was as it should be. At first she went alone, thanks to Caitlin's limitless kindness, then later when she felt it safe to do so, she pushed young Philippe ahead of her, seated ever so smartly in his "new" straw-colored stroller.

Claire's wounds healed, leaving no sign of the devastating blows Victor had heaped upon her person. But they remained with her, nevertheless, in another less visible form.

She became reclusive, rarely leaving the cottage, choosing to remain inside, burying her shame behind drawn curtains and locked doors.

From time to time, Melinda tried to coax her out.

"Wouldn't you like to see the lilacs that are blooming in your garden? They smell heavenly," she teased. But it only served to upset Claire, and Melinda gave it up as useless.

After one such visit, Melinda returned home feeling extremely hollow and depressed. Entering the gate, she released Philippe from his safety harness and put him down on the walk. Just a few days before, he'd found the courage to take his first shaky steps. With a death grip on her index fingers, they walked through the yard, lingering to sniff the fragrance of the open rosebuds on the trellis. On the other side of the rectangle of grass, three magnificent dogwood trees bloomed in pink and white profusion, framed against a clear azure sky. Melinda soaked in the purity of their beauty much in the way something parched absorbs moisture. Spring! How glorious it was. Gone in an instant were the bleak memories of bitter winter, and the desperate turn of events in Claire's life. New life was flourishing all around, and new hope was taking root in Melinda's heart.

Scooping up the boy, she whirled him through the air, delaying a bit longer the tantrum she knew would follow the mention of naptime. She looked up again into the branches of the trees. A final look to store a memory on. Suddenly, something beyond the trees caught her eye. Resting against the windowpane of the second floor tenement opposite hers was a crudely printed sign bearing the words SEAMSTRESS WANTED: APPLY WITHIN.

She stood, attempting to decipher the words, then whirling the boy one last time, she hustled him indoors.

During the afternoon, Melinda kept returning to the window, reassuring herself that the sign was still there. By the time her son awakened from his nap, she'd looked at it at least a half-dozen times. Going to the closet in her bedroom she removed the gray woolen coat she'd made in preparation for her journey here. Lifting the boy into her arms, she carried him down to Caitlin's.

"Well now, won'tcha look at who's comin' to visit! The little prince himself, it is. Come here to Caitie, darlin', and give her a sweet kiss." Reaching out she took him to her. Melinda controlled a flinch as she saw Caitlin press her lips directly onto the child's mouth. "Just like one of them pink rosebuds, that mouth of his." She kissed him full on the lips again.

Going to the window, Melinda pointed to the sign. "What does that say, Caitie?"

"Oh, that," she answered, darting a finger in its direction. "That's Miroff's sign. It goes up now and then when he gets behind in his work. For all I can tell, not a soul ever pays it any mind."

"What does Mr. Miroff do?"

"He's a tailor. You know, a man who makes clothing. He's after lookin' for someone to sew for him." She pushed and pulled on an imaginary needle.

Melinda nodded her head.

Caitie's smile turned into a scowl. "And may I be askin' why yer so interested, miss?" Her flashing eyes came to rest on the gray woolen coat lying across the back of the chair.

"How's Mr. Mulvaney feeling today?" Melinda asked.

"Now don'tcha be changin' the subject, girl. Yer not after thinkin' of goin' over there, are ye now?"

"Yes Caitie, I am."

"Well now, why on earth would ye be doin' that?"

"To earn a few extra dollars, that's why!" She hadn't meant to be short, it just came out sounding that way.

"Well, I hope ye know what it is yer doin'. He's a Jew, he is, and he'll be after gettin' his money's worth from ye. And that's no lie."

"Will you see to Philippe for a bit, Caitie. One way or another, I shouldn't be long."

"Ye know I will. Now be gone with ye." Her scowl followed Melinda out the door.

Ramrod straight, her head held high, Melinda started across the rectangle of grass that separated the houses. Mounting the steps to the open porch, she stopped and smoothed over the gores of her pongee skirt. Taking a deep breath, she blew a kiss to Caitlin, who stood at the window holding Philippe in her arms. Grasping the doorknob, she went into the vestibule and up the steps to the second floor.

Chapter Eight

Samuel Aaron Miroff passed his hands over the brown paper pattern, making sure it was laid out smoothly. He was a meticulous man in every way, but especially so when it came to his work.

Business had been good since he and Natalia had come to Riverton a year and a half ago. This was the third suit of clothes he'd cut out in as many weeks. Sure, it had taken a while for word to get around; miracles didn't happen to Sam Miroff. But after the first six months, he'd had a steady stream of customers coming to his door. Lately his wife Natalia had been giving him some help with his finishing work. Hand stitching took a great deal of time. She hadn't complained. Natia (as he called her) seldom complained about anything, but she had her hands full, what with the house and little Sarah. A two-year-old could keep you going from morning till night—and then some. Last night she and Sam had worked way past midnight in order to finish Oscar Valiera's new summer suit.

"So," Natia'd said, folding the trousers. "I'm finished, thank God. I wish this could have waited until morning, Sam. Black is so hard on the eyes at night." Taking off her glasses, Natia wiped them with a handkerchief. Her eyes weren't the best; she'd worn heavy lenses since she was a girl.

"I know, my Nushka, and I'm sorry about that. I've put up the sign again. Maybe this time we'll have better luck."

"Don't count on it, Sam. For what we can pay ... well, you know what I mean."

In the beginning, when they'd first come here from New York City, it had been good for Natia to keep busy. It kept her from thinking too much about her sister Mila, and the friends she'd left behind on Hester Street. What a strange mishmash of people they were, ranging the spectrum from streetwalkers to cart pushers to holy Hassidics. Sam swore that every Jew who left Ellis Island ended up on Hester or Delancey streets.

Going up the stairs to the flat that they shared with Mila and Sol, Sam often encountered the mingled smell of cabbage and fish that was enough to take a hungry man's appetite away. But Natia, God love her, she'd grown to care for these people, and whenever anyone needed a bed, she'd manage to fix something up for them in a corner of the kitchen. Sam never knew when there would be another gaunt, starving immigrant sleeping alongside the chimney breast.

All well and good, but Hester Street was not Sam's kind of place and he would not remain there. Rubbing elbows with that mass of humanity made his flesh crawl, and there was always some kind of bru-ha-ha going on out in the street. From the window of their fourth floor tenement, they could hear people yelling and screaming at each other in Italian and Yiddish. From morning till night. No—goddamit, he had not left Russia to come here and live in another stinking ghetto. He wanted a decent home somewhere, and to be respected in his community. More than anything, he wanted that for himself, and for Natia and the child.

It hadn't been easy convincing Natia that there were better places to live than on Hester Street. She had a stubborn way of clinging to the old, comfortable ways.

"I'm a simple woman, Sam," she'd argued. "Fancy people and fancy places I don't need to make me happy. I have the freedom I came to this country for, right here on Hester Street, and a little bit of family to comfort me, besides. When I speak Yiddish, they understand me. They don't drive me meshuggah like those high-toned schlemihls uptown. I can go to the butcher's and the fishmonger's without I should take an interpreter with me."

"See? There you go! The old ways again. Learn the language, for heaven's sake!! This is America!"

Sam prided himself in the way he spoke English. A little accent, to be sure, but he'd get rid of that in no time. He refused to speak Yiddish to anyone, including his wife. It was time to forget the past and get moving on the future.

Every so often, Sam's thoughts went back to the old country too. Hell, he wasn't made of stone. His family in Odessa was close to his heart always; but especially so when he wrote to his parents on the first Sunday of every month.

That was sometimes difficult for him to do. Memories of his life there would come rushing back. Voices ... faces ... sounds. Little sisters singing as they picked berries in the woods behind their house, streaks of sunlight caressing their burnished hair. He missed them all so much, but he never knew quite how to put it down on paper. How he wished that they could all have come to America with him.

"It's too late for us, Samuel," his father had said. "It grieves me to say that I am no longer young." A wistful look had crossed the old fellow's bearded face. "Sixty-four years come this summer, and I don't have the energy to begin my life over again. Even if I did, your mother would never agree."

He was right. For them it was too late. It broke Sam's heart, but it didn't change his mind. He left anyway, without them.

Ever since boyhood Sam had suffered from recurring nightmares. Frenzied, terrifying dreams of sword-wielding horsemen thundering through their village, setting fire to the synagogue and riding roughshod over their fields. He dreamed of Cossack raids and brutal, bloody purges. They'd pillaged and raped, and left traumatized women and children to die in their wake. Often as a boy, he'd awakened, lying in a pool of his own urine. Memories of those horror-filled nights still returned to plague his sleep. Not often anymore, but the fear was still there, deep in some corner of the mind, waiting to return at a moment's notice. So far, his family had

been lucky, but many of their friends and neighbors had perished in the pogroms.

As Sam grew older, his plan to flee Russia began taking
shape, and when the time was right he'd taken Natalia, along
with his father's blessing, and left for America. Never once
had he regretted it. But to this day, there were those who
would criticize. Those like his brother Nathan, who chose to
believe that he had deserted his people.

A persistent sound pulled him back to the present.
Straightening from his work, he braced himself for the jab-
bing pain that he'd come to expect. As he walked to the
door, he rubbed his back with his strong, supple fingers.

Sam immediately recognized the young woman standing
in the hallway. He'd seen her coming and going from
Charles Mulvaney's house, pushing her baby in an old
stroller. *Attractive girl up close,* he mused, *with the most arresting blue eyes I've ever seen.*

He bade her enter, and after presenting his wife, asked
Melinda to be seated. "Now then, young lady, what is it I can
do for you?"

* * *

Melinda clenched and unclenched her hands as Mr. Miroff examined the buttonholes of her gray woolen coat. Bent
over it as he was, his eyes and fingers probing her work, she
couldn't help but notice the thick shock of black curly hair
and the alertness of his clear, gray eyes. Mr. Miroff was of
Joseph's size and stature, except for being narrower through
the shoulders.

Looking up at her, his lips curved into a pleasing smile.
"Forgive me if I seem overly particular, but my work, well,
it's my name, my reputation. You know what I mean?"

Melinda nodded, a little uncertainly.

"What you sew for me," he pointed at her and then at
himself, "will also be considered *my work.* You understand?"

She nodded again, this time more assertively.

Putting the coat down on one of the chairs, he turned and faced her. "I thought that my wife's needlework was the finest I'd ever see, but yours is finer still, Mrs. Durand. What more can I say? I can't pay you very much right now, but when it gets better for me, it'll get better for you. The job is yours if you want it, young lady." He smiled and extended his hand.

After closing the door behind her, Sam walked to the window and took away the sign. He stood looking out, still rubbing at the tightness in his back. Hearing the downstairs door thud closed, he watched as Melinda walked across the yard. *Extraordinary woman, this Mrs. Durand*, he thought as he turned and went back to his work.

* * *

For the remainder of the afternoon Melinda went about the house rehearsing aloud what she would say to Joseph. He would not be pleased with what had been agreed to between herself and Mr. Miroff.

She had hoped to get it over with as soon as possible but when Joseph arrived home, one glance at the slump of his shoulders and the downturned corners of his mouth gave her reason to change her mind. She waited, hoping that the soporific effects of his meal would help soften his attitude. Fully aware that having a working wife might undo a man's self-confidence and blemish his masculine pride, Melinda was prepared for resistance. But she was not prepared for the bitter argument that ensued. *Joseph was seething with anger.*

"Let me be sure that I understand what you're saying." His voice was harsh and the deep blue veins in his temples swelled. He said the word slowly, emphasizing each one: "You have agreed to go to work for the man who lives next door."

"Exactly," Melinda answered, her head nodding affirmatively. "Mr. Miroff is a tailor, Joseph. He's hired me to do some sewing for him. I can work right here at home. Isn't it wonderful?"

Joseph got up from his chair. Flinging his napkin down on the table, he confronted her. "Do you really have so little faith in me, Melinda? Are you that afraid that I won't provide well enough for you and Philippe?"

"That's nonsense, Joseph. You know that I have every faith in you. That's not what this is about. The fact remains that we've made no headway of any kind this winter." She detested having to remind him of such things. "If we are to be realistic about returning home in five years, we must take advantage of every opportunity. I intend to take advantage of this one."

"I FORBID IT!" he shouted. "No man worth his salt would—" He didn't finish.

She looked at him long and hard before responding. "I'm sorry that you disapprove, Joseph, but I must go against your wishes this time."

Rising from the table, she poured hot water from the kettle into the dishpan. As she went about the business of washing up the supper dishes, Joseph stalked headlong into the bedroom.

They'd had their share of quarrels, to be sure, but this was by far the most serious. Finishing her work, Melinda waited, hoping that Joseph would regain his composure and return to finish reading his newspaper. When he didn't, she too felt anger, like hot pokers reaching down inside her.

Why hadn't she had the gumption to tell him that she'd given Caitlin only half the rent on the first of the month? And that this evening's poultry had been put on a charge ticket at the butcher shop? Why hadn't she mentioned that she had but thirty-five cents in her purse to do them until payday on Friday? Enough for a loaf of bread and a pint of milk for the boy. Would his knowing these things have changed anything? She thought not. Melinda deeply regretted having this impasse between them, but they were slipping into debt and the thought of that frightened her more than her husband's wrath.

She knelt on the bedstep and said her prayers. Climbing

into bed, she curled herself into a ball. Feeling frightfully alone, she was suddenly engulfed by a plethora of memories. Of Le Baie and her family ... of happier times, when admiration and love were the only things she saw shining from her husband's eyes. Eventually she drifted off, her lips longing for the sweetness of a goodnight kiss.

Chapter Nine

While holding at arm's length the garment he'd just finished pressing, Sam muttered, "A beautiful piece of work, even if I say so myself."

Alex Friedman, an up and coming young lawyer, would be pleased to have his suit two days ahead of schedule. Since hiring Melinda Durand, Sam was getting his work out much faster.

He walked to the closet and hung it away. Turning, he looked at the clock on the mantle. It was almost noon and the good smells drifting in from the pantry suggested that Natia would be serving their meal at any moment. Seating himself at the head of the table, he began to salivate.

"How long does a starving man have to wait for his food?" he called out as Natia came through the door carrying the soup tureen. She placed it on the table in front of him. Lifting the lid, he ladled a bowlful for himself and his wife.

"What about Sarah? Is she having this?" Sam asked.

"Only a little meat and broth. The cabbage gives her gas."

Sitting between them, Sarah amused herself by rolling an empty spool around on the tray of her highchair. Her dark, tousled hair, still moist from her bath, turned up in ringlets at the ends. Her jet black eyes gleamed like shiny new shoe buttons as they darted from one exciting thing to the next. Natia brushed Sarah's hair back from her face, exposing a milky white forehead. Theirs was an exquisite child, and Natia never tired of doing for her.

Sam ate with his usual relish. For a thin man, he managed to ingest half again more food than the average person. Dipping his bread into the broth, he made an effort to chew

73

slowly. Natia always gave him "her look" whenever he ate too fast. Pushing his empty bowl aside, Sam reached for the plate of fruit in the center of the table. Leaning back in his chair he ate an apple and sipped his tea leisurely.

"What's wrong, Sam? You're not gulping your food today. You're feeling all right, aren't you?" Natia always fussed over him. Always worried too much.

"Natia, how could I eat such a meal if I weren't feeling well? Besides, why should I rush? I need this table to do my cutting on."

Natia jumped from her chair. "I'll hurry to clear."

"No, sweetheart." Sam reached for her arm. "No need. I don't think I'll be working anymore today."

"THERE—I knew it was something with you."

"NO, NO! It's nothing with me." Sam tried hard to keep a straight face. "I'm just going to take the rest of the day off."

"SAM, what are you talking about? You never take an hour off, never mind the rest of the day."

"I know, I know. But today ... it's different," he teased. Lifting the child up out of her highchair, he sat her on his lap. "You see what I have to put up with, Sari?" Sam always shortened everyone's names. "Kvetch if I work too hard, kvetch if I don't. Some people you never please. I don't know about that mother of yours." Looking at his wife from across the table, a sardonic smile emerged. "If you *must* know, dear lady, I'm going out today, and you for one will never guess where I'm going."

Natia wasn't smiling back at him. "Talk straight for a change, Sam."

"All right, if you insist." The smile faded from his lips and his voice deepened. "Last night I saw an ad in the paper. An ad for a tailor shop. I'm going downtown and see about renting it."

Natia's brow wrinkled into a frown. "Why, for heaven's sake? You do beautiful work right here," she said as she thumped her palm down on the tabletop.

"You're right, I do," he said, "but my back is killing me. A man should have proper tools to work with, and a proper place to do it in. It's time. I need more space than I have here. For once, already, I'd like to fit a pair of pants without shoving my wife and child into the bedroom. I'm getting more business all the time, Natia. I can't work on your kitchen table anymore. No, Natalia, it's time."

"OY! Sam, you and your crazy hunches. Don't go doing anything meshuggah."

Her hand reached for his. He placed his other on top of it.

"This scares me, Sam. It scares me a lot," she muttered.

"Me too, a little. But I ask myself, what have I got to lose? I can always come back to your kitchen, my Nushka." He patted her hand gently again, his eyes gleaming with excitement. "Just think of it, Natia—Miroff and Son."

"And son? Now I know you've gone crazy, Sam Miroff," she said with a grin.

"Well, maybe I'll leave that off the sign until after we've paid the moyle. I can always add it on later." He leaned and kissed her forehead. "Don't worry, my Natia, let me do that for all of us."

"Oh Sam, you're the best." Again she wondered why a handsome, adorable man like Sam Miroff had chosen to marry a homely girl such as she.

Natia was short, barely reaching five feet in height, and always, even as a child, she'd carried a little too much weight. Her ash brown hair was as fine as that of an angora kitten, and at best all she could do was pull it back neatly into a knot at the back of her head. Looking at him through her thick, silver-rimmed spectacles, she said, "Go, my Sammy ... find yourself a wonderful shop."

The first place he looked at, the one advertised in the newspaper, was just the ticket. But when he was told the price, he winced and walked out the door. Finding his wonderful shop might not be a simple matter.

Standing on the corner of Maincrossing Road, Sam felt a little bewildered. He wanted to go home and say, "You're right, Nushka, like always," and go on as he had been. Instead he went into the tobacconist shop and bought the latest edition of the newspaper.

Back outside, he leaned against the building as he scanned the real estate columns. Another "suitable" place caught his attention, but again no price was given. He'd look at it anyway. What the hell, the day was already shot, and it was on his way home.

Arriving at the address, he climbed a set of rickety stairs leading to the second floor, above a dry goods store. Following the landlord inside, Sam cleared his throat and said, "Before we get too far ahead of ourselves here, I need to know what you're asking for this place."

"Two-fifty a week," the man replied curtly. "Cheap at twice the price. Downtown this would go for at least five bucks. Stay, look around for a while. I'll be in the store by the cash register."

It was definitely more modest than the one he'd seen earlier, but it was on the corner of Pleasant Street, a fifteen minute walk from home, and close to the bustling mill district. It also had very good light, a must for any tailor shop. Sam sat on the dusty floor, his back against the wall between a pair of large windows. Taking off his hat, he put it on the floor next to him.

"A wide counter," he imagined aloud, "up front, next to the door. And a curtain, across that other corner over there. A big enough place to change in and out of your clothes." He stood up again and turned the other way. "A cutting table would fit nicely in front of these windows." He felt the adrenaline pumping faster and faster as he stood there mentally making his dreams come true. He could afford the two-fifty—no problem with that—and after he'd fixed the place up, no one would even recognize it. *I'll tell Natia about this tomorrow,* he thought, *otherwise she'd lie awake the whole night with excitement.* He pushed his hat onto his head and walked down the rickety stairs.

Natia rushed up to him the moment he entered their flat, a look of anticipation on her face. "So tell me ..."

"Sooo ... I'm thinking things over."

The following morning, as soon as he dared, he asked her

to dress the child. "I want you should both come with me."

"Now?"

Sarah was sitting on her hip, naked except for her diaper.

"It's only eight o'clock, Sam. I haven't given Sarah her bath yet."

"Never mind the bath, just clean her up a little. I want you should come with me this instant."

She could see the color mounting in his neck and the stubborn set to his jaw. This was an important thing he was asking. Not something to stand around and argue about.

"Right away, Sam."

Entering the room above the dry goods store, Natia immediately noticed the dirty windows and greasy dust balls gathered in the corners. She put the child down regardless of them, and tried to feel what her husband was feeling. To see the place through his eyes.

"Well—what do you think?" Sam asked.

Natia didn't answer immediately, but continued looking around the room. *What will it look like when he fixes it up?* she wondered. She closed her eyes and tried to imagine it.

"Well?" Sam asked, his toe tapping against the floor.

"I think your shop is wonderful, Sam."

"Then I should take it?"

"Of course you should. It's perfect; it's what you've been waiting for."

Moving closer to him, Natia put her short, plump arms around his neck. He laughed and hugged her tightly. She felt the rough brush of his beard against her cheek.

"I think it's perfect too, my Nushka."

On Monday morning as he sat eating his breakfast, Sam had to admit to feeling tired. For two days he'd schlepped stuff up that goddamed crooked flight of stairs. He'd refused to wait until Monday and hire a man to help him, as Natia'd suggested. Instead they'd broken Shabbat and worked like dogs throughout the entire weekend. Having made his decision, Sam seemed compelled to get started.

On Saturday, Natia'd gone with him, carrying her mop and broom, scouring the place from top to bottom with lye soap. She soaked off the caked-on grime from the window-sills and polished the glass to a fare-thee-well. She scrubbed the floor until the grain reappeared and she sealed it with a coat of lemon oil.

After breakfast on Sunday, Sam gathered his equipment together and made numerous trips down Tremont Street with Sarah's baby carriage crammed to the hilt. One at a time, he moved the heavier pieces, then the remnants were piled into the buggy along with boxes of thread, scissors, pins, chalk, tape measures, buttons, bindings and flatirons. There seemed no end to it. It was hard to believe he'd managed to store so much stuff in the cupboards and drawers in their flat. As he carried the last bolt of fabric up the stairs to the shop the clouds opened up, and Sam stood in the middle of it all, rest-ing, listening to the raindrops hitting against the window-panes.

Overnight the weather cleared and this morning the sun shone brightly through the dotted Swiss curtains in the Mi-roffs' kitchen. It promised to be a beautiful day, but Sam didn't even notice; he wasn't feeling himself today. As he lifted a cup of coffee to his lips, his hand shook and he felt all wiggly inside.

He looked at Sarah who sat next to him in her highchair, her soft-boiled egg smeared all over her hands and face.

"You shouldn't let her feed herself, Natia," he snapped. "She isn't ready for that. She looks like a piglet sitting there with food all over her face. On her eyelashes yet, for God's sake. Neatness is something you must teach to a child early in life."

"You can't be serious, Sam, she's just a baby. Pfhew! Such a business!" she uttered under her breath, more than a little annoyed with his criticism.

"But I am serious!" Sam retorted impatiently. "You spoil the child, and later on you'll regret it."

He lifted the napkin from his lap and began vigorously wiping the child's face. She let out a piercing shriek.

"Ach! Look now, what you've done. You've frightened her half to death. Come to Mama, sweetheart." Natia took the child into her arms and went to the bedroom. Hushing her gently, she laid her into the crib.

Coming back to the kitchen, Natia looked angrily at her husband who was still sitting at the table, his head lowered into his hands. Suddenly she realized he was praying! Sam was frightened. Today meant a new beginning, a very important commitment. It meant risking what they'd saved since coming to Riverton. It meant that maybe he could fail.

She watched as he rose and went to the clothespress. After putting on his new straw hat, the one with the black and red striped band around it, he lifted his umbrella from the stand. Slowly, he turned and looked at Natia, who hadn't spoken a word since returning from the bedroom.

"The paper said maybe rain later." He stopped halfway to the door. "Well, I'd better be going."

Natia walked over to him. Their eyes met.

"I'm sorry, my Nushka, I didn't mean—"

She didn't let him finish. She took his face between her hands and kissed him hard on the lips. "Good luck, Sam. I'm prouder than ever of you today."

Standing at the door, she heard him mutter as he went down the stairs, "Only here, in this country, could this happen to a nudnik like me, goddammit."

Chapter Ten

More than once Melinda had heard Caitlin say, "If you don't like New England's weather, just ye be waitin' a minute or two."

She hadn't really understood what she'd meant at the time, but she did now. It'd taken more than a minute or two, but the beautiful weather they'd enjoyed during May and June, had by August given way to unrelenting heat. Dog days, they were referred to hereabouts.

With each torrid sunrise, life in the attic apartment became increasingly difficult. Philippe, whose faltering steps had taken a sudden turn toward running, was now constantly underfoot. He'd fallen victim to a prickly rash that encircled his neck and caused his privates to burn. He whined and pulled at Melinda's skirts as she sat at the table sewing. Lifting him into her arms, she caressed him gently, patting his firm little bottom as she walked to the bedroom to dust him with cornstarch.

"Pauvre Chou-Chou," she sympathized as she smoothed the silky powder over the angry-looking eruptions.

It helped to ease his discomfort for a time, but soon he was back tugging at her again, burying his face in the folds of her dress.

Later in the morning, Mr. Miroff would be expecting to pick up the work he'd left her last week. She needed at least an hour to turn up the hems of the dark blue suit. Becoming a bit desperate, she was on her way down to Caitlin's with Philippe when she ran into Claire coming up the stairs.

Startled at the sight her, Melinda cried out, "Claire! Is it really you, or am I imagining things?"

A few weeks before, Claire had found the courage to venture a few steps from the cottage. "I walked in the garden yesterday," she'd told Melinda, her eyes filled with childlike pride. "And this morning I went over to the park. It's at least ten degrees cooler there than it is inside the house."

Claire had sat on a bench and watched from a distance as mothers and nannies brought their youngsters to frolic on the swings of the playground. A bittersweet pleasure, to be sure.

This morning, upon rising, she'd gone to the window of her room and looked out on a flawless summer day. She thought immediately of Philippe. She hadn't seen him in so long. Disregarding the vestiges of apprehension that still lingered, she'd decided to visit him.

"Let me look at you! My, but you *do* look well, Claire."

"Thank you. It's wonderful to be out and about again. Not to worry, though, I shan't stay very long; I know how busy you are."

"Yes, and I'm woefully behind this morning. Philippe didn't sleep well last night, and he's been teasing for attention all morning. But do come up and sit for a while. I can work while we visit."

Melinda showed Claire to a chair next to the window.

"If there's any breeze at all it will be here," she assured her.

Returning to her place at the table, Melinda picked up her sewing again. Between stitches, her eyes carefully inched over her visitor from head to foot.

"I'm so pleased that you're getting out, Claire." Then, looking Claire in the eye, she added, "Everything is all right at home, isn't it?"

"See for yourself. I'm so pampered I'm actually getting fat! You're not to worry about me any longer, Melinda."

Philippe began carrying on again, this time turning to Claire for attention.

"Poor darling," she said, lifting him into her arms, "you do look uncomfortable. Look at those awful red spots on your cheeks." Carrying him to the sink, Claire moistened a towel and sponged his face. "It's terribly close in here,

Melinda."

"I know, and every window in the place is open."

"Why don't I take Philippe over to the park? There are always children to play with there, and it's ever so much cooler."

Raising her eyes from her work, Melinda hesitated before replying. "He'd enjoy that, I'm sure, but are you sure you feel up to it, Claire? He's been a bit of a grump this morning," Melinda warned.

"We'll be fine, won't we, my love?" Tightening her hold on the boy, she nuzzled the moist, velvety folds of his neck. "Being with him is like—" Claire stopped without finishing her thought.

A few minutes later they took to the door, armed with a thermos of lemonade and a few of Philippe's favorite playthings.

Chapter Eleven

At about the time that Claire and Philippe were leaving for the park, Victor Durand walked out of the Union Mill yard. He had just been let go from his job. "A necessary cutback of the work force" was the reason he'd been given by the foreman, who'd wisely chosen not to arouse this volatile young man.

Victor had been observed drinking on the job and later caught sleeping it off in one of the storage ells. Many a grievance was tolerated by the corporation's executives, but sleeping on the job was not among them.

Leaving the mill yard, Victor walked down Bedfordgate for a few blocks before turning into a rum shop—one of the many that had popped up on every street corner between the mills and Charrington Mews.

The place was empty at this early hour, save for a solitary patron who lay slumped across a table in a darkened corner of the room.

As he started toward the bar, Victor raised two fingers and the barkeep reached for a bottle and poured him a double measure of Scotch whiskey. He swallowed it down in one gulp, then raised his fingers again. When he left a half-hour later, he'd had enough to drink to make him walk unsteadily.

Heading up Tremont Street, he muttered to himself and by the time he'd reached Sladesferry Landing, his rage had reached a fever pitch.

"That son-of-a-bitch will rue the day he sacked the likes of me," he ranted, brandishing a fist in the air. "When I have done with him, he'll curse the filthy womb that bore him."

Through a thick haze of alcohol, Victor thought of his

brother Joseph. "Salt of the earth," he said aloud. "Poor, stupid bastard. He'll be riding that rig of his down to Stoneheep about now. Glad I'm not the one sitting behind that horse stink on a day like this. PeeeeU!" Victor threw his head back and laughed, the raucous sound of it turning the heads of two pedestrians ahead of him.

After several more blocks of weaving his way forward, Victor found himself on Sladesferry Landing looking up at the windows of Joseph's and Melinda's flat. Beacons of rage ignited afresh in his eyes.

"That bitch!" he snarled, spewing saliva into the air. "I've a few things I want to straighten out with her." With an angry shove he pushed open the gate and lurched into the yard.

* * *

Standing next to the stove, Melinda clicked a hot flatiron out of the handle as Sam Miroff made his way up the stairs. His knock was gentle, his smile a welcome ray of sunshine in an otherwise hectic morning.

"Good day to you, young lady! I hope I'm not too early."

"Not at all, Mr. Miroff." Melinda was not the least bit inclined to divulge how fretfully she'd had to scamper in order to finish her work on time. "Here you are, Mr. Miroff," she said, lifting the coat from the ironing board and laying it across his arm. "It's a beautiful suit."

"Thank you, but a lot of the credit is yours. You do good work, Melinda. Maybe soon I can come nearer to paying you what you deserve. To tell you the truth, I'm already a little embarrassed. I wasn't expecting you to have both of these suits ready for me today. I guess our signals get a little mixed up every once in a while, eh?" He grinned. "I hope I have enough money to pay you," he added, digging deeper into his pocket..

"That's all right, Mr. Miroff, you can pay me the next time."

"You'd trust me for it, would you? Well, no need," he said, placing the extra money down on the table. "Now then, enjoy this hot and humid day, if that's at all possible," Sam joked as he went out the door and down the steep curve of steps.

As Sam was approaching the last flight, the door burst open and came to a halt with a bang on the inside wall. He stopped dead in his tracks. Old memories of Odessa swiftly stirred up old fears.

A swarthy, disheveled man entered and turned into the stairwell.

Sam flattened himself against the wall as much as he could, and as Victor Durand went by, he looked directly into Sam's eyes. Sam vaguely remembered seeing him before. Waiting, he listened as Victor continued on up to the attic apartment. Sam felt uneasy. There'd been something menacing about the man.

Get going, Miroff. Go on about your business, he told himself as he hurried out into the street.

* * *

Victor didn't bother to knock; he simply threw open the door and leaned against the frame.

Seated at the table, Melinda was about to sort the bundle of work Mr. Miroff had just left her, when the door flew open. Her body started noticeably when she realized who it was.

"Victor! Gracious! You frightened me," she said breathlessly. "You're the last person I expected to see here this morning."

"I'm sure that's true," he replied, looking over his shoulder, down into the stairwell.

Victor closed the door with a bang. Instantly the room took on a terrible tension. Melinda stopped what she was doing and watched as he moved closer to her.

"What are you doing here at this hour, Victor? Why aren't you at the mill?" she questioned. When Victor didn't answer, Melinda's face paled. "Something is wrong! It's Joseph, isn't it?" she asked, her voice accelerating higher.

Victor took three steps, and she heard the sharp intake of her breath as his hand hit hard upon the left side of her face. Shaking with shock, she sat riveted to her chair, the red imprint of his blow rising from her flesh.

"Just what kind of a fool do you take me for?" Victor asked, his voice sinking lower, his face so close to hers that the vileness of his breath filled her nostrils. "You don't give a whore's damn about my brother!" The words spat from his mouth like so much filth.

Groping to gather her wits, Melinda found the strength to rise from the chair. Victor stalked her every move. Still in shock, unable to think clearly, Melinda tried to collect herself, desperately hoping she would not enrage him further.

"That's not true, Victor," she said as calmly as she could, "you know it isn't." Courageously she turned and faced his accusatory stare. "You're not yourself this morning."

She tried easing away from him, toward the door, a few inches at a time. But he put himself squarely between them.

"Please Victor, leave now, and I'll try to forget what's happened here this morning."

"My, how very gracious of you." His words were a hateful mockery of her voice.

"I've obviously offended you somehow, Victor." She now suspected that he had discovered her long, covert vigil over Claire. "Whatever it is, I'm very sorry."

Victor appeared unmoved by her apology.

A desperate thought rushed into Melinda's mind. "Let me get you a cup of coffee. There's some still hot on the stove."

She visualized herself tossing the steaming hot liquid into Victor's face and running to safety below. She took a tentative step toward the stove, and just as swiftly he blocked her way again. She was trapped, totally defenseless against this man.

After what seemed an eternity, he spoke again. "What has Claire been telling you about me?" he demanded through clenched teeth, a crazed look in his eyes.

Melinda shivered with cold in the ninety-degree heat of the attic. "Nothing. I swear it, Victor. Claire has never confided anything to me about you," Melinda lied. "She's a good friend, that's all." Inside her head Melinda prayed, *Blessed Mother, let this danger pass away from me.* "Claire's very fond of Philippe," she added, smiling a bland little smile.

"Wouldn't you say it was a bit more than fondness?" Victor's eyes narrowed and they no longer looked like those of a sane person.

"I don't know what you mean."

"I MEAN, she's *obsessed* with your child!"

Relishing the power he held over her, he toyed with her like a cat would a mouse. It felt deliciously sensual. His body throbbed with a passion that flowed like molten lava through his chest, down into his loins. Melinda Bérard was his captive. That sweet little girl he'd watched from the road WAS HIS TO USE AS HE PLEASED!

Sensing his thoughts, Melinda moved further from him. Again he stalked every step she took.

"She's told you about the baby, hasn't she?" Not waiting for an answer, Victor went on: "She blames me for that. She thinks I killed her child." He stopped talking, seemingly confused for an instant, and for a crazy, hopeful moment Melinda thought that he might leave. When he looked at her next, she knew he would not. His eyes were aflame with passion.

"I'll take some of what you've been passing out to that Jew bastard," he said, looking over at the money that lay on the table. "I saw him leaving here just now—your *gentleman caller. Cuckolding my brother, are you?*" he yelled. "Well, you'll pay dearly for your pleasures, Miss High and Mighty."

"No, Victor! *Please*, I beg you—don't do this!" Melinda tried to scream but her voice was unable to rise above a whisper.

Victor reached for her.

"Don't touch me!" she begged, so feebly he could barely hear her.

Retreating backward, Melinda moved from one side of him to the other like a cowering mongrel. Panic swept over her and she tried to scream again. Suddenly she felt the corner of the table come to rest against her buttocks. She could retreat no further.

"Victor, I beg you. If not for me, then for Joseph," she said between sobs.

Like lightning his hands were upon her, one pulling at the back of her hair, forcing her downward, the other clawing at her clothes.

She struck out at him with her fists, then tore at his face with her short, sharp nails. *Please God, please ... please help me ...*

Melinda's primal instincts came to the fore and she fought with the strength of a tigress. But his powerful body pressed down against her and pinned her to the floor. Opening the front of her dress, Victor ripped away the batiste camisole that lay beneath it. Tiny pearl buttons flew through the air like glistening raindrops and hand-stitched seams tore apart like tissue paper, completely exposing her small, firm breasts. Frantically he fumbled with the opening in his trousers. Melinda tried again and again to scream for help, but no sound came from her parched and burning throat. She felt the wetness of his tongue slither across her chest and a quiver of revulsion ran through her. He pulled up her skirt, forcing her legs apart with his knees, probing with his hands. Brutally, he thrust forward and entered her, and a veil of black dropped over her eyes.

When Melinda opened her eyes, the sun was shining through the windows. She became aware of burning pain and the sticky wetness of blood. She lay without moving for a long time, holding reality at bay. She floated in and out of a nightmarish sort of awareness.

From what seemed like a long way off, she heard the clock ticking on the wall. Opening her eyes, she looked up at it. Almost eleven o'clock.

She thought of Claire, and her son, and her heart began pounding fiercely. Claire could return with Philippe at any moment. A rush of adrenaline burst within her, bringing clearer thinking with it. She forced herself to breathe deeply as she pushed herself up from the floor.

She raised herself to a seated position. The room spun sickeningly, and for a moment she thought she would lose consciousness.

I must get to my feet—I must!

She groped for the leg of the table. Clutching it between her palms, she pulled herself to her knees, then gripping the edge of the tabletop, she stood.

Making her way to the armchair next to the window, Melinda eased herself into it, leaning her head against its high, curved back. Her eyes closed, and she fought off hysteria. Soon the tears ran down her face, warm and salty as they trickled into the corners of her mouth.

Please God! Let this be a nightmare from which I shall awaken.

But the banjo clock on the wall ticked on and the nightmare continued. Grasping the arms of the rocker she rose and took a few deep breaths before walking into the bedroom.

She removed her torn, stained clothing and threw them into a corner of the closet. Pouring water into the basin from the pitcher on the commode, she bathed herself, washing her body with harsh, painful strokes. *Will I ever feel cleansed again?* she wondered.

After putting on a freshly laundered dress, Melinda powdered the fading red mark on her cheek and brushed her hair into place. She walked into the kitchen. Bending, she picked up the buttons from her camisole and righted the chair that Victor had knocked to the floor in his haste to leave. Looking around, she saw no further evidence that would bear witness to the worst thing that had ever happened to her in her life. She sat at the table and began sorting her work again, waiting for Claire and Philippe to return. Later, and for the rest of her life, she would have no memory of having done any of these things.

Chapter Twelve

Day followed day, when Melinda's strengths and weaknesses were severely tested. She learned to lie, something she abhorred having to do, but in doing so she managed to keep others from learning about her monstrous secret. When she was alone, she alternately battled rage and depression. She scrubbed at her flesh until it was raw, attempting to purge herself of the filth she imagined still clung to her.

At night, she dreamed of Victor: of his menacing eyes as they followed her, of his hands as they stripped her of her honor. Awakening in a cold sweat, she'd lie sleepless for hours, dreading the possibility that she might cry out his name. She did whatever was necessary to protect her husband from learning the truth. For if it were ever revealed to him, she knew he would surely slay Victor. Perhaps in another time and place Joseph could have thrown down the gauntlet, and in some misty field at dawn, avenged her.

As it was, he would go on believing her to be his own innocent love, the virgin unspoiled, that he had anointed on their wedding night.

Melinda faced Claire. Just the sight of her brought everything back so vividly, Melinda came near to losing control.

"Are you all right, Melinda?" Claire asked. "You look so tired."

How could she explain or tell Claire that her visits had become an unbearable ordeal, a sickening reminder of what Melinda so desperately wanted to forget. How could she say, *Stay away from me, Claire, I can't even look at you without thinking of Victor."*

Instead she answered: "I'm all right, dear. As a matter of fact, since cutting two teeth last week, Philippe has been quite the little angel." For a moment she paused, not knowing if she should say anything more. Then, girding herself she added, "Really, Claire, there's no need for you to come by every day any longer. We've imposed on your good nature too long as it is." *THERE—I've said it, and without flinching!*

Claire flushed, obviously disquieted by the turn in the conversation. "Well, if you'd prefer that I don't ... then of course I shan't."

"Please don't be offended, Claire. We truly love seeing you, but I feel guilty about taking you away from more pleasurable diversions." She thought, *Don't look at me with those tender eyes. It hurts me so much to have to hurt you—but I must.*

Claire'd sensed that something was wrong for some time, and now she was certain of it. More than once recently she'd caught Melinda staring with a peculiar look in her eyes. Perhaps in her zeal to be of assistance, she'd come too often and stayed too long.

Claire said, "That's nonsense. I've enjoyed every minute I've spent with Philippe. But, if as you say, you no longer have need of me ... I've been asked by Mother Superior to assist with the children's choir. I'm sure I'd enjoy the experience. The nuns are planning something exciting for Christmas this year." Claire looked at Melinda. She sat with her eyes cast down. "I think I'll accept her invitation to join them," she added.

"That sounds wonderful, Claire."

"Yes, it does. I haven't worked with music since my father died, and I've missed it." Reaching for her purse, she prepared to leave. "Do bring Philippe to rehearsal. He likes music. When we walk, I sometimes hear him humming."

She left them and rushed down the stairs. When she got to the sidewalk, she broke into tears.

* * *

Later on when she was able to, Melinda entered into the darkness of the confessional. She entered seeking solace, but none was to be found there. "I was attacked, Father! Viciously, and with malice, by my husband's half-brother. My life can never again be what it was—NEVER!" She managed to put into words the unspeakable details of what Victor had done to her. Her voice shook and tears welled in her eyes.

Her pastor listened, passively at first, then she heard the quickening of his breath and he went on to probe deeper. She answered his questions honestly, even though it deeply humiliated her to do so.

After a long pause the voice beyond the screen spoke again: "I feel with certainty that you are withholding some things from me. Do not risk committing a sacrilege, my daughter. Reexamine your conscience," he urged her. "When you are able to confess everything and truly forgive those who have trespassed against you, then and then only, shall God's Grace be once again upon you."

She heard the wooden slide snap shut. Somehow, in some way, it seemed that she was being held accountable for Victor's despicable act.

Melinda left the church in a state of controlled hysteria.

"Forgive those who have trespassed against you," the priest had asked of her. *Blessed Mother of Jesus, how can I ever do that?*

While walking home Melinda searched her mind furiously, going back fifteen years in time: to the classrooms that she and Victor had shared as children; to her father's fields where, as a boy, he'd picked vegetables and fruit; to the rutted dirt road that led to the village where he'd walked alone, this dark and brooding boy escaping for a while the taunts and jeers of his brothers. She could not remember ever having slighted him. She'd been too "bien élevée" to do that. No—there had been no slight, no insult, no reason for his consuming hatred of her.

Reaching home, she stood looking up at the windows of her flat, and beyond them to a cloudless cerulean sky. Her hand rested inertly upon the gate. She ached to remain outside. *Run, Melinda ... hide ... forget.*

She wiped the perspiration from her face. Straightening herself, she walked inside.

Chapter Thirteen

Joseph stood at his place at the head of the table carving the Sunday roast. Thick slices of succulent pork fell from the bone and rested in their golden juices on the platter. In the center of the table were a plate of roasted potatoes and a bowl of buttered carrots. Laying his carving tools aside, Joseph heaped a generous serving onto Melinda's plate.

"I just don't understand Victor," he said as he set the food down in front of her.

Reaching for the collar of her blue chambray dress, Melinda fumbled nervously with the tatted edging. "What is it you don't understand, Joseph?"

"It's been weeks since he or Claire have been here," he complained while carefully cutting Philippe's portion of meat into child-sized pieces. "They're avoiding us for some reason, I'm sure of it."

"Perhaps Victor is uncomfortable about facing you, now that he's lost his situation at the mill," Melinda suggested, her fingers still twisting the lace on her collar.

"Nonsense. That was well over a month ago. Besides, he's found other work."

"Where did you hear that?"

"I stopped for a mug of ale at the tavern last Friday. I'd heard he'd been spending a lot of his time there. He wasn't about, but one of his cronies told me he'd started last week at the Sagamore." His brow again pleated into furrows. "I've a mind to go over to the cottage and find out what's going on."

"I wouldn't press him, Joseph. It's maybe something personal."

"Personal or not," he said between swallows, "if he's got

something stuck in his craw, I'll have it told to my face."

An hour later, after failing to discourage him, Melinda watched apprehensively as Joseph left the house for the cottage on Queens Lane.

Her hands shook as she rinsed off the plates and stacked them next to the sink. "Stop it!" she cried aloud, flinging down the dishmop. "Your secret is more than safe with Victor."

Fighting to control herself, she finished tidying up and read a story to Philippe. As she sat holding the book of fairy tales, her son stretched languidly across her lap, a sudden rush of bile filled her throat. A dizzying nausea sent her scurrying to the water closet. With her son bawling out his protest from the kitchen, she hung over the seat, retching violently. When all had risen, she washed her face and rinsed the bile from her mouth.

Returning to the kitchen, she found Philippe asleep on the floor, his beloved volume tucked under his arm. She stooped and lifted him into her arms. *Oh my sweet, precious son. You're the only joy left to me in life.* She carried him into the bedroom and laid him in his crib.

Still feeling somewhat unsteady, she lay on her bed and closed her eyes. Barely asleep, she opened them again when she heard the door to the apartment open, then close. She lay waiting, her spine as rigid as a steel rod, until Joseph appeared at the door of their bedchamber.

"Are you all right?" he asked.

"Yes, of course. I thought I'd rest until you returned."

She sat on the edge of the bed and slid her feet into her shoes. "You're back sooner than I expected." She dared not look at him to search his face for clues, but listened carefully to the timber of his voice.

"Victor wasn't there. Neither was Claire."

Melinda's back relaxed and she emitted an audible sigh. "Claire rehearses the children after Mass on Sundays. Perhaps they went to the hotel for dinner afterward. They sometimes do that."

"Who knows," Joseph answered, sitting on the bed next to

her, his hand reaching to caress her neck and shoulders. Instantly he felt her body stiffen. "Why do you do that? Why do you tighten up when I touch you?" This wasn't like his wife. She'd always welcomed his advances.

She didn't answer his question. She couldn't.

He leaned and kissed the curve of her throat. "I love you," he whispered, his warm breath fanning the contour of her neck.

Gently she withdrew from him and stood looking at the disappointment in his eyes. "I'm sorry, Joseph, I haven't felt myself this afternoon. I think the pork was a bit too rich."

He nodded, accepting her explanation without further comment. He left the bedroom and Melinda followed him into the kitchen.

"Have you and Claire had a falling out of some kind?" he asked as he filled his pipe from the humidor on the table next to his chair.

"No, we haven't. She visits less often since taking charge of her choir. She's extremely serious about her work with the children." Turning, Melinda looked at him, then lowered her head. "You're worrying needlessly, Joseph."

"I don't think so. Liam Steele tells me Victor spends most of his time drinking in the bars down by the mews. He's at it heavily again." Joseph lit his pipe and pulled on it two or three times. "I'd hoped that was all in the past, left behind in Le Baie with the rest of that trash. But it would seem I was wrong. Why the man is so drawn to the riffraff in those places, I'll never comprehend." He shook his head as if to clear it. "And what sort of wife is it who can't keep her man at home with her? I warned him about marrying Claire. I warned him well." Turning impulsively, he walked to the door. "I'm going down to the mews to see if I can find him. Someone has to pound some sense into that head of his before it's too late."

"No Joseph, DON'T!"

If Victor were drunk and his tongue loosened enough, he might very well boast about what he'd done.

Melinda added, "The rum shops are closed on Sundays."

An act of God had helped her to remember that. "I'll speak with Claire tomorrow." Melinda put a restraining hand on his arm. "I'm sure she'll tell me if anything's wrong. Come, lie down with me for a while."

He looked at her a bit uncertainly. "Women!" He smiled and put his hand on her hip. "How can a man ever be expected to understand them?"

* * *

The clock tower at the high school was striking ten as Melinda left the house the following morning. She pushed Philippe's stroller into the park and sat on a bench with a clear view of the cottage. It was a chilly day with an overcast sky; an early harbinger of the grim months ahead.

Philippe ran in circles, gleefully chasing a fat pigeon through the dried leaves. They waited, half an hour at least, before Claire came out of the house.

Scooping up her child, Melinda dropped him into the seat of the stroller and hurried after her. Closing the gap between them, she called out, "Claire ... wait for me ... please!"

Claire spun around at the sound of Melinda's voice, a look of surprise on her face. "Melinda?"

"I've been waiting for you, Claire. I didn't want to chance going to the door. I wasn't sure—"

"Of course, I understand. But you needn't have worried. Victor isn't there." Claire stooped and kissed her nephew's cheek.

When she stood again, Melinda impulsively wrapped her arms around her, shocked for a moment by the thinness of the frame that lay beneath Claire's sweater. "I've missed seeing you," Melinda whispered, and suddenly she began to tremble.

"Melinda, what is it? Can't you tell me? I've known for weeks that something was wrong."

"I'm sorry, I still can't explain, but I couldn't bear to leave things as they were. You're the dearest friend I've ever had, and I don't want anything to come between us. I have personal problems to deal with, Claire. Serious problems that I'm not free to talk about. I beg you to trust me ... as my friend."

"I do trust you, and always shall."

They embraced again.

"I've suspected that something was going on," Claire said, "but I didn't want to interfere. It does help to talk about it though. I, if anyone, know that for certain."

Melinda nodded. "I will when I'm able to."

They stood looking at one another.

"Now then, enough about me." Melinda skillfully parried Claire's forthcoming question. "Tell me, are you all right?"

Claire looked aside, unable to meet Melinda's gaze. "Well enough, I suppose."

"What do you mean, well enough?"

A rush of color came, then quickly faded from Claire's face. "I truly don't know where to turn, Melinda." Her voice was oddly crisp. "Victor's all but deserted me. He spends his days in the saloons on Bedfordgate and his nights with the whores who frequent them. He's seldom at home, and when he is, he's either in a drunken stupor or ranging around like a madman. I'd like to leave him and return to Canada, to my aunt's in Montreal. I've lost all pride where that's concerned. But I haven't a cent to my name."

"What about your inheritance?"

"Everything was deposited in Victor's name. He controls my life by keeping me penniless. Last week I slipped the passbook from his pocket while he was asleep. Really, I'd stoop to anything to be free of him. I tried to withdraw a few dollars from the bank." She made a brittle kind of sound. "Ha! But you see, they refused me. Only *he* has use of the passbook. Whitehead's have cut me off because payment on my bill wasn't forthcoming. I don't know how long I can go on like this."

"How much do you owe at the market?" Melinda asked, opening her purse.

"No, please don't. I can't take money from you." Claire's colorless lips pressed tightly together as she fought to keep from breaking down.

Melinda took her by the arm and shook her gently. "Claire, listen to me. Last winter, you were so generous to us, and I know that you denied yourself in order to do it." Claire tried to interrupt, but Melinda went on. "Truly, I don't know how I would have managed to get through those months without your help. Please—now that I'm able to—let me in some way repay your kindness."

Claire turned her back, but Melinda remained undeterred.

"I've saved some of what I've earned from my sewing. It's not enough to get you to Montreal, but I can afford to give you something. It will remain strictly between us."

Claire closed her eyes and, without a word, accepted the bill that Melinda tucked into her pocket.

"Now then, go do some marketing. And please, Claire, come to see us whenever you like."

Crossing the park on her way home, Melinda walked with a somewhat lighter step. Nearing the south end, she stopped to look at a row of maple trees whose leaves were turning to crimson. Les Érables and the road that led past the orchard rushed before her eyes. A crushing loneliness wrapped itself around her. She looked down at Philippe who'd laid back in his seat and was fast on his way to slumber. *Not to worry, my innocent one. We'll see this through, and be the stronger for having done so.* Shaking off the wave of homesickness, she pushed on toward home.

Inside the gate, Melinda found a sheltered corner and left Philippe to finish napping. In some places, the clouds were parting and patches of blue were coming through. A golden shaft of sunlight fell across the steps to the veranda, and as Melinda seated herself in the center of it, Caitlin appeared at the door.

"Well now, isn't this turning into a pleasant day? And a blessin' it is for 'himself' in there. His cough is ever so much worse when it's damp."

Melinda nodded knowingly.

"Ye've been strollin', I see," Caitie observed, dropping

down beside her.

"Yes, we've been visiting Claire this morning."

"Really? I've not seen a thing of her comin' or goin' of late. I've wondered about her. Is she well?"

"She's fine. Busy, as we all are." Melinda looked away. Caitlin was very hard to lie to.

There was a long, uncomfortable silence.

"What is it, love? Yer not yerself at all—at all."

Melinda didn't answer, nor did she dare to turn and face those penetrating eyes.

"I'm not after steppin' out of me place very often, but 'tis only an imbecile wouldn't be seem' how unhappy it is ye are. Can't ye be tellin' Caitlin what it is that's botherin' ye, dear heart?"

Melinda turned, sighing deeply.

With a slow wink of her eye Caitlin added, "Maybe I can help ye to set things to rights."

"Oh, thank you, Caitie."

"For what, love?"

"For caring. For that great heart of yours." Melinda knew that sooner or later Caitlin would see the problem for herself. Deciding to pocket her pride, Melinda added, "As usual, your intuition is right on the mark, but the truth of it is, no one can help me with this. I simply have to be patient and see where it all ends." She took Caitie's hand into hers and pressed her cheek against the back of it.

"Well then," Caitie said as she pulled her hand away, a bit flustered by such a display of overt tenderness, "just ye be knowin' that I'm always here if you're ever needin' me help."

Melinda nodded and forced a smile.

"And don'tcha be lettin' Miroff overwork ye, ye hear? You're lookin' downright peaked these days."

"Caitie, please believe me. Mr. Miroff never asks any more of me than I'm able to do, and lately that hasn't been much."

"Then ye are ailin'! I knew it by the looks of ye!"

"I'm not ailing, Caitie. Just a little tired, that's all."

Melinda wanted so much to believe her own words, but this morning she'd again had to rush to the privy, a bare ten minutes after taking her breakfast. Her head even now felt light and floaty as she rose to carry Philippe upstairs.

Two weeks passed and her time came and went for the second month in a row. She felt her body hardening, as it had done when she'd conceived the first time. She knew for certain now that she carried life in her womb. And as the fetus grew, so grew her hatred of Victor Durand.

Chapter Fourteen

It was worst when all was still and Melinda lay sleepless alongside her husband, listening to his slow, regular breathing. She would touch herself, feeling the firmness of her belly, wondering, *Are you or are you not my husband's seed?*

Another autumn passed and winter again poised itself to deal them a withering blow.

On the last day of November the first flurries of snow skittered past Melinda's windows. Laying down her scissors, she gathered up the strips she'd been cutting from a swatch of woolen remnant. She went to the window and carefully pressed them between the sash and the frame with the blade of a table knife. For some days now, she'd felt a cold chill creeping across her shoulders as she worked at the kitchen table.

Philippe was asleep. Every now and then she heard him cough. A dry, unproductive cough that gave him little relief from his first cold of the season.

After plugging the last of the drafty windows, Melinda began preparing herself a cup of cocoa. She stood next to the stove, relishing the smell of it as it came to the boil. For weeks, tea had been all she'd been able to tolerate. That, along with the tedious bowl of broth.

Seating herself in the big chair next to the window, she sipped the cocoa slowly, savoring its flavor in her mouth for a few seconds before swallowing.

She was enjoying a second cup when she heard sounds in the stairwell. She guessed who it was even before going to the door.

"Who is it?" Melinda called as she stood with her hand curled tightly over the lock.

"It's Claire."

Turning the knob, Melinda released the bolt. "You're just in time for a cup of cocoa."

Claire looked thinner and more drawn than ever. "Is Philippe awake?" she asked, her thin brows drawing together slightly as her eyes scanned the room.

"I'm sorry, Claire. I put him to bed half an hour ago," Melinda explained as she poured from the steaming saucepan. "He's coughing and feverish this morning. I couldn't bear the whining a minute longer," she admitted, placing the cup on a saucer.

"It's all right, really. I haven't come to call. I've something important to tell you."

There was a pause when neither said anything.

Claire moved around the table and sat in the chair opposite Melinda's. "Where to begin? ..." She sighed and laced her fingers together. "On my way over here, I gave a lot of thought to how I would say this."

Instantly Melinda felt a flash of heat race through her body.

"I decided that there was but one way—straightforward, and all of it." Then in a low voice she added, "Every miserable bit!"

"What's happened, Claire?"

Against all normal expectations, Claire laughed. "He's gone! Victor has disappeared. I've not seen him since last Friday."

Pressing her hands together tensely, Melinda waited for her to go on.

Rising from the chair, Claire walked toward the window and she spoke as if to an empty room. "That scum!" The words cut through the air like a rapier. "Not only did he defile me and beat me, now he's run off with everything." Her hands reached up to cover her face.

Melinda rushed to her. Taking her by the shoulders, she wrapped her in her arms. "He'll be back, Claire. ... He's just

103

off somewhere drinking."

"No, Melinda, he won't come back this time, and whatever the case, I don't ever want to see him again. I wish he were dead! I wish I had had the courage to kill him!"

Melinda drew in her breath. "Don't say that! You don't mean it."

"I *do* mean it. I despise him! He's stripped me of every decent emotion I've ever had. All that's left is fear and shame."

"Claire, please ... don't."

"No, let me finish. I fear Victor because of the cruel beast that I know him to be, and I'm ashamed because I didn't have the courage to leave him." She ran her tongue across her parched lips. "I've been such a fool." She paced the room. "I can't believe that I once trusted him enough to hand him control of everything. *I gave him the lot!*" she ranted. She faced Melinda. "He never wanted me, Melinda! It was the money he was after," she declared through tightly clenched teeth. "He even went so far as to go through my things before leaving." A sob caught in her throat. "He took my parents' wedding bands from my jewelry box. How despicable can a person be? They were all I had left of them. I'd saved them thinking if we are ever blessed with children ..." Her voice trailed away to a whisper.

"You should have come to us, Claire. We might have helped."

"How could I come to you? Victor is Joseph's brother. Don't you understand?"

Melinda's head slowly, deliberately inclined. "Yes. Yes, of course I do."

"But in the end, I am here, beseeching your aid like a beggar."

"You're not to worry. We'll see this through together." Melinda reached out and took hold of her hand.

Somewhere deep within the timbre of Melinda's voice, a faint yet unmistakable tinge of hope was heard. Victor Durand had fled from their lives. A blessing she had not dared hope for. Perhaps in time, even she might begin to live again.

104

When her lease was up on the first of January, Claire walked one last time in the garden behind the cottage on Queens Lane. Melinda waited on the sidewalk outside the gate. She wore an increasingly lugubrious expression as she watched Claire stooping to touch the dormant rosebushes she'd planted last spring.

"I wonder how they'll survive the winter?" she asked herself aloud, brushing away the powdering of snow from the mulch at the base of the stalk. She'd carefully hilled them in October, before the frost had come. Melinda watched as in turn Claire carefully examined each of the bushes.

As recently as yesterday, Melinda had urged her to come and stay with them.

"Thank you. But you've barely room for yourselves."

"We'll manage ... at least until you find employment."

But Claire had stubbornly refused, insisting instead on taking a room at Mrs. Connerly's boarding house.

Walking from the garden, Claire passed her hand lovingly along the trellises next to the gate where Melinda stood waiting. In a voice that bore little sign of the emotion that choked her, she said, "I'll miss not seeing them bloom this year. Especially the pink ones. I dearly loved those little pink ones."

Victor and Claire's belongings had been sold for a pittance. Everything had gone, except a desk that she'd offered to Melinda, and of course, the piano. She'd found it soon after moving into the cottage, on one of her excursions to the second-hand store. Caitlin had haggled with the shopkeeper until people began gathering 'round, and in desperation he'd let it go for much less than he'd wanted to. Ancient though it was, its keys yellowing with age, Claire could not give it up. It had gone along to the rooming house yesterday, together with the trunk she'd brought with her from Le Baie.

Her room at Mrs. Connerly's was not the same turreted, overlavishly chintzed one at the front of the house that she'd shared with Victor upon their arrival in Riverton. It didn't overlook the confluence of High Point and New Boston roads, where the gentry nested comfortably behind the elms that lined the wide, swerving boulevard. No indeed, it was the narrow room at the back of the kitchen, more or less "done over" to bring in the extra dollar.

There was but one set of windows in the room, that in the center of the east wall. They let in a dollop of weak morning sun to the wicker stand of ferns in front of them. Against the inside wall, a metal bed covered with a worn "wedding ring" quilt was cozy enough, warmed as it was by the flue from the scullery stove on the opposite side of the wall. T'would be far less inviting come midsummer, when its heat was still filtering through the layers of plaster of Paris. She would deal with that when the time came. Presently, her overburdened brain was unable to give quarter to something so far in the future. Spartan though it was, the room cost nearly nothing, and even that paltry bit was more than she could properly afford.

No sooner had Claire settled into her new accommodations, than she hastened to look for work. She went each day to the Office of Employment on Maincrossing Road. Ill-equipped as she was, it was not surprising that after hours of waiting, the names called out never included her own.

On Friday afternoon she returned to the rooming house weary and discouraged. She stood in the entryway drenched through to the lining of her coat, from a rain that was quickly turning to sleet.

Removing her galoshes, she placed them neatly on the fiber mat next to the door. She was well on her way to her room when Mrs. Connerly came into the hallway.

"Heavens to Betsy, Missus Durand. Y'er all but frozen stiff from the look of ye. Come have a tad of something hot."

Claire followed her into the big, open kitchen.

"Miserable weather, ain't it?" she commented as she reached into a large tin and took out several homemade pastries. "These are fresh from the oven this morning."

Claire took off her coat and sat at the table as Mayre Connerly poured coffee from the ever simmering pot on the back of the stove.

"Any luck?" Mayre queried, passing a hand over her disheveled salt-and-pepper hair.

"I'm not sure. There could be a housekeeping position for the Fathers at Blessed Sacrament, but it's not available until the first of the year. To be honest with you, Mrs. Connerly, I'm fast on my way to financial ruin."

"Aye. I thought as much. Caitlin Flanigan tells me yer man has run off on ye." Her piercing black eyes studied Claire's reaction. There was little.

"Yes, he has. And please, dispense with condolences, Mrs. Connerly." Claire raised her hand in protest. "I'm far better off without him. That is, if I can ever find work."

"I'm that surprised, I am. He seemed a fine gentleman," Mayre remarked as though thinking aloud. With a shake of her head, she nudged herself back to the conversation. "Well now, ye need something for sure, and it was just that I was fixin' to talk to ye about. Ye remember Mave, me son Davey's wife? Lovely girl, that. ... She's waitin' on her first any day now. She's not been well of late, dear little soul." Leaning closer to Claire, she whispered, "It's that worried I am about her." Leaning back into her chair again, Mayre continued. "Be that as it may, it's left me without help. I've taken eight boarders as ye well know, not countin' me own brood. I can't keep up with the cookin' and cleanin' all on me own, not to mention the warsh on the first of the week. I'll be needin' someone to do for me—here in the kitchen." With a firm slap of her hand against her thigh, she brought any doubt about that to an absolute end. "Ellie, me sis, comes in at five most days to help serve the supper, but I can't always count on her bein' here. It's that frivolous she is." She clucked her tongue several times. "And at her age, imagine." She covered her mouth with her hand, suppressing a throaty chuckle.

"Are you offering me employment, Mrs. Connerly?" Claire cut straight to the core, certain that Mayre Connerly would have gone on and on, into the lurid details of her younger sister's wayward ways.

"Well, in a manner of speakin', I am. I can't pay anything

107

much, mind you, but I'm willin' to give you room and board as well as a little extra sum in exchange for services rendered."

A scullery maid. That was the size of it. But there was no time to wallow in false pride or petty vanity. She was on the cutting edge of being destitute and this, unfortunately, her only available recourse.

"Thank you, Mrs. Connerly. I'd much appreciate the opportunity."

"Ye can call me Mayre, if you've a mind. This evenin' then, for the supper?"

* * *

The work was hard. Claire rose at dawn to light the fires and bake the loaves for breakfast. At night it was usually after eight before the dishes were washed and put away and the dining room carpet swept. Afterward there were puddings to bake for the following day, and yeast dough to set to rising. She couldn't ever remember working so hard, not even when she lived on the Durand farm. Her hands grew red from the caustic soap, and her knuckles cracked open and bled. At night she covered them with glycerin and wrapped them in flannel rags to heal.

On Sundays, Mayre Connerly left the house early to attend Mass at Saint Mary's Cathedral. Afterward, she visited with her friends and kinfolk up in Corky Row.

Before leaving, she set currant buns and soda biscuits on a lead crystal platter that she placed in the middle of the credenza. Coffee was brewed and left to keep hot on the back of the stove. Otherwise, for all intents and purposes, Mayre's kitchen was closed in strict observance of the "Lord's Day."

Freed of her chores for a few hours, Claire looked forward to sleeping later and attending the nine o'clock Mass. While in the loft, listening to the purity of the children's voices echoing through the vaults and arches above her, she was able to forget, for a time, the drudgery her life had become. But alas, it returned all too swiftly on Monday morning when she was back at work stoking the fires and rubbing bedsheets on a board alongside the incessantly jabbering Mayre Elizabeth Connerly.

"Of course," she ran on, "it would all depend on what ye'd charge, but I'd like to see me granddaughter have a dash of the culture. There's a limit to what I'll give for it, though." She turned to Claire, who looked straight ahead, not having heard a word. "Well then ... how much?" Her shrill, high-pitched tone got through to Claire this time.

"How much for what, Mayre?"

"For the piano lessons—for my Meagan?"

"Oh gracious, I haven't taught in years."

"Well that may be, but I've ofttimes heard ye playing in yer room. It goes straight to me heart, it does. I've always wanted to play the piano, but me Ma brought eleven youngsters into this world, so it was out of the question, of course. That's why I'd like for our Meagan to learn. She could play for me in me dotage."

Word went into the neighborhood by way of Mrs. Connerly's waggling tongue, and in less than a month Claire had three more piano students.

For four hours on Sunday afternoons, she taught her sweet, pale-skinned Irish girls the staffs and the fingering. Precious little was paid for this labor of love, yet meager though it was, it added up week after week. God willing, there was again hope that one day Claire Durand would free herself from the ranks of the feckless poor.

Chapter Fifteen

Charles Mulvaney died on Good Friday. It was a shock, even though it was not unexpected. He'd rallied several times and Caitlin had felt encouraged. But as sure as God made the "little people," he'd taken a turn for the worse again. The previous week, after several days of rain, his cough came on worse than ever before.

On Monday his eyesight began failing, and the following day when he awakened he could see nothing.

"Don'tcha be frettin' now," Caitlin reassured him with a pat of her hand on his. "I'll send straightaway for the doctor."

Doctor Burns examined Charlie and left him a stronger medicine. But when he walked into the parlor, out of earshot, the doctor confided the bad news to Caitlin. "There's nothing more to be done, Miss Flanigan. He's struggling for every breath he draws. The man is doomed. I suggest that you send for his priest while there's still time for him to receive the sacraments."

Caitie stood on the veranda and watched Doctor Burns's buggy leave, then, moved by the urgency in the doctor's voice she called out to the young Sullivan boy, "Francis! Run and fetch Father McNally."

From that moment she hardly left Charlie's side. On Friday morning in the wee hours before dawn he breathed his last.

Dozing in a chair at his bedside, Caitlin was awakened with a start. His racking cough had ceased; the room resounded with a disturbing quiet. Charlie lay on his side in the big brass bed, his eyes wide open, as if staring at the brilliant red stain on his pillowcase.

Caitlin hung out the crepe (satin, and black as midnight, it was) and had him done up in his finest. She bought five large floral pieces to place around the casket that stood in the curve of the parlor windows.

One by one they came to the wake and filed past his bier; his friends, his neighbors, and a few curious onlookers. They knelt to say the rosary with Caitlin and Father McNally, and later they partook of Caitie's buffet and drank the Old Bushmills long laid aside for this day.

They sat beside his earthly remains and spoke glowingly of his "grand ways" and the goodness of old Charlie's heart.

The days that followed the funeral passed slowly for Caitlin who, without "himself" to care for, was lonelier than she'd ever thought she could be. Except for a very few, folks stayed away after the burial, and within a month Charles Mulvaney and his "grand ways" were forgotten by all but his housekeeper.

Through long-standing habit, Caitie continued to rise at five and turn out her baking for the day. Later in the morning, she'd climb the stairs to the third floor, carrying saffron buns and the extra loaf of bread in the folds of her apron. She'd sit for a spell and sip a cup of tea with her dear little friend who waited patiently for the coming of another baby and had more to do than a body ever ought to.

* * *

There were those who were shocked to hear that Mr. Mulvaney had willed everything he owned to his housekeeper, including his house and the two adjacent properties in the yard on Sladesferry Landing. A goodly amount of cash had also been put by in the Riverton National Bank. With his death, Caitlin Bridgit Mary Flanigan became a wealthy woman. She would never want for anything for as long as she lived.

At Samuel Miroff's suggestion, she visited the office of Alexander Friedman, an adept young attorney who'd befriended Sam on his arrival in Riverton. After examining the documents, Alex returned them to her.

"Other than a few legalities, Miss Flanigan, these documents speak for themselves. It was Charles Mulvaney's wish that you inherit his entire estate. I foresee no problem of any kind."

Caitlin walked home from Friedman's office garbed in her mourning black. Atop her flaming tresses lay a pert hat tied under the chin with shiny black ribbons. She sat in the musty, seldom used parlor and asked herself, *WHY?*

She'd known that he'd had no family here, but there was a brother in Ireland. Charlie'd spoken of him a time or two while recalling his boyhood in County Limerick.

"Like as not, he's dead and dust by now," Charlie'd remarked, the brogue still heavy on his tongue, his words free of the nostalgia usually heard in Irishmen's voices when they spoke of the 'Old Sod.' I had a stepsister, Ivy. She was a good many years younger than I. Pretty girl, she was. I've not seen nor heard of her in upward of fifty years. And there was her mother. A witch of a woman, that one. Drove me brother off without a penny in his pocket. 'Shiftless and lazy,' she'd called him. After my father passed on, she took the girl and went back to Scotland to be with her family."

At the age of sixteen, young Charlie Mulvaney had been left on the farm to shift for himself. He'd written his stepmother in Scotland but a year later, after not having heard a single word, he'd sold the place to his neighbor to the north. Taking only his share of its worth, he'd left the rest of the money with his parish priest and crossed over to America to seek his fortune. He'd worked hard, plunging every penny he'd earned into a savings account. Later he invested most of it in real estate. Tall and handsome, with laughing Irish eyes and a thick head of curly white hair, he'd remained a bachelor all his life. 'Twas said he'd courted a lady for many, many years. She was for some reason beyond his reach, and he never gave his heart to another.

Eleven years it was, next month, since Caitlin had come

down from Boston to serve him. Eleven years since she'd become more family to him than he had ever known.

* * *

January of 1889 was unbelievably mild. There were cold snaps to be sure, but often it was warm enough to walk around the pond in Hutchinson Park in the afternoon. But Caitlin couldn't seem to get up the gumption for it. Most of the time she sat inside and watched from the window as others took advantage of the unusually pleasant weather. The days were dreadfully long in passing, as were the months that followed.

Spring, as usual, was rainy and it made Caitlin restless and cranky. On the last day of April, after a dismal month of overcast skies, the sun finally came out. At the sight of it, Caitlin was filled with a newborn energy and impulsively decided to rid the house of Charles Mulvaney's wheelchair. It had stood like a specter in the corner of the kitchen, next to the Franklin stove, his brown and yellow afghan folded neatly over the back. She was bumping it down the cellar steps when Melinda called down from the landing.

"Be careful at the turn, Caitie, the steps get narrower there."

"Aya, darlin', that I will."

After moving the chair into the corner behind an old bedspring she'd hauled down there in the fall, Caitie covered it with a piece of sheeting and went back up the stairs.

Melinda had waited for her in the entryway, holding Philippe in her arms. "I wish you'd ask Joseph to help you with things like that, Caitlin. He'd be only too happy to be of service."

Caitlin smiled and looked directly into Melinda's eyes. "Practice what you preach, Miss. It's no harder for me to take that chair down to the storage room than it is for you to be carryin' that heavyweight up to the third floor."

She leaned and kissed Philippe on the tip of his nose. Stepping back, she got a full view of Melinda's girth. She

113

was enormous!

"Come in and sit for a spell, Melinda." Looking at Philippe, she teased, "I baked a batch of ginger cookies this morning."

"We'd like to, Caitie, but we can't stay long. I've frittered away most of the morning feeding a flock of pigeons."

"Well, you needed a bit of sunshine, the Lord knows, and another few minutes won't make a bit of difference now, will it?"

As they entered the flat, the smell of spices and confectionary sugar made Melinda's mouth water. For about a month now, she'd craved sweets. Awakening at night, she'd tiptoe into the kitchen and spread soda crackers with peach preserves or honey.

"Any sign of ... well, you know what it is I'm askin'," Caitlin stammered.

"Not a sign, but I've still two weeks to go before I'm due." Melinda washed down her cookie with a gulp of milk and reached to the plate for another.

"Bless me, girl. I do believe yer the biggest 'lady-in-waitin'' I've ever seen. For yer sake I hope it isn't much longer. That babe is big enough now to stand on its own two feet."

Melinda sighed and nodded agreement. "All in good time, Caitie, all in good time."

* * *

May 10th dawned gun-metal gray, with moisture-laden clouds racing every which way across the sky above the choppy waters of the bay. Wind noises in the eaves awakened Melinda to the consciousness of pain deep in the small of her back.

Sitting up, she reached down to the foot of the bed for her robe and felt the warm trickling of her waters as her membranes ruptured. Rising quickly, she stood inert for a stunned moment, then lifting her gown, she saw blood-streaked mucous trickling down the insides of her thighs. Hurrying to the

114

washstand, she took hold of a towel to sop up the flow. It had begun, and as much as she'd yearned for this day to be here and gone, she now wanted to hold it back.

Taking her clothes, she went into the kitchen. She sponged herself and dressed as usual. She brewed the coffee and put three eggs into a pot to boil. When Joseph seated himself to breakfast, she sliced the bread and mentioned nothing of what had taken place earlier. Caitlin would fetch the doctor when the time was right. No need for hurrying. It had taken fifteen hours before she'd been delivered of Philippe. She couldn't bear having everyone hovering over her for that long again.

After her husband left for work, Melinda tended to the boy and did the routine chores, but as the morning progressed, so did the frequency and intensity of her pains.

* * *

During his first trip of the day down to Stoneheep, Joseph was preoccupied. Melinda was two weeks overdue and this morning she hadn't seemed herself. She'd hardly spoken a word and she'd asked him to fetch the boy from his crib—something he'd never been asked to do before. He decided to go home at noon to reassure himself that everything was as it should be.

Halfway up the stairs he could hear Philippe crying. He raced the rest of the way up, taking the steps two at a time.

He found his son sitting on the floor banging a wooden soldier against the foot of the bed. Melinda lay across it, her knees pulled up to her middle, her face buried in the pillows. Joseph scooped Philippe into his arms and ran downstairs to Caitlin's.

"The baby's coming, Miss Flanigan—I'm off to fetch the doctor," he shouted excitedly. Handing her his son, he rushed away, running the four blocks to the physician's office on East Prospect Street.

Fifteen minutes later he returned with the doctor in tow

and found Caitlin upstairs sitting on the edge of the bed next to Melinda, the youngster contentedly seated on her lap sucking his thumb.

Caitlin stood and handed him the child. "Here, take him below and feed him something. I'll be a sight more help up here than you will, Joseph."

Doctor Picard rolled up his shirtsleeves and examined his patient. "This should go quickly," he predicted a bit smugly, but after an hour of punishing labor, Melinda'd made little if any progress.

Her pain had become so severe, she could barely concentrate on the effort at hand. She moaned and groaned, tossing her head from side to side, pulling hard on the rungs of the metal bedstead. Seated at the bedside, Doctor Picard looked at Caitlin, his bushy brows pulling together. "I'm afraid she's losing ground. We'd best get the forceps sterilized."

"Nonsense!" was Caitlin's reply.

Caitie approached Melinda from the other side of the bed and wiped her face with a moistened cloth. She'd seen a lot of birthin' as the daughter of a midwife and she wasn't about to give up so soon. Stooping, she gave Melinda a sip of tepid water.

"There now, love, that's better, isn't it? Rest a spell, dearie, rest. ... Just take it easy now. No need to worry about a thing. Caitie'll help you push out that big, lazy babe."

"Oh Caitie, help me." Melinda's voice was shrill, and her eyes had a hollow, sunken look.

"I'm here now, darlin' girl. Just ye be takin' me hands in yours. Push now, hard as ever ye can, PUSH!"

A series of deep groans escaped Melinda's throat as she strained, pulling tightly on Caitlin's hands throughout another contraction.

"It's coming!" Picard announced excitedly. "The crown has started into the canal."

"Only a little longer, darlin'."

Melinda gripped Caitie's forearms, her nails digging into the alabaster flesh, while another gush of perspiration drenched her from head to foot.

All at once there came a cry that cut through Caitlin to her very heart. Seconds later she heard the infant's wail.

Caitlin bathed Melinda and changed her into a fresh gown. Caitlin lifted the baby out of the cradle and carried the newborn boy, wrapped in a worn flannel blanket that had swaddled his brother Philippe, to the bedside. Strands of his dark, moist hair fell across his forehead, and long, sweeping lashes laid soft shadows on his cheeks. His full lips, slightly parted, had the look of a cherub's mouth.

"Such an angel! Never have I seen a more beautiful boy. Look at him, love. Look at your darlin' son."

Melinda turned her face away. "I can't, Caitlin. Not yet. Please let me rest for a while."

The smile vanished from Caitlin's lips. Only rarely had she seen a mother turn away from her infant, no matter the ordeal in bringing it into the world. Strange ... very strange indeed. Melinda Durand would have been the last one she'd have expected would do a thing like that.

Chapter Sixteen

Five Years Later, 1894

Sam Miroff and his family were returning home from the first vacation they'd taken since coming to Riverton. Standing alongside the railing of the *Bristol* (one of the Glory Ships of the Riverton Steamship Lines), Sam couldn't help but reflect on how many things had changed in the years since then. All for the better, he was happy to say. Thank God—everything had paid off like manna from heaven. And not just for them. In New York where they'd visited this week with Mila and Sol, things were going full blast ahead for them too.

It had been exciting for Sam to hear what his energetic young brother-in-law had had to say. Sometimes Solly made him feel like an old man. He ran around like a sixteen-year-old, his thinning brown hair disheveled, his long, nervous fingers constantly raking through it. He was always on the lookout for a faster, better way of doing things. The safe, conventional way seemed to bore Solly to death. It made for some chancy undertakings, but most of the time he managed to come out smelling like a rose.

They were direct opposites, these two. Sam was a cautious man, his appearance neat and never flamboyant. His brilliantined hair always neatly combed, with a part that looked as though it had been put there with a surgeon's scalpel. The only thing similar about them was their eyes. Not the shape or the color, but the alertness. Sam, like Solly, never missed a thing. They got along—even if their thinking was often poles apart.

"I kid you not, Sammy," Sol said on their first day together in the city, "in ten years a tailor will be a luxury in this country. Only the wealthy will wear custom-made clothes. The rest of the world will buy from the rack. *Ready-to-wear*. It's the coming thing. Hell, it's here now in New York City." His hands went through his hair again, doubtlessly uprooting a few more strands from his scalp. "Go ahead, laugh! But don't forget who told you this!"

The following day he and Solly went back to Seventh Avenue, to the Crown Manufacturing Company where Sol was employed as a floor manager. They climbed the stairs to the fourth floor of the red brick building with the embossed metal façade.

Inside the factory, Sam followed Sol through row after row of women working at electrically powered sewing machines. The men stopped every now and again to watch one of the operators do her job. Sol stood at Sam's elbow and spoke above the whirring of the motors.

"We have fifty-four girls working for us now. We hire anyone we can train to sew on these machines. Some of them can't speak a word of English, but they do their job and they do it good. If not—out they go on their asses. We can always find others to fill their chairs." He hunched his narrow shoulders callously and walked on. "Each of them works on a different part of the garment. Piece work, it's called. That way, they get to know how to do it *very well, and very fast.*"

Sam watched intensely as a buxom German woman went through her procedure for them. The needle sped through the fabric so fast it was unbelievable. She was stitching collars onto the body of a shirt, and doing it with incredible accuracy.

They moved past the women toward a green door at the far end of the room. Solly opened it and went inside.

"Hiya Georgie ... Al. Ya see, fellas, I can't stay away from here even when I take the day off."

They all laughed, and he introduced Sam to the cutters.

"I just wanted to show this guy how we do things in the big time."

They laughed again. Sam shook their hands, but his eyes were riveted on the giant, circular blade on the long table.

"Twenty layers it cuts through," Sol said. "And look, over there. Patterns, all laid out by sizes." He looked Sam in the eye. "Make sense?" Before Sam could answer, he added, "You bet your weenie it does!"

From there they walked into the shipping area. Hanging from moveable metal racks were the finished garments, freshly pressed and ready to go to the customer. "It's here to stay, Sam. You mark my words."

* * *

Looking from the ship's railing toward Riverton as the city drew nearer and nearer, Sol's words were still ringing in Sam's ears. As a matter of fact, all the way home he'd been thinking about what he'd seen down in the garment district.

"You're somewhere else again, Sam." Natia's voice broke into his thoughts. She was standing alongside him, gripping her restless child by the hand.

"Let go, Mama, I want to feed the seagulls," Sarah whined.

"Don't talk like that to your Mama," Sam scolded. "She knows what's best for you. Here, come over by Papa."

They stood all three at railside as the *Bristol* approached her mooring.

"What a sight, eh, Natia? I never cease to be amazed." Sam's eyes looked up at the three giant stacks as wave after wave of silver-winged gulls followed the *Bristol* into her berth.

The ships of the Riverton Lines carried passengers from New York City, down Long Island Sound, past Point Edith, into Mount Hope Bay. They served the people of coastal New England and served them lavishly. They strolled her three open decks and dined in luxury in the plush walnut-paneled salons.

The *Bristol* carried eight hundred and fifty passengers in

her staterooms, and below on the freight deck a cargo of forty-eight freight cars sailed the sound with them, bringing bales of cotton from the Carolinas and as far away as Egypt. Bales that might very well be loaded onto the low gear driven by Liam Steele and hauled up Anawan Hill to the Union Mill yard.

As they made their way toward the gangplank, Sam looked around for Alex Friedman, who was to meet them on their arrival. It was like looking for a needle in a haystack, what with the hundreds of passengers disembarking and heading for the trains that stood waiting to take them into the city.

Sam stretched his neck, trying to look over the heads of the people in front of him. As he reached the bottom of the gangplank, he spotted Alex leaning against a building across the street.

It was hard to miss Alex, even in a crowd like this. He sported a thatch of blond hair that anyone over the age of puberty would have envied. Along with it were a pair of gray-green eyes the color of salt water. He stood over six feet tall, with the physique of an athlete. "Outstanding" was the only word Sam could think of to describe him.

The man never wore a hat, summer or winter. When Sam asked him about it, he'd explained, "I can't stand the things. They give me migraines."

Maybe so, but Sam suspected Alex enjoyed showing off that golden mane of his.

Apart from his striking good looks, Alex Friedman was a fine human being. Early on, he had steered a lot of business Sam's way, and Sam would never forget that.

Catching sight of them, Alex loped across the street and shouted above the din. "WELCOME HOME! We've missed you—all of you, but ESPECIALLY YOU!" He took Sarah from her father's arms and hugged and kissed her.

She adored Alex, and wrapped her arms tightly around his neck.

Natia liked Alex, too. He was so different from any other man she knew. And his wife, Erica—she was something special! So self-assured and beautiful, always the last word in fashion.

At one time, Natia had tried to emulate her and had bought an expensive, trendy dress. Sam had burst out laughing when he saw her in it. He'd stopped when he saw the hurt come into her eyes. She'd never worn the dress again. Her square, shortwaisted figure didn't lend itself to frilly things and her broad features were too blunt for the kind of hairstyles that Erica Friedman wore. She'd wasted a lot of her husband's hard-earned money trying to be something she could never be, and she would never do it again.

On the way home in the carriage, she sat quietly as Sam and Alex talked business. Most of the time she only half listened to what they were saying.

"You really should see it, Sam. C'mon, it won't hurt anything to look at the place," she heard Alex say. "It's the kind of house that you and Natalie should have."

He always insisted on calling her Natalie, even though she'd corrected him any number of times.

"Okay, for Chrissakes! I'll look at it—just stop harping about where I live."

"Great, Sam, you won't be sorry. This place is one in a million. Sarah will love it, won't you, honey?" He patted her lovingly on a pink cheek.

* * *

Known as the Kraegen House, it was up on High Point Road where "the Yankees" lived. Sam felt out of place up there. He'd never thought of himself and Natia as "Hill People." Sladesferry Landing, where he lived now, was a kind of melting pot. His neighbors were Irish, French-Canadian and Portuguese, with here and there an Italian family. They all blended well together. He'd never felt he had to apologize for living in that neighborhood, even though Alex considered it less than grand. Sometimes Alex's tastes were a little too uppity to suit Sam.

On first impression it looked to be a large house, and Sam

turned to leave.

Alex grabbed him by the arm. "Let's go inside."

"Give me a break, Alex! I don't need the Taj Mahal to live in. What are you—meshuggah or what?"

"Come on! It's not as big as it looks."

It was Queen Anne in architecture, turreted, with a multi-level roofline and a broad veranda circling around three sides of the house. Flowering shrubs and evergreens nestled at its base, while six perfectly shaped elm trees lined the semicircular drive up to the front door.

Entering reluctantly, Sam followed Alex from room to room. He didn't say anything, but Alex could hear him grunting as he walked across the parquet floors.

"Genuine Italian marble fireplaces, Sam. Have you ever seen anything more beautiful?"

Another series of unintelligible noises made their way out of Sam Miroff's mouth.

Exquisite French wallpaper in pastel florals enhanced the living room, and crown moldings bordered the ceilings. Solid walnut paneling enriched the walls of the library, dining room, and the butler's pantry. This was indeed a very special house.

They walked into the large kitchen with its terrazzo floor and a bank of mullioned windows overlooking a gazebo in the center of the garden.

Sam stopped right in the middle of it. "You've got to be nuts if you think I can afford anything like this. Why the hell are you wasting my time?"

"Because you *can* afford it, Sam. Listen, I'll try to explain." Alex took a hefty breath. "It's part of the Leonhardt Kraegen estate. He was a founder of the union here. He died three years ago. His wife preceded him by a year, a suicide, and there were no children."

"A suicide?" Sam couldn't imagine such a thing.

Alex nodded his head. "I'm not at liberty to discuss that with you. The heirs live in Germany, and they're very anxious to settle. There are a lot of problems." He put his hand on Sam's shoulder. "Honestly, I'd never have suggested this to you if I didn't think it was an extraordinary deal, Sam."

When Sam said nothing, Alex went on. "If this isn't your style—well then, forget it. But at this price, I wanted you to have a shot at it."

"What price, goddammit!"

"Let's go downtown to the office."

Sitting alongside Alex, Sam looked at the sheaf of papers spread out across his desktop.

"Are you sure this isn't some kind of mistake? How can it be for such a house?"

"There's scandal associated with Kraegen. Ergo, the suicide. I can't go into details, it's confidential. But the heirs don't want to adjudicate."

"Adjudicate?"

"Go into the courts and have it all come out. They're willing to settle for much less if they can do it privately through their lawyers. Well, what do you think?"

"I think this is insane! But ... all right, damn you, I'll do it. And God protect your fancy ass if anything goes wrong here."

"You won't be sorry, Sam. It's a hell of an investment."

Chapter Seventeen

Melinda watched from her window as two burly men made their way down the porch steps of the tenement house across the yard from hers. They were loading Sam and Natia Miroff's belongings onto a moving van that was waiting out in the street. She was sorry to see them leaving, but she had learned that in America, moving was the thing to do. In August a year ago, she and Joseph had moved down to the second floor flat made available upon Mrs. O'Leary's demise. After the funeral, Caitlin had offered them the place for little more than they were paying for the attic apartment.

At first Melinda had not fully appreciated how wonderful it would be. It was only after the boxes and barrels had been unpacked and stored away that she looked around and saw all the space. She and her husband were alone in their bedroom for the first time since leaving Les Érables.

Philippe and his brother Marc now shared a bedroom across the hall from theirs, and albeit small, there was even a third one that she had set up as workroom. Finally, she was able to confine her mess to an area away from the rest of the house.

He had not said so, but this pleased Joseph, who still found the clutter an abrasive reminder of her stubborn, headstrong ways. He was not yet fully reconciled with the way she had handled things, and probably never would be, but ... had it not been for the money she'd earned, they would still be nesting upstairs, with two growing boys sharing their bedroom with them.

Joseph's attitudes confused her at times. To this day she could not understand why he had accepted her working for

Sam Miroff as a form of personal betrayal. Many women worked in the mills, and in Boston a group of staunch feminists were making the headlines.

Turning away from the window, Melinda looked again at the letter that lay on the end table next to her. Slowly, she slid the pages from the envelope and reread the last paragraph:

Papa is unable to speak and I sometimes wonder when I look into his eyes whether or not he knows who I am. Except for the family, Pastor Lucier and Doctor Savard, he sees no one. He is so weak his heart is barely able to beat. Mama, of course, suffers it all with him.

Marie-Élise's words drew forth a grim scenario.

Michèl Bérard had suffered a stroke and was left partially paralyzed and unable to speak. Melinda innately sensed that he, the man she had loved more than any other save her husband, was very close to death. Her heart ached at the thought of never again seeing a smile crinkle the corners of his eyes ... or never walking through the orchard arm in arm with him, her face so close to his shoulder that she could smell the fragrance that was uniquely his. Could she bear having him gone forever, this gentle person whose lips were as soft as the brush of silk against her cheek?

She walked into her workroom, to the desk that Claire had given her. Lifting her pen, she dipped it into the inkwell. But her hand shook and she was unable to think. Perhaps tomorrow the words would come.

Three weeks later, another letter came from Les Érables. Upon opening the envelope, a black-edged photograph of her father fell into her lap. She lifted it, and stared into Michèl Bérard's face. Turning it over, she read aloud the simple prayer printed in gold lettering on the reverse side. On September 7th, her father had gone to sleep and never reawakened. Pressing the photograph to her lips, she kissed him one last time. Walking to her bedroom, Melinda opened the Bible that lay on the bedside table and placed the photograph between its pages.

For the longest time, in that moment just before sleep came, or the moment just after she awakened, Melinda thought of her father. Memories of him ebbed and flowed and she would lie in the curve of her husband's arm and weep. Not to have been there, not to have shared his loss with the rest of her family, left a hollowness inside her. She wanted to feel her mother's hand in hers and to grieve with her. Instead she wrote:

Dearest Ones,

I have dreaded this day, for I am here and you are so far from me that we cannot reach out to each other. Across the many miles that separate us, I can but share this sorrow with you in spirit.

I have not words to express the deep sense of despair I suffer at not having been by your side when Papa left us.

Dare I hope that things will change in the foreseeable future? I seriously doubt it. So much has happened to make our returning to Le Baie impossible. Joseph works ever so hard, but I think that he has given up his dream.

I wish that Papa could have known our children. They are happy, healthy boys and we are pleased with them -- for the most part.

Philippe troubles me at times. He is so intelligent, so sensitive, and yet his grades this past year have not reflected this.

He seems unchallenged by his studies. A common affliction in a boy of his age, I'm told. Perhaps I worry needlessly, but I do so want him to succeed. He is Claire's most improved piano pupil, however, and his music lessons have become important to him.

Claire has done well. You would be proud of her. She has many pupils now, and enjoys both her work with them and with the children's choir. She has recently come to share Caitlin's home with her, and we are delighted in having her close to us again.

Claire had survived. She seemed to have successfully put tragedy behind her. She was not as she had been and never would be, but they had all changed, each in his own way.

Still holding the pen in her hand, Melinda paused. Her mind wandered off. Where was Victor Durand, she wondered? Had he returned to Baie de Saint-Jacques, or was he lurking somewhere nearby, watching them with scorn-filled eyes. Almost five years had passed since he'd disappeared from their lives. No one ever spoke of him, not even Joseph. It was as though they'd made a pact never to remind each other of Victor. But a day never passed when she was not reminded of him. He was ever there in the presence of her son Marc, whose face she scanned unceasingly for traces of resemblance. The dark, nearly black hair, straight, as was Victor's, with a satiny sheen so brilliant it was beyond describing. His eyes were hers, as blue as forget-me-nots except for a deeper, violet tinge in the center. He was a gentle, obedient boy, and the apple of Caitlin Flanigan's eye.

* * *

October blessed them with a glorious Indian summer. It wasn't until the third week of the month that the frost touched the earth and the full palette of autumn color spread itself across the countryside. It ended all too abruptly, when November's winds brought the scarlet leaves tumbling earthward. Then grayness filled the skies above the bay as winter sharpened its claws.

January, 1895

On the eighth day of the new year, Father Jean's letter arrived from Sherbrooke. It had become an annual blessing upon Melinda and Joseph's house, a reevaluation of the year just past. A sort of cleansing of the mind and spirit in preparation for a new, hope-filled future. Melinda devoured every word, reading it aloud to the family. This year, in addition,

Father Jean had added a paragraph intended for her alone, one that took her completely by surprise:

In one of your letters to the family, you made mention of Philippe's lack of interest in his schoolwork. From what you wrote, I gleaned that the school is obviously failing him. Sometimes in these new parishes, the nuns have not yet had enough experience to set sound standards for their pupils. This will come in time, but your son may be the loser because of it. I would like you to consider sending him here, to me, to l'Académie, the elementary school at Saint Charles. We are the finest, and I hope that you will forgive my arrogance in stating this fact so unequivocally.

At first she totally rejected the idea. IMPOSSIBLE! She knew only too well that they could not bear the financial burden of a private school like l'Académie.

"He doesn't need a school *like that,*" were Joseph's exact words when she broached the subject to him. "Besides, he'd be away from home for most of the year, and that's not fair to a boy of his age."

Melinda didn't agree, and pointed out that youngsters were flexible, more able to adjust to change.

"Hordes of children go away to school, Joseph. At the very least, Philippe would have his uncle and the family in Le Baie to support him." The more she spoke, the more the idea appealed to her. "Philippe would get to know our people," she continued. "They are, after all, his flesh and blood."

An almost giddy exhilaration began pulsing through her. It quickly subsided when she again remembered the stress this would place on their already overburdened budget. She tried to dismiss the idea from her mind—but it kept returning. Father Jean's proposal refused to die a natural death.

Later that night when the house was quiet, Melinda walked down the hallway to the room where her sons slept. She stood in the doorway and looked down at Philippe, spread out across his bed, his long, lean legs straying out from under the covers. *He will be tall,* she thought, *like the*

Bérard men. Stooping beside his bed, she brushed back a lock of hair from his forehead. Time passed so quickly; Philippe would be eight years old on his next birthday. Soon he would cease to be a child. *Somehow his future must be assured.* She rose after pressing her lips to his forehead and returned to the kitchen.

Melinda slept poorly that night. Wrapped as she was in a cocoon of uncertainty, she kept tossing and turning into the wee hours.

With only two hours of sleep to refresh her, she rose at five the following morning. She waited until Joseph had left the house, then went directly to the bottom drawer of her dresser. Reaching behind her underthings, she pulled out a leatherbound bankbook. In the last year she'd saved a goodly sum of money by taking on a larger workload. Something she had intended doing ever since Philippe had entered school. She had not given up their dream, even if Joseph had. But she would willingly do so if it meant that Philippe would reap the benefit.

She held the bankbook in her hand, looking down at the figures. It wasn't a lot, but it could be a beginning.

Dare I oppose Joseph again? she asked herself as she sat crosslegged on the floor. Jumping up, she went to her workroom and sat at the desk. She would not deal with that question yet! There were other things she must take care of first. Picking up her pen, she wrote Father Jean in search of answers. Before the end of January, she had them.

Furthermore, you'll be happy to know, that as a member of this faculty, I am entitled to offer any member of my family a considerable reduction in tuition fees. In addition, I will be happy to absorb whatever discrepancy might be outstanding. I can think of no better way of investing what I have, than by assisting you in this effort.

The seeds were sown, and slowly they germinated. ...

* * *

It was a difficult summer. Philippe fought tooth and nail against the idea of leaving to study in Sherbrooke, and Joseph withheld any support he might have given his wife.

"I will not do battle with you against the boy, Melinda." He gave notice as he stood at the washstand sponging his arms and chest. He was tired and irritable, his skin prickling from the residue left from the bales. "I've stated and restated how I feel about this." His voice deepened and the corners of his mouth turned downward. "Because of your insistence, I have agreed to a trial. But that is as far as I will go."

Weighted under a mantle of guilt, Melinda verged close to surrender. Caitlin, Joseph, Philippe. Everyone opposed her—everyone except Claire, who'd said, "What sort of chance will Philippe have if he remains here in Riverton? Will it in any way compare with what Father Jean is offering him? He's young, Melinda, he'll soon forgive you for loving him so much."

The subject of l'Académie was avoided during the rest of the summer, especially when Joseph was at home.

"If there's any more quarreling over this issue, I will put an end to the whole affair," he warned her.

With this dictum resounding in her ears, she had no choice but to take him at his word.

In August, Melinda purchased a bolt of fine navy blue serge from Mr. Miroff and began working on Philippe's suits. He stood before her, a tape measure encircling his waist, his lower lip curling down.

"I'm going there, aren't I?"

"Yes, Philippe, you are."

* * *

The night before his scheduled departure, Joseph trimmed Philippe's hair and clipped his fingernails. The boy stared at him, tears gathering at the edges of his lids.

Joseph felt his throat tighten. "Go along with you now, you need your rest," he told him briskly.

Philippe made his way to his room, his stomach muscles knotting, his shoulders slumping. All was lost. His father had been his only hope, and now he too had abandoned him. What was one to do in the face of such abject betrayal?

Rising before dawn the following morning, Philippe moved like a sleepwalker as he made his way across the kitchen to the bathroom. He stopped and looked at his mother, fully dressed and at the stove preparing breakfast.

"Hurry, Philippe, wash yourself and brush your teeth. I'll lay your clothes out on your bed."

He took a step and then another and stopped. He stared disdainfully at his younger brother who sat at the table, still in his nightclothes.

"Why isn't he going too?" he challenged in a surly monotone.

"Marc is too young to leave home." Reluctantly and with one last, menacing look in the direction of his sibling, he continued on his way to the privy.

Philippe put on his trousers and a clean shirt, and over that a sleeveless red sweater presented to him last Christmas by his Aunt Claire. His new clothes felt tight and itchy and he scratched at his neck and backside. Picking up his cap, he set it on his dark, tousled hair. For a long moment he stared down at his suitcase on the floor at the foot of his bed.

Father Jean, he thought. *I hate him and I don't even know what he looks like.* Then, a more chilling thought occurred to him. *What if he hates me? What if he doesn't remember who I am?* With a hopeless shrug, he conceded defeat. Picking up his bag, he walked out of the room.

As they rushed through the railroad station to the platform in the rear, Philippe's hand felt cold and numb. He tried to twist it, to free it from his Mother's grasp, but her grip would not be broken. While he held onto his ticket with the other hand, she led him quickly to where they would meet the young seminarian who would see him safely to Sherbrooke.

Adrien Marchand greeted them with a smile, and as he

shook Philippe's hand, the bright light of the locomotive appeared, making its way around the big loop of track into the New York, New Haven and Hartford yards. Soon it came to a grinding halt alongside them.

Panic, like flashes of white light, once again filled Philippe's being. Melinda took the boy into her arms. She felt him shaking.

"Be a good boy, my darling, and work hard." She kissed him and held him close.

"Mama!"

His shrill voice was like a blade cutting through her. His hands gripped her forearm. Freeing herself, she half-walked, half-ran from the platform.

Sitting in the rear of the electric car, Melinda could hardly breathe. Her fingers fidgeted with the ruffle on the cuff of her calico blouse. She kept seeing her child's tear-streaked face. He'd looked so desperately forsaken. She bit her lip so as not to break down here in this public place. Remembering Claire's words helped to sustain her, and deep inside where it mattered, she knew that studying under the Dominicans at Saint Charles was the chance of a lifetime for her son.

She started at the sound of the clanging bell as the streetcar made its stop at Tremont Street. Getting off, she began to climb the hill, then turning on her heel, she headed in the opposite direction. Ten minutes later she stood on the corner of Pleasant Street, looking up at Mr. Miroff's shop windows. Without hesitating, she went inside.

She opened the door and leaned against it. Looking up from his work, Sam jumped to his feet. The moment their eyes met she burst into tears. She felt his arms go around her, holding her tightly to him.

"Come on ... come on. No more of this stuff or you'll have me bawling too. And that's an ugly sight." Holding her at arm's length, he looked into the stunningly beautiful eyes. "He's gone, your boy?"

Slowly she lowered her head.

Sam put his fingers under her chin and lifted it. "No more

tears. You've done a wonderful thing for your son. It would have been so much easier *not* to do it. It's hard right now, but before you know it, he'll be back pestering the bejesus out of you."

She straightened. Taking a handkerchief from her purse, she dabbed at her eyes. "Oh Sam, I'm so sorry. What must you think of me, behaving like such a fool."

"A mama you are, a fool you're not. And thank you for finally having the chutzpah to call me, Sam. I thought it would never happen." He smiled and took her hand into his. "Go home, get yourself busy. It'll do you a world of good."

On entering, the house seemed strangely different, as though she'd been gone from it for a long, long time.

On her way to the workroom, Melinda stopped at the boys' bedroom door. She looked in at Philippe's bed, still unmade, his nightshirt strewn across the pillow, his tattered bedroom slippers askew on the braided rug. Slowly, she approached and picked up the nightshirt. Lifting it to her face, she drew in the fragrance of him, feeling anew the keenness of his loss. She sank to the edge of the bed and let the tears flow once more.

"Why are you crying, Mama?" Marc's frightened voice filled the room and she felt his thin arms wrap themselves around her. "Please, Mama, don't cry anymore."

Instantly Melinda jerked away, releasing his arms from around her. "I'm all right, Marc. I just have something in my eye. Come, I'll fix your lunch."

Perplexed and shaken, he looked up at her.

Returning to the kitchen, Melinda opened the icebox and removed a plate of food. The raven-haired boy still stood in the hallway looking at her.

"Wash your hands, Marc, everything will be ready in a minute."

Melinda chided herself, *Why did I recoil from my child in that way?* She despised herself for having done so. Why hadn't she been able to bridge the chasm that, since his birth, had stood gaping open between them?

Chapter Eighteen

As had become his custom since moving to Highpoint Road, Sam Miroff came and went twice a week to the house of his seamstress on Sladesferry Landing. He was usually in and out in no time, but on this particular Monday morning he lingered, graciously accepting the cup of tea that Melinda offered him.

"Any news from Quebec? It's been three weeks already," he noted, his gray-blue eyes following her as she went about fixing their tea.

Melinda nodded and pulled a letter from her apron pocket. "I was about to tell you, Sam. Philippe's first letter arrived on Saturday. I've read it a dozen times." She heaved a burdensome sigh. "I'm afraid Philippe is finding l'Académie enormously challenging. He complains that the priests are rigid, and overly strict with the boys. But he likes his new roommate, a boy from Montreal named Paul Tremblay, and one of his teachers, a Father Sebastien, has allowed him to play the chapel organ a time or two. He was thrilled about that, and has asked for permission to take lessons."

"Well now, more good news than bad. ... Isn't that a wonder?"

"I miss him so much, Sam." Pressing her lips together, she put the letter back in her pocket.

"Of course you do. What kind of a mama is it who doesn't miss her son?"

Their eyes met.

Melinda knew that Sam understood her as perhaps no one else did.

He said, "I have something important to discuss with you.

I'm planning a little surprise for Natia. We'll be married ten years next month, and I want to do something special for her. I'm going to close the shop for a week and take her to Boston for the time of her life."

Melinda filled the cups and handed him one. "That's wonderful, Sam."

"Natalia needs to get away for a while. She needs to rest. Moving to Highpoint has been an exhausting experience for my wife. She puts her heart and soul into everything she does and she's worked herself to a frazzle." He lifted his cup to his lips and drank. "Excellent tea, Melinda. Boston is someplace we've always wanted to go. So now we'll go." Putting the cup to his lips again, he drained it. "You're not to worry, though, I'll leave plenty of work with you before I leave. Your wages will go on as usual." Sam pressed the napkin to his mouth. Standing, he reached for his hat. "As soon as I get back, I want to discuss a plan I have for enlarging the business."

"Enlarging the business?"

"Yes, I've bought five electric sewing machines. They'll be delivered to the shop at the end of this month. I'll explain everything to you when the time comes."

* * *

Boston

Despite all of the carefully laid plans, Sam and Natia's anniversary trip did not come off as he'd hoped.

They stayed in a suite at the Parker House, the best the hotel had to offer: a large canopied bed, draped in rose velour and held back by cords with golden tassels, filled the center of the boudoir, a chamber within a chamber, intimate and private, with lace pillows scattered across the counterpane.

The sitting room walls were covered with a delicate wallpaper, a subtle green print, a bit oriental in feeling. A white loveseat and an imported leather fauteuil were grouped together with a low table facing the fireplace.

The weather was pleasantly warm in the afternoon, and he and Natia strolled along the crushed stone pathways of the Commons and the Public Gardens, arms linked together. When the wind blew in from across the harbor, Natia moved closer to Sam.

"Cold?"

"No, darling, not at all."

Natia denied the truth, even to herself. She wanted to relish every inch of this great city as her husband was doing, but each day she became a little more tired. Just bathing and dressing for dinner left her exhausted.

On their last night there, as they sat in the dining room beneath the immense chandelier, Sam looked at his wife. She'd worn her blue crepe, his favorite dress, with a single strand of pearls, but even in the soft, flattering light she looked wan and colorless.

"What is it with you, Natalia? You're not yourself." He looked from her face to the plate of food in front of her.

"Nothing is with me, Sam. I'm fine."

"Then why are you pushing a meal that's costing me a fortune around and around on your plate? Don't lie to me. I know you too well for that."

"All right! So I'm a little tired. I guess I'm not used to all this ... whatever." She made a deprecating little gesture with her hand. "Maybe the food is too rich or something."

"Tell me the truth." His face reddened.

"Sam—please—don't make a scene." She looked from under hooded lids at the elegant people seated around them. "Why is it so terrible if I'm a little tired? I've had a lot to do with the house and Sarah."

"Ah! So now it's the house."

"Sam! DON'T! Don't spoil everything by making a fight with me." Her eyes lowered and she looked down at her hands.

A tense moment followed, then she saw his hand reaching out across the table. After a moment she put hers into it, and looked up at him.

"I'm sorry, my sweetheart," he said sincerely. "It's just that I've been worried about you." His voice was soft and loving once more.

"Meshuggah! That's what you are. But I love ... love ... love you, Sam Miroff."

He lifted her fingers to his lips and kissed them. "Come, my sweetheart," he murmured, "let's go upstairs to that fancy bed and make a baby boy to take home with us."

* * *

After returning from Boston, Natia saw the blood again. Little spots of it at first, then more and more every day. *No baby boy for Sam,* she'd thought when she'd first seen it. When it continued, she went to Doctor Sofrenko, her friend and physician. He advised a thorough examination. That was when they found the lump in her uterus. Natia Miroff had cancer.

She returned to Boston, to the magnificent new General Hospital overlooking the Charles River. There the doctors cut the mass from her body, leaving her close to death. But she fought hard; Natia wasn't ready to die yet.

She came home to the house on Highpoint Road to recover, but alas, her struggle proved a hopeless one.

In a matter of weeks Doctor Sofrenko discovered another tumor. He said nothing to Natia, but went directly to see Sam at the shop.

"We can't risk another surgery, Sam. She would never get through it alive. She's too weak—nothing but skin and bones."

Sam's hands flew to the sides of his head. "What then?" His voice was tight and at least an octave higher than usual. "If you can't operate, what *can* you do?"

"I'm sorry, Sam. It's spread to her liver. We've done everything we can do for Natia."

"The hell, you say! There are other doctors. I'll take her to New York! She'll have the very finest there is."

"She wouldn't survive the trip, Sam. Believe me when I

tell you that this is killing me, too."

Sam didn't hear the last of what he said. He had collapsed into a chair and was sobbing his heart out.

Natia continued to swallow the medicines the doctor brought her, but after a while her stomach revolted and she couldn't even do that. She grew visibly weaker by the day and her skin took on a sallow, unhealthy tone. Finally she gave up the fight and took to her bed, leaving Sam and Sarah in the hands of a housekeeper. Natia never left her room again.

During the last three weeks of her life, Sam kept a constant vigil at her bedside, reading to her from *Ruth* and *The Prophets*, his free hand under the bedcovers holding onto hers. She heard little of what he read, but the soft drone of his voice comforted her. In the final week, her kidneys failed, and her groans became heart-wrenching cries. Nathan Sofrenko gave her the morphine and prayed for it all to end.

The instant it happened, Sam knew. It was as if her last breath struck a hammer blow to his brain.

* * *

Sam threw himself into his work. The less time he spent in that memory-ridden house the better. Since Natia's death he'd not been able to sleep in their bedroom, imagining there to be a fragrance of her lingering in the bedding and among her clothes hanging in the closets. And perhaps most difficult of all, he could not yet look, without breaking down, at the wisps of hair caught in the bristles of her silver hairbrush on the vanity.

He found no comfort in being with Sarah. Trying to answer her questions, to bring to his child some measure of understanding, drove him close to losing his own tenuous grip on himself. The only time Sam could truly function was when he was dealing with work.

He began a search for new quarters to house his business. He found a place he liked in the east end of the city, a new building with electricity to power his new equipment. He oiled and installed the machines himself, and was down on his haunches until all hours of the night bolting them to the floor.

When everything was ready, he ordered a new sign to hang on the building above the door. SAM'S TAILORING now became:

MIROFF MANUFACTURING COMPANY
Second Floor

* * *

"Well?" Sam asked Melinda after she'd had her first lesson on one of the new machines. "What do you think?"

"It's very exciting, Sam. I just hope I can learn to use it properly."

"You will. If I can do it, you can do it."

And she did. Within a week she was comfortable with the speed, and her accuracy was almost flawless.

There were no two days alike anymore, everything was changing so fast. Melinda no longer worked at home. Every morning at seven-thirty, she took the streetcar to Flint Street. Sam had hired three more women, and she was training them to use the machines. What had once been a good little tailoring business had all of a sudden become something else.

Not long ago, in a darkened room on Highpoint Road, a dream had ended for Sam. It had changed his life forever. There would never be another Natia, another round-faced woman with a glowing smile, whose joy in life was bringing joy to him. But kneeling now on the still soft earth of her grave, he spoke to her and he knew she listened.

"You should see the new shop, my Nushka. It's going to be quite a place. Already I've ordered five more machines. They'll be coming the first of the year ...

* * *

140

L'Académie
Saint Charles Seminary
Sherbrooke, Quebec, Canada

Had she realized how badly his first weeks at Saint Charles had cowed young Philippe, Melinda would have been truly distressed. He moved through life in a shroud of self-pity, his homesickness all consuming. He suffered crippling attacks of stomach distress and vomited frequently after taking his meals. In addition, he'd awaken in the dead of night with cramps gripping his bowels. Rising, he'd run down the long, unheated corridor in his nightshirt, praying that he would reach the lavatory before everything inside him burst open. Every scrap of dignity was being stripped from him, one way or another.

When at last he was restored to health, he was either too early or too late for everything, or in the wrong place at the wrong time. No one seemed to care a fig about him. Not surprisingly, his grades reflected this turmoil and it all ended with his sitting on a stool before his uncle in his office.

"I'm sorry, young man, but excuses won't do here. I'm aware of the sort of work you're capable of, and I will accept nothing less. I'm also aware that you are lonely and homesick. All the boys experience that to some degree. But one must learn to be manly about such things. You cannot permit yourself to wallow about. It just won't do. It's time you buck up, my boy." Father Jean waggled his finger ominously close to Philippe's nose. "Unless things improve, you shall remain 'in house' over the Christmas holiday."

Rising, he walked around his desk and stood next to Philippe's stool. "We would miss having you with us in Baie de Saint-Jacques, my boy."

Philippe stared down into his crotch, not wanting his uncle to see the tears welling in his eyes.

Patting Philippe gently on the shoulder, Father ended by saying, "You're a good boy, Philippe. I'm sure you'll rise above all this."

"Yes, sir, I'll try."

His "rising above" was slow but steady, and as the holidays approached, Philippe was found to be once again in his uncle's good graces. Word was sent by way of his dormitory master, to prepare himself for departure to Le Baie on December the 22nd.

That morning found him on the train heading north through the hilly Laurentien countryside, with Father Jean pointing out the more interesting landmarks through an early morning haze.

The north country looked exactly as Philippe had thought it would: snow-covered farmhouses nestled in groves of birch and maple, gray threads of smoke rising into the sky from the sturdy brick and fieldstone chimneys; village churches with Gothic steeples; and narrow, stained-glass windows looked for all the world like a Renoir painting as the sky began to clear.

It was like a dream he'd once had, coming to life before his eyes, and for the first time since leaving Riverton, Philippe felt a sense of belonging.

* * *

The beaming faces of his Aunt Marie-Élise and her family greeted them at the station house in Saint-Denis. From there they drove by sleigh to Les Érables, the adults in one, he and his three cousins, all girls, in another.

Dominique, the eldest of them, passed him the reins as the horses pulled them along the narrow country road. "Try it, Philippe, it's fun."

It was cold, but Philippe had never felt so much warmth in his life.

Turning into Les Érables, he steered past the orchard, down the narrow lane to the big farmhouse beyond. As they passed the barn Philippe noticed a large wreath hanging on the front door, adorned with bunches of holly and a huge red satin bow.

"It's beautiful," Philippe remarked, mostly to Dominique,

who sat close at his side.

"Thank you, Philippe. Mama and I made it yesterday."

The sleighs drew to a stop at the side of the house and everyone hurried to get indoors, where a fire burned in the open hearth and hot apple cider awaited them. Muguette, the family cat, awakened as Uncle Daniel opened the door. Dropping soundlessly down from her perch on the window ledge, she scampered out to her safe haven in the barn.

"Par içi, Philippe."

Dominique hurried to show him his bedroom on the other side of the kitchen. She smiled constantly, and grasped at his hand a time or two. He blushed, feeling embarrassed, even though he much admired his new cousin.

She was taller than he, with thick, dark braids that hung over her shoulders, and soft brown eyes that followed his every movement.

Pointing to the door next to his, she spoke in a hushed voice. "That's where Rita sleeps."

"Rita?"

"She's the Indian woman who helps Mama. She looks scary, and talks funny. That's because she has no teeth. But you'll like her anyway. Muguette sleeps in there with her sometimes."

Promptly at six they sat down to supper. Rita placed a large tureen at the end of the table, and Marie-Élise ladled a thick potage into their bowls. As they passed them down from one to the other, the aroma of lentils and onions made Philippe's mouth water. But he waited until grace had been said and his aunt had taken up her spoon. Father Jean smiled and nodded his head, noticing that he had remembered his manners. Meanwhile, a platter of braised beef and vegetables was brought over and placed on the sideboard.

His aunt nodded to the servant. "Thank you, Rita. See to Mémère now, if you please."

As Uncle Daniel stood to carve the roast, the room reverberated with chatter from one wall to the other. The sound of so many high-pitched voices fairly set Philippe's ears to buzzing. Everyone wanted to talk to him, and they did it at the same time. He was undeniably "La Premiere Étoile."

Mama'd been right when she'd told him not to worry: "Your cousins will love you, Philippe. You're all from the same blood."

After finishing their chores, the girls sat at the kitchen table painting pinecones to decorate the big fir tree that lay on its side on the veranda.

Dominique interrupted her work to remark, "Wait until you see the church, Philippe. It's more beautiful than anything. Grandpère Michèl carved the Nativity scene. It took him six years to finish it all." Without stopping to take a breath, she added, "I'm so happy that you're sharing Christmas with us, Philippe." Leaning over, she placed a chaste kiss on his cheek. "I hope you come every year."

Philippe felt himself coloring again.

He was about to excuse himself and retreat to his room, when Marie-Élise called to him from the doorway. "It's getting late, dear, and there's something you must do before you go to bed."

* * *

A fire glowed in the blue tiled fireplace in the room at the front of the house. An old woman sat in a rocking chair, her thin shoulders draped in a heavy shawl, her needlework resting in her lap. On a round table in the corner next to the window, a single candle leaped and fluttered before a plaster likeness of the Blessed Virgin.

Nudging Philippe ahead of her, Marie-Élise approached her mother. "Mama? You have a visitor."

The old lady squinted at him.

After a moment Marie-Élise came to her rescue. "This is your grandson Philippe. This is Melinda and Joseph's son," she explained, her voice wavering ever so slightly.

Emilie had long since lost hope of ever seeing her grandson again. Staring at him now, her expression varied from doubt to disbelief. Then a slow smile pushed the skin on her face into a thousand tiny wrinkles.

"Philippe? Ç'est notre petit fils?" A pair of ancient eyes searched his. Lifting her hand, she beckoned him nearer. "Quel joli garçon! Vien ... içi, près de moi."

He moved closer to her, and in a moment was in her embrace.

She smelled of talcum powder, the kind his mother smelled of. Standing before her, his hands entwined with hers. She asked question after question of him, about his mother, his brother Marc, and his father. While he was answering them, she let go of his hands and a vagueness came over her features.

He knew that she was no longer listening. Stopping, he looked up at his aunt.

She smiled knowingly and took him by the hand. "Grandmother is tired, Philippe. We'll speak with her another time."

They left the room, the smell of candle wax and talcum powder following them into the hallway.

On the following day, two figures trudged through a sea of swirling snowflakes along the road to the village. In minutes, the shoulders of the woman's cape were covered with snow, as were those of the young boy's coat. They walked a half-mile down the road from Les Érables, toward a neighboring farmhouse, a weather-beaten old place whose shutters were almost all nailed closed.

Lifting the knocker, Marie-Élise struck at the door. Minutes passed without an answer, and she struck again. She was about to turn and leave when Louis Durand, Philippe's grandfather, opened it and peered out at them. Recognizing Marie-Élise, he stepped back and allowed them to enter.

He looked old, his clothing was tattered, and his face was covered with a grizzle of salt-and-pepper stubble. He appeared, if that were possible, even more neglected than when Marie-Élise had last seen him.

Assisted by a cane, Louis walked with obvious pain, his chronic bouts with gout having over the years left an aftermath of enlarged, inflexible joints.

145

Philippe fidgeted as yet another appraisal of him got underway.

"You're a lot like your father, I think. Taller than he was at your age, but the face is the same." Louis Durand shuffled his way to the foot of the staircase. Holding onto the newel post, he called out, "LAURA!! COME DOWN HERE!"

He paced at the foot of the stairs, muttering blasphemies under his breath. When she failed to respond, he struck a blow at the post with the head of his cane and returned to the kitchen.

"She's not been well," he explained, looking at Marie-Élise, "and she can't hear a goddamned thing." He took a deep breath and turned to Philippe again. "I hear you're studying at Saint Charles," he commented, openly disdainful. "Like as not they'll make a priest out of you too." Pausing, a half-smile twisted his lips. "You'd make a damn sight better farmer, from the looks of you. Priests—fops—all of them. Couldn't do a man's work if their lives depended on it." He walked to a chair. Hanging his cane over the back of it, Louis seated himself.

He didn't invite them to do likewise, so they stood awkwardly in the middle of the room.

"I'm sorry. I seem to have chosen a poor day to visit," Marie-Élise apologized.

Taking hold of Philippe's coat sleeve, she directed him toward the door. They were almost there when Laura appeared, barefoot, clad in a dirty flannel robe.

Her hair, white except for a few streaks of faded brown, was extremely long and hung down her back in a mass of unkempt tangles.

She stood without speaking, staring down at her grandson. "So you're Joseph's boy," she said finally, her voice cracking as though she'd not used it in a long time.

"Yes, Grandmother," Philippe answered timidly, his great eyes widening at the sight of her.

Laura broke into raucous laughter. She came closer, a vile stench preceding her. "Are you afraid of me, boy?"

"Yes ... a little."

146

Marie-Élise interrupted the bizarre exchange between the two. "We should be leaving now."

"NO! WAIT! Just one more minute." Laura turned and went quickly to the sink. Reaching to a shelf above it, she took something from a small glass bowl. Returning to where Philippe and his aunt were standing, she held out a tightly clenched hand.

Philippe hesitated and looked at his aunt. She nodded.

"Here—take it! Un cadeau de Noël." Laura threw open her hand, revealing an object that glinted in the light.

Philippe reached out and took it. It looked and felt like a coin. "Thank you, Grandmother." After closer scrutiny he saw that it was not a coin, but a shiny new "miraculous" medal.

"Father Lucier left that on the table the last time he was here. I want you to have it. It'll bring you luck."

"Crazy old fool," they heard Louis mumble as they went out the door.

* * *

On Christmas day, church bells began ringing at dawn, their sound drifting across the rooftops into the meadows and up the hillside as far as the banks of the river.

Philippe and his family could hear them as they boarded the sleighs for the short trip into Le Baie.

As people strode across Place de la Sainte Eglise, the organ could be heard sounding the canticles of the Yuletide. Inside the church, the smell of pine bows mingled with incense and burning tapers.

Philippe followed Dominique down the aisle to the smallest altar to view Grandfather Bérard's crèche.

Mary, Joseph, and the Infant Jesus looked back at him from their niches in the roughly hewn manger. They were about half life-sized. With them were a shepherd boy holding the weakest of his flock in his arms, and the hand-painted figures of the Magi kneeling in adoration, their heads bowed in deep homage.

Philippe felt his heart beating faster. What a superb sculptor his grandfather had been! Would that he could have remembered him, even just a little.

Taking their places in the pews, they waited for the Mass to begin.

Father Jean assisted the pastor at the altar, his clear and mellow voice resounding throughout the edifice. A great pride welled up in Philippe.

To be God's chosen servant, to sing His praise, to nurture His flock, was a life he felt he truly could aspire to.

Upon his return to l'Académie, the gates of Saint Charles no longer frightened Philippe as they clanged closed behind him. They suggested a protective air instead of the punitive, as he had previously perceived them. After chapel that evening, he hurried to his room to write home, while sleigh rides and holly wreaths still vividly glowed in his mind.

* * *

Philippe revisited Les Érables again at Eastertime, and at least for the present, Dominique continued to be the favorite of his cousins.

She understands me, he wrote home, *she's really so like a boy.*

They rode together atop La Bête, the old mare who somehow kept her patience with these boisterous, energetic children who gave her no peace. They led her through the orchards and down the road to the village, where they visited the blacksmith at his forge. Monsieur Fortin, a giant of a man with enormous, hairy forearms, taught Philippe how to shoe the horse.

His letters were filled with excitement. He wrote of days spent in happy exploration with his cousins, doing the things that Melinda had done as a child, in the places where she had done them, and she savored the bond that was growing between them.

Elizabeth is sick with the croup. She isn't allowed to go

148

with us into the village this afternoon, he penned in his large, sometimes slipshod hand. *She cried hard, and when Dominique saw her, she cried too. With the spending money I have left I'm going to buy her a book. We can read it together tonight after supper.*

Simone is very nice, but she doesn't care a hoot about what we do. She's always in her bedroom playing nun. I find that very boring.

I'm anxious to return to Sherbrooke this time. I've truly come to enjoy it here in Le Baie, but I can't wait for this year to be over with, to be back in Riverton with all of you again.

Sometimes Melinda brought some of Philippe's letters to work with her and shared them with Sam. Especially the humorous ones that Joseph enjoyed.

"Ahaaa! Sleigh rides! ... They remind me of another boyhood. Did you know that there are bells on the troikas, Melinda? Funny thing ... I haven't thought of them in years, but just now when you were reading, I could swear I heard them ringing." Sam looked up from the battered desk where he sat to do his paperwork. "I guess you don't ever forget the good things, do you?"

"No, Sam, you don't ever forget the good things."

For a moment his thoughts turned inward and he stared blankly at the desktop. He was home again, in Odessa, frolicking through deep swaths of powdery snow. His smile gradually faded as he returned himself to the present.

"I wish Sari would go away to school," he said, out of the blue.

"Why, Sam?"

"Because she's so alone up there in that house. I hate to admit it, but I feel guilty about leaving her with Mrs. Acot all the time."

"You shouldn't. You have your work to do. Besides, she's in school a great deal of the time."

"In a few weeks school will be out for the summer. Then what?" He shook his head, as if trying to shake away his frustration. "It's just that she's growing up so fast. Soon she'll need to know things." His face flushed a little. "She

149

needs a woman to share these moments with her."

"If I can ever help, Sam, you know I'd be happy to."

No, dear girl, thank you, but no. We'll manage it some-how. But I can't help getting angry sometimes."

"Angry?"

"For Chrissakes, Melinda, if God sends you a kid, why the hell does he take her mother away?"

Melinda left the office quietly. There was nothing more to be said. Sam was still grieving and only time would take away his bitterness. Walking into the factory, she carried some of the hurt that Sam was feeling with her. *Soon it will be summer,* he'd said. Suddenly the thought of being re-united with Philippe filled her with excitement. It had truly been a long year, for all of them.

* * *

On the day of Philippe's arrival, Melinda paced the floor of the terminal. They had only been waiting for fifteen min-utes or so, but it seemed like hours to her. When he finally turned the corner into the open room, all he could see was her eyes. They blotted out everything else in the place. He ran into her outstretched arms, his body trembling with emo-tion.

Over her shoulder, Philippe could see his father smiling down at him. He looked different. His hair was grayer and he had grown a handlebar mustache. Aunt Claire was there to greet him too, and next to her, looking very dapper indeed, was his Marc. His brother'd grown so tall in just a year that Philippe would not have known him. How wonderful it was to be home, to be with his loved ones again!

All during the spring semester Philippe had tried not to think about "la fin de l'année." He'd needed his wits about him to study for final exams and to pull down grades that would keep him in the upper ten percent of his class—a to-tally unexpected priority placed on him by his uncle after the Easter holidays. But when the month of May arrived, Phil-ippe began drawing Xs through the numbers on his calendar,

150

and his final week in Sherbrooke became almost as unbearable as his first one had been.

With Father Jean waving goodbye, young Philippe and Adrien Marcal boarded their train for "the States."

Rounding the corner onto Sladesferry Landing, Philippe caught sight of Caitlin waiting on the veranda. Dashing into the yard and up the short flight of steps, he threw himself upon her, burying his face in her warm, familiar bosom.

As was to be expected, the excitement generated by his homecoming began to pale after a week or two, and a regrettable return to normalcy began taking place. Small chores were once again pressed upon him. Going to the bin with the day's accumulation of trash was more than a little punishing to his over-inflated ego, and he grumbled to himself as he went about collecting it for disposal.

Mornings, his parents left for work before he and Marc rose for the day, so it fell upon him to see to his younger brother's breakfast. Fortunately, they ate with Caitlin at noon, after which he was allowed to go off on his own until four in the afternoon, when he returned to face still more "responsibilities."

Moreover, when he *was* free, he was constantly followed about by his sibling, who seemed to prefer trailing around after him rather than seeking out playmates of his own.

"Don't you have any friends?" Philippe asked rather scornfully, as he tried in vain to rid himself of Marc.

"Yes, but I'd rather play with you, Philippe."

What a bothersome pain in the neck he is, the older brother brooded. With Marc underfoot, Philippe could not risk some of his more pleasurable pastimes. Smoking cigarettes was out of the question, as well as the use of some of the more interesting profanities he'd learned at school this past year. "I'm really beginning to hate it here," he mumbled under his breath.

By midsummer, Philippe had already engaged in a number of fisticuff encounters in the park with the Portuguese boys from Plain Street. Having risen victorious from his share of them and never once turning to run, he began gaining the respect of their leader, a handsome, swarthy young colt named Rego.

As Philippe entered the park on a sultry July afternoon, Rego approached and stood facing him, his legs spread apart, his hands provocatively planted on his narrow hips. He was older than Philippe, with a smattering of dark, silky hair shadowing his upper lip and jaw. With his entourage of toughs standing close at hand, he confronted Philippe.

"You know anything about soccer, Frenchie?"

"Yes, a little."

"Would you like to play a game, or would you rather fight one of the boys here?"

"I'd rather play."

"All right—*let's go,*" hollered Rego, spinning the soccer ball on his middle finger. "But just remember, this doesn't change nuthin'. I still own Hutchinson Park. You got that?"

"Whatever you say, Rego." Philippe acquiesced, a grin making its way slowly across his lips.

The Portuguese boys were excellent soccer players, having learned from their fathers, who'd learned from theirs in the old country.

Rego tried to teach Philippe some of the finer points of the game, but despite his help Philippe usually finished up by getting knocked to the ground and scraping his knees to the quick on the gravely dirt of the soccer field. In addition, he tore and stained his clothing, thus evoking a rare expression of displeasure on his mother's face.

"Really, Philippe. I should think that a boy of your caliber could find better companions, with better things to do than kick a ball around in the dirt all afternoon. I've a good mind to forbid you—"

"Leave the boy alone, Melinda," Joseph interrupted. "There's nothing wrong with playing soccer. The Portuguese boys are rough, I won't argue that. Philippe will learn to take care of himself or he'll perish in the trying."

"But his clothes are always ..." She didn't finish, realizing that Joseph would turn a deaf ear to such an unmasculine bit of trivia. But before conceding defeat, she tossed him a parting shot. "It's obvious you care little about the mending I have to do, Joseph. I just hope he doesn't come home with a broken nose one of these days."

She looked up to see them grimacing at each other. This was not the first time that they had joined forces to form a united front against her. Not having been reared with brothers, this was simply another example of a good many things that Melinda didn't understand about the opposite sex.

Philippe's enthusiasm for Rego and the soccer field was, in the end, dimmed by the oppressive late summer heat. He chose instead to do some reading, a book suggested to him by Father Jean before he'd left for home.

Now and again as he sat in the big wicker chair on the veranda, his book laid aside for a moment, his thoughts began turning to Sherbrooke. In a few weeks' time he would be back with his classmates at l'Académie. He felt a ripple of delight pass through him at the thought of seeing his old roommate, Paul Tremblay, and of being shucked of Marc once and for all. He longed for the rugby games, and pillow fights, and resuming his studies at the organ with Father Sebastien.

During his final week at home, he struggled with boredom and found it difficult to suppress his eagerness to be in Sherbrooke, reunited with his fellow classmates once again.

To Philippe's way of thinking, the next three summers were a carbon copy of the past one: his return for the summer hiatus was always a "cause célèbre"—at least for a day or two. His father's hair was always a shade grayer and his mother began heaping responsibilities onto him the moment he'd emptied his suitcase. His soccer didn't improve, nor did his relationship with his younger brother. Nothing ever changed, at least not noticeably.

It wasn't until he had matriculated into the upper grades of L'école Supérieure at l'Académie that Philippe began enjoying the status he felt he deserved at home. His father, ordinarily a man of few words, began engaging him in semi-adult conversations. Philippe was more than pleased when Joseph listened to his opinions with what seemed to be genuine interest. Joseph even made a few suggestive little jokes. They'd embarrassed Philippe at first, but later on he perceived them as a mark of his imminent adulthood. At seventeen, he felt a kinship with his father he'd never felt before.

Marc, inches taller and admittedly more handsome than he, now regarded him with appropriate respect rather than the cloying adulation of a pubescent younger brother. Growing up, so far, had been fraught with its share of upheavals, to be sure. Hopefully, maturity would prove the struggle to have been worthwhile.

* * *

Young Philippe wasn't the only one dealing with growing pains. Sam Miroff was also caught up in somewhat of an upheaval.

By nature, Sam wasn't given to impulsive decisions, but what Alex Friedman was asking him to do now—well—that was impulsive!

"Why are you looking at me like that?" Alex asked him from across the dining room table.

"I'm sitting here wondering if you're playing with a full deck, that's why."

Erika tried not to giggle as she cut into her scaloppini.

"Oh, for God's sake, Sam."

"This has got nothing to do with God, Alex, it has to do with shekels. And I for one don't want to jeopardize everything I've worked for all these years."

"Trust me, Sam, you won't lose a dime."

"Easy for you to say with all your millions."

Erika couldn't help it. She laughed out loud. She enjoyed sitting in on Sam and Alex's dinner "conferences." They were so equal to each other. What one didn't think of, the other did.

Sam trusted Alex completely. He had his finger on the pulse of everything worthwhile that went on in the city. But confidence and trust aside, this was a huge decision he was asking Sam to make. Out of nowhere the previous week, Alex had proposed that they join forces and go into the manufacture of women's ready-to-wear.

"I've never made anything but men's clothes. I've never wanted to. Women are too picky—all those pleats and laces. Not to mention fittings! That could be touchy, if you'll excuse the expression."

Alex did not acknowledge the clever double entendre. "This is different, Sam. You'd never have to deal with the consumer—only the buyers. But first and foremost, you'd have to stop thinking of yourself as a tailor."

"I'm not sure I can do that. Granted, my operation is bigger than any other in this area, but I'm still a tailor, goddammit!"

"Things have changed, Sam—it's 1904. Listen, if you're worried about losing money, I'll let you off the hook. What I have in mind is going to take a guy with the guts to lay it on the line."

"Just hold on a minute! If you're saying I don't have what it takes to do this, well, you're wrong—I do."

"That's great, Sam! You won't be sorry, believe me. You put up your half of the capital and I'll take care of all the legalities. The business will be yours to run as you see fit." Alex stood up and raised his glass. "Mazzel-tov, partner."

Sam's head was swimming. What the hell was he getting himself into? "What about Melinda?" Sam questioned. "Where does she fit into the picture?"

"Wherever you want her to fit, Sam. She's entitled, too."

"Okay, big spender, you've got yourself a deal."

* * *

Alex had made it sound so simple, but getting this project off the ground was no small chore. Again a new location had to be found to accommodate the additional machinery. In the beginning, thirty operators would make up their payroll, plus the cutting and shipping room personnel. But, all in all, Sam couldn't complain. Alex carried more than his share of the freight, and, as always, Sam had Melinda to help him survive.

He marveled at her versatility. She did everything she was asked to do, and did it well. She had a good kephale on her shoulders, that girl; it was as simple as that.

From her desk at the old factory, Melinda hired the new employees, then trained them to work on power machines. Later, she took over the office as manager and freed Sam up to work out on the floor with the women. In six months' time M and F Manufacturing was shipping their "Gibson Girl" shirtwaists all over the Northeast.

Keeping her life on an even keel became a constant struggle for Melinda, and as Caitlin had foreseen, it all became too much for her.

"Land sakes, girl," she scolded, "ye do the work of three women. What ye need is a housekeeper."

"Joseph wouldn't like that, Caitie. He's a very private man. He isn't comfortable with changes."

"And more's the pity, if yer askin' me."

Melinda whirled around, a look of surprise on her face. "I don't recall that I did ask, Caitie. Please, try to understand. Joseph does the best he can."

"Aya, if you say so." Caitlin rarely stepped over the line, but she worshipped Melinda and couldn't help mothering her every once in a while.

"I know you mean well, Cait, but I won't let you speak ill of my husband."

Caitlin's face flushed a beet red.

"I do think you're right about a housekeeper, though. Maybe you can help me with that."

With the aid of her hopelessly indelicate friend, Melinda found Costanza Mira, a fortyish Portuguese woman with a pleasant demeanor and two gold teeth shining from the middle of her mouth. She spoke incredibly poor English, yet between them they managed a unique way of communicating.

A meticulous housekeeper, Costanza soon had the furniture gleaming and the cupboards rearranged to her liking. And as time went on, she took on the laundry and the preparation of their evening meal.

Not surprisingly, she cooked her native Azorian dishes. One, a pungent fish chowder laced with chunks of salt pork and paprika; the other a hot, spicy sausage she called chourico, that she fried together with onions and little hot peppers. It wasn't long before everything in the house reeked of olive oil and garlic.

It was hardest on Joseph, just as Melinda had feared. He could barely tolerate Costanza's meals, and he abhorred having her puttering around the place.

"I don't have a minute's peace with that one fussing about and talking her gibberish at me."

"Try to be patient, Joseph. You can't have forgotten how difficult it is for those who haven't full use of the language."

Apart from considering her a terrible cook and a nuisance in general, Joseph also suspected Costanza of rummaging through their private belongings when she had the house to herself. He set cunning little traps that in the end simply served to prove her innocence. Melinda cajoled and placated, promising to get rid of Costanza if and when she proved herself unworthy.

On Sundays when they were alone, Melinda pampered him, granting his every wish, and little by little, week by week, Joseph got used to Costanza and the olive oil ... the garlic ... and the little green peppers.

This arrangement should have proven to be the answer to Melinda's dilemma, but the less she did at home, the more she took on at the factory. During their rare moments together, she often felt guilty that she and Joseph shared so little of their lives anymore.

Finishing her grocery list one evening, Melinda looked over at her husband. He sat quietly smoking his pipe, the newspaper resting on his lap. She rose and approached him.

"There's something I'd like to talk to you about, Joseph."

He looked up at her over the silver rim of his reading spectacles.

Pausing for a moment, Melinda tried to appraise his mood. "What would you say to our going to Philippe's graduation in May?"

A smile touched his lips, then quickly disappeared. "I'm afraid that's impossible. I'm only allowed the first week in July. You know that."

"Tell them it's a family matter. Ask them to make an exception."

"They don't make exceptions, Melinda."

"How can you know that? You've never asked them to."

"I just know. Now get the idea out of your head."

"Joseph, please—we haven't been home in so long."

He looked at her. She was biting down on her lower lip. He thought, *Oh, how I wish I could grant this request.* Not wanting to hold out any false hope, Joseph didn't openly agree to anything. But during his lunch hour, he went to the supervisor's office and made an appointment to see him. Much to his surprise, his request was granted. He would forfeit his pay, to be sure, but Liam Steele and low gear would be waiting upon his return.

Melinda had to stop herself behaving idiotically when she heard. She couldn't help but give herself little hugs. In her dreams Les Érables was the same at it had been; nothing and no one had changed. Even her father returned to life and she walked with him along the road to the orchard. The waiting became so difficult.

In April she shopped for luggage, and gifted Joseph with an Italian leather valise.

"It's very handsome," he acknowledged, running his hands over the grain. "It must have cost a small fortune."

"We can afford a few luxuries, Joseph," she assured him as she watched him undo the heavy brass fittings.

"You can afford them, Melinda. Let's not deceive ourselves about who the breadwinner is in this family."

"Oh Joseph ... dear sweet Joseph." She cupped his face

between her palms. "What does it matter where the money comes from? I want this trip so badly I can taste it. I want to be with you, my love," she said lowering her voice. "We deserve this time together."

"And we shall have it."

He pulled her to him. His arms went around her and their lips met. For the first time in years something burned between them. He lifted her into his arms and carried her to their bedchamber.

Chapter Nineteen

On the day preceding their departure, Melinda sat at her desk in the office and went over her checklist. Everything seemed in order.

Marc's needs would be tended to by Claire and Caitlin, his devoted surrogate mothers. She was certain he'd give them no trouble; Marc was an exemplary boy.

Drawing a line through the final item at the bottom of her list, she threw it into the wastebasket. In the morning they need only pick up their suitcases and close the door behind them.

After lunch she sat making a few notes for Sam to refer to while she took leave of her duties. Nadine, the new book-keeper, would be there to assist him, but there were so many things about the business that were entirely in her hands. She knew that the moment the train left the platform, he'd be ranting and raving: "Where the hell is the bill of lading for this?" and "What's happened to all that black sateen that I ordered?"

As she sat writing, she became aware of someone entering the office. Looking up she saw a tall, gaunt man in his mid-thirties walking toward her desk. She didn't recognize him at first, for it had been years since she'd seen him last.

"May I help you?" she asked politely. She was positive she knew him; why couldn't she remember his name? All at once it came to her. Before he could reply, she said, "You're Liam Steele, aren't you?"

"Yes ma'am, I am him." He seemed to have difficulty speaking. "Ah, Missus Durand ... I ... I come here to tell ye some fearful bad news."

"What is it? What's happened?" In a flash, Melinda was on her feet.

"'Tis yer man, ma'am, he's been hurt, he has."

"Hurt? How?"

"An accident, ma'am. They be after takin' him up south to Saint Anne's. He—"

She didn't wait for him to finish, but ran into the factory to find Sam.

"Jesus Christ! How bad is it?" he asked.

"I don't know. ... He says it's bad. I'm going to go with him to the hospital."

"Go, go. I'll come as soon as I can."

Melinda quickly hailed a cabbie, and on their way to the hospital the Irishman unfolded his story.

"T'was our first trip o' the day. A rain shower ended just as we turned into The Hill. Of a sudden, our lead horse Fee slipped on the cobbles and fell to her knees. Slick as ice they were, with the wet and all." He clapped his hands together. "T'was as quick as that. Hard as she tried to regain her footin', she just kept on slippin' further away. She began pulling Toby down with her. He put up a fierce battle, the old fella did. T'was a sight to see, missus. Like bloody hell itself."

The Irishman took a handkerchief from his back pocket and wiped the sweat from his brow. "Jody, he jumped down from his seat while I kept hold o' the reins. Moved right quick he did, squeezing hisself awteen them, tryin' to get hold of Fee's mane. She got undone at the sight o' him and started her legs to kickin'. She caught him with a hoof in the chest right off, and he went down on the cobbles next to her. Then, old Toby, he spooked. He rose on those hind legs o' his and come down on Jody three, maybe four times, afore breakin' his lead and boltin'. As still as a dead man he lay, Jody did, his blood all over them stones."

At the hospital Melinda learned that her husband was being cared for by a staff physician. She waited in the hallway outside the room, her mind leaping crazily from one thing to another. *How can this be happening?* she asked herself over and over again.

A moment later she heard hurried footfalls coming down the corridor. Looking over her shoulder, she saw Sam.

"Thank God you're here. Stay with me, Sam ... please."

"As long as you need me, I'll be here."

Neither of them spoke. Only the sounds of the sick were heard as they drifted into the corridor from the transoms above the doors. They waited, for what seemed an eternity. Just when she thought she could bear it no longer, the doctor came out of Joseph's room.

"Mrs. Durand, I'm Doctor Van de Meier. I'm sorry to have kept you waiting so long." He paused, clearing his throat. "I'm afraid I have little encouraging news."

Melinda's nails dug into Sam's palm.

"Your husband has sustained severe injuries to his head, right shoulder and arm. The arm itself has literally been crushed. I personally can do nothing more for him. I suggest you send for a specialist."

"I'll get someone," Sam said while releasing himself from Melinda's hold. "I'll get him the best. ... Trust me."

"I do, Sam, I do."

He walked, then ran down the passageway past the nursing station and out the doors.

Looking up at the young physician, Melinda asked, "When will I be able to see him?"

"You may see him now if you wish. But I must warn you, he's drifts in and out of consciousness. When he's awake, there's a lot of pain."

She nodded and followed him into the room. The shades were drawn and the room was cloaked in somber stillness. Melinda slowly approached the bed.

Joseph lay unmoving, his eyes closed, his chest heaving slowly. The acrid odor of disinfectant stung the membranes in her nostrils. His shirt lay in tatters on a chair nearby, the blood stains covering it already darkened to a murky brown. She moved nearer to the bedside. Leaning close, she whispered his name. When there was no response, she looked fretfully at the young intern.

"Is he, is he ..."

"He's unconscious, Mrs. Durand."

Large magenta abrasions stretched vividly across his parchment-like skin. Some of the hair had been shaved from his head and it gave him a curiously unbalanced look. The wounds to his arm and shoulder were covered with a loose-fitting dressing in the center of which a bloodstain slowly spread into an intricate, web-like pattern. She wanted to touch him but she dared not.

Again she spoke his name and waited, looking intently at his mutilated face.

She was about to speak again when she felt the doctor tug at her arm. She straightened and followed him into the hall-way where he left her to attend others in need of his care.

Feeling desperately alone, she stared at the closed door behind which her husband lay. The deathwatch had begun.

Sam returned. He put his arms around her trembling body. "Doctor Hauffman will be here as soon as possible. Any news?"

She shook her head.

"Hauffman will know what to do. He's a fine doctor." He patted her shoulder reassuringly.

"No one can help him, Sam. He's dying. I can feel it." She put her hand to her diaphragm, to the cavern inside her where dwelled the tragedies of her life.

"Hey! That's not you talking. You don't give up without a fight."

"I don't know if I can fight anymore."

"Well then, give it to God. When you can't fight any-more, He does your fighting for you."

Chapter Twenty

A telegram arrived at Saint Charles Seminary early on Saturday morning. Father Jean was holding it in his hand when Philippe entered his office.

His nephew smiled and his eyes shone with anticipation as he approached the mahogany desk. "Good morning, Father."

"Philippe, my boy. Please, sit down."

Sensitive as he had become to Father's every mood, Philippe was immediately aware of the solemnity in the older man's tone.

"We may dispense with formality for the present. This is a family matter."

Philippe's frown deepened as he waited for his uncle to go on.

"I have sad news for you, Philippe. Your family won't be coming for the graduation ceremonies." He stopped and took a deep breath. "There's been a tragic accident, my boy. Your father has been badly injured in the course of his work."

Philippe could not speak. He could not make a sound.

"I've informed Monsignor, and you are dismissed as of this moment." Reaching down, he picked up an envelope from his desk. "Here is enough money to get you to Riverton. Hurry, my boy, your mother needs you."

For a moment Philippe was unable to do anything, then a rush of adrenaline pumped through his arteries into his limbs, and he sprang from the room.

On the train, Philippe paced the aisle restlessly.

"Don't die, Papa—please—don't die," he prayed, sometimes aloud, impervious to the eyes of curious onlookers. They mattered not. Only his need to beg for his father's life mattered now. "Ever just and merciful Lord, spare him, and in return I shall dedicate my life to your service."

* * *

The sun made a feeble stab at breaking through the clouds when Philippe arrived in Riverton on Sunday afternoon. It was hot and humid as he carried his bag to the streetcar stop on the corner of Maincrossing Road. He waited fifteen minutes or more before the car going south finally came into sight.

He was tired and drenched with nervous perspiration, his shirt sticking uncomfortably to his chest and back. Except for the sugar and milk in the dozen or more cups of coffee he'd drunk since leaving Sherbrooke, he'd taken no nourishment of any kind.

As he rode, he looked listlessly from the window at the familiar landmarks passing by. Whitehead's Market: on the left, next to the door, a barrel of pickles cured in a brine. It was the first thing you smelled when you stepped inside onto the sawdust-covered floor. They were New York delicatessen style, the best pickles Philippe had ever tasted. Fryars Tobacconist Shop: another well-known landmark in Riverton. He'd bought a Kay Woodie pipe there a very long time ago—a birthday gift for his father. The Emporium, the First National bank, the city hall clock with its immense gold hands. All fell today on bleak, despairing eyes.

At Middle Street Philippe descended from the streetcar. Feeling a touch of lightheadedness as he walked across the street, he stopped and rested for a minute before turning up the hill toward the hospital.

Passing through the big double doors, he left his bag with the nun at the desk, and followed her directions to his father's room at the far end of the corridor.

Sitting in an alcove across from it, on a cluster of folding chairs, were his Aunt Claire, his brother Marc, and Caitlin Flanigan.

Catching sight of him, Claire ran down the hall to meet

him. "Philippe! Thank heavens!"

He felt her body shake as she held him tightly to her.

He hugged his brother briefly. Looking into his handsome features, he saw a terrible anguish there.

"Are you all right, Marc?"

"Yes."

"And Mama?"

"It's been hell for her, Philippe. She's all twisted up inside. She can't even *cry*," Marc added, himself hovering on the verge of tears.

The only measure of calm to be found was within Caitlin's embrace.

"You look dreadful, love," she murmured, caressing his back with her hand.

"Don't worry about me, Cait, I'm fine. Is Mama in there?"

She nodded, looking toward Joseph's room.

* * *

When Philippe opened the door, he found his mother sitting in a chair next to the bed. Looking up, she hastened to raise her index finger to her lips.

He mouthed the words "Hello, Mama."

The air in the room smelled foul, and Philippe's already sensitive stomach lurched. He quickly controlled an impulse to vomit, and approached her.

She reached for his hand, pressing it to her cheek. Looking up at him, she smiled a very wan, very sad smile. He leaned and put his lips to her forehead. As he did so, his eyes came to rest on the figure of his father lying beneath the sheet.

"Dear God!" he uttered aloud. The intake of his breath made a sharp, sucking sound.

Melinda rose and they left the room together.

Closing the door, she looked again into her son's grieving visage. "They took his arm this morning," she whispered hoarsely.

Her face blanched and as her knees gave way, Philippe swooped her into his arms. The soft sound of sobs began escaping her throat as he held her to him. It escalated until it became a cry that tore at the souls of everyone who heard it.

Day after day, the three sat together and watched Joseph's struggle for life. Septicemia invaded his bloodstream, and his doctors fought the onset of gangrene. The putrid flesh in his stump caused his fever to rise to an alarming degree, and his pain sometimes seemed beyond enduring. But the man was a Goliath. He endured it all, with dignity and what seemed superhuman strength.

* * *

One day ran into the next and Melinda lost all sense of time. From early morning, far into the night, she and her sons continued their vigil. Without fail, they ended the day kneeling together in the chapel, pleading for yet another miracle.

Arriving home late one evening, Melinda gathered her boys to her.

"I want to thank you both for helping me to survive this ordeal. I truly don't know what I would have done without you. But I must go on alone now."

She raised her hands and interrupted a barrage of protests.

"Marc, you have a wonderful opportunity to work for Alex Friedman this summer. I want you to take it. Alex is an exceptional man and you'll learn a great deal from him." She turned her gaze to her other son. "Philippe, I want you to rest. You've been with this every living moment since you boarded the train in Sherbrooke. Tomorrow, I will sit with your father alone."

* * *

Melinda entered the darkened room, a now familiar place, her eyes having long since probed every bump on the ceiling, every crack in the wall, from her chair at her husband's bedside.

Joseph lay semiconscious, his eyes closed, his lips slightly parted, calm except for brief moments of delirium. He was in the eleventh day of postoperative trauma. *So weak,* Melinda thought each time she reentered his room, *so wasted. How much longer can he go on fighting?* The thought brought with it a chilling reality. One that she chose not to entertain. Weary and almost drained of hope, she dropped her head into her hands. Moments later she sensed something happening. Raising her head, she looked into Joseph's eyes.

They were open and clear, and the meekest of smiles turned up the corners of his parched lips.

"Joseph! Dearest! Can you hear me?"

With obvious effort, he nodded his head. Falling to her knees, she buried her face in the bedclothes and wept.

* * *

Each day thereafter brought a fraction of progress. Little as it was, it gathered, and in three weeks' time Joseph was released from the hospital.

As his sons led him through the gate of the house on Sladesferry Landing, the eyes of his neighbors looked on. Not many would have recognized Joseph as the man they had known. His hair was a wisp of white, his eyes faded to the color of weak tea. He was bent and broken, but he was alive.

Marc carried him up the stairs to his bed. After settling him into his pillows, Melinda sponged his brow with a linen cloth while Philippe and Marc watched anxiously from the foot of the bed. Joseph's lids closed before they had time to take their leave of him.

Later in the day, Philippe listened at his father's door for any sign of stirring. He'd risen perhaps ten times during those few hours to do that very thing. Slowly, noiselessly, he opened the door an inch. He closed it just as soundlessly when he heard his father weeping.

Joseph gradually regained his strength, each day adding a bit to that of the day before. With immense frustration, he learned to button his shirt with his left hand, and pull on his socks and trousers—an effort that sometimes left him weak to the point of having to retreat to his bed for an hour to recover.

"Are you all right, Papa?" Philippe asked as Joseph lay back onto the bed.

"Yes, I'm all right. I just feel as if I have no bones."

Relearning the simplest things brought about violent fits of temper. After a clumsy attempt at feeding himself, Joseph sent his plate crashing to the kitchen floor.

Philippe, who had taken charge somewhere along the way, restrained him. "Don't worry about it, Papa. I'll clean it up. We'll try again tomorrow."

So many times during that summer Melinda had wanted to intercede, to take up Joseph's spoon and feed him, to put his shoes upon his feet. But she respected what Philippe was trying to do, and difficult as it was, she supported him.

"I think it would be best if we were alone," Philippe finally suggested. "Go back to work, Mama. It shames Papa so, to have you see him like this."

After countless attempts, Philippe succeeded in getting his father to leave the house. Joseph was fretful, and walked only a few steps beyond the gate.

"Let's go to the park, Papa. We can watch the boys playing ball."

"Not today. Some other time, son."

When Philippe persisted, anger—like molten lava—welled up and spilled over. "For God's sake, leave me alone," he begged.

At first Philippe found it hard not to think of his father as a rancorous old man. But soon he realized that Joseph wasn't ready to face the world, to submit to its scrutiny with an empty sleeve dangling from his shoulder.

After the first month in which Joseph made a respectable

amount of progress, he reached a plateau, a place where he seemed content to remain.

At first he feigned illness. He'd awakened "with a throbbing headache," or "the pain in his stump had returned to plague him during the night." Later he made no excuses; he simply refused to cooperate with Philippe at all. Muttering to himself, he returned to his bedroom and remained closeted inside for hours. Philippe decided not to press him further, lest they both grow sick at the sight of each other.

This decision left hours in the day with little for Philippe to do. His healthy young body craved some kind of activity to relieve his pent-up energies. It was then that he thought of the garden.

"Caitie," he called as he strode through the door into her kitchen. "Do you mind if I dig up that patch of dirt alongside the tool shed? I'd like to plant a few seeds."

She walked over from the sink, wiping her hands on her apron. "Yer more than welcome to try, love, but that's a lifeless bit of soil. Nary a self-respecting weed has grown there in many, many a moon."

"I'll give it try anyway, if that's all right with you."

* * *

On the first morning as Philippe worked with the spade, he noticed Joseph watching him from the kitchen window. He carried on, paying him no heed, mixing a pile of manure into the sterile soil.

The following morning as he was raking out the stones and twigs, he noticed Joseph coming out of the cellar door. Moving slowly toward a rickety bench that leaned against the house, he seated himself and looked on. Again Philippe gave no indication of having seen him.

All at once, Joseph called out, "It's pretty late in the season to plant a garden."

Philippe had hoped to arouse his interest, yet he was none the less startled when he heard his father's voice.

Leaning on the rake handle, his hair glinting red-gold in

the sun, Philippe looked at Joseph directly. "It's only July, Pa." Dropping the rake to the ground, he walked over to where Joseph sat. "What do you suggest I plant?"

"Greens ... radishes, maybe a few tomatoes."

"That's fine. I'll plant a salad garden." Turning, he started toward his plot again, then stopped. With his back still to Joseph, he spoke in a low voice. "Will you help me with it, Papa?"

There was a silence, when all that was heard was the rustling of leaves in the branches.

Joseph walked to where Philippe stood. Taking the rake from his hand, he replied, "I'll try, Philippe."

It wasn't easy relearning something that had once been second nature to him. Something he'd done with such facility that he'd hardly given it thought. Gripping the tool tightly, he hugged the handle to the inside of his bicep. Tediously, painstakingly, he gained control of it. He worked feverishly for several minutes, the sweat running from his brow into his eyes. Stopping, he wiped them with his handkerchief.

Joseph tired quickly but he fought his way through it to a second wind, and when he released the hoe an hour later, a slight tremor shook his hand.

"Are you all right, Pa?" Philippe asked anxiously.

Joseph nodded. Stooping, he picked up a fistful of dirt and let it trickle to the ground through his fingers. "I think it's getting better, son. ... I can feel some substance in it now."

When the delicate, thread-like seedlings sprouted, Joseph sat on the ground and skillfully pulled away the weeds that grew along with them. After supper, when the heat of the day had passed, he trudged down to the pump in the cellar. Filling and refilling a rusted old watering can, he sprinkled the herbs and radishes, and the pale saffron lettuce leaves beginning to break through the ground.

Their harvest was abundant enough to be enjoyed not only at their table but at a number of neighboring tables as well. From a beam in the cellar, Costanza hung bunches of dill weed, chives, and parsley to dry, and in September Caitlin added them to her jars when she put up the last of the season's tomatoes.

"It's time we tidied up the garden for winter, Papa," Philippe suggested on a crisp morning touched with a tinge of frost.

Joseph nodded, and they went about doing the job together. Afterward they rested on the rickety bench next to the house.

"If you'll carry this bench into the cellar before you leave for Sherbrooke, I'll repair it this winter."

Philippe's brows drew together, his expression perplexed. *I've not mentioned a word about leaving for Sherbrooke.* "I'll bring it in tonight, Papa."

"When do you plan on leaving, son?"

"Oh, when everything is up to it."

"It is, Philippe ... it is." Reaching out, Joseph stroked his son's forearm. "I don't know how to thank you, son."

"No need, Papa. It is I who thank you."

* * *

A thin veil of mist hung in the air. It hovered over the brackish waters of the Takonnet River as it flowed on its unceasing journey into the bay. It swirled about the church spires that rose through the treetops on The Hill. Philippe turned toward Riverton and looked at it one last time before boarding the train. He was on his way back to Sherbrooke once more, on his way to fulfilling a promise he'd made to God Almighty.

Part Two

Philippe:
The Seminary Years

After entering the gates of Saint Charles, the first thing that Philippe did was to go to the office of the administrator to be officially received as a first year seminarian. At the same time he received his schedule of study and his cell assignment. He was on his way to his quarters when, directly ahead of him, he spotted an all too familiar gait. He quickened his step, then loped down the tree-lined walkway toward his friend Paul Tremblay. Philippe grabbed his shoulder and whirled him around.

"Philippe!" Paul yelped. "I've been thinking of you all morning. Must be some kind of telepathy, eh?" he suggested, shaking Philippe's hand and clapping him on the back. "Why the devil didn't you write me this summer, you mangy dog?" His tone became serious when he added, "I've heard some grim reports about your father's accident and I've been worried about you. How are things, anyway?"

For a moment Philippe hesitated, then all at once the closeness returned. "Under the circumstances, I'd say pretty good."

"Then he's okay?"

"It's hard to explain, Paul. He's well enough, physically, and he's learned to deal with the handicap." Philippe inclined his head, then raised it again. "I sense that a lot of his manhood was lost along with his arm, Paul."

"I'm sorry. Gosh, I can imagine how hard this has been on you."

"It's been hard on everyone. My father needed someone who'd force him to start living again, and that turned out to be me. He could've easily let himself go right down the

173

drain."

"How's your mother doing?"

"Better than I thought she would. That's not to say she doesn't have her moments, though."

Philippe had forgotten how uplifting it could be to share his feelings with Paul. Ever since he'd first arrived in Sherbrooke ten years ago, Paul had been there for him, loyal and supportive. And as the years passed, a deep bond had grown between them. Only once during that time had they been separated.

Upon graduating from the eighth grade, Paul's father had insisted that he leave l'Académie and study at Longchamps, a prestigious private school on the outskirts of Montreal. At the time, Edgar Tremblay had held strong reservations about what he considered "a totally stifling, academic environment." He wanted to mold Paul into a well-rounded man, one to whom he could later turn over his lucrative importing business. But Paul had failed to measure up, and it was only through the pleadings of his mother that he was returned to l'Académie the following year.

Walking with him now, feeling the pressure of Paul's arm slung across his shoulders, Philippe was grateful for the trust and respect they shared.

Nearing the dormitory they would inhabit along with ten other seminarians, Philippe suddenly blurted out, "I've really missed you, Paul."

Paul came to a halt in mid-step. "I missed you too. I was tickled to get your telegram. I didn't think you'd be coming back. What made you change your mind?"

Philippe grinned, the dimple in his left cheek deepening more than usual. He was a lot thinner and Paul noticed his usually compelling gaze was lackluster. A lot had happened to his old buddy since he'd seen him last.

"It's personal, Paul. Suffice to say I made a deal with someone. My apologies for not writing. I have no excuse to offer other than the tense situation at home. I thought of you often, though." Hoping to change the subject, Philippe added, "How was your summer? Was your father awfully upset by your decision to go on to seminary?"

"Well ... let's just say it was an interesting time for all concerned. To be fair to the man, he just can't fathom having a son who's a priest. It's beyond his ability to even perceive it. You know, I wish I'd had a brother or a sister. From the day I was born he's focused on me. He's planned every moment of my life, and he deplores having lost control of things." Paul drew in his breath, then sharply expelled it. "Who knows, Phil, maybe someday he'll take some pride in what I'm doing." A rueful smile twisted his full lips. "My mother is ecstatic, though, and that helps to make up for a lot of it."

They moved up the stairs to the door of the building. Inside, they went their separate ways.

The week that followed was crammed with activity. Each day dealt with another facet of their lives as seminarians. New curriculum, new professors, etcetera, as well as being subjected to probing interviews that would hopefully reveal where their aptitudes lay, and more specifically where they would eventually become most useful to the Dominican order.

"I'm not surprised, Phil," Paul remarked a week later when they'd finished with all the preliminaries. "You've always been good at languages, and your music—that goes without saying. Are you disappointed in their appraisal of you?"

"No, not a bit! I could have saved them a lot of time and trouble if they'd only asked me right off."

"They have their methods. Pretty good ones at that. It didn't take them long to peg me as a bean counter. I really enjoy working with figures. It's like a game for me."

"You'll breeze right through this stuff, Paul."

"I hope so. Hey—whaddaya say we get out of here for a while? Once classes begin, we won't have a prayer of leaving this place for weeks."

Philippe grinned at Paul's unintentional aphorism.

"Whaddaya say, Phil," Paul repeated, "let's go for a walk."

They rose at once and dashed out of the building toward the gates.

Morning had brought the city a cloudless autumn day that was warmer than the norm for October in Sherbrooke. Montmorency Street was filled with young students enjoying their last precious moments of freedom browsing through bookstores and gift shops along the broad, tree-lined avenue.

No sooner had they lost sight of the school, Paul shouted out a familiar challenge. "Race you to the park."

"You're on," Philippe answered. Pulling his cap from his head, he burst forth, dodging and bobbing in and out of the pedestrian traffic.

Paul was a slow starter but he regained his ground and lost the contest by a mere half-stride. "I'll get you next time," he said breathlessly.

"No you won't. I always beat you," Philippe contradicted haughtily, breathing as hard, if not harder, than his worthy but vanquished opponent. Taking his jacket off, Philippe slung it over his shoulder.

They walked side by side, kicking up crisp fallen leaves that covered the grounds of the park.

"Great, isn't it, Paul?"

"Yeah. It's a relief to be outside the walls for a while."

"I meant the foliage, birdbrain."

Paul looked up at the trees and nodded. "Uh huh. Beautiful."

"You know, Paul, I didn't realize you felt so hemmed in at school."

"Oh ... sometimes I do and sometimes I don't. Forget it, it's just a mood."

They left the path and walked through the glen to the edge of the pond. This was a special place, each of them having come here many times before to skate, to join in a game of rugby, and to toboggan down the hill in the newly fallen snow. Today, there were no eager voices to be heard, no pucks or footballs to be chased after. But for the rustle of leaves, all was still.

The water of the pond was motionless, mirror-like, reflecting the brilliant sunlight. Pulling down their caps, Philippe and Paul shaded their eyes and watched a small flotilla of ducks bobbing its way across to the far shore. Paul sank to the ground and Philippe did likewise.

"Do the responsibilities of priesthood bother you, Philippe?"

"Not anymore. I've decided it will work itself out before I'm ordained. Why—are they bothering you?"

"Yes, a little."

"I can't believe this. I thought you had everything all figured out."

"I thought so too. Maybe it's because I'm standing on the brink of the precipice, so to speak."

By now, Philippe's eyes were widening noticeably.

"Don't be alarmed," Paul reassured him. "I want priesthood very much ... most of the time. I guess it's just normal to miss the little extras once in a while."

"Well, you've had a lot more *little extras* than I've had, Paul. I guess I can understand how you feel."

Sprawling out in the grass, Paul rolled onto his stomach. He picked a blade of grass and stuck it between his teeth. Philippe followed suit. Each in his own private way savored the moment, enjoying the warmth of the sun on his back and the time for thinking private thoughts.

A young couple approached and sat nearby. They caught Philippe's eye immediately.

They were lovers. Oblivious to the world surrounding them, they lay on the grass holding tightly onto each other. They kissed—long, passionate kisses that made Philippe feel like looking away. But he didn't. He watched as the heel of the man's right hand came dangerously close to touching the woman's breast, the left lost in a maze of curly blonde hair.

A rush of excitement pulsated through Philippe's body.

Paul, who'd also been looking on through semi-closed lids, observed churlishly, "That's normal too, you know."

Philippe started. Moments ago Paul had seemed to be dozing.

"What are you talking about?" Philippe turned and glared at him.

"I'm talking about what you're feeling right now, old buddy. Don't deny it, it's normal ... it's healthy. It's called sexuality. It's the thing that in the tenth grade, Father Christian told us we must learn to control at all times under penalty of sin. Impure thoughts, remember?" Paul sat up and spit the blade of grass from his mouth. "I wonder how many decades it takes to rid your body of all its natural impulses?"

"Don't be absurd, Paul. You're talking nonsense."

"Oh! Forgive me. It was stupid of me to have thought that you would be *normal*."

Paul's sarcasm was beginning to eat away at Philippe's hide. Rising without a word, Philippe headed toward the park entrance on Montmorency Street.

Paul hurried after him. "Wait a minute, Phil. WAIT, will you?"

Philippe stopped long enough for Paul to catch up.

"I am sorry. I didn't mean to shove my ugly mood off on you."

"Really? You could have fooled me."

"Hey! I have an idea. Let's go to the Inn. I'll buy you a lemonade or a cup of coffee. Whaddaya say?"

"No thanks, I have some things to take care of. Okay?"

"Sure."

Reaching his cell, Philippe dropped onto his cot. Yellow-white streaks of sunshine spilled through the shutters at the window and stretched across the floor in long, thin lines.

His unpleasant go-around with Paul had not diminished his memory of the lovers embracing in the park. To the contrary, his anger and frustration seemed to have intensified it. Visions of the girl's curving hip, her lover's hands fondling her ... floated round and round beneath his closed lids. Rolling onto his stomach, he pounded his pillow.

This was not the first time that he had had to contend with the sexual demands of his body. It had happened with increasing regularity throughout his high school years. Out of nowhere, the merest glimpse of something would trigger a strong sense of desire. He'd laughed it off, joked about it, as the other boys had done, and from time to time sought relief in one of the bathroom stalls. But it was different now. He felt guilt, and oftentimes shame, even when it happened during a dream in the middle of the night. Celibacy hung like a weight around his neck.

He lay still for a long time, then his fists uncurled and his hands lay open at his sides. It had passed. Sitting on the edge of his bed, his head in his hands, he rested a minute before deciding to join Paul at the Inn.

Chapter Twenty-One

The dreaded first semester of seminary life was coming to an end, and both Philippe and Paul had survived it. At first it hadn't seemed more difficult than studying at l'Académie, merely different. Only later did one realize the very subtle changes, made ever so gradually, that brought about a new way of thinking.

Philippe learned the value of parsimoniously scheduling his time, and when the holidays approached he found himself in excellent shape academically. His study habits had truly undergone a metamorphosis this term.

There'd been an added incentive to keep on top of things, however. A month ago, he'd been invited to spend Christmas with Paul and his family at Terrebonne, and he was keenly looking forward to it.

There was but one distasteful bit of business he would have to take care of first: explaining to Father Jean why he would not be at Les Érables with the family this year. He prepared himself for a stiff argument and spent quite a bit of time rehearsing his rebuttal. However, when the time came and he was face to face with his uncle, the best he could manage was to courteously ask his permission to leave. Much to his surprise it was graciously granted, and on December twenty-third, he walked through the gates with Paul.

* * *

Arriving in Montreal, they were met by Gaston, the Tremblay's groomsman. He chatted with Paul while Philippe dashed into a nearby florist to buy a bouquet for his hostess.

The city was enchanting. Church bells rang, and lights winked and glittered from shop windows beckoning the children who stood gazing in awe at the toys and sweets.

At Terrebonne Paul and Philippe were greeted by a prim-looking maidservant who relieved them of their outerwear. Philippe looked excitedly around him as he stood in the magnificent marbled foyer. He'd visited here before, but never would the splendor of this great house fail to excite him.

"Hello, darling!" Paul's mother strode into the foyer and warmly embraced her son. She was a tall, slender woman with steel-gray hair, once as dark as Paul's, Philippe suspected. She wore red silk draped at the waist and caught by a glittering broach at the curve above her hip.

"Mother!! My, you look festive. Something new?" he asked as he appraised her dress.

"No dear, not at all. Philippe! How very good to see you! We are indeed delighted to have you with us this year."

"Thank you, Madame Tremblay. Needless to say, I'm delighted to be here." He handed her the red roses wrapped in delicate pink tissue paper.

"Aren't these lovely!" she exclaimed as she leaned to sniff their fragrance. "Thank you, Philippe dear. Wherever did you find them this time of year?"

"At a little shop near the railway station."

"You shouldn't have," she said. Then with a twinkle in her dark, expressive eyes, she added, "But I'm glad you did. They're my favorite flower."

"My pleasure, madame," Philippe assured her, bowing slightly from the waist.

Philippe's attention was then drawn to the large Christmas tree in the rear of the foyer. It soared to the second floor of the house, its gold and silver ornaments dangling gracefully from the boughs. He was about to express his admiration when Madame Tremblay hooked her arm through Paul's and said, "Come along now, your father is anxious to see you."

* * *

Applewood burned in the fireplace of the richly paneled library. As they entered, Edgar Tremblay put down his cigar and rose from his leather chair.

"Ah! There you are, Paul ... Philippe. I thought I heard you come in. I understand from Gaston, a helluva storm is getting underway. His arthritis predicts it will be the worst of the winter so far. Tell me, how was your trip?"

"Excellent, sir, thank you." Philippe said, reaching to shake his hand.

"Well, gentleman, what can I fix you? Something to warm you, perhaps? A cognac? Some sherry? What will it be, Philippe?"

"A sherry would be fine, thank you, sir."

"Paul?"

"The same for me, please, Father."

"Marielle? Care for something, dear?" he queried as he moved to a bar set up on a table behind the sofa.

"A sherry, please ... a small one."

"Very well," he agreed as he poured from the crystal decanter.

Edgar Tremblay was a dapper man. Not as tall as his son, who was almost six feet, nor did he possess Paul's classic physique. He was finer boned and narrower through the chest and shoulders. His clothing, however, hung impeccably from his erect, medium-sized frame, the cinnamon-colored smoking jacket lending him an air of panache, as did the paisley foulard folded at his throat. A trace of reddish-blond stubbornly mingled with a predominance of silver in his thinning hair and his neatly trimmed moustache. His eyes, not quite blue, not quite gray, were quick and sharp, reminding one of a bird of prey. Genetically, Paul favored his mother; the broad forehead and proud aquiline nose, a distinctive trait carried by the men in her family.

"Well, Mother, what's on the agenda?" Paul asked, albeit a totally superfluous question since he more than suspected she had scheduled her usual round of holiday affairs.

"You usually complain that I plan too much, Paul, so please feel free to decline whatever you choose."

"You know I love your parties, Mother."

"I know you do, dear. I was mostly thinking of Philippe."

"He'll love it," Paul assured her before Philippe had a chance to protest for himself.

"I did leave tomorrow open until five," she began, "after which we are having a small reception for some of your father's associates. Just some champagne and canapés, nothing big. At eight, we will dine here with Monsignor Charbonneau and four of the priests from the chancellery."

Paul pulled a wry face.

"We do it every Christmas eve, Paul. They've come to expect it." She drew in a fresh supply of oxygen and continued. "I'm sure you've celebrated Réveillon with your family in Baie de Saint-Jacques, Philippe. It's a Christmas tradition that's been observed for centuries in Québec. We'll join the family at Gilberte and Martin's this year."

"Now, that's a party Philippe can't afford to miss!" Paul exclaimed. "All the family skeletons come out to dance between midnight and 2 A.M."

"Such nonsense, Paul." Marielle shook her head as she gently chided her son. "Anyway, most of the family will be there." Pausing briefly to sip her sherry, she went on with her litany. "I thought we would wait until Christmas morning to open our gifts. It's always so late when we get home from Réveillon. We can even sleep in for a bit in the morning. Mass isn't until eleven. By the way, Paul, Marie-Collette will be soloist at Sainte Anne's this year."

Paul looked at Philippe with diffident eyes. "Marie-Collette is my second cousin thrice removed, or some such."

"That's more nonsense," Marielle was quick to retort. "She's my sister's daughter. May I continue, please?" she said, looking directly at Paul.

He rose from his seat and feigned a grand bow.

Philippe thought, *They play interesting games with each other, these two.*

"After Mass we're invited to luncheon at Uncle Germain's and Tante Annette's. He is Edgar's brother. I hasten to add that bit of information lest my son make up some silly story about him.." She cleared her throat genteelly. "The remainder of Christmas day, we'll be at home, just the four of us. Does that please you, gentlemen?"

A burst of applause rose from the three men.

"Take a bow, Mother, another memorable performance, I must say," Paul teased.

Marielle stood and, taking a pinch of her dress between her fingers, she curtsied in their direction.

The lighthearted banter continued at the luncheon table set for them in the morning room. It was a leisurely repast, and they watched from a long row of windows facing the garden, as the storm gathered intensity. At around three o'clock, Philippe was shown to the guest room on the third floor.

It was more like a suite than a bedroom, having a sitting corner with a blue-green chair and ottoman next to the fireplace and an adjoining private bath.

Philippe unpacked his few things, hoping they would serve well enough for Marielle Tremblay's soirées. Afterward, he turned back the bedspread and lay on the antique four-poster. He wasn't tired—he was far too excited for that. He simply wanted to "déroule" or stretch out. Lunch and the glass of sherry had left him with a lush, lazy feeling. He lay quite still, listening to the sound of snowflakes tapping against the windowpane.

Philippe awakened with a start to the chimes of the clock on the mantel. Craning his neck in its direction, he looked at the time. He had less than an hour to bathe and dress for dinner at seven-thirty. Bolting from the bed he raced into the bathroom.

As the immense marble tub filled, he proceeded to shave. The older he got, the more he loathed this daily ritual of scraping his skin with a razor. He'd tried growing a beard, hoping to end it forever, but alas, he could not endure the itching that resulted and promptly shaved it off.

Finishing, he rinsed his face with cold water, then sank into the tub.

"How absolutely decadent," he said aloud. "How in the world will Paul manage to give it all up?" *Hmmm, that is dedication!* To Philippe, the amazing part of it was that Paul and his family took it so much for granted. Hot water running from the mouth of a bronzed fish. Maids who knocked at the door, bearing heated bath linens and soaps imported from the south of France. Aaah ... the sheer ecstasy of it was almost too much to bear. A far cry from Sladesferry Landing and the little tin tub that was brought into the kitchen. Almost instantly, the exhilaration fled. "What the devil am I doing here anyway," he asked himself as he climbed out of the tub onto the black and white marble floor.

He dressed and shook off his distasteful mood, and promptly at seven-thirty he appeared in the drawing room looking splendid in his black serge and at peace with the world. He'd barely seated himself on the blue damask sofa when Marielle Tremblay entered the room.

"Don't get up," she hurried to say, but he rose anyway.

Resuming his seat next to her on the sofa, he looked at her admiringly. He hadn't thought it possible, but she appeared lovelier in her framboise taffeta gown than she had that afternoon.

"Paul's late, as usual," Edgar Tremblay noted as he entered the room soon after her.

"Please, Edgar, don't make a fuss."

"Very well, my dear."

Within minutes Paul appeared wearing a black suit of silk and wool, a new fabric imported from China. It gave off a sheen that complemented the glow of his olive complexion. Jade cuff links encircled in gold gleamed from his wrists and a burgundy silk tie finished off his dashing ensemble.

Marielle's eyes rested admiringly on her son. "My, but you *are* handsome this evening. You all are," she was quick to add, turning with a smile to her husband and houseguest.

It didn't take Philippe long to assess the adulation shared between Marielle Tremblay and her only child. Philippe looked across at Edgar, wondering how long it had been since the dignified head of the household had been relegated to an afterthought. How long since he had become the encore instead of the main event. His train of thought shifted sharply when a servant called them to the table.

They began the meal with a "terrine de dinde," a rich mingling of wild turkey, veal and aromatic spices—a piquant combination that stimulated the taste buds and aroused the olfactory sense. It was followed by a "potage Crecy," a velvety soup of pureed carrots laced with cream and finished with a dash of nutmeg. The main course, a filet of beef wrapped in a fluffy pastry, was done to perfection. Rare, but moderately so. Several spears of white asparagus "au buerre" and a small roasted potato lay alongside it. They finished with a lemon mousse, so light and glistening that it threatened to slide from Philippe's spoon as he attempted to raise it to his lips. It was a culinary achievement the likes of which Philippe Durand had never before enjoyed.

They left the dining table two hours later, going into the drawing room where demitasse and brandy were served.

After pouring, Marielle excused herself. On occasions such as this, it was customary for the men to be left to their liqueurs and tobacco. As little as a year ago, Paul had risen and left along with his mother. But since celebrating his nineteenth birthday in June, he'd gained a quasi-adult status in the family.

Sometime between the brandy and the coffee, Edgar Tremblay began to question Philippe about his life at Saint Charles. They were not the usual garden-variety questions asked of a young man preparing for priesthood. They were of a more personal nature.

"I've been told there is a special sort of intimacy that grows between seminarians. Tell me, Philippe, is there any truth to that rumor?"

"Intimacy?" Philippe repeated, the innuendo striking a nerve. He thought for several seconds before answering. "There's a definite closeness among us. After all, we live together and are all reaching for the same goal. But intimacy? That word somehow conjures up a different relationship in my mind that I'm sure you didn't intend. Let me put

186

it this way: I've known most of my peers most of my life. I think that *brotherhood* better describes what we feel for each other."

"But surely some of you are closer, one to the other, are you not?"

Philippe stifled an urge to laugh. Across from him, sitting in a gilded Louis XV armchair, Paul's jaw worked furiously.

"Absolutely!" Philippe conceded, hurrying to offer an answer before Paul had time to throw himself headlong into the fray. "You have a perfect example of that between Paul and me. I couldn't hope for a better friend."

Philippe turned to face Paul, who now ogled the pattern in the carpet.

"Come on, Father," Paul finally said, "Philippe is our guest. He's on holiday. He doesn't want to be reminded of school."

"No, Paul," Philippe contradicted, "it's all right. People are curious about us. I really don't mind setting them straight."

"Well, I do mind. I'll answer your questions, Father, all of them, but at some other time." The chill in Paul's tone put a definite end to any further discussion.

"I'm sorry, son, I was merely interested in hearing another point of view. Why do I always forget how oversensitive you are?"

Looking away from Paul, he apologized to his guest. "I hope I haven't offended you, Philippe. I certainly hadn't intended to. I have the utmost respect for the clergy, as Paul well knows."

Looking over at his son, he said, "For some reason, Paul becomes arbitrary and defensive when we get on the subject of priesthood. Most unbecoming, my boy." He lifted his hand in an expostulating gesture, as if to dismiss his son along with the subject.

The wonderful mood created earlier that evening had vanished and after a period of mundane conversation, Philippe excused himself and went up to his room.

At the top of the stairs he turned and looked down into the

foyer, over the top of the shimmering Christmas tree, to the open doors of the drawing room. Paul and his father still lingered there, but all was grimly silent. Turning again, Philippe continued on to the upper floor.

Nestled under the comforter, Philippe mentally reviewed what had transpired that evening. It was obvious that Edgar Tremblay had bitterly opposed Paul's commitment to the priesthood. Philippe had known that for a long time. But he had not known that Tremblay considered his son less than a man for having done so.

Paul's father was complex—compulsive by nature, needing to control the lives of those who surrounded him. Paul had denied him that pleasure, and he wasn't about to forgive him for it.

After a time everything began blurring. The wine and the cognac had at last defeated Philippe. He closed his eyes and drifted into sleep.

* * *

Philippe awakened but was reluctant to rise from the warmth of his bed. The fire had burned out completely and there was a frosty chill to the room. Curled into a ball beneath the featherbed cover, he lingered in a soft, shadowy half-world, remembering snatches of a dream that had lingered after he'd awakened.

A rap at the door jolted Philippe back to reality. Holding the bedclothes up over his chest to keep warm, he rose to a seated position.

"It's open, Paul," he called out.

Paul's smile brightened the room as he entered carrying a tray. Not a vestige of last night's petulance was in evidence on his face.

"You lazy so and so, it's almost ten. You've missed breakfast! Do you plan to spend all of your time sleeping?"

Philippe grinned at him sheepishly. "I'm sure you'd never allow it. I'm sorry, Paul. I had no idea of the time. I've been lying here daydreaming for almost an hour. I haven't heard a sign of life, not a sign. I swear it."

"I know, it's wonderful up here. I sometimes use this room when I'm at home."

"What's on the agenda?" Philippe asked.

"Well, I'm not sure that you'll approve, considering your penchant for lying abed, but I thought we'd go for a sleigh ride." Paul stood next to the bed looking handsomely casual in his tweeds.

"Ah! This time you're wrong. I most heartily do approve. I happen to love sleigh rides."

"Then get up, will you?" Placing the tray of coffee and croissants on the bedside table, Paul walked toward the door. "By the by, Phil, I hope you weren't too upset by the old man last night. He gets a bit outrageous when he's had too much to drink."

"I'm not upset, Paul, but I am surprised that a man of his stature would even entertain such misconceptions. He seemed to be insinuating perversion." Philippe again felt an urge to laugh just as he had the night before.

"I'm sure he doesn't believe that, really. I think it's his way of getting back at me for leaving him stuck with the business. The ultimate insult, so to speak."

"No need to explain, Paul. We all have our share of stuff to deal with."

"I think you've hit it right on the head. See you at the stable in half an hour. Wear something warm under your sheepskin—it's bloody cold out there." He disappeared through the doorway and dashed down the hall.

* * *

The two magnificent Morgans pulled the sleigh effortlessly along the deserted country road. A light, powdery snow blew back into Paul's and Philippe's faces as the runners cut through its untracked, virgin whiteness.

Gaston skillfully handled the reins as the two young gentlemen sat snugly beneath a pair of bearskins.

189

"It must be below zero!" Philippe said as he felt the skin on his nose stiffen.

"Very possibly," Paul said with a chuckle. "We'll stop down the road in a little town about six miles from here. I have some friends there. I'm sure they'll give us a hot lunch."

Up to a foot of new snow had fallen overnight, leaving the landscape looking like something out of a fairytale. Philippe had been on sleigh rides before, but never on one such as this. It was to be a memorable day—deep down inside he could feel it!

"Here ..." Paul handed him a handsome silver flask.

Raising it to his lips, Philippe took a swallow of the fiery liquid.

Taking it back, Paul did the same. "Tastes good," he said, tapping in the heavy silver stopper.

It took almost an hour for them to reach Nicolet. About two miles north of the village, Gaston turned the team into a road that led to a sprawling country house nestled into a grove of firs.

As they left the sleigh, Philippe and Paul plunged through the drifts toward the entrance to the house. Approaching the door and noisily stomping the snow from their boots, Paul reached for the knocker. Before he could lift it, the door opened.

"Paul—Paul!" she cried, throwing herself into his arms. Her pale blond hair swung like a silken pendulum across her shoulders, wisps of it catching on the back of her pale blue sweater. Flushed with excitement, her skin reminded one of flawless porcelain. "How heavenly to see you!" she exclaimed in a hushed, breathy voice. "When did you get home?" Her lips drew into a smile, uncovering lustrous white teeth and a deep dimple near the left corner of her mouth.

Philippe stared, unable take his eyes from her. Releasing her, Paul was about to make introductions when she interrupted him.

"Please, come inside, it's much too cold to be standing

out here."

The foyer was immense, and a gracefully turned staircase in the center of it spiraled to the second floor where it divided and led to wings on the right and left.

Paul made another stab at introducing the two. "I've been looking forward to this for a long time," he began, clasping his hands together. "Dionne, allow me to present Philippe Durand, my fellow seminarian. I think you'll agree that he is one very special fellow." Turning the other way, he said, "Philippe, this is Dionne Caron, whom I have been fortunate enough to have known all of my life, and who is undeniably the loveliest young woman I have ever known."

Dionne smiled shyly, another flush of color rising to enhance her already stunning features.

She is more than beautiful, Philippe thought. *I have never seen anything like her in my life!*

"Paul's spoken of you often, Philippe. I'm truly pleased to meet you at last."

Philippe suddenly felt tongue-tied.

Noticing, she graciously returned her attention to Paul. "You didn't answer my question. When did you get home?"

"Yesterday."

"And it's taken you all this time to come and see me?"

Their laughter was interrupted by a tall, ruggedly handsome man who was making his way down the staircase. "Well, look who's here!" he said in a deep, sonorous voice. Bounding across the polished floor, he pulled Paul into his arms. "God, it's good to see you!"

Paul's voice became husky and a bit emotional. "And to see you, my friend."

In that instant there seemed little left of the blasé young man that Philippe knew Paul to be.

Regaining his aplomb, Paul went back to the introductions. "Meet François Caron, Philippe, my boyhood friend and Dionne's older brother."

A maid appeared and took their caps and sheepskins.

Looking at Paul, it struck Philippe that he had never seen him look so vibrant, so alive.

Dionne took hold of Paul's hand and led him into the great room. It was a delightful room, with shafts of winter sunshine flowing through the sheer curtains, spilling onto the Persian rug, raising its reds and oranges to an even more brilliant level of color. Other than the carpets, everything was done in a shade of yellow. The walls, washed in its palest tint, cosseted the overstuffed furnishings ranging in tone from a creamy beige to brilliant maize. Ornately gilded frames enclosed French Impressionist art, and an Oriental sculpture, stark in its simplicity, adorned a marble-topped credenza.

A Chinese silk shawl covered a baby grand piano that stood in the far corner, close to the windows. This was eclecticism in the finest sense of the word.

"I love this room," Paul said, "it's so ..."

"Cozy?" Dionne filled in for him.

"Not even close. Exotic would be the adjective I'd choose." Before being seated Paul walked to a tall curio cabinet on the far side of the room. Stooping slightly, he looked inside at a grouping of figurines. "Still collecting, I see," he commented, looking over his shoulder at Dionne.

"Every chance I get. Every once in a while I find something irresistible beckoning to me in one of the antique shops on Rue du Saint Sepulchre."

"They're lovely," Philippe chimed in, having at last found his voice again. Feeling a bit more at ease, he ventured to add, "I also like your Christmas tree. It's beautiful."

"Thank you for noticing, Philippe. I did the tree by myself this year." She threw a look of disdain at François.

"Really?" François retorted. "And who do you suppose cut it down and hauled it in here for her?" Looking at Philippe, he grinned. "I truly go wanting for appreciation around here. Tell me, how long will you be at Terrebonne?"

"I'll be there through the New Year, but Philippe has to return to Sherbrooke for services next Sunday. He's conducting the Offertory music at the cathedral. Quite the honor, right, Phil?"

Philippe nodded shyly.

"I'm sorry you'll be leaving us so soon, Philippe," said François. "I hope we'll at least be seeing you tonight at Réveillon. Dionne and I will be staying with Gilberte and Martin for the holidays."

Paul once more hurried to answer for both of them. "You can count on us. Wouldn't miss it for anything. By the way, where are your parents?"

Dionne said, "You won't believe this, Paul. Mother finally convinced Father to take her to Geneva for Christmas." Turning to Philippe, she explained, "It's been over twenty years since my mother has spent a holiday with her family in Europe. She actually threatened to go alone if Papa refused to take her." Her eyes, rimmed with thick, swooping lashes, changed color with the light, from rich amber to pale saffron.

"How about something to eat?" François asked.

"Thank you," Paul replied, "we'd like that. I was afraid you weren't going to ask."

"Dionne, please tell Celine, and have her fix something for Gaston as well. I'll pour us a glass of that Château Margaux that Papa brought up from the cellar." He rose and walked to the liquor cabinet. Taking out four wine glasses, he uncorked the bottle and filled them halfway.

"Philippe?" François offered him the first glass.

Philippe reached up and took one from the tray, seriously questioning the wisdom of this action. The brandy they'd warmed themselves with in the sleigh had quickened his pulse and he felt it racing through his bloodstream still. He set the glass down on the marble-top table next to his chair.

Dionne returned from the kitchen just as François shook up the fire and put on another giant log. Seating himself on the floor in front of it, he rested his back against the stone of the hearth.

When resuming the conversation, Philippe was surprised to hear François ask: "How are things with your father these days, Paul?"

"About the same. He was in cock-fighting form last night, but Philippe put the damper on by running off to bed. It's really frustrating though. Just when I feel that I'm gaining a little ground, he takes me up short with a tasteless remark." Perplexed, he shook his head slowly. "At any rate, he's still allowing me in the house, so I guess things could be worse."

Philippe felt his hands grow moist; he was glad when they went on to another subject.

Luncheon was simple, similar in many ways to the food Philippe was accustomed to having at Les Érables. He ate with unusual gusto, anxious to add something substantial to the alcohol running amuck in his system.

Seated across the table from Dionne, Philippe made an effort to refrain from staring at her. From the occasional glimpses that he did steal, he saw that the pupils of her eyes were outlined with a circle of black, as if put there with an artist's brush. *How rare,* he thought, *for one endowed with so much perfection, to be so seemingly unaware of it.*

Finishing, they lingered over coffee, still reliving old times they'd enjoyed together in the past.

"We must be boring you to death, Philippe. I do apologize for our bad manners," Dionne hastened to say.

But before Philippe could reassure her, Paul got up from the table. "Bored or not, we have to be on our way. My mother is expecting us at a reception she's holding this afternoon. I'm afraid we've already stayed too long."

Moving ahead of them into the hall, François collected their gear.

Standing next to Philippe, Dionne smiled and extended her hand. "It's been nice meeting you, Philippe. I'll look forward to seeing you this evening at Réveillon."

"I'm looking forward to it too, Dionne." He had not, until now, had the aplomb to address her by her given name. "Thank you for a very enjoyable day."

"No thanks are necessary—just promise to visit again sometime."

"I promise."

Gaston took up the reins while Philippe and Paul burrowed beneath the heavy fur robes. The sun was setting and the temperature plummeting. There was little conversation on the return trip to Terrebonne; Paul dozed on and off, and Philippe quietly daydreamed beside him.

Admittedly naïve when it came to the opposite sex, Philippe found himself fascinated by Dionne Caron. Lavished as she'd been with the best that life had to offer, she seemed so unsullied by it all. She was pleasingly shy, yet at the same time she possessed a world of self-confidence. He mentally reviewed every word that had passed between them.

Looking at his watch, Philippe was startled to see it was nearing four-thirty. They would be late in arriving for the Tremblay's reception. This wouldn't sit well with Paul's father, Philippe feared. Edgar Tremblay seemed obsessive about promptness.

When they arrived at Terrebonne, the senior Tremblay greeted them jovially as they entered, their absence for the first half-hour seeming to have made little or no difference at all.

As Philippe hurried to change, music from a string ensemble playing in the conservatory drifted upstairs, adding a festive air to every corner of the mansion. Downstairs, servants passed canapés on sterling silver trays, and conversation flowed as rapidly as the brut.

Paul moved among the partygoers, chatting easily, joking with the men and women who over the years had become a part of his life.

More reticent, Philippe stood back, twirling the thin stem of his glass between his thumb and forefinger, feeling a bit "mal à l'aise," as if he didn't belong there. He walked unnoticed into the library and looked out from the long, narrow windows across the snow-covered expanse of the grounds, wondering if Tante Marie-Élise had begun to bake the "tourtières" for the family festivities later tonight. He could almost smell the cloves in the ham, browning slowly under a maple sugar glaze. He thought of Dominique, perched precariously atop the ladder, affixing the Christmas angel to the top of the tree. He envisioned his grandmother being carried down from her room in Daniel's arms to join the family for dinner. His thoughts were still in Le Baie when he heard Paul's voice from behind him.

"I'm sorry, Paul. What did you say?"

"Where *are* you, Philippe? Are you sure you're all right?"

"Yes of course. Why wouldn't I be?"

"How the devil would I know? You were so quiet at the Carons this afternoon, and now you're hiding in here."

"I'm not hiding. I was just taking a few moments to think about my family."

"Not overwhelmed by all this gaiety, I hope."

"Not at all," Philippe denied. "Just a little homesick, that's all."

"Well, just wait until the next contingent arrives. They'll put you back into the Yuletide spirit—I guarantee."

And he was right! The dinner for the priests was a huge success.

Philippe listened intently to the conversation as they discussed the local political climate, as well as a number of well-chosen diocesan problems, disagreeing heatedly with each other at times.

Edgar Tremblay, his predator eyes darting from one cleric to the other, chose to challenge much of what was said. He was indeed an unorthodox host, but Philippe was beginning to crack his veneer. Once in his cups, Tremblay relished conversational sparring. Anger brought out bigotries and sacrosanct opinions otherwise kept under wraps.

Personally, Philippe didn't contribute to the conversation very much, but he swelled with pride when the stout old prelate seated next to him occasionally asked that he offer his opinion. The soirée carried on in a similar vein until almost ten o'clock.

Philippe and Paul helped with the cloaks and saw the guests safely into their carriages.

After the last had pulled away from the portico, Marielle dashed into the kitchen and passed out the customary Yuletide envelopes to her staff.

Up in his room again, Philippe made a stab at freshening up, but instead he found himself reaching for his nightshirt and robe.

Donning them, he sat by the fire and held his rosary beads tightly. He closed his eyes and began to pray, but through the blackness of his closed lids came the face of Dionne Caron.

Paul knocked. He stepped back gingerly when Philippe opened the door, appraising him from top to bottom. "Hey, old buddy ... your choice of dress for this evening is rather unique. Wish I'd thought of it myself."

"Sorry, Paul, I'm going to pass on Réveillon. I'm exhausted." Putting his hand up to his head, he groaned a bit. "I won't need anything more to eat or drink for a very long time."

"No problem, Phil. Sleep well, see you in the morning."

Kneeling beside the four-poster, Philippe felt as if a weight had been lifted from his shoulders. Holding the cross of his rosary beads to his lips, he uttered softly, "In the name of the Father ..."

Chapter Twenty-Two

Moments after returning to Saint Charles, Philippe was informed of the death of his grandmother. She had succumbed peacefully in her sleep on Christmas Eve. Would he ever be able to forgive himself for not having been there?

The depth of his grief moved Father Jean. He'd witnessed the love that the two had come to share in the years since Philippe had returned to Canada, and he desperately wanted to comfort him.

"She was eighty-six, my boy, and God took her with a gentle touch of His hand. She never suffered, not for an instant. I know it doesn't help you to hear this just now, but it will, later on, when you've had time to give it some thought." He put his arm around Philippe's shoulders. "She's where she wants to be, you know. With Papa and her babies."

Philippe lowered his head and buried his face in his uncle's shoulder.

* * *

February and March were the coldest they'd ever been since Philippe had come to Sherbrooke. Wind cut like a stiletto through the layers of his clothing, and the snow piled so high that he and some of his fellow seminarians were pressed into duty shoveling the many paths that connected the seminary complex. It was even cold inside, despite the new boiler's struggle to warm their drafty cells.

He wore long woolen underwear beneath his suit, and he slept with it and his socks on. It was the longest, dreariest period of his life.

Spring, when it finally came, did not fulfill its promise. It sleeted and rained, a dismal combination of elements that delayed the blossoming of the flowers and shrubs usually blooming at this time of year.

All of this did little to raise Philippe's already sagging spirits, and he continued to be plagued by feelings of guilt. He couldn't seem to reconcile himself to the events surrounding the death of his grandmother. During a conversation with Dominique, he'd deduced that Mémère had passed from this earth at about the time he'd stood listening to the music in the conservatory at Terrebonne, a glass of champagne in his hand. This bit of information simply served to add fuel to his daily regimen of self-deprecation.

He spent hours in the chapel praying, denying himself his "off" hours normally spent in recreation.

Paul tried to snap him out of it. "I can't understand your thinking, Phil. You behave as though you'd been off on a decadent fling somewhere."

"I should have been with my family, Paul. I let them down."

"Your grandmother was ill. This could have happened at any time. Get a grip on yourself, man. I'm starting to worry about you."

By the end of June, his exams somehow successfully behind him, Philippe left for a three-week vacation in Riverton.

He found his family much the same as when he'd left them last: his mother overburdened with work despite the load that Costanza carried for her; Marc excitedly planning his future; his father living somewhere on the fringes of things, seemingly oblivious to them all.

Crossing the veranda after supper one evening, Philippe tripped over Marc's legs as he sat sprawled in a chair watching the sunset. "Those things are lethal, little brother. How tall are you, anyway?"

"Six three. ... Philippe, can we talk about something?"

"Sure. What's on your mind?"

"I applied for admission to Boston University. They've accepted me."

"That's terrific, Marc! They have an excellent law school. You'll do well to have a degree from there."

His voice took on a serious tone. "Well, it's not all that cut and dried."

"Why not?"

"I don't have the money. I'll have to save for tuition and living expenses. It will take me at least a year to get started."

"Wait a minute, I'm confused."

Marc pulled himself out of a slouch and sat upright. "I can't take any money from Mama, Phil. She doesn't believe in what I'm doing."

"There must be some misunderstanding, Marc. Mother has always—"

"Let me explain," Marc interrupted. "It's basically a difference of opinion. I told her last year that I wanted to go to Boston and study law. She gave it short shrift then as she does now. She said I'd be wasting my time and her money in law school. She mentioned other opportunities here in the city. By that she means a job at Miroff and Friedman's, or clerking in Alex Friedman's office after I graduate. That was when I made up my mind to go it alone." His cheeks puffed and he blew out a stream of pent-up breath. "I don't like talking about Mother behind her back like this. She's been very good to me. I'm not forgetting that. But I don't want to give up my dreams—not without a helluva fight first. Alex has connections in Boston. He said he'd do what he could to help me find a job when I get there. Until then, I can go on working part-time in his office."

"I see." Philippe thought for a moment. "Do you want me to talk to Mama, Marc?"

"No! That's the last thing I want. I just wanted you to know where things stand, that's all. Don't worry about me, I'll make it."

"Well, I wish you all the luck in the world, and if you should change your mind, I'd be happy to talk to Mother about this."

Marc shook his head vigorously. "No, thanks. I appreciate your wanting to help, but I can handle this on my own."

There were times during his first week at home when Philippe awakened in the middle of the night with a diaphanous image of Dionne Caron imprinted before his eyes. Even after six months, she returned with regularity to his dreams. He'd lie awake for a long time, listening to the sounds of the night, then he'd rise and dress, and quietly leave the house.

In the eerie half-light before dawn, he walked the streets of Riverton before returning to have breakfast with his father.

Philippe enjoyed the walks. They gave him the solitude he needed to think clearly, as well as the perspective to be found in looking, even if briefly, into other people's lives.

As the first streaks of crimson edged over the horizon, he began encountering mill workers heading toward their jobs, dinner pails dangling from their hands, abject acceptance to their lot in life reflected in the dullness of their gaze. Life had offered them little, other than drudgery and the slow draining of their aspirations.

Returning home, he saw their children playing in the streets. Little girls with long braids, jumping rope, others playing "one potato, two potato, three potato, four." Oblivious to the hardships endured by their elders, they frolicked in the morning sunshine. Would drudgery and hopelessness be their legacy as well? Would it seep into their lives like a defective, disfiguring gene?

Turning onto Bedfordgate, Philippe heard the clanging of the streetcars, the blaring of the fishmonger's horn, the rag man begging "rags, bottles, rags." The city stretched and came to life.

He ran up Tremont Street to Sladesferry Landing. Closing the gate behind him, he went beyond the house to the garden. Squatting, he reached into the bed and lifted the leaves of a vine. The first of Papa's strawberries were ripe for the picking today.

During his final week in Riverton, Philippe felt more at

peace with himself than he had since the death of his grandmother. Returning to his roots had somehow helped put things into a healthier perspective. With the aid of his Father Confessor, he'd forced himself to admit a number of humiliating truths to himself. Although deeply saddened by Emilie's demise, it had not been at the root of his depression. His guilt and confusion had more to do with the passion that meeting Dionne Caron had aroused in him.

"We are vulnerable, Philippe. Guard against it. Never for a moment allow yourself to forget it."

* * *

Philippe went into his second year conference with Monsignor Ébert, hoping that the grueling year ahead would at the very least prove more fulfilling than the past one.

"You're looking very fit, Philippe." Monsignor smiled and gripped Philippe's hand. "Your sabbatical seems to have restored your vigor. However, before we get started I'd like to ask about your family. Is your father well?"

"His health is good, Monsignor, but he's become more and more withdrawn. He no longer takes part in family activities. He seems to have lost interest in life—except for his garden. When we are out there working side by side, he seems quite as he had been before his accident."

Father Ébert wove his fingers together and stretched them. "Perhaps with time," he suggested encouragingly, "we must pray for that to happen. Now then, I'm sure you want to get on with business. This year we are going to be giving our young gentlemen some additional challenges. We've chosen a teaching assignment for you, Philippe. A seventh-grade music class at l'Académie. I think you'll enjoy working with the boys."

"Thank you, Monsignor, I'm sure I shall."

Leaving the meeting, Philippe grinned with satisfaction. A seventh-grade music class! He couldn't have hoped for a better assignment.

***

In general the boys were spirited, sometimes unruly. Much as Philippe had been at their age. Fortunately, he was able to cope with their problems, not having forgotten how perplexing life can be at thirteen.

After classes Philippe sometimes played ball with his students, and later in the year he took them to the park on ice skating and sledding excursions. He encouraged them to ask questions and to seek his counsel during stressful times.

Easter recess found Philippe on retreat at the Dominican monastery in Ottawa. No sooner had he arrived, when he ran into Paul in the corridor. He hadn't seen much of him this year, their curriculums having taken them in different directions. Paul seemed as unflappable and as debonair as always. Except for a couple of dark circles under his eyes from burning the midnight oil, he hadn't changed at all.

"I wish we had time to talk for a while," Paul said, exasperated with the rigidity of his routine.

"So do I, but with services and the silent hours, I doubt that we will."

They walked into the great hall together for the first of the lectures, this one being given by a Redemptorist missionary, a native of the Belgian Congo.

"We'll get together later, in Sherbrooke," Paul whispered as they took their seats.

Spring slipped into summer, and the hoped-for reunion with Paul never materialized. They waved in passing and once in a while they shared a meal together. Philippe missed Paul keenly, and regretted that they were drifting apart.

Summer passed almost as swiftly as did the following year, when Philippe was chosen to assist the parish priest in Lac Bellrive. Time became so elusive that he sometimes didn't know one day from the next.

Returning to Saint Charles in September, Philippe's final year of seminary got underway. In May he would be ordained a Dominican. There seemed now an urgency to have done with preliminaries, to embrace the life for which he'd been preparing for so long. He'd cherished his years at l'Académie and Saint Charles, and the men who'd guided him through them, but he hungered to taste of the future.

Philippe barely noticed what went on outside his class-rooms, so grueling was his workload. Seasons changed and before he realized it, it was the end of April, and May loomed ahead of him like a tidal wave, poised to sweep him away.

With great discipline, he succeeded in keeping his nose firmly pressed to the grindstone right to the very end. He managed it, that is, until the evening that Father Jean arrived at his quarters unannounced, carrying a small package wrapped in brown paper.

"I have something for you, my boy. A small but significant gift. Go ahead, open it."

Philippe pulled away the wrapping, uncovering beneath it the invitations to his ordination, engraved in fine gold script.

"I'm very proud of you, Philippe." Father's voice was filled with pride. "I know what you've been through, and I couldn't love or respect you more if you were my own son. It's important to me that you know that." He stopped speaking and took Philippe's hands into his. "Pax vobiscum, my friend."

Chapter Twenty-Three

That very evening Philippe addressed and mailed the invitations to his family. Thereafter, he anxiously awaited the post each day to bring him their replies. Tante Marie-Élise's was the first to arrive.

The entire family in Le Baie will be honored to attend your ordination, including Sisters Marie-Agathe and Marie-Adèle.

He was pleasantly surprised to read the latter. It was a long trip for these elderly women to make, especially Sister Marie-Agathe, who'd been ailing most of the winter. A week later he opened his mother's letter.

My Dearest,

When I opened the envelope to find the invitation to your ordination, I felt goose bumps rise up all over me. It seems as though I've been waiting for this moment since the day you were born. I won't try to express my love and pride in this letter. I will wait until you are in my arms to do that.

Marc and I will be coming, as well as Aunt Claire, but it grieves me to tell you that your father will not. Don't be alarmed, my darling, he is quite well physically. But his mind is far from what it was the last time you were here. He is confused much of the time, so much so that I feel sure there are moments when he does not know who we are. The doctor believes that it goes back to the head injuries he suffered in the accident.

Caitlin has agreed to care for Papa while Marc and I are away. A truly unselfish sacrifice on her part, as I know she would like to have been with us. Between her and Costanza, he will have the best of care, I assure you.

I will let you know the exact date and time of our arrival in Sherbrooke. I cannot tell you what sharing this blessed moment with you means to me.

Mama

On the day of their arrival, Philippe witnessed the sunrise from a bench in the park. He'd not slept a wink all night. He sat for almost an hour listening to the birdsong and watching a fiery dawn spread itself across the horizon.

At seven o'clock he attended Mass in the chapel, then took breakfast with a number of his fellows in the refectory. Returning to his room, he nervously prepared to greet his family at the railroad station.

While dressing, he was frustrated by fingers that fumbled, and socks that twisted as he tried to put his feet into them. He felt like lashing out at these conniving thieves of his time.

Promptly at half past ten, decked out in his best, he walked through the seminary gates. He turned north, down the hill on Montmorency Street, past the great cathedral, to the terminal in the heart of the city. He arrived a good twenty minutes early.

Choosing to wait outside the building, he paced back and forth. He wished he'd asked Paul to come with him, or better yet, his uncle. *How stupid of me not to have asked Father Jean!*

At eleven-thirty, after forty-five minutes of waiting, he heard the distant rumble of the locomotive.

"Thank goodness," he uttered as he dashed through the building to the crowded platform behind it. There, a gathering of students as well as clergy milled about waiting excitedly to welcome friends and relatives.

The train pulled in slowly, grinding to a halt with a gigantic wheeze.

Philippe's heart pounded in his chest. Marc was the first one he saw. His six foot, three inch frame towered over everyone who was descending to the platform. Stepping down, Marc turned and held out his hand to assist his mother. Side-stepping and squeezing around people, Philippe hurried toward them, calling out and waving his arms above his head to attract their attention.

Marc saw him. "Philippe!" he called out.

Gradually they made their way toward each other through the crush. Melinda threw herself into her son's arms.

"Oh, my sweet boy," she whispered against his ear.

He held her closely, gently patting her shoulder, breathing in the familiar fragrance of her hair.

"Welcome to Quebec, Mama. Welcome home."

She continued holding onto him, not wanting to let go. Suddenly he felt her body quiver, and her arms dropped to her sides.

"Jean," she said as she pushed past him into her brother's embrace.

They stood for a long time, not speaking, the tall gray-haired priest weeping along with her.

Twenty-one years had passed since that bleakest of partings in the Montreal railroad station. Long, often difficult years, but here and now in this tender moment, time fell away.

Father Jean greeted Claire and shook hands with Marc, the nephew he'd never known.

"I'll get the baggage, Mama."

"Not yet, Marc," Father Jean said, "not yet, I haven't had my fill of you." Jean looked long and searchingly into the startling eyes that were so much like Melinda's. "You're your mother's son, all right! Magnificent! Simply magnificent!" he said, turning to Melinda. "I should have known that he would be."

At the Inn, the sight of Melinda's three sisters evoked an equally powerful outpouring of emotion. Time had changed them. Marie-Élise was heavier, her lush dark hair noticeably thinner and streaked with gray. Sisters Marie-Agathe and Marie-Adèle were as frail and fragile as ever, their narrow faces deeply etched with lines. But the love they'd shared had endured—unaltered by the years.

Chapter Twenty-Four

"Emitte quaesumus ..." (Send forth, we beseech ...)
[from the prayer of consecration for the Oil of the Sick]

The strains of Handel's "Largo" filled the massive Cathedral of the Sacred Heart, its incomparable beauty swelling into the huge dome high above the congregation.

The twelve ordinants gathered in a waiting room at the front of the church. Leading the procession would be the master of ceremonies, carrying a bronze crucifix, followed by Monsignor Ébert, director of the Seminary of Saint Charles. The deacons and subdeacons, resplendent in their white and gold vestments, would follow Monsignor. Behind them, twelve altar boys in red cassocks formed a vanguard to usher in the candidates, garbed in hooded robes of common homespun.

They took their places and awaited the chord that would signal the start of the procession.

Inside the church, Melinda and Marc were shown to the side altar, where Philippe would later celebrate his first Mass. They knelt on ornately gilded prie-dieux and waited for the ceremonies to begin. Marie-Élise and the Sisters, as well as Claire and Father Jean, were seated further down in the nave.

Calla lilies adorned the great altar from which His Eminence Cardinal Richard Lemieux would consecrate these twelve men into the service of Almighty God.

Without pomp, His Eminence appeared on the altar. After genuflecting before the tabernacle, he walked to the Communion rail and stood facing the congregation.

The organist let loose a resounding chord that reached into the soul of every participant. A hush fell over the gathering and the processional began.

As the young men advanced, everyone turned to look at them, much as they would have a bride coming down the aisle to be wed. Reaching the transept, they bared their heads. The altar boys and deacons took their places on the altar alongside His Eminence.

Philippe Durand was the first to prostrate himself before God and the assemblage. Rising, he knelt at the Cardinal's feet and was questioned as to his worthiness. Placing both hands upon Philippe's head, Cardinal Lemieux sang the "Emitte Quaesamus," a consecratory prayer.

Philippe was then vested with chasuble and stole, and his fingers anointed with oil. A chalice and patent were delivered into his hands, signifying his right to sing Mass. Carrying the chalice, he proceeded to the side altar followed by a deacon who would assist him in singing his first Solemn High Mass.

When all had been consecrated, the seminary choir sang out with a joyous "Alleluia" and the Masses simultaneously began.

* * *

Young Father Durand's hand shook slightly as he lifted the first Host from the chalice and presented it to his mother. One by one his family approached and stood in single file before him. In an instant all tension disappeared and was replaced by a serenity Philippe had never known before in his life.

Half-hidden behind Father Jean, who was slowly drawing away, the last of the communicants approached the altar. Dionne Caron knelt before him, her hands tightly folded at her breast, her large-brimmed hat shadowing her face. Slowly she raised her head and looked into his eyes.

Chapter Twenty-Five

The following morning Philippe awakened feeling drained. He packed his books and clothing into boxes despite the headache that threatened to waylay him. Later he went down the hallway to the "salle de bain" where he bathed and prepared himself for his appointment with Monsignor Ébert.

Back in his room, he brushed and re-brushed the coat of his new suit, picking away any traces of lint. After dressing, he appraised himself in the mirror, re-angling the brim of his hat. The Roman collar at his throat once again took him a little aback.

He walked briskly from his old quarters toward Monsignor's office in the administration building. As he went, his conversation with Paul earlier that morning ran through his mind. Paul had rushed in right in the middle of his packing.

"You'll never believe where my assignment is—*never!* Try to guess, Phil."

"Forgive me, Paul, but I'm too tense to play games. Please just tell me what it is."

"The CHANCELLERY! In Montreal! I'M THRILLED!!"

"One would never guess it," Philippe replied dryly. "Just wait until your father hears the news. I'm sure he'll be thrilled too." Philippe stopped what he was doing and extended his hand. "Joking aside, Paul, I'm very happy for you. You'll do a great job for them there. Congratulations!"

"Have you seen Ébert yet?"

"No. I have a ten-thirty appointment," Philippe answered, looking at his watch, "and I'd better start getting ready."

Philippe had sincerely meant what he'd said to Paul ear-

211

lier. He was a brilliant accountant. Combined with his savoir-faire, he was perfect for the chancellery. Paul would have been bored to death in some dinky parish counting up the weekly dole.

Running up the stairs to the second floor of the building, Philippe walked directly into the reception room of Monsignor's suite of offices. Two Brothers sat working at their duties. Philippe coughed to get their attention.

"Father Durand ... your timing is perfect. Monsignor will see you right away." Rising, Brother Julien ushered Philippe inside.

"Good morning, Father." Monsignor's voice was as robust as ever. "Please take a chair," he added, indicating the one facing him across the desk. Reseating himself, he clasped his hands across his middle, and began. "I know how anxious you are to learn of your assignment, Father, and I won't keep you waiting. Let me preface what I am about to say by telling you that this has not been my decision. It is a collective decision. We try very hard to place our priests where they will be most effective." He turned his head aside and coughed. "Now then, we have found you to be skilled in many areas, Father, but your most outstanding work has been with Father Sebastian. Your music. He speaks very highly of your talents, and since we have been searching for someone qualified to assist him, we have decided to be selfish and keep you here at Saint Charles. Does this please you, Father?"

"Yes, of course, Monsignor."

"Your tone seems a bit resigned. I hope we haven't disappointed you."

"I'm sorry, I didn't mean it to be. I've liked working with Father Sebastian and the boys."

"Good. Well then, I won't keep you a moment longer. Get on with your holiday, Father. You do indeed deserve it. We'll look forward to seeing you in two weeks' time."

* * *

Still in the grip of the crestfallen mood he'd felt since leaving Monsignor's office, Philippe knocked at the door of his mother's room at the Inn. His wasn't a bad assignment. Indeed, it was quite flattering to be kept on to teach at l'Académie. But he'd have preferred to have gone to a parish. Teaching was fulfilling, to be sure, but he'd never thought of it in terms of being his life's work.

"Good morning, Mama." He greeted Melinda with a kiss and held her to him for a moment "I see you're about ready to leave," he remarked, looking past her at the suitcase on the floor next to the bed.

"In a little while. I was hoping we'd have a few minutes to talk."

Philippe looked at his watch. "The train to Le Baie doesn't leave for an hour."

"Tired?"

"Yes."

"That's not surprising. You've been keyed up for so long. You'll get some rest at Les Érables. Do you feel like talking?"

"Of course, Mama. Let's sit down."

Melinda said, "I've been thinking about Marc ever since he and Aunt Claire left this morning. He'll begin his second year at the university this September. Time passes so quickly, doesn't it?" Melinda shook her head, not really expecting an answer.

"I was disappointed he wasn't staying longer," Philippe said. "I wish I could have spent more time with him."

"He had to get back to Boston. He's working for that law firm again this summer, Klein, Klein and Adamson—Alex's doing. Marc's earning his own way through school, Philippe."

"I know, we've been corresponding."

"I've tried to be fair with him, but we've had a difficult time agreeing about his studying law. I guess some of the options I've suggested have offended him. No—more than that—insulted might be a better way of putting it. Ever since then, he's flatly refused to accept any financial assistance from me. Frankly, I feel more than a little guilty about how I've handled things. Has he mentioned any of this to you?"

"Yes, we've talked about it."

"What did he say, if that's not betraying a confidence."

"Just that, since you didn't approve of his choices, he wanted to go it alone."

The distress in her eyes deepened. "I feel awful about this. I really thought it was just a whim. He adores Alex and I thought ... hero worship. Well, I was mistaken, and it seems he will not forgive me for it."

"Don't take him so seriously, Mother. It won't hurt Marc to get along on his own. If he needs help, I'm sure he'll come to you for it."

"I hope you're right. I'm probably overreacting at this point."

Philippe looked at his watch again. "We'd better be going." Picking up his mother's bag, Philippe walked to the door. Holding it open for her, he added, "Don't worry, Mama, it's all right. Marc knows how much you love him. That's what matters in the long run."

* * *

Marc

Boston, 1908.

A year previous, when Marc Durand went to Boston to study at the university, he'd instantly fallen in love with the city. It wasn't just the school that excited him, it was the pulsating everyday life of the place that he found so fascinating. It had an energy uniquely its own, like no other anywhere.

At first, getting around in Back Bay was more than a little challenging. It sometimes seemed to Marc as if he were running around in circles. Streets crisscrossed confusingly and their names changed, often without warning of any kind. Several times when he'd struck out on his own, he'd finished up by getting lost. He'd soon learned it didn't pay to stray too far from his own neck of the woods.

Considering what he was able to afford, he'd been very fortunate in finding good lodgings. Mrs. Hinton's was one of the best boarding houses on the south side of town. Hers was a pleasant home, and immaculately kept. She charged a slight bit more than the others he'd looked at, but she cooked well and would do the odd bit of laundry for him from time to time.

"Pegeen," as she was known to her friends, was a friendly woman with a ready smile and a gentle, motherly manner.

"It wasn't an easy time, mind you, but with the good Lord's help, I managed to raise them," she'd said of her three children the morning Marc met her. "Grown and gone now, except for Catherine," her youngest and only daughter. "She was barely eight when my Dennis was taken. Ten years since. My, how the time does pass."

Catherine was a tall, striking girl who worked as a nanny during the week for a well-to-do family on Beacon Hill. She wore her wavy auburn hair drawn back neatly into a thick braid that she wrapped around her head at least twice. Luminous jade-green eyes (bordered by dark, sweeping lashes with just a glint of copper at the tips) looked out at the world from under thin, arching brows. There was something very special about Catherine, Marc realized the very first time he saw her.

On weekends, she sometimes went off with Arthur Jameson, another of Pegeen's boarders, and more and more as time passed, Marc found himself wishing that it was his arm that Catherine Hinton was holding onto on a Saturday night.

Having attended a Catholic boys' institution all during his high school years, there'd been little opportunity for Marc to meet girls before coming to Boston. He'd gone to one or two of the high school socials every year, but these were strictly chaperoned affairs, where dancing twice with the same girl was frowned upon. What with a part-time job in the summer and chores to attend to at home, there was never any time to get to know a girl well enough to ask her out for an evening. Little had changed along those lines since his arrival in Boston.

Just before semester break last autumn, he'd attended a performance of the symphony with Jeremy Hill, another student who roomed with Mrs. Hinton. Sitting in the great concert hall listening to the sound of the orchestra playing Wagner's "Overture to Tannhäuser" was an experience like none Marc had ever known. Unfortunately he only rarely indulged in such pleasures.

When the walls of his room began closing in on him, Marc would sometimes walk to the Fenway. He'd sit on one of the benches outside the conservatory where he could hear the music students at work. Music made him feel things, special things, and it was during those times that he'd again dream of courting the beguiling Miss Hinton.

Brief respites such as those made sticking to his rigid schedule more bearable when December gales rattled his windowpanes and bleak winter settled in for a four-month stay. He'd sit cross-legged on his bed and work far into the night. His grades were always above average; they had to be if he were ever to obtain scholarship money for law school.

* * *

On Easter Sunday of that first spring, Catherine donned her finery, and she and her mother walked the five blocks to attend services at their neighborhood church. The weather was unusually fair, feeling more like a morning in June than April. Marc stood looking at them from the window of his room until they were out of sight.

Never had he seen anything more fetching than Miss Catherine in her bright green dress and matching Easter bonnet. Tiny daisies adorned the brim and a cluster of white satin ribbons fell at the back, all the way down to her shoulders. They bobbed every which way as she walked, and the fabric of her ankle-length dress clung provocatively to her lithe, long-waisted torso. As he watched, a wave of desire

216

suddenly spread through his body.

Marc forced himself back to his studies, but after an hour and a number of useless attempts at concentration, he quit his room in favor of the narrow stretch of yard between the houses. Sitting in the grass with his eyes closed, he savored the warmth of the sun upon his back.

As usual, it was quiet around the Hinton house on Sunday.

"You'll have the place to yourselves, you and the other boys," Pegeen had informed him on the day he'd leased his room. "I visit with Bryan or David every Sunday after nine o'clock Mass. But be on your best behavior, young man, for I'll not abide any shenanigans."

More often than not, Catherine accompanied her mother, especially on a holiday such as Easter. Consequently, it surprised Marc to see her crossing the lawn toward him.

"Happy Easter!" she called out.

"Thank you! Happy Easter to you! I thought you'd be at your brother's for the day." Marc scrambled to his feet.

"I should be, I know. But sometimes the little ones—well, I'm with children so much during the week."

"Of course."

"Please don't misunderstand, Marc. I love children, and Bryan's are grand to be with. It's just that today I wanted to do something else," she confessed, lowering herself slowly to the ground. "Like a summer morning, isn't it, Marc?" she said, looking into the cloudless sky. "Seems like I wait all winter for this. I get so restless I can hardly wait for the flowers to start."

He sat next to her, watching as she fingered a blade of grass. His question had been personal—perhaps too personal—and he wished he hadn't asked it.

He was about to apologize when she spoke: "I don't see Arthur anymore."

"Oh? I'm sorry, I thought ... well ... you were together a lot this winter." He felt stupid and bumbling, and didn't know what else to say.

"No reason to be sorry, Marc. Not for him, nor for me. It

was never anything special. We liked each other well enough, but mostly ... we're friends, that's all." She stopped and turned to look at him.

"What is it, Catherine? You seem to have something on your mind."

After another pause, she said, "Marc. May I ask you a question?"

"Of course."

Her eyes held his for a long moment, then turned aside. "Oh ... maybe I shouldn't."

"Please, Catherine, don't do that to me. ... Go on with what you were saying."

She gave him that same intense stare. "Tell me whether or not I'm wrong, Marc, but I've had the strongest feeling that you've wanted to ask me out. Been right on the verge of it, so to speak, then for some reason or other, you'd change your mind. Was I mistaken in thinking that?"

The question surprised him. He'd not thought of Catherine as a girl who'd "go after a man."

"No, you're not mistaken," Marc admitted. "I've thought of asking you out. What guy in his right mind wouldn't? There are a couple of reasons why I haven't, and I'm sure you know what one of them is."

"Arthur."

"Arthur. He's not just a friend, Cathy. I happen to know he's crazy about you."

"Well, I don't feel the same and never have done. What's the other reason?"

"Money."

"Oh," she replied, a little embarrassed by his candor. She pondered for a moment, then went on. "Having a date doesn't have to cost much. Walking, for instance, or going on a picnic to the beach—only a bit of carfare."

"Yes, I know," Marc interrupted, "but some girls might feel that was cheap."

"Well I wouldn't! I think it would be fun. Could we do that sometime, Marc?" Catherine's aggressive approach continued to dismay him.

"Sure we can ... if you'd like to."

Glimmers of light shot from her eyes, betraying the excitement building inside her. "When?" she asked, pursuing the subject quite shamelessly.

"I don't know ... when I have time. Between my studies and my job there isn't very much." His words sounded cavalier, but he hadn't intended them to.

Catherine rose, brushing bits of grass from her dress, looking somewhat rejected.

Marc rose too, and stood next to her. Leaning close to her ear, he whispered, "Like today, for instance."

Her smile reappeared instantly. "Do you mean it?"

"Yes, I'd like to get away for a couple hours."

"Well then, we'll have a picnic, an Easter picnic!" she shouted, as she ran toward the house. Turning as she reached the door, she said, "I'll be ready to leave in ... twenty minutes." Her voice trailed off as she disappeared through the kitchen door.

After cutting several slices from Saturday's roast for sandwiches, Catherine put a few eggs on to boil. Then choosing two apples out of the fruit bowl, she polished them with a tea towel. She dashed upstairs, her heart beating like a trip-hammer, and changed into her white lawn dress. Pulling an orange grosgrain ribbon from her dresser drawer, she wrapped it around her waist. She undid her braid and brushed out her hair, fluffing it loosely around her shoulders. The sunlight coming through the bedroom window sent titian darts sparkling throughout the undulating mass.

Moistening her lips with her tongue, she reached for her sweater, then glanced one last time in the mirror before fetching the picnic basket down from the attic.

Conversation flowed easily as they rode the trolley down to the waterfront, to Catherine's favorite picnic spot on Gullwing Beach.

Despite it being early in the season, a good smattering of people were enjoying the spring-like day, walking or merely looking out across the harbor from the vantage point of the pier. Marc and Cathy chose to sit next to the seawall where they were sheltered from the still cool breeze.

"I love this place," Catherine said breathlessly, looking out at the pounding surf. "The sea is so haunting. Listen to it with your eyes closed for a minute."

"Yes it is. Now open your eyes and look way out there beyond the horizon. Can you see Ireland, Catherine?"

"Sure and begorrah I can," she said with a laugh.

"If you could walk across the water, would you want to go there and live?"

"Oh no! I love it here in this beautiful country. I'm truly proud to have been born in America. My dad used to tell me stories about Ireland when I was a little girl. Sad stories about the famine and the war, neighbor killing neighbor. He told me that America was the greatest country in the world, and never to forget it. He sold everything they owned to get them here." She shook her head sadly, trying to imagine the hardships. "Bryan was just a tot when they left, and Davey, a wee one in arms still sucklin'. No, I don't want to live anywhere other than here. Do you?"

"I don't think so. Tell me, do you come to this beach very often?"

"Oh yes, I do. I even come in winter. I walk the shore when there's snow on the sand. It's here I do my best thinking."

"What do you think about?"

"Oh, lots of things. I think about my dad. More and more as the years pass, he's becoming a blur. I still dream of him now and then, but he's always looking the other way. Mama has a picture of him on her vanity, but it's getting old and faded. I hope I don't forget what he looked like." Then, another thought leapt into her mind, a happier thought. "He had red hair and green eyes like mine, you know." She seemed quite child-like when she spoke of her father, and even now, so many years after he'd gone, Marc could sense how much she still missed him.

"What else do you think of, besides your father."

"Just silly stuff, I suppose. I wonder about my life and what will happen to me."

"I don't think that's silly. Everyone wonders about their future. I know I do, a lot."

A furrow marred the smoothness of her brow. "You're very ambitious, aren't you, Marc?"

He thought, *God—she keeps throwing these curves at me!* He waited a moment before answering. "I guess you could say that. I've set certain goals I would like to reach in my lifetime." He didn't elaborate further.

"Well, you're on the right track, I'd say. The law is a good profession for an ambitious man. It gives you a lot of choices, a lot of directions to go in."

Marc wondered what had happened to the little girl he'd been talking to just a few moments ago. "That's what Mr. Klein thinks. He's my boss, and a darned good attorney. One of his sons is running for mayor of Quincy. I hope he makes it, but I doubt that he will."

"Why not?"

"He's a Jew. A Jew doesn't have much of a chance of being elected to office around here. He knows that, I'm sure. But if nothing else, he's making his name known to the big-wigs, and that might mean something further on down the road."

"Is that what you want, Marc?"

"What?"

"To become mayor or governor someday?" She didn't smile. She was in deadly earnest.

He laughed aloud; he couldn't help himself. "WHOA! I have a lot of ground to cover before thinking of anything quite so lofty as that. Right now it's study, and work, and one day at a time."

As they walked hand in hand down to the pier and beyond it to the grassy dunes, Marc curled his fingers around hers. Stooping every now and then, Catherine picked up seashells and put them in her pocket. Later they playfully raced each other back to the seawall. She was captivating. One moment child-like, the other, seductive; the next, a tomboy he could race with.

Catherine opened the picnic basket and spread out the cloth. They sat side by side peeling their eggs and enjoying their roast beef sandwiches.

"I'm ravenous," Marc admitted. Then he asked, "Why does everything taste so much better here?"

"I call it beach hunger. I'm never this hungry anywhere else."

They walked again after they'd finished, barefoot this time, braving the cold, wet sand left by the receding tide. Chilled, they returned to the seawall and sat close to each other, talking quietly as the afternoon passed into evening.

Noticing that almost everyone had gone and the beach was now nearly deserted, Marc wondered aloud: "Shouldn't I be getting you home?"

"Not unless you have to study."

"Won't your mother be worried about you?"

"My mother doesn't get in until bedtime on Sundays." She waited for him to comment one way or the other. When he didn't, she reached across him for the picnic basket.

Marc took hold of her arm and pulled her to him. "Not yet. ... I could stay here with you forever." His voice was deep and husky. He lay down on his back and looked up at the darkening sky.

Catherine lay down next to him.

He moved nearer to her, his thigh almost touching hers. Turning on his side, he propped his head on his hand and whispered, "You're so beautiful, Catherine."

Her eyes searched his face. "You're the one who's beautiful, Marc. I've never seen anyone more beautiful than you."

"Men aren't beautiful."

"Of course they are. My dad was beautiful, but not so much as you."

"I'd like to kiss you, Catherine," he heard himself saying.

"I'd like that too." There was no hesitation, no coyness in her reply.

Lowering his head, his full lips parted slightly, brushing hers lightly, once, twice, three times. Then his mouth pressed down on hers, gently at first, then harder, more passionately.

Releasing her, he said, "We'd best be going."

In the privacy of Mrs. Hinton's yard, Marc kissed her once again, holding her to him, his long, slender fingers caressing her shoulders. His head was spinning. Everything was happening so fast.

The warm spell continued. Despite trying hard, there was little accomplished in the way of study for the next few days. Marc couldn't stop thinking about the sweetness of Catherine's lips under his, or the velvety feel of her skin. When he heard her laughter from his open window, he wanted so much to go down to the veranda and sit on the glider next to her. To smell the fragrance of her, to touch her. But he resisted the impulse. He needed time to think about this.

* * *

Upon his return from his brother's ordination in May, Marc realized just how much he'd missed Catherine during the time he'd been away. He couldn't wait to hold her close, to feel her in his arms again.

If it were possible, she came to mean more to him each time they were together. She was sweet, and responsive, and seemed intuitively to sense his every need. They explored each other's hearts, learning things, private things ... things that lovers shared.

Marc discovered that they had a common interest in politics, something he would never have suspected. She listened intently as he read editorials to her from the Sunday edition of *The Herald*, while dangling her feet in the lagoon of the Public Gardens.

He enjoyed going into the city with Catherine. She so loved watching the gentry as they walked up Beacon Hill of a Sunday noon on their way home from worship at Christ Episcopal Church. Later in the day she and Marc would catch the streetcar to Duffy's down on the beach for a bowl of hot chowder. He lived for the hours when they were to-gether, when everything but Catherine faded into oblivion. She had become the most important thing in his life.

Chapter Twenty-Six

While en route back to Sherbrooke after visiting his family in Riverton, Father Philippe Durand arranged to meet with his brother in Boston during a two-hour layover between trains. They found each other despite the throngs crowding the steamy little lunchroom across the street from the station.

Being with Philippe wasn't the same anymore. The priestly garb somehow precluded any discussion of Marc's romance with Catherine, which was ever in the forefront of his mind. It seemed tasteless somehow to talk to a celibate about women. He even had difficulty knowing how to address his brother. "Father Philippe" sounded strange, and just plain Phil, somewhat irreverent under the circumstances. Thus, he avoided calling him anything at all.

"Mama tells me you're working for a very prestigious firm, Marc."

"Yes. I didn't realize quite how important K, K & A were until I landed the job last summer. I'm glad I didn't—I would have been scared to death."

"Mama's concerned about you. She thinks that you're carrying too big a load. Don't you think you and she should talk things over again?"

"No, I don't. We understand each other perfectly."

"I don't think you do, but I won't debate the point. I hear there's a young lady in your life these days. Anything serious?"

"How did you know about that?" The idea of disclosing anything about his relationship to Catherine made him cringe inside.

"I have my spies on you, little brother," Philippe teased.

"It has to be Caitlin. She's the only one down there I've told about Catherine. I hope she isn't blabbing it all over the place."

"She isn't. Don't be so defensive."

"Sorry. How do you like teaching?" Marc asked, anxiously hoping to change the subject.

"It's all right. I'll know more about it after classes begin in September. Come on, Marc, tell me about her."

"There isn't anything to tell. Her name is Catherine Hinton, and she's the daughter of my landlady." He rolled his eyes. "It isn't anything serious. We just go out once in a while." *Rats! Why do I feel as though I'm under a microscope?*

Philippe patted him gently on the shoulder and went on to speak of other things—impersonal, unimportant things. After an hour he picked up his bag and prepared to leave. "Get down to see Papa if you can, Marc. He misses you."

"Papa thinks I'm ten years old."

"I know, but he misses you all the same."

* * *

For two weeks in August, Leon Klein closed his offices and joined his family summering on the North Shore. Marc decided it would be a good time to spend a few days in Riverton with his parents. Not that Philippe's remark had laid any guilt on him, mind you. Until last year he'd always been there for them, which was more than his brother could ever say.

He arrived in town feeling a bit hollow at the thought of not seeing Catherine for a while, and depressed at the prospect of finding his father more "out of it" than the last time he'd seen him.

Before going upstairs, he stood at Caitie's door and called out, "Anybody home?"

Instantly he heard her heavy tread as she came from the kitchen.

"Well, if it isn't my darlin' come home to visit! Come in,

226

love, come sit for a spell."

"What smells so good?" he asked as she released him from a bone-crushing hug.

"I'm puttin' up some tomatoes. Now then, let me get you a glass of lemonade. It won't take but a minute."

"I can't stay, Cait, I have to get upstairs."

"Well now, ye don't either. Costanza was just after leaving ten minutes ago. Your Papa is sound asleep. He naps every afternoon around this time."

"All right, lemonade sounds good."

She ran to the ice chest and poured each of them a glass. "Come sit in the parlor, love," Caitlin suggested," it's hot from the cookin' in here. Now then, tell me everything. I want to know what's going on up there in Boston."

"There's nothing much to tell. I'm working at Klein, Klein and Adamson's full-time this summer. That's why I had to leave Sherbrooke right after Philippe's ordination. In a couple of weeks I'll register for my sophomore year. I hope I have enough money saved to pay for my tuition and books."

"Then what?"

"Then I work part-time at the law office and carry a full schedule at the university."

"Gracious, it does sound a lot for a young lad to do."

"It is a lot. Sometimes I think Mama was right. Maybe I should just get a job and get married."

"Married?" Caitlin raised her hands to her cheeks. "Land sakes, you're just a baby!"

Marc looked away, his jaw tightening a little.

"Tell me about your Catherine."

"She may never be *my* Catherine, Caitie. I have nothing to offer her, and I'm not sure she'd be willing to wait until I do."

"Well then, she's not the sort I'd be choosin' if I were you."

"You don't understand, Cait."

"Oh, I'm not so old as all that, love."

"Look ... uh ... I've gotta go."

227

"It's real good to see you, Marc. If you've a mind to, bring your Pa and yourself down to breakfast in the morning."

* * *

The door to their apartment was slightly ajar. Quietly tiptoeing past, Marc glanced into his father's bedroom, only to find that he wasn't there.

"Papa? Papa, where are you?" he called out. When there was no response, he hurried from one room to the next, then down the stairs to Caitlin's again.

"My father's not in his room, Caitie. I've checked everywhere. He's gone," he informed her, wringing his hands, his heart thudding a mile a minute. "Does Costanza always leave him alone like this?"

"Now don't ye be frettin', darlin'. Have ye looked out back in his plot? He never goes very far anymore." Pushing aside the curtain, she peered out, with Marc looking over her shoulder. "I don't see a soul out there, do you?" she asked, an anxious falsetto creeping into her voice. "Sure and he must have decided to go to the park after all. Run over there, love. I'll have a look 'round the neighborhood."

Joseph wasn't sitting near the fountain, nor was he watching the boys on the baseball diamond. Marc's heart beat faster and faster as panic mounted. Running up the hill to the upper level near the picnic grounds, he searched the area thoroughly. Just as he was about to look elsewhere, he spotted Joseph sitting on a bench at the far side of a small grove of pines. He broke out in a sweat as relief washed over him, giving way, in a moment more, to anger.

Joseph wasn't alone. Sitting on the bench alongside him was a man Marc didn't recognize. The stranger rose and hurried away as Marc approached. Joseph stood, looking after him with a bewildered expression on his face.

Marc's tone of voice was as if he were talking to a child. "Papa! What are you doing here? Who was that person you were talking to?"

Joseph looked at him with a smoldering rage in his eyes. "He's my friend," he answered through clenched teeth, still staring in the direction the man had taken.

"I know he's your friend, Pa, but what's his name? Why did he leave like that?"

"I don't know what his name is. I can't remember!" he snapped. "You scared him away. He won't come back anymore." Joseph began to cry.

All of Marc's anger dissipated as he recognized, perhaps fully for the first time, what a pathetically lonely person his father had become. He took him gently by the arm.

"I'm sorry, Papa. Let's go home now."

After Joseph had gone to bed for the night, Marc mentioned the incident to his mother.

"So there is someone!" she exclaimed. "He's talked about seeing a man—a friend—but I thought ... well frankly I thought it a figment of his imagination. I wonder who it could be? What did this man look like, Marc?"

"I didn't get a good look at him. He's a lot younger than Pa, and a lot bigger."

Marc walked to the bedroom door and looked in on Joseph. He seemed to be sleeping soundly. Closing the door again, he said, "Let's go into the kitchen. I don't want him to hear us talking about him."

Sitting across the table from his mother, Marc spoke in a hushed voice. "For some reason, this man is very important to Papa, and I'm more than a little uneasy about how he ran off when he saw me coming. In the future, Costanza must watch him more carefully, Mama."

Costanza was alerted to the problem and thereafter, whenever Joseph left the flat she followed him. Without fail he'd turn and go to the tool shed, his new "friend" seemingly forgotten—another victim of Joseph's ever diminishing memory. After several days of this, everyone heaved a sigh of relief, and Costanza took to leaving again as soon as Joseph went to lie down for his nap.

* * *

Less than an hour after Marc left for Boston on Friday, Caitlin threw open her kitchen window to hang a few things from the pulley line. Her attention was immediately drawn to Joseph standing next to the fence behind the tool shed. He was talking to a man she didn't recall seeing before.

The stranger was thin, and there was the look of the destitute about him. Her curiosity getting the better of her, she slipped out through the cellar door and stood close to the corner of the house, listening. She heard a muffle of words, then Joseph laughed—something he rarely did anymore. The man reached over the fence and shook Joseph's hand. Then he left, crossing the neighboring yards down to Sladesferry Landing. Joseph stood looking after him until he was gone from sight.

After a few minutes, Caitlin went and stood by his side. "Good day to ye, Joseph. I see ye've had a visitor."

He turned to her, a smile on his lips. Without saying a word, he walked past her toward the house. Upon reaching the walk, he stopped abruptly, turning to look at her once more.

"He liked my garden," he called back. After taking a few more steps, he stopped again. His eyes crinkled and he smiled broadly." I remember now, I remember his name. His name is Victor." Grasping the doorknob, Joseph went inside.

Caitlin listened for the upstairs door to close behind him.

Poor old fella, she thought, shaking her head from side to side. *Now, where's the harm, I ask ye.*

* * *

Catherine jumped up when she heard the doorbell jangle. She'd been in Marc's room lying on his bed, daydreaming. She'd done this routinely while he was away in Riverton.

Pulling Marc's sweater up over her head, she folded it neatly and placed it on the bureau before rushing downstairs. Reaching the last of the steps, she could see, through the nar-

230

row glass panel at the side of the door, Marc putting his key into the lock. He entered before she had time to reach for the knob.

Her long, slender arms wound around his neck as he drew her into his arms.

"Never leave me again," she begged him, her voice breaking, her breath leaving sensual little tingles across the side of his neck.

He could not speak, the sight of her having taken all logical thought away. His lips sought and found hers, and he felt a passion beyond any he'd ever felt before.

"Don't let go, darling. Don't ever, ever let go," Catherine murmured.

He pressed her to him tighter still, burying his face in her hair. All of the tension fell away. All of the turmoil and anxiety he'd accumulated in Riverton disappeared as he let himself sink into the warmth of her love.

Chapter Twenty-Seven

Marc tore the month of August off the calendar on his desk at K, K & A. Things had piled up during his ten-day visit in Riverton. Several new briefs had to be drawn up, and a number of other documents awaited his attention.

Glancing across the room at Alicia Blackmann's meticulously organized desk, he wondered how she managed to always keep on top of things. Soon after, he heard the clicking of her heels against the hardwood floor as she walked down the hall from Leon Klein's office.

Seeing him, she raised her hand in greeting. "Hello there, young man. Welcome back to the salt mines."

Alicia Blackmann had been managing this office for the better part of twenty years. She was petite and svelte for her age, which office gossip had determined to be about forty. She was known in the building as the "Iron Maiden."

Marc sometimes wondered why she hadn't married, since she was far more attractive than average. He'd allowed himself several flights of fancy on that subject, envisioning her as Leon Klein's secret paramour who'd sacrificed hearth and home with some other man for one night a week in the boss's arms in one of the downtown hotels.

Alicia lived with her mother in Brighton in an old Colonial house, and never to Marc's knowledge had she mentioned having a date or any gentlemen friends.

"How was your vacation, Marc?" she asked without looking up.

"Fine, Alicia. ... How was yours?"

"Short. Oh—I almost forgot. Mr. Klein asked to see you the minute you got in."

The muscles in Marc's abdomen knotted together and a flurry of "what ifs" ran through his mind.

Walking down the hall, he prayed he would still have a job when he walked back to his desk. Taking a deep breath, he knocked on the door of the "Sactum Sanctorum," the office crew's name for Leon Klein's elegant suite of offices.

Klein smiled as Marc entered. "Marc! It's good to see you, my boy. Come in!"

"Good morning, sir," he replied, shaking the hand of his employer.

"Please sit down, Marc. I have something important to discuss with you."

A strange sensation spread across the back of Marc's calves as Leon Klein reached for a folder that lay atop a pile on his blotter. "This, young man, has to do with you." He held up the folder and shook it firmly. "And I know you'll be as happy about it as I am."

Marc couldn't imagine what the hell he was talking about.

"A few days ago, a legal representative came to this office on behalf of a client whose identity I cannot divulge. The purpose of the visit was to engage this firm to handle an extraordinary transaction." He stopped and looked steadily at Marc. "Now, hang onto your britches! This person wishes to underwrite all of your college expenses, through to the successful completion of your law degree."

Marc sat facing him like a piece of petrified wood.

"I'm sorry I can't tell you more about this," Klein said, "and you must have a million questions. But it is the wish of the client that he remain anonymous." Noting Marc's stunned expression, Leon added, "I know this comes as a shock to you. It rather shocked me at first."

"I don't understand, Mr. Klein. Why would anyone want to do this for me?"

"I can't answer that, Marc, but these are the facts. And let me add that this is not a loan, it is a gift."

A wry smile slowly covered Marc's lips. "This anonymous client couldn't possibly be my mother, could it, Mr. Klein?"

"No, Marc, I assure you it isn't. There is no family connection of any kind here."

"Well then, why? Why would anyone give a damn about me?"

Klein shrugged his shoulders. "I can't answer that either, except to say that this person is interested in helping a conscientious student, and rather than give the money to the school toward a scholarship fund, prefers to do it himself." He got up and came around the desk, resting his hand on Marc's shoulder. "I can see this is difficult for you to cope with. Why don't you go home and think it over for a few hours. We can talk about it again tomorrow. I do want to assure you that it is all very legal and above board. I personally think you're a very fortunate young fellow."

Back at the boarding house Marc kept hearing Mr. Klein's voice over and over again, and the same bewildering question returned to his mind: *Why me? Why Marc Durand? This is absurd. ... There must be some mistake!*

The secrecy involved bothered Marc. If he could have shaken this man's hand and thanked him face to face, it might have made some sense.

Later that evening he went over the whole bizarre episode with Catherine.

"I think it's wonderful, Marc! You must be thrilled!"

"THRILLED? Catherine? I can't accept this!"

"Not accept? Why, you'd be a fool not to."

"Think about it a minute, sweetheart. ... Try to understand how I feel."

"Well, I understand one thing, Marc. If you don't take it, someone else will and you'll be the loser."

Marc awakened a dozen times that night tossing and turning, only to fall again into a restless, nightmarish sleep. In his dream he saw Catherine standing at the end of a long passageway. He hurried to reach her, but no matter how fast he ran, the distance between them remained the same. Then people began crowding between them. He pushed and shoved trying to make his way past them. He heard her laugh, and then he stood before her looking into her eyes. She no longer laughed. Instead, her lips curled with contempt as she repeated the words, "You're such a fool, Marc."

He opened his eyes and saw light filtering through the window shade. He lay for a long time looking up at the ceiling, feeling more tired than when he'd gone to bed the night before.

"She's right," he said aloud, "I'd be a damned fool not to take it."

He rose to face his day.

With many misgivings yet unresolved, Marc went to Mr. Klein and accepted the endowment. But even as he stood there receiving his instructions, he half-expected his employer to tell him it had all been a regrettable error.

"I'd like to stay with my job for a while, sir, if that's at all possible. I'd prefer to take only a minimum of assistance. Tuition and books. ... I can pay for my personal expenses myself."

"I'm sure that can be arranged, Marc, and we'd be happy to have you stay on with us for as long as you like. You've been a valuable addition to our staff."

After a while Marc stopped thinking about the endowment every waking moment, as he had in the beginning.

But every now and then he probed his mind for clues. Alex Friedman was a good possibility. He'd always treated him like the son he'd wanted and never had.

Another was Sam Miroff! They'd talked often of his ambition to become a lawyer when he was working at the factory during his high school years. Good men, both with the wherewithal to do such a thing.

On the other hand, it didn't make a lot of sense. Most assuredly, they would have taken him aside and discussed it with him. Neither Sam nor Alex was the type to go in for this cloak-and-dagger stuff.

As time passed Marc gave up trying to figure it out.

The three pin oaks on Massachusetts Avenue where K, K & A. had its offices gradually turned a fiery red as another autumn settled over New England.

Marc stood mesmerized by the trees when a striking young woman entered the reception room. She looked his way briefly, with lively ink-black eyes, then went directly to Alicia's desk.

"I don't want to interrupt anything, but I would like to see Mr. Klein if he has a free moment. I'm an old friend who'd like to say hello."

"May I tell him who's calling, please?" Alicia asked in her best "maybe yes, maybe no" tone.

"Just tell him it's Sarah Miroff," she answered, seating herself to wait in the chair next to Alicia's desk.

Marc looked across the room at her, and she soon became aware of his gaze.

"Is anything wrong?" she asked, staring right back at him.

"No, no! Aah ... please forgive me, but I think I know you. Or I did, a long time ago. Aren't you Sam Miroff's daughter?"

"That I am. And who might you be?"

"I'm Marc Durand. I'm sure you don't remember me, but—"

"You're ... Marc ... Durand? *Little* Marc Durand?"

"That's right." He chuckled, rising to show off his full six feet, three inches of height.

"My, but you clean up nice. The last time I saw you, you were sitting in the backyard making mud pies. You must have been all of five."

They both laughed, and Marc noticed how white and even her teeth were.

"How wonderful to see you again, Marc. What are you doing here in Leon's office?"

"I work here part-time. I'm a student at the university. What brings you to Boston, Sarah?"

"Well, I guess you could say that I'm a student too. I've just enrolled at Amery, a school of design a couple of blocks from here."

Alicia appeared and interrupted them. "He'll see you now, Miss Miroff."

"Talk to you later, Marc," Sarah called back as she followed the receptionist down the hall into Mr. Klein's office. After about fifteen minutes, she came out and walked over to his desk.

"I can't tell you how much fun it's been seeing you, Marc. I wish we had more time to reminisce, but I have an appointment at Amery in ten minutes," she explained, putting out her hand.

He took it into his. "It's been fun for me too, Sarah." Rising, Marc walked around his desk and helped her on with her coat.

"Thank you," she said as she plunged her arms through the sleeves.

Sarah walked out and closed the door behind her. Soon it opened again and she stood in front of Marc's desk, grinning.

"Forget something?" he asked.

She shook her head. "I was just wondering if maybe we couldn't get together and talk over old times?"

"I'd like that very much."

Taking a pad from her purse, she scribbled down her address. "How about a week from tonight? Are you free for dinner?"

"I think so ... yes."

"Good, I'll see you then."

Laying the paper down on his desk, she hurried out the door. Marc rose again and ran down the hall after her. "Hey ... what time?"

She stopped and turned toward him. "I'm sorry, Marc. Anytime after four."

* * *

It was easy to see that Sam's Miroff's daughter had all of the good things in life. Her chic apartment house was nestled among the better buildings just west of the Commons. Marc took the elevator to the third floor. Finding her place at the end of the hall, he removed his raincoat before knocking.

A fire burned in the fireplace of the intimate room furnished with an elegance that reflected its occupant's impeccable taste.

A silk charmeuse blouse in a deep shade of peach complemented the olive tones of Sarah's skin. A black velveteen skirt hugged her narrow hips and flowed in widening gores to below her calves. She wore no jewelry except for a cameo at her throat and Natia's antique silver combs in her hair. In the candlelight she was a delectable sight to behold.

"I hope I'm not too early," Marc remarked timidly.

"Not at all. Your timing is perfect. And please, Marc, call me, Sari."

"Sari—I like that. It suits you."

"It should. Sam has called me that ever since I was a baby. He likes nicknames. He thinks they're very American. ... Can I offer you a glass of wine?" she asked, walking to a round table set for two in the center of the living room.

"Thanks." His eyes followed her in the candlelight.

She was short, perhaps one or two inches above five feet, but with her jet-black hair piled in a mass of ringlets at the top of her head, she gave the illusion of being taller.

Filling two glasses, she handed him one. "To you, Marc," she toasted.

He lifted his glass and touched hers. "To you, Sari, and our meeting again after all this time."

They walked toward the fireplace, where two floral brocade wingchairs were placed at either side. A driving rain could be heard, beating hard against the French doors behind the sofa, on the opposite side of the room.

"Listen to that rain. I can't believe it. It was so pleasant earlier, I'd planned to entertain you on the terrace."

He waited for her to be seated, but instead of taking a chair she dropped to the floor onto a large velour cushion.

He followed suit, sitting on the one next to hers.

"Forgive me, I'm not feeling formal tonight."

"Nothing to forgive. I like it this way."

For a moment there was silence, then Sari spoke. "Tell me, do your parents still live in the house on Sladesferry Landing?"

Marc nodded yes as he swallowed a mouthful of wine. "My father hasn't been well. He feels very comfortable there."

"I heard about his accident. How's he doing, Marc?"

"He's changed a lot. I don't think he's ever come to terms with the loss of his arm. We found out later that he'd also suffered some brain damage. He was never able to work again and that can do terrible things to a man."

"I'm so sorry." Her voice was tender, and for a moment he glimpsed at another facet of the sophisticated woman sitting next to him.

"Is Caitlin Flanigan still living there?"

Just the mention of Caitie's name lifted the somberness that had momentarily fallen between them.

"Yes, she does. She owns the property now, but that's a long story. My Aunt Claire and she share her apartment. They're very different, but they get on very well together."

"Gosh, it feels good to talk about the old neighborhood," Sari said. "This may surprise you, but I loved it there. All of my memories of my mother were in that house. She was such a simple woman. I think that she was happiest when she was living in that crowded little flat, stretching the dollars from one week to the next." Her hand reached up and touched the broach at her throat. "My little Jewish mother was like a fish out of water in that big house in the Highlands."

Marc rose and refilled their glasses. They sat drinking in front of the fire for a long time.

Suddenly Sari got to her feet. "Gosh, you must be starving! I'm sorry I got so carried away."

Marc walked behind her as she rushed through the living room. He stopped at the kitchen door and leaned against the frame. "Don't apologize. I've enjoyed it as much as you have."

She stopped what she was about to do and looked over at him. *WOW!* she thought, *what a man Marc Durand has turned out to be.* Aloud she said, "I'm not much of a cook. I hope you like brisket. It's the only thing I've learned how to make."

Sari set the platter of beef in the center of the table in the living room. "By the way, how's your brother? Gosh ... I've forgotten his name."

"Philippe."

"Of course."

He told her about Philippe's ordination and his assignment to the staff at Saint Charles in Sherbrooke.

"A priest? Gosh! I never would have predicted that one."

"Why not?"

"He just never struck me as the type. Oh, what do I know anyway? That was a long time ago."

"He seems really happy."

"I'm sure he is. I don't imagine you see him very often."

"He visits for a month every summer."

"You must miss him."

"He's been gone for a long time, Sari. We've sort of drifted apart. Maybe someday we can change that."

"I'm sure you'll change a lot of things, Marc." She went back to the kitchen and brought in the rest of their dinner.

When she returned, he asked, "What makes you say that?"

"Oh, I dunno. I sort of sense an undercurrent in you. A real need to prove yourself. Am I wrong?"

"I'd like to be successful, if that's what you mean," he admitted while seating her at the table. "I try not to look too far ahead."

The evening ended much later than Marc had expected, and the exhilaration of it clung to him all the way home. He let himself in just as midnight sounded from the clock on the landing. Mounting the stairs to his room, he noticed Catherine sitting on the sofa in the parlor, her long, slender legs folded under her.

"Up late, aren't you, sweetheart?" he asked as he descended again and walked over to her.

"A little." She rose and kissed him. "How was your evening?" she asked.

"Good ... very good. Sari is a nice person."

Catherine pressed closer to him, and he gently withdrew, removing her arms from around his neck.

"I still have some studying to do, Cath."

"Well, I ask you ... is that fair?" Pouting, she turned away from him. "Here you spend your entire evening with someone else, and now there's no time left for me."

Marc felt himself bristle with irritation. "I'm sorry, Catherine. It's late, and I still have work to do. Please don't make me feel guilty about it."

She turned to him again and put her arms around him once more. "I'm sorry, I didn't mean to do that." She kissed him, her lips lingering a little longer this time. "Go along to your books. I'll go to bed like a good little girl."

After studying for an hour, Marc found himself too keyed up from his evening to fall asleep right away.

Sari Miroff was like a jewel, each facet more dazzling than the other. He'd never met anyone like her. She was feisty and opinionated, as well as sensitive and charming. He hoped he'd see her again sometime, but doubted that he would, since he possessed few, if any, of the attributes that rendered her so magnetic. *No,* he decided, *she could hardly have found me as fascinating as I found her.*

He lay waiting for sleep to come, his thoughts shifting from Sari to Catherine. He was still a little put off about what had happened this evening. Catherine's petulant remark had miffed him, and the apology that followed seemed less than sincere. It was all too obvious that she'd resented the time he'd spent with Sari. Jealousy—a dimension of Catherine he hadn't seen before. It made him realize how very little he knew about women. In certain aspects, Catherine and Sari were similar; in others, direct opposites. Sari: the uninhibited free spirit, drinking of life to the fullest. Catherine: possessive, needing commitment and security to give meaning to her life. It was all so bloody confusing.

Sleep finally put an end to Marc's dilemma, and he awakened the next morning feeling at peace with it all. Perhaps seeing Sari had thrown him a touch off kilter, or more likely, too much of the vintage Bordeaux had.

Two weeks passed without any word from Sari. Two more found Marc no longer thinking of her. Their evening together had gradually dimmed and faded from his mind. An interlude ... a pleasant one to be sure, but certainly nothing more.

* * *

Sundays continued to be Marc's and Catherine's special day.

On this, the one that followed Thanksgiving, a cold drizzle fell as they ventured into the city to browse through the Fine Arts Museum, one of many such places Marc had introduced Catherine to. Later, at a small downtown hotel, they enjoyed a meal together before returning home.

The house was quiet, Pegeen not yet having returned from Brian's, and Art and Jerry were off doing whatever they usually did on a Sunday evening in November.

Upstairs in Marc's room, Catherine lay in his arms. He kissed her gently, but with each touch, each caress, his need for her grew, until he could bear it no longer. Breaking away, he rose and paced the room nervously.

"What is it, Marc?" she asked as she sat in the middle of the bed, knowing full well what his answer would be.

"We shouldn't be here like this, Catherine. It's wrong," he answered, his voice filled with unspent passion.

"How can you think it wrong when we love each other

so." Her eyes pleaded with him to return to her.

"I feel as though I'm betraying a trust."

"My mother," Catherine said, nodding her head knowingly.

"I just don't feel right about it, Catherine. She'd be upset as hell if she knew what was going on up here. Besides, what if we can't stop one of these times. That would really be awful."

"Would it?" she retorted sullenly, pushing her hair back, away from her face.

"Would you *really* want that to happen, Cath, knowing how I feel about it?"

"Sometimes I don't know what I want anymore, Marc. Let's just drop the subject, it's getting to both of us."

He sat on the edge of the bed, his head lowered.

She crept up from behind and put her arms around him. "I love you so much, Marc. I hate it when you're upset with me."

"I'm not upset with you, I just want to do what's right."

Then marry me, darling, she wanted to say. Instead, she leaned her forehead against the back of his neck.

They sat without moving for a long moment. Through the silky camisole she wore, he could feel the hardness of her nipples against his shoulder blades. He stirred and moved away.

"You're in a mood, Marc. I'll go take my bath. Goodnight, darling."

Hurrying into the bathroom, Catherine locked the door behind her and leaned against it. *Why does he do this to me?* she asked herself, tears hovering at the rims of her lids.

Sighing, she put the stopper into the tub and ran the water. Waiting for it to fill, she undressed and looked down at her naked body, passing her hands gently over the velvety skin of her breasts and belly.

"Is it you, Sari Miroff? Are you going to take him away from me?"

* * *

Marc threw his book aside. It was useless to try to study when he felt like this. Some of his grades had suffered last semester, and that was worrying him. He lay back against his pillow feeling drained. He hated it when anything came between him and Catherine. *Goddamit, she's the best thing that has ever happened to me. Why do I feel so miserable, when I should feel nothing but good?*

His head ached. He closed his eyes. Almost immediately he fell asleep, and as he had so often lately, he dreamed. Sometimes he dreamed the same dream over again. Tonight the dream was different, yet in some ways it was the same.

Walking into a large room, he saw Catherine standing on the far side of it, looking from a window. Sunlight poured over her, lighting her face and hair. He hurried to her. She turned her head and looked at him, then turned away again. Placing his hands on her shoulders, he whirled her around and looked into the face of his mother. "Philippe," she said happily, and Marc shook his head. "No, Mama, it's me. It's Marc." Then the sunlight faded away and he ran through the darkness, groping, feeling frightened and lost. Catherine reappeared suddenly, and he fell into her open arms, his lips crushing hers, his hands sliding under the silkiness of the camisole she wore. "I love you, Marc," he heard her say, and then he smelled the lavender of her bath. The dream ended.

He opened his eyes. Catherine lay beneath him, her body arching to meet with his. He was past caring about right or wrong. Only the fulfilling of this most urgent of needs seemed to matter now.

His hands trembled as he searched for and found all her secret places. As his tongue outlined the curve of her lips he heard her moan softly, her passion challenging, if not surpassing, his own.

"Forgive me, Catherine, forgive me," he whispered, as together they became one.

* * *

When Marc came down from his room the next morning,

244

Catherine was in the kitchen helping her mother with breakfast. Usually she was off to Beacon Hill before he rose for the day. He avoided her eyes—so great was his burden of guilt. Yet, mingled with it was a smoldering anger, for she had seduced him as surely as if she were a streetwalker beckoning from a shadowy corner.

Seating himself at the table, Marc tried to appear as casual as possible, engaging in small talk with Art and Jerry.

Finally, as he was leaving for class, Catherine approached him. "Darling? We should talk," she began, putting her hand on his arm.

"Not now, Catherine. I just can't deal with it yet."

"When?" she dared ask.

"I don't know. You shouldn't have waited for me. I have to leave. I have an eight o'clock class."

For a long moment she simply stared, fear mingling with the anguish in her eyes. "All right. Let me know when you can spare the time, Marc."

She left soon after and went to Beacon Hill, to spend her day dealing with trivialities of children while her world fell apart around her.

* * *

It rained a lot during the next two weeks. It did nothing but add to Marc's already distressed state of mind. He couldn't bring himself to face Catherine, to tear down the barrier that had risen between them. He wanted to ... he just couldn't.

The holidays came and went most unceremoniously. Accompanied by his fellow boarders, Marc ate a mediocre meal at Duffy's on Christmas Day, while Catherine and Mrs. Hinton packed off for the weekend to celebrate with family and friends across town.

Since he and Cathy were still hovering between sixes and sevens, he hadn't expected to be asked to join them. An undeclared truce had been drawn for the sake of civility, but the relationship had suffered a mortal blow.

The passage of time didn't heal the wound inflicted on their relationship. Rather, it seemed to strike the death knell to a union that once seemed carved in granite.

Marc made himself scarce when Catherine was about. He had no taste for a confrontation that would render little but accusations and hostility. Yet, without one, there seemed an unsevered bond tethering him to her. After much vacillating, he decided to seek her out and have done with it.

He found her washing her hair at the kitchen sink and waited until she'd wrapped a towel around her head before approaching her.

"I'd like to talk to you, Catherine."

She looked at him, her eyes narrowing slightly. "Talk? About what?"

"About us."

"There is no us, Marc. Whatever we had together died, up in your room last autumn. We both know that."

"I'd like you to know how I feel."

"You've been avoiding me for months. That speaks for itself. I thought we felt the same about things, Marc. I was wrong. Let's let it go at that."

She left the room, the scent of her freshly washed hair wafting in the air behind her. Marc stood quite still, making no attempt to pursue her.

Catherine was missing from the dining room table every evening of the week that followed. When Marc inquired as to her whereabouts, Mrs. Hinton gave him a brusque reply.

"Catherine's 'living in' at her place of work. Can't say that I blame her any."

Marc sensed a razor-sharp hostility growing in Pegeen Hinton. Preferring not to deal with it head-on, he began taking his meals at Duffy's.

On entering the house one evening, he was on his way to his room when Mrs. Hinton called out to him from the

246

kitchen. The next moment, she stood looking up at him from the foot of the stairs.

"We need to discuss a few things, Marc. I'd like to do it now, if you please."

Nodding, he descended and followed her into the living room.

"Far be it for me to judge or place blame for what's happened between you and my Catherine. But I will say this much. I feel she's been driven from this house because of your presence here, and I've no other recourse than to ask you to leave at the end of the term. That's plenty of time for you to find other quarters."

"Of course, Mrs. Hinton, I understand," he assured her, showing none of the emotion he was feeling inside.

When he reached his room he pounded his fist hard against the desk.

Only once after that had Marc gotten a glimpse of Catherine when she'd come by to visit her mother. He'd caught sight of the two drinking coffee at the dining room table. He'd hurried off before she'd become aware of his presence.

Just the sight of her had left him heavy-hearted the rest of the afternoon. He loathed feeling that way. He hoped his leaving would put an end to it once and for all.

* * *

On his last day at the Hinton house, Marc carried the remainder of his things downstairs and set them onto the tile floor in the front hall. He then went back to the kitchen and paid Pegeen what was due her.

Turning to leave, he said, "I'm terribly sorry about all this, Mrs. Hinton."

"I'm sorry too, Marc. Mostly because I like you so well. I guess in my heart I'd hoped ... but I know my girl and how headstrong she can be. Good luck to you, dear. You're a sweet boy. I wish you only the best."

Marc veered unexpectedly and took her into his arms and

hugged her. "Thank you for saying that. It means a lot to me."

He left, remembering the day he'd come to this house—naïve and a little bit frightened, and he remembered too the first time he'd seen the titian-haired girl sitting on the glider.

He hurried down the street without looking back.

Chapter Twenty-Eight

On the first day of the month a representative of Klein, Klein and Adamson delivered a letter into the hands of Marc's benefactor.

Knowing what to say had been difficult at first, but each time he wrote made the next time that much simpler. This morning, as he wrote at his desk, the words flowed easily from Marc's pen.

Most kind and benevolent Sir:

Since writing you last, I've had the opportunity of evaluating the effect your generosity has had on my life. The most important difference, I believe, has been relief of anxiety. This of course reflects positively throughout my life in general.

Since I am an average student unendowed with an overabundance of gray matter, I must study hard for my grades. But I don't begrudge the extra effort it takes. The end result will certainly have been well worth it. Becoming a lawyer means everything to me.

So often it seemed an impossible dream. Now, thanks to you, the dream will become a reality. How does a man thank another for such a gift? Words alone could never express my gratitude.

It would give me great pleasure to thank you personally if ever you should change your mind about

remaining anonymous. Until such time, I will con-
tinue to keep you appraised of my progress.

Ever respectfully yours,

Marc Durand

* * *

"Hello again."

Marc recognized the crystal clear timbre of Sari Miroff's voice immediately. Looking up, he grinned and jumped to his feet. "Sari! Good to see you again! It's been a long time."

"Yes it has. I tried getting in touch with you in Riverton over the holidays, but your mother informed me you hadn't come home this year."

"That's right. I decided to stay here and get in some extra studying."

After an awkward silence, they both began talking at once.

Sari threw her head back and laughed. "You first," she said, still giggling.

"No, please, go on with what you were saying."

"I was just going to say that you missed a wonderful party."

"What party was that?"

"Why, my unforgettable New Year's Eve gala. I sent you an invitation. You might at least have declined, you know."

"Did you send it here, to the office?"

"No, I mailed it to your rooming house."

"Oh. Uh ... I don't live there anymore, Sari. I'm in a dormitory on campus. I'm sorry, it must have gotten lost in the shuffle. I swear I never received it."

"I'm sorry too," she said. "Maybe we can make up for it. How about dinner tonight?"

"I'd love it!"

"You mean you're free?" she said, exaggerating her disbelief.

"Yes, I am."

Their eyes held. Marc looked away first.

"Well," Sari added, "I'd better get busy. I have some serious shopping to do. Brisket, remember?"

It was his turn to throw his head back and laugh. Suddenly he felt a lightheartedness he hadn't known in months.

Sari moved toward the door, and he followed her.

"Don't you want to see Mr. Klein?" he asked.

"No, I came here to see you." She looked over her shoulder and smiled as her steps echoed down the hall toward the elevators.

About an hour before Marc left for Sari's that evening, it began snowing and a brisk northeast wind blew in from offshore. Deciding to brave the elements, Marc buttoned his overcoat and turned up his collar. In the light of the streetlamps as he walked past them, snowflakes whipped and whirled like soft, fine feathers rising up from the ground as well as down to it. "Raw" was the word Bostonians used to describe a night like this. Once in sight of Sari's apartment, Marc ran toward the building and hurried inside.

The room looked exactly as it had the last time he'd been there, except for a new Victrola in the living room.

Wearing black again, Sari looked more stunning than ever. The dress was simple, clinging but not tight, set off with a long strand of pearls doubled around her neck. This time her hair was unpinned, and it fell down past her shoulders.

"You look unbelievable," Marc said as his eyes took in every fraction of her.

She walked to where he stood and casually took hold of his hand. "I'm so happy you're here. I was afraid I wasn't going to see you again."

"You said you'd be in touch, Sari. After a while I gave up."

"Did I say that? I can't remember. It's been a hectic year." She stopped talking and with her free hand, pulled his

251

head down, brushing his lips with hers. "It doesn't really matter, does it?" she asked huskily.

"No," he murmured as she put her lips to his again.

Under her dress, Sari's hips swayed sensuously from side to side as she walked across the room. Marc felt himself reacting.

"What kind of music do you like, Marc?"

"Whatever you like."

She gave him a sidelong glance as she opened the new phonograph and played a romantic waltz.

"Perfect," he assured her.

As she had the last time he'd been here, she sat on the floor in front of the fire. He stood for a moment, looking down at her upturned face, before dropping down beside her.

"This is wonderful, Sari. ... I've never heard recorded music before. It's remarkable."

"We live in a wonderful world, Marc."

He tilted his head to the side, his expression a bit ambivalent. "Umm ... I guess so."

"Are you religious, Marc?" she asked, her eyes still holding his.

"Where on earth did that come from?" he asked, attempting to sound a trifle shocked.

"I'm crazy with curiosity about you. If the question is too personal, don't answer it."

He hesitated, teasing her a little. "The answer is, yes I am religious. I believe in God, but I think everyone must decide for himself what God is about. I know this must sound strange coming from the brother of a priest."

"No it doesn't. I was raised by devout Orthodox Jews, and I feel very much as you do." She looked up at him, another question hovering on the tip of her tongue. "Have you ever been in love, Marc?" Before he could answer, she hurried to add: "No—don't answer that. It's none of my business."

Marc couldn't help laughing. "Out with it, Sari. What is it you want to know?"

She didn't look the least bit embarrassed. "You must think I'm very rude. I just want to know if there's a woman in your life."

"At the moment, I'd have to say no. There *was* someone, a very special girl, but we're not seeing each other anymore. It got a little too serious. She wanted more from me than I was able to give her. We broke it off."

"You mean you broke it off."

"Yes, I did."

"Do you still love her?"

"I don't think I even know the meaning of the word."

"What happens now?"

"I don't know. I just know I'm not ready for a commitment. I need to learn a lot more about myself before I can do that."

"Then there are no strings?"

"No strings, Sari." He leaned and covered her mouth with his.

They saw a lot of each other throughout the winter months. Sari was always the same—provocative and dazzling! She pampered him, made him feel manly and vain. It was inevitable that they become lovers, and only a matter of time before he moved in with her.

* * *

When Marc walked in, the apartment was filled with the sound of Rudolph Friml. Sari yelled "hello" to him from the kitchen.

Marc left his bags next to the door, not wanting to take them into the mauve-painted bedroom just yet. He stood motionless at the French doors, looking out at the city. For the first time since coming to Boston, he longed to be home in Riverton.

Sari entered the room. "Marc? Are you okay?"

"Sure, I'm fine."

"No, darling, you're not. Having second thoughts?"

"NO! Well, that's not exactly true. I'm feeling a little uncertain, I guess."

"Hey, you don't have to put on an act for me." She put her arms around him.

He closed his eyes and let her sensuality envelop him.

"Let me prove something to you, Marc," she whispered, her breath warm against his neck. "Let me prove that you belong here with me."

She undid the buttons of her emerald silk blouse and pulled it out of her skirt. He slid his hands inside, and fondled her lace covered breasts. Lowering his head, he kissed her, feeling the tip of her tongue pass caressingly close to his. Lifting her into his arms he laid her gently on the white plush carpet in front of the fireplace. She lay without moving, looking at him, her dark eyes half closed, her hair fanned out like petals around her head. Piece by piece, he took the clothing from her, caressing every inch of her body. Their lovemaking was almost obsessive. As if each were striving to fill an overpowering void.

It wasn't long before Marc felt he couldn't exist without her. Therefore, at the end of the spring semester, he decided to take the summer off and go back to Riverton with Sari.

During those months, his emotions swung like a pendulum, oscillating between exciting weekends with Sari and the emptiness he felt when they couldn't be together. He lived to be with her—anything else meant just existing.

Every Saturday morning they took a train somewhere. Sometimes to the Cape for the weekend, other times hiding away in an old hotel in Newport, lazing the hours away under a white-hot sun, or making love under the stars on the open balcony of their room.

Early in the morning when Sari was still sleeping, Marc would walk down to the beach and watch the sun rise over the Atlantic. He'd see the gulls swooping in, exploring the sand in search of savory tidbits. Out of the blue, Catherine would be there filling his mind with tender memories. Why did she so cunningly intrude on him when he was happier than he had ever been?

Sari combined those rapturous hours in Marc's arms with working in a cramped little office at M and F Manufacturing. With her course of study at Amery completed, she strove now to establish herself in the dress designing field. By mid-August, with portfolio under her arm, she headed for New York, hoping to interest manufacturers in her creations.

Toward the end of the month, she arranged to meet there with Marc. He'd never been to New York and she couldn't wait to show it to him.

Sari planned everything ever so carefully, this being their last weekend together before Marc returned to Boston to begin his first year of law school.

Tickets to the opera and a Broadway production of the "Follies" were purchased. They would dine at Delmonico's and Sardi's, where they would sit amidst the celebrities who frequented these glamorous watering holes. People like Florenz Ziegfeld and Billy Burke, David Belasco, and the great George M. Cohan. Sari wanted Marc to see what the good life was all about.

* * *

On the morning of his departure for "the big city," Marc had difficulty keeping his mind on what he was doing. He felt like a racehorse waiting to charge out of the gate.

After changing into his gray pinstriped suit, he gave his shoes a quick once-over with the brush. Then, picking up his overnight bag, he went downstairs.

"So this is your New York weekend, is it?" Caitlin inquired.

"Uh-huh." Marc grinned. He hadn't told her much about himself and Sari, but he imagined she'd figured a few things out for herself.

She waggled a finger at him. "Now don'tcha be forgettin' yer manners, young man."

"I won't, Cait."

"Enjoy it, love. I'll keep an eye on your pa."

Marc walked through the garden, followed closely by

Shenanigans, Caitlin's ever-lovin' tabby. There wasn't a sign of his father anywhere.

NOT AGAIN—NOT TODAY! Marc said to himself as he approached the tool shed. Looking past it, he froze in his tracks. On the ground next to the fence lay his father, face down, unmoving. For an instant Marc stood gaping at him, a strange inertia locking his limbs. Then swiftly, he was beside him, touching him, lifting him into his powerful young arms.

* * *

It was a small group of people that left the church to follow Joseph Durand's remains to the cemetery of Notre Dame. They stood at the gravesite, eyes hooded, heads lowered, listening as his pastor eulogized him. It was a simple ceremony, appropriate for a man so innately private.

Melinda waited next to the bier until all the mourners had gone. A few feet behind her, Marc watched as she placed a white rose on the lid of the coffin. Her hand rested there for a moment of farewell. She stood looking down on the casket for what seemed a long time, her back ramrod straight, her thoughts shutting out the rest of the world.

Marc wanted to touch her but he did not. Nor did he attempt to intrude upon her grieving with words of consolation. He knew she preferred it that way. Like so many other things, he could not share this time of bereavement with his mother. Finally, she walked away.

They reached the road where their driver waited. Looking over her shoulder, Melinda gazed one last time at her husband's resting place.

From the corner of her eye she caught sight of something. From a grove of trees that stretched between it and the cemetery wall, the figure of a man approached the flower-strewn plot.

"Let's go home, Mama," Marc urged, putting his hand to her elbow to help her inside the carriage.

"No, not yet, Marc," she replied firmly. "Wait here, I won't be a minute." Freeing her arm, Melinda returned to the

256

gravesite.

Victor Durand had changed, but never could he change
enough that she would not recognize him.

He made no attempt to flee as she approached; he simply
stood staring at the casket that held the body of his brother.
She stopped several yards from him, repugnance forbidding
she move any closer. She stood stoically, the wind rustling
the folds of her "widow's weeds."

Slowly, with every pulse in her body pounding, she lifted
the heavy veil that covered her face.

"Did he suffer?" he asked in a low voice.

The hatred of a lifetime returned to her eyes. Through lips
stretched taught came the hoarse, raspy reply: "Why would
you care?"

He turned and his dull, sunken eyes looked into hers. He
answered in a monotone, "He was my brother."

She swallowed hard and regained her composure, remembering that Marc stood next to the carriage, out of earshot,
yet witnessing everything. "Tell me, Victor, have you been
hiding in Riverton, spying on us all this time?"

He clenched his fists at his sides and looked away. "No. ...
I went to sea for many years on a cargo vessel out of New
Bedford. ... Melinda—"

"Don't ever speak my name! Go back to the gutters that
you came from and leave us alone." Beneath her outer garments, her skin was bathed in perspiration.

Victor's eyes lifted and looked past her at Marc who was
approaching in their direction. Nothing could prevent their
meeting now.

As he reached his mother's side, she turned to him and
forced a smile. "This gentleman is an acquaintance of your
father's, dear."

Marc offered his hand to the tall, gaunt stranger standing
next to his mother. "How do you do, I'm Marc Durand—
Joseph's son." He looked at the man uncertainly, trying to
recall where he'd seen him before.

Melinda linked her arm through his. "I think we should

leave now, Marc. We're keeping the carriage-man waiting."

On the way home Melinda sat in stony, dry-eyed silence, Marc's words echoing in her ears. *I'm Marc Durand— Joseph's son.* Pain and guilt returned to gnaw at her insides. The never to be answered question returned with it.

That night Melinda heard midnight ring from the tower-clock above the new high school. She hadn't slept but a few hours since her husband's death. She lay with her head upon his pillow and her body in the depression his had made in the mattress. Suddenly she heard a sound ... a key turned in the lock and the outer door opened, then closed. Her limbs stiff-ened and her breath locked in her throat. Remembering that she wasn't alone, that Marc was down the hall from her, she dared rise and look out. She saw Philippe tiptoeing toward his bedroom.

She pressed her head hard against the chest of her first-born, feeling his love and strength flow into her. Tears, un-shed until now, finally spilled from her eyes.

Marc awakened to the sound of weeping. Rushing to in-vestigate, he came to an abrupt halt when he saw Philippe holding tightly onto his mother, weeping with her. He with-drew to his bed again, feeling as if he'd looked upon some-thing he wasn't meant to share.

Mere hours later a cloudy, humid morning found Philippe and Melinda, arms intertwined, standing at the foot of Jo-seph's tomb. By now the flowers had wilted, their shriveled brown-edged petals skittering in the breeze across the freshly filled grave. Later they sat together in the parlor looking through old photograph albums, reliving happier times. Marc left them to their reminiscing, choosing instead to harvest the vegetables wasting away in the garden. He brought them in to Caitlin, who set up her pots and went about preserving them. When he'd finished, Marc gathered up his belongings and returned to Boston.

Chapter Twenty-Nine

It took only his first night alone in the apartment for Marc to know he wouldn't be able to stay there without Sari.

He missed her—mentally and physically—and even the familiar surroundings didn't offer him any comfort. He longed for the sound of her laughter, he wanted to hear the music they danced and made love to, but most of all he craved having her touch him. Everything he looked at served to intensify his solitude. It was almost unbearable. The very next morning, he left and found a room on Burncoat, a street bordering the grounds of the university.

Sari came for Thanksgiving. She was upset when she found that he'd moved his things out of the apartment without a word to her.

"Don't hide things from me, Marc. I'm not the enemy. I want what you want, sweetheart."

"I can't stay here without you, Sari. I just can't."

"Listen to me, darling. I loathe the thought of slinking around in out-of the-way hotels, registering as Mr. and Mrs. Whatever. That would spoil everything. The only reason I signed another lease was so we could be here together. This is our place, yours and mine. I could never think of this apartment in any other way."

"I've been happy here too, you know that. But I hate it when I'm here alone."

"You didn't give it enough time. Try again please, for me."

Sari was so sure of herself. Everything was either black or white; she never wavered in between. Marc didn't even try to argue, he just let the matter drop.

Sensing that she'd said enough, Sari hoped that time would bring everything back into perspective. Suffice that she and Marc were together now, making love in the white wicker bed in the mauve bedroom, filling the vacuum that was always there when they were apart from each other.

They slept afterward. Marc was the first to awaken. Reaching over, he ran his fingers across the soft flesh of her abdomen. Sari opened her eyes, making sensual noises that sent a clear message to him.

"Hey, we can't live on love. How about getting something to eat? I'm starving."

Sari giggled in that incomparable way of hers, the black eyes flashing.

Walking into Brunnetti's, the new Italian restaurant just off campus, it was obvious that Marc enjoyed having Sari on his arm again. He relished the stares of a group of fellow classmates who looked on in covetous envy as they passed. No question about it, Sari attracted a lot of attention.

Seated at a corner table, she brought him up to date on everything she'd been doing: "I'm sorry I wasn't able to get up here before leaving for Europe, darling." She reached and wrapped her fingers around his. "The decision to go to Paris was made on the spur of the moment. Charles Goodman, *the* Charles Goodman of Wentworth Fashions, invited me to join a group who were going to the haute couture shows. Marc! It was the most exciting thing I've ever done in my life!"

No mistake about it, this trip had started juices flowing Sari'd never known were there. It had given birth to some dramatic new ideas.

"Copies, Marc. ... Copies of European originals at a fraction of the cost. God, I can't believe no one's thought of it before. I simply must convince them to go for this at M and F." Her face flushed with excitement. "My father thinks I'm some kind of a nutzo," she added, grinning. "Thank God I have your mother on my side. There are a lot of women out there who can afford clothes like these, and dammit, we're going to make them."

Marc had never heard her carry on like this before, never known how important the "business" was to her.

"Aren't you a little overboard on this, Sari?"

"Yes I am! I have to be. My father, God love him, is dragging his feet. Who can blame him? He's getting on and he doesn't want to risk everything he's accomplished because some Johnny-come-lately tells him he should. Even if it *is* his own daughter. But I'm confident that with Melinda backing me, sooner or later he'll come around."

Marc was sure of it too. Sari usually got whatever she went after.

She left Sunday night in a flurry of hugs and kisses, and in a few hours the grayness crept into his life again. He repressed the lingering passion left inside him and found himself wondering when it would end between them, for he felt sure it would. Weeks passed before he heard from Sari again.

Her letter arrived, crammed with appropriate regrets, underlined and capitalized to emphasize her distress at having to cancel their plans for a rendezvous at the apartment. Due to some unexpected quest for panne velvet and Portuguese lace, it was impossible for her to be there. She ended by saying:

The good news is—Sam has agreed to turn over half of the floor to my designs. As you can imagine, the factory is in a helluva flux. I know you'll forgive me, darling.

* * *

The first time, Marc had coped with it well enough. The second brought a wretched anxiety to bear: *Doesn't she know that everything we've come to mean to each other is in jeopardy? Doesn't she care?*

When she failed to join him a third time, he sat at his desk at Klein's and penned her a scathing letter.

This has been some time in coming, San, for I wanted to be sure of how things stood between us before writing to you.

261

If I had the time, I'd come to Riverton and face you with my decision. Since I do not, this is the way it has to be.

It's been more than two months since I've seen you. Knowing you, I'm sure that by now you have satisfactorily replaced me.

I would have appreciated a more direct approach rather than this choking off of things a little at a time. I think I deserved that much. For what it's worth, it's over between us, and I don't want to hear from you again. Whoever he is, I hope you'll make the joyride worth his while, Sari.

* * *

A bleakness of spirit, so profound that Marc lost interest in his studies, plagued him into the spring quarter. At midterm he failed a crucial test. He was shaken, and after discussing his grade with his professor, he vowed to put his life together again. He decided then and there to register for the summer semester. Whatever reasons he'd had for returning to Riverton in the past no longer existed.

Chapter Thirty

In the weeks that followed his break-up with Sari, Marc anxiously looked through his mail half-expecting there would be some word from her. When none came, her silence merely served to confirm his suspicions.

He took precious little comfort in that conclusion, however.

A July heat wave, whose back simply refused to be broken, eventually drove Marc to abandon his room on Burncoat Street and sit along the grassy banks of the river to study. There was almost always a breeze there, and when he'd put his book down for a spell, there were the ever-present sailboats to watch, dipping and bobbing on the waters of the estuary. He had always liked sailboats. He would have one, one day, when life fulfilled its promise to him, and for a while he'd forget how empty his world had become.

But at night, the foghorn in the harbor forlornly reflected the ache that so stubbornly lingered, and he'd lie on his bed, his mind defenseless against thought.

Turning off his lamp, he tried to shut them out, to flee from them in the blackness of sleep. But even that simple solace was denied him.

Bittersweet memories of Chatham and Newport returned to wound him afresh. Other images, long thought to be forgotten, welled up from that piece of him where memories of Catherine still lived. He heard the sound of the sea and the shrill cry of gulls as the incoming tide rushed over an isolated stretch of beach. He saw again a barefooted, titian-haired girl, her skirts caught up in her hands, playfully chasing after it, the sound of her laughter echoing into the twi-light.

* * *

Marc gave up his job at Klein, Klein and Adamson's at the start of the fall semester. He registered for additional classes with the hope of earning his degree in June. Just when things were beginning to iron themselves out, Sari arrived in town ... unannounced.

It had taken a long time for her to put aside the anger and humiliation she'd suffered upon receiving Marc's letter. Now that she had, Sari was determined to face him. There were a number of things she wanted to put to rest before going on with her life.

She went directly from the train to the apartment and arranged with the manager to ship her personal things to Riverton. Finishing that, she browsed through the kitchen and the bedroom looking for anything that might have been overlooked. In the living room, she sat on the floor in front of the fireplace and listened to some Chopin on the Victrola. In a matter of seconds, Marc's presence filled the room. It all came back—the passion and the pain. She rose and turned the music off.

Sari took the stairs down to the ground level, too unsure of her emotions to chance breaking down on the elevator. Inside the taxi on her way over to Klein's, she braced herself for her confrontation with Marc. She was almost relieved when Alicia told her he was no longer with them.

"I have his address, Miss Miroff, if you'd care to go to his rooming house." Seeing the expression on Sari's face alter, Alicia hurried to add: "But if you prefer, I can have a message delivered to him there."

"Thanks, Alicia, I'd appreciate that. Ask him to meet me in the lobby of the Parker House at four tomorrow."

Marc was the first to speak: "You're looking well, Sari."

"Thank you. You do too. A little thinner, maybe?"

"A lot thinner. It's been a tough year."

"Would you mind going up to my room to talk, Marc?"

He hesitated.

"Don't worry, you're perfectly safe with me."

An oppressive silence hung between them as they rode the elevator to the third floor. Reaching her room at the end of the corridor, Marc took the key from her hand and opened the door.

The room smelled musty. Sari walked over and pushed up the sash. The voile curtains billowed out against the back of the gray frisé armchair.

"Sit down please, Marc."

Taking off her hat, Sari went to the loveseat and sat facing him. "Thank you for meeting with me. I wasn't sure that you would."

He looked at her, his arresting blue eyes darkening to violet. He offered no response to her comment.

Sari rose again and walked restlessly back and forth in front of the windows. "I don't quite know where to begin. I can't ever recall feeling this uncomfortable." She sat again, the palms of her hands pressed together, her fingers lacing tightly. "I want to start by saying that I didn't deserve that letter. You should never have written it."

Marc's eyes bore into hers, but still he remained silent.

"I'm sorry to have let you down so badly, Marc. I tried to explain the crisis I was facing. I guess I didn't do a very good job of it. I truly wanted to be there for you, but ... well, I won't plead my case, other than to say it's been a tough year for me, too."

He continued to look at her, almost indifferently, still withholding any comment.

Sari waited, then went on: "In dealing with this, I've tried to take a number of things into account. I realize that the death of your father was a terrible blow."

"I don't want to talk about that, Sari. It had nothing to do with us."

"Then what had, Marc? What made it go so sour?"

"I think the answer to that is obvious. You lost interest. You got so wrapped up in other things—other people—that our relationship became meaningless. Marc Durand just wasn't big-time enough for you, Sari."

"That isn't true, Marc."

"Yes it is!" he cried. Everything came pouring out: "Admit it, Sari! You were just killing time until a more suitable candidate came along. I was just filling the gap, wasn't I?"

The gauntlet fell at her feet with a clatter.

Her hands stopped trembling and her conciliatory demeanor vanished. "Although I hate to, I'll lower myself to answer that question, Marc. Nothing—or perhaps I should say no one—came along. I'm not the slut you've chosen to think I am. I've been working! I've been trying to help M and F get off the ground with their new line. *My line!* Maybe you don't understand what it takes to set up a design studio, to create fashions, to find appropriate fabrics to implement them. Hasn't your mother told you anything about this? It's grueling work, Marc, but I love it. It's what I want to do." She stood in front of him now, frustration fueling her anger. "I don't know why I'm defending myself to you anyway. You were the one who wanted an open relationship. You do remember saying that, don't you?"

Marc sat motionless, his head lowered, his sullen expression the only visible sign of any emotion. He raised his head slowly and answered, "I thought we'd gotten past that. I thought you knew how I felt."

Sari's voice shook as her upper body leaned forward. "Let me tell you something. I still don't know how you feel. You've never told me." She paused and took a moment to steady herself. Her voice was less accusatory when she continued: "I won't deny that I was playing games at first. You were playing them too. But I came to care deeply about you, Marc, and what we shared together. I don't know ... maybe

266

I'm some kind of a freak ... but loving a man just isn't my whole goddamned life."

"Then why bother, Sari?"

She waited tensely, a decapitating rebuttal on the tip of her tongue. Deciding against it, she rose and went to the door. Given Marc's present attitudes, any further protest was futile. "I know I haven't changed your mind about anything, but I've said what I came here to say. Think about it."

She opened the door, and he walked from the room into the corridor.

"A bit of unsolicited advice before you leave, counselor. Regardless of what is or isn't in store for us, you should resolve your feelings about Catherine Hinton. It isn't fair for a woman to have to compete with her memory."

Sari left Boston that evening but her words remained, falling more harshly on Marc's ears than when she'd first spoken them.

Had he been the self-serving cad she'd made him out to be? Had he used her, as she'd suggested, in order to forget Catherine? How could he have done that, when he would have found such behavior unconscionable in another man.

He forced himself to think back to when he and Catherine were together. And to ask a lot of unanswered questions.

Why had he rejected Catherine so callously, after what they'd meant to each other? Why had he then fled so willingly into Sari's arms? He tried desperately to put the pieces together, to more clearly understand himself and his motives. But the longer he tried, the more confused he became. Pushing it from his mind, he packed it off to an unmarked grave along with a number of other things that he'd buried there. He determined to cease looking back, to look ahead to one thing and one thing only: the successful completion of his final year of law school.

* * *

Marc seldom overslept, but he'd had another restless, uncomfortable night and awakened feeling groggy. Rolling out of bed, he threw his robe on and went down the hall to the bathroom.

Returning, he dressed, and swallowed the remains of a cup of coffee he'd brought up from the pantry. As he drank, he stared down at the stack of books piled on the floor next to his chair. Suddenly, he couldn't bear another day of the grind. Putting his cup down, he grabbed his sweater and slammed the door shut behind him.

Bells rang out to late morning worshipers from the belfry of Grosvenor Chapel on the university campus. Marc walked without hearing them, his head lowered, his hands plunged deeply into his pockets. Lost in thought, he meandered through the quiet lanes bordering the school, into the neighborhood streets beyond. At Fairfax Avenue, he hopped the cross-town streetcar for Duffy's.

It was almost noon when he got there.

Heading for his usual table where he could see the pier and the seawall, he stopped short, realizing that someone was already seated there. His heart skipped a beat when he saw that it was Catherine.

She sat alone, the Sunday newspaper opened up in front of her.

Taking a deep breath, he approached her. "Hello, Catherine." For an anxious moment he wondered if she would even acknowledge him.

"Hello, Marc," she answered, putting down the newspaper.

"Do you mind if I join you for a minute?" he asked. "I promise I won't stay long."

"That's up to you, I suppose."

"It's nice seeing you, Cath. How've you been?" he asked, seating himself in the chair facing her.

"Well enough. And yourself?"

"I'm fine. It's been a long, hard summer, though. I took classes this year instead of going home."

"Really? Your family must have missed you. Especially your dad."

For a split second Marc couldn't speak. "My father died over a year ago, Catherine. He had a stroke."

"Mercy!" she gasped, putting her hand to her mouth. "I'm sorry for your trouble, Marc. That must have been terrible for you."

"Yes, it was." He felt himself choking up. He hadn't talked about his father's death in a long time. Clearing his throat, he turned and looked out the window.

"Are you all right?" she asked, the emerald eyes searching his face.

"Yes. I just miss him, that's all." He paused again, and without thinking he added: "I've missed you, too, Catherine."

She stiffened. "Please, Marc, that's water under the bridge."

"I'd like to say one thing more if I may?"

"What's the point?" she asked, annoyed that she had allowed him to intrude this way. Looking into his eyes, she relented. "All right, if it's really important to you."

"I just wanted to say that I'm sorry about the way things ended between us."

She stared at him for a moment, then looked down at the table. "It's all right, Marc. It was my fault. Believe me, I've learned a lot since then."

"It wasn't your fault, Cath. I behaved like a fool."

She looked at him again, little furrows pleating her exquisite brow. "Yes, Marc, you did ... and I ... I was dishonest," she admitted. "I deserved to lose you, pure and simple. I'm sorry," she added while gathering her things. "I see no point to this." She rose and walked away.

"Catherine! Wait!"

She walked on, ignoring his plea. Outside, she ran down the beach toward the seawall.

He left as well, taking the opposite direction, until he came to a small park a short distance down the road. Going past the salt marsh to the far end, he found a secluded spot out of sight of a couple who was picnicking there. Lying on the ground he looked up into the sky. *Dear God,* he cried, *don't let it be too late.*

His jaw quivered and tears like searing acid flowed, spilling onto his face. Bitter tears, self-pitying tears, tears that should have been shed long ago. Turning over, a groan escaped his throat and he struck out at the ground with his fists.

An hour later, his emotions still churning inside him, Marc dashed from the streetcar, down Fairfax Avenue, past the Hinton house and through the familiar neighborhood. It was only when he found himself standing in front of the church that he became truly conscious of where he was. The sounds drifted through the open doors, into the street. Marc had not entered a church since the day of his father's funeral. He went in and slid into one of the rear pews.

Vespers was in progress. He knelt and cradled his head in his hands.

Benediction began, accompanied by the organist's mellow baritone singing the "O Salutaris."

Marc closed his eyes and stared inside his soul.

A hand came to rest on his shoulder. Startled, Marc looked up to see Father Burke leaning over him.

"The service is over, my son."

Marc looked around at the empty pews. He began to get up but Father restrained him with a touch.

"Let me help you, my boy."

Marc's words came forth guardedly at first, but then there was an outpouring he would not have believed possible. With each utterance, a weight seemed to lift from him. He was like the man condemned who touched the hem of His gown.

"I remember sitting in the kitchen when I was a child. It's as though it were yesterday, Father. I was watching my mother set the table for supper, and my brother Philippe sat nearby, studying his lessons. Mama hummed as she crossed the room to where Philippe sat. When she passed his chair, her arms went around him and she buried her face in his hair.

It was at that moment, a moment of such consummate bonding, that I became aware of the difference between me and my brother. I could never remember feeling my mother's arms around me. Ever after, I've wondered why she couldn't love me—the way she loved him."

"I'm sure that she loved you, Marc, just in a different way."

Marc thought about that for a moment before going on: "No, Father. She cared and she's always been good to me. I can't fault her for that. But I know now, more certainly than I've ever known, that she has never loved me."

Clearly it had been his father's love that had helped Marc thrive, and the kiss that was Caitlin's had in time become a mother's kiss. But neither of these things had taught Marc to believe in himself as a man.

He sat for a time without speaking, with the kindly priest seated next to him.

"Thank you for listening, Father," he finally said.

"No thanks are required. It's what I'm here for."

"My brother is a priest," Marc told him, not really knowing why. "Will you hear my confession, Father?"

"To be sure, my son, to be sure."

Chapter Thirty-One

A pale autumn sun was setting behind the rooftops of the brownstones on Beacon Hill.

Marc waited across the street from one of them for almost an hour before Catherine opened the etched glass door and walked down the short flight of steps to the walk.

Wrapping her black nanny's cape around her, she pulled the hood over her head and started down the hill. Dashing across the street, Marc hurried to catch up with her.

As if sensing his presence, her step gradually slowed, then stopped. Turning toward him, she stood without uttering a sound until he drew alongside her. Even then she didn't say anything; she waited for him to speak.

"I've been waiting for you, Catherine. You must let me speak with you, please."

She bit down on her bottom lip, then slowly nodded her head.

They walked to the corner and sat on a bench in the little square at the end of the street. Marc looked down at his hands, unsure of where to begin. As he'd done with Father Burke, he chose his words carefully at first, and again the barriers collapsed.

"I don't know if you can understand this, but all of my life I've wondered what was so wrong with me that my own mother couldn't love me. I still don't know the answer to that and I probably never will. But that doesn't matter anymore. We matter, Cath—we matter."

As honestly as he could, Marc explained why he'd reacted as he had, why he had hidden from her the deep-seated insecurity that, in the end, had destroyed their relationship. He

272

finished by saying: "I've never stopped loving you. Even when I was with Sari, you were always there. If nothing else, you must believe that, Catherine," he begged her, holding her hands between his. "I was afraid to trust in your love. I was sure that sooner or later you'd take my arms from around you." He lifted one hand to his lips. "Can you ever forgive me for that?"

Her lids pressed together tightly as she strove not to weep. "I do forgive you, Marc. Lord knows, there'll never be anyone for me again—not like you. But there's something you must know. Something you ... may never be able to forgive." She turned her head aside, unable to meet his gaze.

He turned her to him. She was so close he could feel her trembling.

"I want to marry you, Catherine. I want you to be the mother of my children. I want to spend the rest of my life making this up to you."

She leaned her head against his chest. "No, Marc, you won't want that ... not after you know what I've done." She straightened and opened her purse. Reaching inside, she pulled out a tattered envelope and handed it to him. "This is yours, Marc."

A puzzled expression crept across his features. He tugged at the contents, pulling them from inside.

Golden bells and champagne bubbles surrounded the words: A Gala New Year's Eve Affair.

He laughed. A funny little laugh at first, then his head thrust backward and he roared with amusement. Pulling her to him, he said, "I love you, darling. Please marry me."

Chapter Thirty-Two

When Melinda rose in the morning, it was usually dark outside. Today, daylight spread through her curtains and still she lay abed. Her eyes were closed, but she wasn't sleeping. She was just lying there remembering.

Perhaps it was the letter that had come from Marc the previous day that had dredged up so many feelings.

Arriving home late—as had become usual—Melinda'd picked up the mail and gone through it. She was almost to the last of it when she saw the envelope with Marc's handwriting. Tossing the rest onto the table, she hurried to open it. It had been a long time since she'd heard from her son. They'd drifted so far from each other since Joseph died.

Dear Mama,

My apologies for the long delay. I hope in the future to be more prompt in answering your letters.

Don't fall to the floor when you read this, Mother.

I have proposed marriage to Miss Catherine Hinton, and am happy to say she's accepted. The ceremony will take place in Boston after my ordination in June.

He didn't go into detail; Marc never did when it came to anything personal.

I can't say exactly when, but we hope to visit soon. Catherine is looking forward to meeting you. I'm sure you'll get on together. You're really quite alike in some ways.

Marc hadn't talked very much about Catherine. Melinda had supposed it to be over when he'd begun seeing Sari. That too seemed to have gone by the wayside when Sari'd become so caught up in the business.

Sighing, Melinda put the letter down and walked to the bedroom. Opening the door to the closet, she hung her coat away, touching the sleeve of Joseph's robe before closing the door again.

One might have expected that she'd have adjusted by now. That time would have dimmed the pain of losing him. But all of her husband's clothes still hung in the closet. She'd tried several times to pack them up and give them to Costanza for her sons, but whenever she took out a garment, she smelled the scent of Joseph on it. His pipe tobacco ... the witch hazel he'd used after shaving. She'd hold it to her for a minute, then put it back into the closet. No, she couldn't yet rid her life of Joseph's earthly possessions.

The garden had suffered an early demise. She'd tried but she couldn't give it the time-consuming care that it needed to thrive. Without Marc's help, it all went to brambles in no time.

At M and F, so much had changed that for a while they'd all nearly lost their minds. Sari's new line had been introduced to an overwhelming success that no one could have predicted. For months she'd tirelessly overseen the many preparations for the changeover. She was a perfectionist. A relentlessly focused individual who did not deviate from her course—for any reason. It had cost her dearly.

M and F had come a long way this year; longer than Sam had ever intended. Melinda couldn't help but smile when she recalled him standing in the shipping room looking at the dresses about to be shipped out.

Turning to her, he'd shouted, "My God, Melinda, what's a little Jew from Odessa doing in a fancy place like this?"

When she was there in the factory with him, in that world that Sam had created around her, Melinda was never lonely or afraid. It was only at home that she brooded and lived with regret. Oh, how she dreaded facing another winter alone, enduring another holiday season laden with old memories.

Pushing the blankets back, Melinda shoved her feet into her slippers and reached for her robe. Vaguely, the sound of piano music made its way to her ears. Claire's first lesson of the day had already gotten underway.

Taking a fresh set of underwear from the dresser, she went across the hall to the bath.

* * *

The first real snowstorm of the season bore down on Riverton on the 22nd of December. It came in the still of night, covering lawns and rooftops and turning every fir tree in Hutchinson Park into a Yuletide vision. It continued throughout the next day, seeming to reach the height of its ferocity at dusk, just as Melinda was leaving the factory for home.

As she made her way to Maincrossing Road, wind-driven flakes dug like icy darts into her face. Raising the collar of her beaver coat around her cheeks, she held it in place with both hands.

Boarding the trolley she greeted several acquaintances with a nod and "Merry Christmas" as she walked down the aisle and took a seat in the rear of the car.

A number of fabric samples had arrived from Excelsior in Vienna, that afternoon, and Melinda took advantage of the time to look them over. Magnificent quality, all. Cloth had indeed come a long way since she'd worked for Sam at her kitchen table.

In her travels, Sari had found some unusual new sources to buy from—unique patterns and textures that were becoming the signature of an M and F garment.

Descending the streetcar at Tremont Street, Melinda's foot gave way on a slippery patch, nearly dashing her to the pavement. Beneath the snow, a thin film of ice had formed, making walking more treacherous by the minute. A feeling of foreboding overcame her. She was suddenly anxious to be safely at home.

Starting up the hill, hardly able to make out the way ahead of her, she walked guardedly, chiding herself now for not having hired a cabbie.

Darkness fell as she reached Sladesferry Landing. The gas lamps ahead fluttered dimly through the many layers of snow. Again the furtive, uncomfortable feeling she'd felt before washed over her.

She was to look back on this night, in years to come, and swear that she'd sensed his presence full seconds before seeing his shadowy figure standing under one of the lamps. Even without seeing his face, she knew him. Her flesh crawled and she wanted to flee. Instead, she moved on, careful not to hesitate as she approached him.

Victor fell into stride beside her. "Melinda—WAIT." Sounding strained and raspy, his voice was unlike his own.

Melinda walked on, looking straight ahead toward the house less than a block away.

Reaching out, Victor put his hand on her arm. It was gloveless and dotted with scabs. A swift motion jerked her arm away.

"For the love of God, Melinda, have pity."

She whirled and faced him. "What would you know about God, or pity, Victor?" she cried out, her lungs sucking in the icy air. Moving closer, her hatred having conquered her fear, she shouted, "WHAT MORE DO YOU WANT OF ME? YOU RUINED MY LIFE, ISN'T THAT ENOUGH?" She choked and coughed and could not go on.

"Please, Melinda. I beg you! Forgive me! Don't make me die with this on my conscience."

He followed her past the gate, up the stairs to the veranda and into the house. Halfway up the first flight, Melinda heard the door to Caitlin's apartment open. She froze against the wall.

"Melinda?" Claire called up the stairwell.

Somehow she found enough breath to answer. "Yes."

277

"It's a terrible night. I was worried about you."

"I'm fine, dear. The storm delayed me a little, that's all."

"Can I fix you something hot to drink?"

"Not tonight, thank you. I'm really very tired."

"All right, have a good rest."

Melinda felt a little faint as she heard the downstairs door thud closed.

Climbing the rest of the way, she entered her flat and lit the lamp on the credenza. The banjo clock above it struck the half-hour. Turning slowly, she looked at Victor.

His eyelids were red and next to the lashes was a powdery scale. A small stream of spittle ran from the corner of his mouth, and his chest heaved as he breathed. Victor Durand was a sick and dying man.

"Do you remember the last time that you were in this house, Victor? Upstairs ... in the flat overhead?" She spoke with steely self-control. "You stripped from me, and from your brother, the most sacred thing a man and a woman can share."

Dizzy and laboring for breath, he said, "I remember ... I remember all too clearly. I have no defense to offer, except to say that I was insane with drink. I didn't know what I was doing."

"Oh yes, Victor, you knew. You want to destroy me. Your hatred of me and my family was such ..." She couldn't find words adequate enough to express what she felt. "So you see, I cannot forgive you, ever. Not the man you were, nor the pitiable wretch you've become. I HOPE YOU BURN IN HELL, VICTOR."

Opening her purse, she took out several bills and threw them onto the floor at his feet. "I give you this from your brother, who, I believe would have aided you in spite of everything. But this is the last. If ever you come near me again I will have you put away, and never for one second should you doubt me."

She went to the door and opened it. "GET OUT."

Victor looked down at the bills on the floor. Stooping, he picked them up and stuffed them into his pocket. He felt his way down the darkened stairwell, leaving behind him the stench of filth and morbidity.

Melinda stared into the fire, ignoring her half-eaten meal on the tray-table next to her chair. As she sipped her tea, her mind still struggling to deal with her encounter with Victor, she was jolted by a knock on the door. Her cup clattered onto the saucer. Rising slowly, she approached the door. Her hand gripped the bolt firmly as her heart hammered crazily.

"Who is it?"

"Merry Christmas, Mama. I have a surprise for you."

Opening the door, Melinda folded her arms around Marc and drew him to her. So startled was he by this display of affection, that for a moment he didn't respond. Then, lifting his arms, Marc pressed her body to him.

Behind them, Catherine's eyes were brimming with tears.

* * *

Wending his way up Befordgate at dawn, a vagrant slowed his step and came to a stop alongside a snowbank. His dull eyes made the slightest start as they saw Victor Durand's frozen body lying there, his skin an opaque gray, his lips black. Three ten-dollar bills protruded from the dead man's pocket. Looking furtively around him, the hobo knelt and took the money, then hastened away.

Upon returning to Sherbrooke from Boston where he'd gone to participate in his brother's wedding, Father Philippe Durand found a number of messages waiting for him in his box. One of them was from Monsignor Ébert, requesting that he meet with him at his earliest convenience.

As he sauntered toward the administration building, Philippe was still cloaked in the warmth of having been with his family. His visits, though less frequent now, were always something he eagerly looked forward to. This time he'd had the unprecedented pleasure of officiating at the marriage of his brother, Marc, to the charming Miss Catherine Hinton.

Marc was happier than he'd ever seen him. Small wonder, considering his successful passing of the Massachusetts bar, followed two weeks later by his marriage to Catherine. His mother seemed fit, but still there was something missing. Something that hadn't been there since the passing of his father, and perhaps never would be again.

Entering the anteroom to Monsignor Ébert's suite, Philippe exchanged greetings with Brother Julien and was directed inside.

"Good to see you, Father Durand." Monsignor welcomed him, shaking his hand somewhat more firmly than usual. "I dare say the festivities at home seem to have left you aglow."

"They have, Monsignor. It was a happy time for everyone."

"Your first wedding, was it?"

"My second. I married my cousin Dominique to a fine young man in Baie de Saint-Jacques last summer."

"Aaaah." Monsignor nodded, bringing the small talk politely to a close. "You're aware, Father, that from time to time, the members of my staff meet to review our priests and their present assignments. You've been with us for five years now, and I wish to state straight away that your work has been exemplary. We are most pleased.

"What we are about to discuss has nothing to do with your teaching. It's simply a matter of ... mmm ... broadening your priestly horizons." Rather pleased with his choice of metaphor, he smiled again. "So, Father, before you become too comfortable in your quarters, let me tell you that it is our intention to send you to Nicolet as soon as you are able to prepare yourself. And you're not to worry about your students. They will be well served by Father LeClerc."

Philippe's calm exterior belied the tumult that was running rampant inside him.

"Let me explain more fully," Monsignor continued. "We have received word that Father Augustin Tullie, the pastor of Saint Basil's in Nicolet, has suffered a serious heart attack. At present he is in hospital in Montreal, and the diocese has called upon us to choose a man to carry on his duties."

"Am I to assume his parish?"

The question brought a benign smile to Monsignor's meaty lips. "Not to worry, Father, the parish is small, and their needs, like the people themselves, are simple. When may I tell them to expect you?"

"Three or four days, I suppose. Sooner if necessary."

Monsignor lifted a pale, smooth-skinned hand. "No need, no need. Three or four days will be quite soon enough." He stood and extended his hand again. "Good luck, my boy ... good luck."

* * *

Nicolet
June, 1913

No one met Father Durand upon his arrival in Nicolet. After waiting for a reasonable length of time alongside the deserted old depot, he picked up his bags and carried them down the dusty, unpaved road. He trudged a quarter-mile or more before coming upon what he assumed was the village of Nicolet.

Up ahead a small fieldstone and timber church nestled amid a cluster of low-roofed houses. He quickened his step, for the eighty degree heat was withering, and the handles of his valises had begun burrowing into his flesh.

Coming to a stop in front of a dwelling next to the church, he read the crudely crafted sign attached to the door:

Presbytère: Augustin Tullie, O.S.D.

Walking up to it, Philippe impatiently jangled the bell.

The door opened and a robust, florid-cheeked woman appeared.

"I'm Father Philippe Durand, you are ... expecting me, are you not?"

"Aaahh, mais oui, mon Père. I'm sorry dey was no one to meet you, but the bedeau, my 'usband Pierre, he works ever day at the saw mill."

"On Saturdays as well, madame?" Philippe blew away the dust that covered his hat, and swiped at the cuffs of his trousers. Never had he been so unceremoniously received.

"Bin oui, mon Père ... .ever day 'cept Dimanche. Then 'e sees to the work 'ereabouts." She looked genuinely apologetic as she stood there, her hands clasped across her ample middle.

Philippe managed a flimsy smile. Acquiescing, he shrugged and entered the house.

"Must be you are tired, Father. Let me show you to your chambre-a-coucher upstairs."

Philippe gingerly stepped over the body of a massive black Labrador stretched across the entire entryway.

With a quick clap of her hands, the woman commanded, "Va tant, Lago, va tant," and he lumbered off to the kitchen. "Two year ago, Mademoiselle Caron, she give dat animal to Father. Since den I 'ave nothing but trouble around 'ere."

"Really, he seems quite friendly."

"'Es a hunter, mon Père, he chases everything that moves in de village."

Philippe chuckled. Turning to more serious matters, he asked, "How is Father Tullie progressing, madame?"

"From what I 'ear, 'e's improving. But very slowly, mon Père."

They climbed the flight of stairs that went up from the vestibule, the roughly hewn steps creaking under the burden of Marguerite Boucher's two hundred pounds.

His quarters were austere—a rather grim reminder of his student days at l'Académie. The luxuries that life after ordination had afforded him had too soon been taken for granted.

After removing his collar and shirt, Philippe poured water into the basin atop the washstand. It felt refreshingly cool as he splashed it against his chest. Running his hands through his hair, he dampened it thoroughly before attempting to pull his comb through the tangles.

He had almost finished buttoning a freshly laundered shirt

when he heard the tinkling of a bell.

Hurrying down the stairs, he found Madame Boucher, clad in a starched, white ruffled apron, standing next to the dining room door.

"De dinner is served, mon Père."

So incongruous was the scene that Philippe came dangerously close to dissolving into laughter. Taking hold of himself, he squelched the impulse and thanked her politely.

Entering, he found it to be a small but pleasant room, with its lace-curtained windows opened to the sultry evening air.

Atop a crisp linen cloth, old Limoges graced the rectangular table, along with odds and ends of burnished silver.

Walking to the credenza, Philippe poured himself a glass of wine from the decanter. He sipped it slowly as Madame Boucher prepared him a plate of roast chicken and steamed vegetables, selected that morning at the village marketplace. She left him to enjoy every delectable bite.

Licking the last of the pudding from his spoon, Philippe ran his napkin across his lips. He was rising from the table when Madame Boucher reentered the room.

"That was excellent, madame," he said as she went about clearing away the dishes.

Following her into the kitchen, Philippe perched on a stool next to a small serving table. The housekeeper chattered nervously as she washed the dishes. The moment she paused for breath, Philippe hurried to get in a word.

"I wonder," he began, then rephrasing his words, he said, "I'm sure that there are many things that have been put aside since Father Tullie's illness, madame. I wonder if you might be able to help me with some of them?"

Her head spun around and her eyebrows arched anxiously. "I do what I can for you, mon Père, but I 'ave my 'ands full."

"No, no. I didn't mean that. I just need some information about the parish—the people."

"Well, I do know de people in dis village. I'm née in Kamouraska, but I've been 'ere a long time. Maybe I know what it is you ask."

"Frankly, madame, I'm at a loss as to where to begin. Perhaps you can tell me where the need is greatest."

She embarked on a long monologue that summarily ended with Father Tullie's collapse on the altar.

"Since then, mon Père, not much 'as been done for dese people. Dere are some who are sick, who need for you to take them the Eucharist, and Marie-Berthe Archambault's baby boy hasn't been baptisé." Her face suddenly clouded and she approached him, wringing her hands together. "Just after dey took Father Tullie to Montreal three weeks ago, there was an accident at the mill. Roger Cassavant, 'e was kill. His famille, dey need you bad, Father."

He hastened to make notes, jotting down names and vague directions to their homes.

She spoke next about the people who lived outside the village, where Tullie rode on horseback to bring the old and the bedridden the sacraments.

Finally, Philippe held up his hands. "That will be fine for now, Madame Boucher." His head was spinning. The needs of these people, it seemed, were not so simple after all.

Before leaving the kitchen, Philippe took a kerosene lamp from the wall and lighted it. Leaving the house, he turned onto the walk that led to the church.

The Pascal candle burned in the sanctuary and a myriad of vigil lights flickered on a stand to the right of the Lady's altar. Raising the lamp, Philippe walked down the aisle, his footfalls echoing against the stone floor.

Kneeling, he made the Sign of the Cross and looked up at the great hand-hewn crucifix that hung above the sanctuary. Lowering his head, he prayed to the gaunt and bleeding Christus that it bore. "I am Thy servant, Lord. Guide me in my ministry of this parish."

Returning to the rectory, Philippe found Madame Boucher standing on the walk, her shoulders wrapped in a cotton shawl, a large pocketbook dangling from her forearm. Lago sat waiting at her side.

"I'll be going now, mon Père, if you don't need me no

more çe soir."

"Going where?"

"Why to 'ome, Father. I don't live 'ere in the rectory."
She felt her face flushing. "Pierre and me, we will be 'ere at
six in the morning. 'Ave a good night, Father." She walked
past him down the walk, then halting, she called out: "It's
good to 'ave you at Saint Basil's, Father Durand. Welcome
to Nicolet."

Lago remained sitting as she walked away. Leaping up,
he followed at Philippe's heels into the house.

* * *

It was nearly eleven when Philippe finished unpacking
and prepared himself for bed.

As he lay in bed, going over the events of his day, the air
coming in through the bedroom window rustled the curtains.
He could hear the brook, the croaking of frogs and the chirp-
ing of crickets in the woods near the cemetery. Gentle, comforting sounds—so unlike the sounds of a city. Pulling the
coverlet up over his shoulders, Philippe drifted off to yet another unfamiliar noise. The sound of the huge black dog
snoring on the braided rug at the foot of his bed.

Philippe was awakened at dawn by a family of sparrows
in the walnut tree next to his window. Getting up to close it,
he watched the sky change from silvery-purple to a warm red
as the sunrise bathed the low roofs of the little village in a
shimmering light.

Going below to the kitchen, Philippe heated some water.
He was back in his room shaving when he heard Madame
Boucher arrive at six. He finished dressing and went downstairs. Approaching the kitchen, he called out a cheery "Bon
jour!"

Pierre Boucher rose from a stool, hurrying to set down his
steaming cup of coffee.

"Good morning, mon Père." Marguerite Boucher left her
spot in front of the stove and walked toward him. "Dis is
mon man, Pierre. 'Es a bit hard of hear, Father, so if you

don't mind to speak up."

"How do you do?" Philippe put out his hand. "Please, don't let me interrupt. Go on with your breakfast."

Marguerite looked away, embarrassed. "We usually fast, Father, but since Father Tullie is gone, Pierre is too shy to make his confession to the strangers who come up from the cité."

"No need to explain, madame." Philippe returned his attention to Pierre. "I understand you are our caretaker."

"For twenty years now, mon Père." Pierre Boucher did not speak with the same heavy accent as his wife.

"That's a long time, Monsieur Boucher."

"Please, Father, just call me Pierre."

"Of course ... thank you. Were you born here in Nicolet, Pierre?"

"No, Father, I was born in Boisvert, about five miles from here, but I've lived in this village for most of my life. I was wondering, Father, if you need for me to help you on the altar this morning. The altar boys, they disappear in the summer." He grinned, his lopsided smile softening his harsh, craggy features.

"That's good of you, Pierre, thank you."

"Pas du tout, mon Père, pas du tout."

They walked single file across the stretch of concrete that separated the church from the rectory. Entering through a side door, Philippe found himself in the sacristy, a long, narrow room tucked behind the altar.

Opening the doors of an ancient armoire, Philippe found the vestments inside and to the right, a cupboard that held the accoutrement necessary for the singing of Mass. A dozen or more candles and a container that held unconsecrated hosts were stored in a drawer below it.

Returning to the armoire, Philippe lifted out a number of garments. As he examined them, he noticed that some were badly soiled and smelled strongly of perspiration. He folded and put those aside. Choosing the best of the lot, he began dressing for Mass. Just as he donned the stole, he heard Pierre ringing the bell, announcing the start of the service.

The parishioners—mostly women with young children—sat in widely spaced clusters in the first few rows, while five or six other people chose to sit further back in the shadows. Altogether there were perhaps twenty-five in attendance at Father Durand's first Mass at Saint Basil's.

With Pierre at his side, he moved across the altar, feeling their eyes on his back. The priest was always the subject of careful scrutiny, especially in outlying parishes.

About half the people approached the Communion rail, the rest no doubt remaining away for the same reason that Pierre Boucher had. God willing, in the weeks to follow, he would win their trust.

Then, like déjà vu, it was the day of his ordination again and she was the last to approach the altar. Philippe steadied his hand before placing a Host on the tongue of Dionne Caron.

She looked much the same; time had made no visible changes in her perfection.

Since his arrival here yesterday, Philippe had been briefly reminded of her when Madame Boucher mentioned the gift of the dog, Lago, to Father Tullie. Nonetheless, he had assumed that the Carons worshiped in Montreal at the cathedral, or at Saint Ignace, down in Val Dorin. He had not expected to see any of that most venerable family kneeling at the altar rail of this poverty-stricken church.

At the close of the service, Philippe followed Pierre down the aisle, out to the steps at the front of the church where he waited to greet the parishioners as they exited onto the walk.

Most went their way without pausing. Others waited with shy smiles upon their lips, to shake his hand and express their gratitude for his having come to serve them. They too hurried way, after extending vague invitations to come by for supper some evening.

Now, only Dionne remained. He went to where she stood under the branches of a giant elm. Her large-brimmed hat softly shadowed her face, and the white silk dress that she wore enhanced the pastel hues of her Dresden-like complexion.

"Welcome to Saint Basil's, Father Durand."

He hadn't forgotten the crystalline quality of her voice. "I'm pleased that you remember me after all these years, Mademoiselle Caron."

Her tawny eyes glimmered with catches of light and the small dimple at the corner of her mouth quivered as he shook her hand. "Oh, it's not as many as all that, is it, Father?"

"Five. It seemed a long time to me." As soon as the words escaped his lips, he regretted having said them.

She seemed not to have noticed his small transgression. "We've known for some time we would be greeting a new priest who would take charge until Father Tullie returns. Are we so fortunate as to have it be you, Father Durand?"

"For better or worse, mademoiselle." He felt incredibly inept and was saying all the wrong things.

"I'm sure you'll do it superbly, Father. I just hope that you won't find it too dull here in Nicolet."

"Thank you. I'm sure I won't."

"Well, I'd best go along and leave you to your duties. I'm sure they are many." They walked to her carriage. Taking hold of her arm, he helped her inside. "À bientôt, Father," she called as the carriage slowly drove away.

"Yes ... à bientôt."

Philippe stood and watched, following the carriage with his eyes until it took a turn in the road and was out of sight. He remained motionless for some moments, surrounded by her delicate fragrance that still hung in the air.

Chapter Thirty-Three

On the first day of August, the three Ursuline Sisters who operated Saint Basil's Elementary School returned from their motherhouse in l'Ongueil to their quarters in the "sous-basement" of the school. Sisters Melanie, Bernadine, and Marie-Solange were received at the presbytery soon after their arrival. They were a delightful trio who proved to be of enormous assistance to their fledgling rector.

Even on the hottest days they could be found, their veils pinned high atop their wimples, down on their hands and knees scrubbing the floorboards of the vacant classrooms. Or atop a rickety ladder polishing the countless panes of glass in the windows of the elementary school. To Philippe's delight, they carried their buckets and brooms into the church, culminating their gargantuan cleanup with the laundering of the altar cloths and vestments. But only the surface of their talents had been exposed.

Pumping vigorously at the recalcitrant pedals of her ancient instrument, Soeur Melanie brought music to their Sunday services. Her dainty feet poised atop the pedals, her veils swirling a touch too lustily, she attempted to conduct a hodgepodge of choirboys from her bench at the wheezing organ.

Soeur Bernadine, the eldest of the three, rode herd on the children when they arrived for the eight o'clock Mass. Standing austerely at the front of the church, she led them to the section of pews reserved for them, controlling their every movement with her "claquoire," sounding it once to sit, twice to rise, and three times to kneel.

With the aid of Soeur Marie-Solange and what remained

of Father Tullie's loosely kept records, Philippe was able to compile a list of the members of the parish. Working together, they sorted the dead from the living and those who'd remained in Nicolet from those who hadn't. Then on a balmy evening, without warning, Father set out on his first "Visite de la Paroisse."

His birreta placed squarely on his head, he strode down the center of Main Street, the hem of his cassock sweeping in the dust, his hands wrapped around a cruet of holy water.

The long summer twilight had all but disappeared when he rapped at the door of Louis Carpentier's modest domicile.

Louis' wife stood behind him, bestowing a jittery nod as he entered. A child clung to her, peeping at him shyly from behind her skirts. Eventually, Philippe lured the little one to him with a piece of peppermint candy he pulled from his pocket.

"She's your youngest, madame?"

"No Father, there are two younger than she. Janine is five, although she doesn't look it. I'm afraid she's the slow one in the family. She's not been strong, not since birth. Gaston is the youngest. He's almost a year."

"How many children are there?"

"Eleven, Father. I bore sixteen, but two died at birth, the others from the diphtheria."

"Dear Lord," Philippe uttered, shocked to the core at this cruel statistic.

"They were gone within a week, Father, all three of them," she announced stoically.

The woman's dulled eyes met with his. He turned away, unable to answer the question in them.

Bringing as many of the children together as could be found, the Carpentiers knelt, and he blessed them. The hovel they shared for a moment seemed a brighter, happier place. Kissing Janine's cheek, he slipped another piece of candy into her hand, and went on to the next house, and the next.

Within the week he'd visited them all, the same dismal scenario repeating itself all too frequently.

Little by little, they trickled back into the pews on Sundays. A few at a time, until the church once again pulsated with life. Philippe had, in two months' time, worked a minor miracle.

* * *

On the very first day that he found no new, compelling challenge to focus his energies on, Philippe took the brief train ride into Montreal for a visit with Augustin Tullie.

Reaching l'Hospice at mid-morning, he was led to Tullie's room by a spry old nun dressed entirely in white. Her large, winged headdress rose and fell rhythmically as she walked ahead of him, bringing to Philippe's mind the graceful flight of a gull.

Entering the room, he approached the elderly gentleman and introduced himself.

"My apologies for not having come sooner, Father, but it's been a hectic summer. I readily concede to being a neophyte when it comes to dealing with the problems of a parish."

Listening from his armchair in a bright corner of the room, Father Tullie seemed a fragile man, with no outstanding physical characteristics save for a head of lustrous, silver-gray hair.

"But don't be alarmed," Philippe hurried to reassure him, "I'm happy to report that all is well at Saint Basil's."

"That's excellent news, Father Durand. I've been eager to hear how you've managed with my people."

"Of course you have." Philippe promptly felt most remiss at not having visited sooner. "I'm sorry, Father. It was thoughtless of me not to have sent you some word."

"Don't apologize, please. I know all too well how limiting the confines of Saint Basil's can be. I personally had not ventured more than a few miles away in the twenty-five years I'd been there. Not to worry or concern yourself about me, you've more than enough to cope with as it is." A smile came to his lips. "I must admit that I've gleaned a few snippets of information from time to time, from my dear little

291

friend Dionne Caron. She visits quite often and tries to keep me abreast of things." As he spoke, Philippe noticed that the left side of his face sagged and his speech was slightly slurred.

"How is your convalescence going, Father?"

"That's a difficult question to answer. Today I feel quite well, quite strong. But tomorrow, who knows. I'm in God's hands, my boy." He rested for a moment or two before going on. "I suffered a severe heart attack in May, and since that time I've had a number of small strokes. There is some paralysis, as you can see. But despite the setbacks, the doctors seem optimistic."

"Well, Godspeed, Father. I hope that it won't be much longer. Your parishioners miss you."

He told Father Tullie of his pastoral visit, and as closely as he could remember them, gave details concerning each family. Most of the people in Nicolet were old and dear friends of Augustin Tullie. He had come to them as a young man, and had never once left them until his health failed this spring.

"I deeply regret having to tell you that Roger Cassavant was killed in an accident at the saw mill. Madame Boucher told me that you and he were very close. I'm sorry I don't know more of the details."

The old man stared and shook his head from side to side. "Roger ... Roger. Mon pauvre. How unfair can life be to a man?" He gripped the arms of his chair, struggling for composure.

"Are you all right, Father?" Philippe now questioned the wisdom of his having been so blunt.

"Yes, yes. ... I'm all right. I knew Roger well. We came to Nicolet together. He helped me to build my rectory. Before that, I depended on the charity of my parishioners for bed and board. He was the strongest man I have ever known. He could split a shingle with his bare hands. We were like brothers." He took a handkerchief from his bathrobe pocket and wiped the tears from his eyes. "I failed him, Father Durand. I should have been there when this happened."

Philippe went on, hoping to cheer him with some light-hearted anecdotes having to do with the children. But he failed to lift the old man's spirits.

Before he had time to say anything more, a nun carrying Father's luncheon tray appeared at the door.

Philippe rose and shook Tullie's hand.

"I've made a few mistakes, Father, and I'll probably make a few more, but rest assured, I'll do my best to keep your parish intact until you return."

"I'm confident you will, my son." A wan, melancholy smile appeared on his sparse, bluish lips. "That may not be for a long time, you know." Tullie took a deep breath. He was tiring visibly.

Philippe picked up his hat, promising to return again within the month. He walked down the long corridor and out into the fresh air, feeling his heart break a little for Augustin Tullie.

Philippe took his noon meal at a little café not far from the hospital. It occurred to him as he lingered over his coffee, that the chancellery was just minutes away. Swallowing the last sip, he left and headed down Rue de la Charité.

Passing under the arches of the white-columned building, Philippe walked through a massive set of bronze doors embossed in a bas-relief, bringing to mind those of the great basilicas of Florence.

Across the foyer a young man sat at a desk reading *L'Aurore*, Montreal's controversial morning newspaper.

"Good afternoon."

Philippe's greeting swiftly brought the young man's eyes up over the top of the pages. "Good afternoon, Father. How can I be of assistance?"

"Is it possible for me to see Father Tremblay? We're old friends from seminary days, and I have only an hour to be in the city."

"Of course, Father. If he's in the building, I'm sure it can be arranged. May I have your name, please?"

"Father Durand—Father Philippe Durand."

"I'll check with his office. Please take a chair, I may have to track him down."

Picking up a section of the newspaper, Philippe chose a chair to the left of the desk. Making himself comfortable, he scanned the front page as he waited. In less than ten minutes, he saw the young fellow returning.

"Success, Father, he'll see you immediately. This way, please."

Reaching the top of a flight of steps, Philippe could hear Paul's voice echoing down the long corridor. Soon he came rushing up to him.

"Philippe! You old son-of-a-gun! Gosh, it's good to see you! It's been ages!"

Years of separation slipped away the moment Paul's arms went around him. Walking into Paul's office, the feel of his hand still gripping Philippe's shoulder, they seated themselves in front of the fireplace.

"Now tell me what you've been up to. I haven't a clue. I must have written you a dozen times, Phil."

"I know, I know. I'm sorry, Paul. I'm the worst when it comes to letters. I did enjoy hearing from you, though," he teased. "Sounds like life is pretty exciting around here."

"It can be," Paul said, grimacing. "But what about you? How are things at Saint Charles?"

"I'm sure nothing has changed since I left there."

"What? What the devil are you up to?" Paul repeated, feigning exasperation.

"I've a new assignment. I've been sent to Saint Basil's in Niclolet to replace Father Tullie while he convalesces from a heart attack."

"Saint Basil's? Good heavens! How long have you been up there?" From his tone one might have believed Philippe had been dropped into the "Black Hole of Calcutta."

"Since June. Really, Paul, it's quite an assignment. I hope I'm up to the challenge. Those people have been left to shift for themselves up there."

"Really? I hadn't heard."

"Well, to be brief, a priest was sent up to sing Mass on

Sundays, only to beat a hasty retreat back here afterward. Honestly, Paul, Saint Basil's is barely surviving. There isn't a hope of meeting the budget. Frankly, I don't know how we're going to heat the place this coming winter. I can't understand how Tullie's managed for all these years on the pittance he gets in the collection basket."

"Please!" Paul covered his ears with his hands. "Don't go on, it's too depressing."

"I won't—but give a thought to these poor fellows in the small parishes. They have a tough job to do."

"I know they do. I often feel guilty about the luxuries and advantages that are showered on us here in the city." He dwelled upon that for a moment, then asked, "Why didn't you tell me sooner that you were up there? Maybe I could have gotten some help to you."

"I know you won't believe this, but I haven't had the chance. I work well into the evening every night. This is the first opportunity I've had to make myself known to Tullie."

Paul leaned forward in his chair. "Well, they picked the right guy for the job. If anybody can save Saint Basil's, you can. But promise me something. Promise you'll let me know if I can help. I can always rustle up a few dollars here and there. That's what I'm good at, remember?" He reached across and gripped Philippe's forearm reassuringly. "Tell me, have you seen the Carons yet?"

"No, I haven't. Well, that's not quite true. I spoke with their daughter very briefly one morning after Mass. She's the only Caron that attends Saint Basil's."

"That's not surprising. What surprises me is that *she* does."

"She's there every Sunday, and often attends daily Mass."

"I'm sure they would all enjoy seeing you, Phil. Maybe we can get together sometime during the holidays."

"I doubt it, Paul. I never know when the bell will ring, night or day. I'm the only priest in the rectory. I can't leave the place unattended."

"Oh, come on. Just for an evening, for pity's sake."

"I can't promise. We'll just have to wait and see."

"Hey, have you eaten? Can I offer you some lunch?"

"No thanks, Paul, I have to be leaving. I have some sick calls to make before dinner."

"Well, let's have some coffee at least."

Paul returned to his chair after Philippe left, and sat thinking about what they'd discussed. Unlike Philippe, he'd never been required to grapple with the hardships of the poor or the miseries of the sick and dying. If the truth be known, he doubted that he could have hacked it. Fortunately, some astute Dominican had seen the frailties that lay beneath the surface and had put him exactly where he belonged.

He would remember Philippe and the people of Saint Basil's on the altar tomorrow. That was the least he could do.

Chapter Thirty-Four

Philippe remained faithful to his promise. All through autumn and early winter, he visited Father Tullie every other week. He grew genuinely fond of the man, and learned much about the business of running a parish. On his most recent trip into the city, he'd seen a slight but perceptible improvement in Father Tullie's condition. God willing, it would continue.

Often after these visits he would join Paul for lunch at the chancellery. Paul was a good listener. His objectivity allowed him to thresh out some of the issues that stymied Philippe, and his encouragement helped Philippe work his way through the quagmire of problems that at times seemed so impenetrable.

Returning home, hope renewed in his heart, he'd make his sick calls before supper, then with Lago at his feet, he'd read for an hour in front of the fire in his bedroom.

Philippe retired early. He'd adopted this habit soon after coming to Nicolet, when it became apparent that he could be called from his bed to administer extreme unction or, as on one occasion, to assist in the premature birth of a child. That had without question been the most maturing experience he'd encountered since taking on his ministry here.

Dazed and groggy, he'd been raised from his bed by a young husband frantically pulling at the bell at four o'clock in the morning. Philippe put on his trousers and made his way downstairs. Donning his boots and cloak, he'd followed the man to the bedside after they trudged through the foot or more of snowfall that had gathered since sunset. In those few but tumultuous hours, he'd become a part of the world again—the naked, unprotected world outside the gates of Saint Charles. A world he'd known very little of till now.

After a more recent night at a bedside, Philippe returned home and fell into a deep sleep, only to be roused again by his alarm clock in less than an hour. Bleary-eyed but none the worse for wear, he sang the seven and eight o'clock Masses. Walking back to the rectory afterward, eagerly anticipating his breakfast coffee, he looked up to see water cascading down from the roof of the church. A thaw! A rare but welcome respite from the cold that had come late in October and never once relented.

This would be a day to cherish, for there might not be another until spring. A day to shovel away the foot or more of snowpack on the roof, and to knock down the icicles dangling from the eaves, threatening life and limb should they chance to break away. A day to split logs and rebuild the woodpile, to sweep out the barn, and exercise the horse.

After a hearty meal and at least three of Madame Boucher's buttermilk biscuits, Philippe began with the logs. He'd worked for over an hour and was about to put the axe away when he heard the sound of bells in the distance.

As the sleigh approached carrying its cargo of frolicking passengers, he recognized Paul, as well as Dionne and her brother. Moments later, François Caron reigned in the horse and jumped from the sleigh.

"Good morning, Father," he called out, making his way toward him.

"Good morning!" Philippe leaned the axe against the house and went to greet him.

"A belated welcome to Nicolet, Father Durand," François said.

"Thank you, François. I'm pleased to be among you." For the first time, he felt himself really meaning it. "Come in, please, I'll have Madame Boucher prepare some coffee for us."

"Please, Father," Dionne interrupted from where she was seated in the sleigh next to Paul, "we were hoping you would join us."

"Thank you. I'd really like to, but I have a number of chores to take care of this morning."

"Oh, for heaven's sake, Phil! Can't it wait for an hour?" Paul asked, becoming impatient with all of this dedication.

"I wish it could, Paul, but I really must take advantage of this weather. Please forgive me."

"All right, Father," François agreed, "we won't keep you from your work, but you must join us for dinner this evening. My parents have forbidden me to take 'no' for an answer." François was a persistent young fellow, one who was used to having his way with people.

Philippe hesitated for a moment. "Thank you, François, I'd like that."

"Then you'll come, Father?" Dionne stood up in the sleigh, her eyes beaming with excitement.

Philippe looked at her and nodded.

"At six, then?" she asked.

"At six."

* * *

Confessions seemed interminably long that afternoon. After the last person had gone through the door, Philippe went to the altar and knelt for a moment of prayer. Then he bolted for the rectory.

As was usual on Saturdays, Madame Boucher had left the premises after starting his bathwater to heating on the stove.

Tossing his cape aside, Philippe plunged his finger into the copper boiler. He rapidly withdrew it, his face grimacing with pain. Opening the door to the storage cupboard, he pulled out the galvanized tub and placed it in the center of the room. Locking the door and drawing the blinds, he emptied the boiler into it, and as the water cooled, he ran upstairs and selected his clothing.

He didn't linger in his bath very long, despite the relief it brought to the muscles of his lower back. The next time there was a thaw, it would behoove him to be less zealous about chopping wood.

After dressing, Philippe slipped his silver cufflinks into place. They were a gift from Dominique when he was ordained. Turning the lamps as low as possible, he picked up his cape from where he had tossed it, and headed for the barn.

It was about two miles to Maison Caron and by the time the big bronze lamps at the entrance appeared, darkness had fallen.

Agnes, the chatelaine, admitted him and after taking his things, she led him into the sitting room. It had been years since he'd seen it, but the magic was still at work there.

As he entered, the men stood and François, with his usual aplomb, made the introductions.

"Father Durand, I'd like to present my parents, Leo and Monique Caron."

Monique Caron was tall, fair, and as elegantly poised as was her beautiful daughter. Her husband Leo, a very large man, stood protectively at her side. Expensive European clothing gave him a quasi-debonair appearance, but there was something about him that belied the country gentleman persona. Leo Caron had worked hard to get where he was, but despite the trappings, it showed.

After introductions were made, Philippe seated himself on the sofa next to Paul. His eyes came to rest on a priceless "new" Matisse hanging above the mantle.

"Exquisite," he remarked, glancing in Monique's direction.

Still where he remembered it in the far corner of the room stood the rosewood curio cabinet containing Dionne's collection of porcelain figurines.

Her favorite, a ballerina in shimmering white and gold, stood alone in the center of the middle shelf. Looking at Dionne, it occurred to him that she might well have been the inspiration for it, so closely did she resemble the figure.

Dionne's hair was drawn high upon her head and twisted into a smooth coil at the crown. She wore a white crepe dress that swirled about her legs in a flurry of tiny pleats. Around her neck hung her grandmother's pearls, passed on to her on her twentieth birthday.

In the beginning, the conversation dealt with Saint Basil's and Philippe's new assignment there. When that, in time, exhausted itself, Paul and François parried amusingly back and forth, to the delight of the others. Later, a trend to more weighty conversation surfaced. Inevitably, it dealt with the war in Europe.

"It seems so impossible. I can't believe what I read in the newspapers." Monique explained: "Barely a year ago when Leo and I were in France, there seemed not a single indication of trouble. Is there truly a danger that Canada will become involved?"

François was first to offer an opinion. "I don't see how it can be avoided. Not with Britain hanging so precariously in the balance."

"What about America?" Philippe asked.

"I think the U.S. will bide its time," Paul assured him, "but eventually ..." He pressed his lips together and shook his head.

François shuddered as the dreaded words escaped his lips: "Global war."

"We must hope that it never comes to that. It could drastically change the world as we know it today," Leo reasoned. "In the meantime, I suggest we leave the burden of such fearful decisions to those who are charged with them."

Paul and François quickly diverted their dialogue to a less serious subject—the local political scene. Arguing and dissenting fiercely at times, they carried it into the dining room with them.

Philippe had only once been seated at such an impressive table. That, at Terrebonne years ago while visiting with Paul and his family. In so many ways, Maison Caron and Terrebonne were synonymous. The wealth, the people, the things that made them tick.

Havilland china complemented the finest Belgian linen, accompanied by Lalique shimmering in the candlelight. Compared to the modest kitchens in which he'd partaken in town, it seemed a disturbing amount of luxury, blatantly taken for granted.

The same uneasy feeling Philippe had experienced at Terrebonne so many years ago returned, along with a flurry of memories, not the least of which had to do with Dionne. Never would he forget the moment he had first seen her.

Noticing that his thoughts had veered away from the conversation, Dionne very gently nudged him back to the present. "A penny for your thoughts, Father."

Looking up, he grinned apologetically. "I'm sorry, I'm not very good at this sort of thing. Since coming to Nicolet, I've more or less drawn away from what goes on in the city. I don't even read the newspaper half the time."

"Not to worry, Father. Paul and François thrive on this sort of thing. Challenging each other has become a way of life for them. Why don't you talk to me? I'm not nearly as controversial as they are."

"What? No opinions carved in stone?"

"Not really. Politics interests me only in as much as it affects people. People interest me."

"I feel much the same way. I understand you work at Misericordia Hospital. Tell me about what you do, Dionne."

"Actually, I'm studying there. I hope to become a nursing professional when my training is completed this spring."

"An administrator?"

"Oh no, Father. That kind of work would not suit me, worthy as it may be. I want to care for the sick. Children, specifically. It's what I've always wanted to do."

"What about marriage ... children of your own? Or is that too personal a question?"

"Not at all. Perhaps, one day, but not in the foreseeable future."

They drank their demitasse in the living room where the fire still burned. Later, Dionne played some Mozart for them on the piano. The ambiance all seemed so like a fantasy.

It was later than Philippe realized when François helped him into his cape.

"It's been a splendid evening. Thank you all."

302

"It's we who thank you, Father," Leo Caron replied sincerely. "Please don't wait for an invitation. Come whenever you like."

"Our home is always open to you, Father," Monique Caron added, "as it was to Father Tullie."

Paul reached for Philippe's arm. "Good grief, I must be losing my mind. I've something very important to tell you, Philippe. Monsignor Ébert has resigned his post as Director of Saint Charles. Father Jean-Philippe Bérard is to succeed him."

"You're not serious—"

"Absolutely! It was announced at the chancellery this morning."

"This will mean elevation! How wonderful for him! I can't wait until my mother hears about this!"

Chapter Thirty-Five

February, 1914

Britain was at war ... sinking deeper each day into the quicksand of death and destruction.

Canadian men, eager to demonstrate their allegiance to the king, enlisted by the thousands. They boarded transport vessels as their families looked on and military bands played "O Canada" and "It's a Long, Long Way to Tipperary."

Women wept soundlessly and children clung to them with fear shining from their eyes.

Dionne Caron worked her shift at Misericordia Hospital and after her hours on duty were over, she rolled bandages for the armed forces overseas.

François was gone, having volunteered the day after England declared her position. His father'd begged him to wait, but he could not ... would not.

Since then, Leo Caron had become shorthanded at the mill and was spending ten to twelve hours a day there striving to keep things going. They were busier than they'd ever been at the yard, due to a number of government contracts they'd received. Barracks were cropping up like weeds all over eastern Canada, and Leo Caron's lumber was helping to build them.

Monique worried about her husband. He came home at night too tired to eat, interested only in his glass of whiskey and his bed. He had lost a worrisome amount of weight since his son had gone. Dionne offered to help in any way she could, but he'd rejected her offer, saying: "A lumber yard is no place for a woman."

She'd felt the rejection keenly. She had hoped to do something that would restore her father's faith in her.

Things had not been good between them since late the previous year when she'd refused to be courted by a young gentleman, the son of a wealthy contractor that Leo did business with in Montreal. Apart from this particular disappointment, there was his daughter's reluctance to commit herself to anyone. He could not fathom it! Over the years, she could have had her pick of a multitude of young suitors, many of whom the family would have approved of.

Indeed there were times when he thought she would have done well had she chosen to embrace the veil and live her life in a nunnery somewhere.

Given her father's state of mind, it was probably a good thing that they so seldom encountered one another coming or going these days.

Like him, Dionne was seldom at home. She spent two nights each week at Saint Basil's Elementary School, where she joined the village women in preparing and packing used clothing to be sent to wartorn Europe.

Father Durand assisted them with the relief program when he was able, nailing shut the heavy crates and carrying them to the storage room, where they would be collected by the Red Cross and shipped overseas. They seldom spoke, yet he could not help but sense the passion with which she did this work. Dionne Caron was as selfless a human being as he had ever known.

"Don't you ever get tired?" he asked one evening after the others had gone and she'd remained, mending yet another little garment. He sat on the bench beside her.

"Yes, Father, I get tired. But the need is so great."

"I know Dionne, but you can't fill it all by yourself."

"I can try."

"At least let me fix you a cup of tea. Come, take a rest from this. It'll do you good." He took the garment she was working on and laid it aside.

She followed him into the pantry where a kettle simmered

305

on the gas-plate. "Let me," she said as Philippe took down the pot and a tin of tea leaves from the shelf above.

They sat on a pair of folding chairs put there by the nuns for the use of the Women's Guild.

"It's awful, isn't it, Father?" Dionne asked as she handed him the steaming cup. "I can't understand why God asks some to suffer so much more than others. Can you?"

"No, Dionne, I can't. I just pray and keep telling myself that there must be a reason, a very good reason, and that someday there'll be a reward greater than anything they could ever have imagined."

"I don't just mean the war, Father. Look at some of the people here, in Nicolet ... the children. They have so little."

"I know. ... I wish there was more we could do for them, but our means are so limited."

"Let me help you to help them, Father."

"You are helping, Dionne. You're Saint Basil's most generous contributor. I can't ask you to do more than you already do. But thank you so much for wanting to."

She looked away, disappointed in his answer.

"Go home, Dionne. You're tired and you need your rest. I'll stay and pack what's left of this."

She looked into the warm brown of his eyes. "How blessed we are to have you, Father, even for just a little while."

* * *

On a bitter, cold day when it hurt to breathe, Philippe headed into the city for his visit with Father Tullie.

He stood by the outer door of l'Hospice knocking the snow and ice from his boots, relieved to at last have reached his destination. He had barely entered the building when he was approached by Father Tullie's physician.

"May we have a word, Father?" the doctor asked.

"Of course. Good news, I hope." Since the first of the year Philippe had seen a good bit of improvement in the old fellow's condition. He'd gained some weight, and color had returned to his sallow cheeks.

"Excellent news, Father. I believe that in a week or two, Father Tullie will be ready to return to Nicolet."

"You're sure."

"Absolutely. Of course he'll have to pace himself, but there's no need for him to be hospitalized any longer."

"That's wonderful! When will you tell him?"

"Knowing Father, I'll wait until just a few days before discharging him. Otherwise there'll be no peace around here. So, mum's the word, Father."

After spending a half-hour with Father Tullie, Philippe became restless and politely took early leave of him. "Official business at the chancellery," he explained. A white lie that for the time being would allow him to delay telling Father the news.

Philippe had hoped that the Christmas collections would be generous enough to put something toward the fuel bill that had risen so dramatically after the first of the year. A few parishioners were able to add to their usual offerings, but not enough of them to make a difference. That very morning a letter had arrived from the coal company denying them further delivery until some payment was forthcoming on their burgeoning account. He hated to, but this time he might have to go begging to Paul.

It was snowing. The wind blew hard against his back as Philippe walked down Rue de la Charité toward the cathedral. He hadn't intended to stop there today, but as he passed he ran up the steps and through the big double doors.

Dropping a coin into the poor box, he walked down the center aisle and slid into a pew. His hand reached into his pocket for his rosary. Lowering his head, he offered a ducat in thanksgiving for the old priest's recovery, then he prayed for some answer to Saint Basil's financial crisis. Finished, he was leaving his pew when he noticed Dionne standing next to one of the confessionals. She didn't look his way as he walked to the outer vestibule of the church, where he stopped

307

and waited.

Before long, Dionne came through the archway and saw him. "Father!" she exclaimed. "What brings you into the city on such a dreadful day?"

"Good morning, Dionne. Oh ... my usual visit to Father Tullie. I'm happy to tell you that I won't be making them very much longer. He'll be returning home to Saint Basil's in a few weeks' time."

"That's wonderful news!" Then, looking up at him, a sober expression quickly replaced the jubilant one. "I suppose this means we'll be losing you, Father?"

"Yes, I suppose it does. But not until Father Tullie is able to handle the parish by himself again. There are problems I don't think he's ready to deal with ... not for a while."

"I see," she said, walking out into the street with him.

"Are you heading for home, Dionne?"

"No, Father. I have an appointment to see someone at the International Red Cross this afternoon."

They walked down the street, unmindful now of the wind or the swirling snowflakes that so quickly blanketed their clothing.

"Don't tell me—let me guess. You've volunteered for another relief program."

"Something like that, Father," she said, then laughed.

"Really, Dionne, you're amazing. I wish I had a fraction of your energy."

"Thank you, but it's nothing compared to what others are doing. When I think of my brother and men like him who've had to leave their homes and give up their families—perhaps even their lives—it's little enough to do in return for their sacrifices."

"What do you hear from François?"

"Nothing. I expect we will soon. You do think he's safe, don't you, Father?" she added, searching his face for a reassuring answer.

"Of course. The army is so complicated. He's probably moving around a lot. You'll hear soon, I'm sure of it."

Despite his words, her concerned expression changed little.

He heard himself asking, "Won't you join me for a bite to eat? That is, if there's time before your appointment."

The question hung like a lead weight between them. He hadn't really intended to ask it.

She turned, her eyes fixed on his, hesitating.

"It's all right. Really. Priests have friends, you know," he reassured her, a knowing smile spreading slowly across his face.

Again she thought how warm and caressing it was. "I'd be happy to, Father."

He took her to La Bonne Soupe, an unimpressive little bistro he frequented on his jaunts into the city from Nicolet. The moment they stepped inside, every eye turned toward them. Ignoring it, Philippe chose a table in the center of the room. They chatted as they waited to be served, enjoying the coziness of the place and the savory aromas drifting from the kitchen.

"This is very nice, Father," Dionne commented, looking around at the colorful array of tablecloths. "At times, the war can seem so far away. Like a bad dream that you vaguely remember."

"Try not to dwell on it, Dionne. Just pray for it all to end."

"Is that enough to do, Father? Is praying enough?"

Philippe didn't answer her question. He really didn't know how.

Each of them enjoyed the house specialty: a steaming bowl of "soupe aux pois" and a plateful of crusty bread still warm from the oven.

Afterward they lingered over tea, making easy conversation for half an hour or more.

Looking at her watch Dionne said, "I must be going, Father."

He rose and helped her on with her coat. "I've kept you too long," he said. "I'm sorry."

"Please don't think that. I've enjoyed every moment, Father. I can say things to you that I can't say to anyone else." She held out her hand, and he took it into his.

"Goodbye, Father. Take good care of everyone."

Philippe sensed Dionne's absence the moment he set foot at the altar. Looking to where she usually sat, he saw Mirelle and Lorette, the Caron's kitchen girls. But Dionne was not with them. He was sure she wasn't in attendance when she failed to be among those receiving Communion. Questions began hammering his mind.

Had he unwittingly offended her when they were together on Wednesday? Had she therefore decided to worship elsewhere? No, he refused to believe that. More than likely she had taken ill—a cold or a debilitating case of the grippe.

After the final service Philippe changed into his cassock, his brain still searching for an answer. Picking up the collection basket, he hurried across to the rectory.

Philippe ate without appetite at noon, and it took all of his self-control to remain poised. He called himself every kind of a fool for wanting to rush to Maison Caron and reassure himself that Dionne was all right. Instead, he read his offices and tended to other parish business.

Passing the dining room later in the day, Philippe noticed the collection basket lying on the table. Taking it up, he began counting the offerings—a demoralizing bit of business if ever there was one. The first envelope he opened was empty and only a few sous in most of the others. Below them, near the bottom of the basket, he noticed a larger envelope with his name written boldly across the front of it. His fingers fumbled with nerves as he lifted it out and hurried to tear it open.

Inside was a bank check in the amount of five hundred dollars. Clipped to it was a piece of notepaper with the words, "Keep them warm, Father" written across it.

Dionne was absent from her pew again on the following Sunday, and the one which followed as well. Philippe now felt it within his priestly duties to find out why. Hitching up the gelding, he drove out to the Caron house.

He was shown into the library, where he pretended to browse among the books while he waited. Soon thereafter,

Monique Caron appeared. She greeted him most cordially.

"It's been too long since your last visit, Father. Please, sit down." She motioned him to a large "fauteuil" next to the fire. "May I offer you some coffee or tea?"

"Nothing, Madame Caron, thank you." *Where do I begin?* he asked himself. "I was wondering if you'd had any word from François," he started, carefully avoiding any mention of Dionne.

"Yes, Father, just this week as a matter of fact. We were nearly beside ourselves with worry." She rose and went to the Louis XV desk and opened the drawer. Pulling a letter from inside, Monique read it aloud.

François had left England but was not at the front, as they had feared. He was stationed with the Quartermaster Corps near Strasbourg, in France. Safe—at least for the time being.

"We're so relieved, Father, you can't imagine. What with Dionne's leaving to serve with the International Red Cross, we were about at our wits' end."

He tried to speak as naturally as possible: "The International Red Cross?"

"I'm sorry, Father, I was sure she'd told you. She left more than two weeks ago for England. From there she'll be sent to Geneva." Monique passed her hand across her brow. "Dionne wasn't able to bear it any longer; she so much wanted to contribute in some meaningful way. It all happened very fast."

WHY? he wondered. *Why had she not told me what she was intending to do?*

As though reading his mind, Monique Caron said, "She was so pressed for time, Father. At first she'd planned to work in the city with the families of the fighting men, but then she changed her mind. Her father was appalled when she told him she'd requested overseas duty. I'm sorry she failed to reach you before leaving."

His hands clenched and unclenched and his lips pressed tightly together. "I hope for all our sakes, she'll not be in any danger," he managed to get out calmly.

"We hope that too, but from what we hear, these volunteer medical people go very near to the fighting sometimes."

He rose, and they moved out to the foyer.

"Thank you for seeing me, madame. When you write her, tell Dionne I was asking about her." He hurried to leave before everything inside him came apart.

* * *

The return of Augustin Tullie to Saint Basil's was the cause for much celebration. He was frail, to be sure, but a healthy glow emanated from him like a nimbus. And if one could predict from the manner in which he relished his food, it wouldn't be long before he was strong and vigorous again.

The climb to his bedroom on his first day at home threatened to undo him, but after several hours of rest, he descended to the living room under his own power.

In no time at all he was receiving his parishioners at the rectory. To Philippe, it simply drove home an incontrovertible fact: "Le curé" had returned to the helm.

When the preliminaries of his homecoming were over and done with, Father took to touring the premises with Philippe, marveling at what he had managed to do. The plywood had been removed and the broken windows in the barn replaced. Philippe had painted the water-stained ceiling of the sacristy and patched up the leak in the roof above it. He'd tacked felt stripping to the frames of the doors and windows, hoping to keep the heat from seeping away through the cracks, and— wonder of wonders—he'd built a handsome stone wall along the path to the graveyard. Tullie truly envied Philippe's youthful enthusiasm, knowing that he would never again have the energy to take charge as this young, inexperienced prelate had done.

"You've done yourself proud, young man. Saint Basil's will miss you sorely when you leave, and so will my—our people."

"And I shall miss being here, Father."

Spring approached, and as more and more of the pastoral

duties were returned to Father Tullie, Philippe began looking ahead to when he would hear from the chancellery. A restlessness had begun stirring inside him now that his work here was winding down. It was time to get on with it, to see about returning to his post at Saint Charles.

When several weeks passed without his hearing a word, Philippe wrote for an appointment to see Father Dussault at the chancellery.

A rainy mid-May morning found Philippe seated in Dussault's office. He was already beginning to lather when Dussault arrived, more than ten minutes late for their appointment. As they spoke, Philippe was further upset by the vagaries in his superior's answers.

Leaving him, Philippe hurried to find Paul. Tense and agitated, Philippe recapped their entire conversation while Paul listened attentively.

"I'm sure it's simply a matter of time before they clear the way for you, Philippe," Paul assured him. "Have a little patience, old buddy."

"Patience is fine, Paul, but what am I supposed to do in the meantime? Tullie's made a remarkable recovery. He's completely in charge again."

"That quite amazes me, really," Paul said. "To be truthful, I didn't expect he'd recover at all. I was afraid you'd be stuck there for the rest of your life. Well, listen—I'll have a talk with the powers that be, but I can't promise you anything."

"Thanks, Paul, I'd appreciate that. By the way, have you had any news from François or Dionne?"

"Not personally, but Leo came by when he was in town last week. The last they heard, Dionne was in Switzerland training with a medical unit. François is still in Strasbourg, as far as they know."

"I was shocked to hear she'd asked for overseas duty."

"So was I," Paul agreed. "Dionne can be impulsive at times. She's not your average young woman. I'm sure that by now, you've come to realize that."

313

"She could be hurt, Paul." A look of intense concern spread across Philippe's face.

"Hey—don't worry about her. She'll take care of herself."

They walked through the doorway of Paul's office and down the long corridor.

Philippe said, "It's really none of my business, except ..."

"Except what?" Paul's gaze bore down on him.

"She's a very special person. I care what happens to her."

"That's fine, Phil. As long as you don't care too much."

Philippe was suddenly motionless and his voice filled with suppressed fury. "What the devil are you insinuating?"

"All right, all right." Paul threw up his hands. "Don't overreact! Just remember, we're as vulnerable as anybody else. Maybe more so."

"I'd better leave ... NOW." Philippe strode quickly down the short flight of steps toward the bronzed doors.

Paul followed him out. "I'm sorry, old buddy," he apologized. "I've always thought we could be completely honest with each other." This time Paul feared he'd gone too far.

Philippe stopped. Turning to Paul, he stuck out his hand. "Forget it, Paul. I'm feeling pretty rotten today."

As he rushed down the busy thoroughfare, Philippe's head began to ache

* * *

In spite of the handshake, Philippe continued to bristle as he rode the train back to Nicolet. Why had Paul even suggested such a thing? His behavior, as far as Dionne Caron was concerned, had never been other than above reproach. Yes, he admired her! Was that some sort of mortal sin? And yes, he'd enjoyed what little time they'd spent together. But never had he allowed himself to think beyond friendship.

Entering the rectory, Philippe went directly to his room. Throwing himself onto the bed, he closed his eyes. His head throbbed with the pain of an oncoming migraine. Almost asleep, he sat up with a start when there came a knock at the door. Nauseous and dizzy, he rose and opened it.

"I'm sorry for to bother you, mon Père, but dis came to-day. I thought it might be important." Madame Boucher handed him a letter. Noticing the sag of his body, she wondered if he were sick. "Will you take any supper çe soir, mon Père?"

"No, madame, not this evening. Please offer my apologies to Father Tullie."

"Is dey anything else I can do for you, Father?"

"No thank you. I just need to sleep. I'll be all right in the morning."

Philippe sat on the edge of his bed and stared down at the envelope. It was postmarked Geneva and had been mailed weeks before. He ran his finger under the flap and ripped it open.

Dear Father,

Let me first apologize for not having come to say goodbye before leaving for England. It was a troubled time for me and for my family, and my departure was a very hectic one.

Although it may have seemed so, my decision to come here was not made frivolously. I'd thought of it on and off ever since François left home. Now that I'm here, I know that it was the right thing to do.

You are undoubtedly on the verge of returning to Sher-brooke, if you haven't already done so. They will miss having you at Saint Basil's. I know how fond of you the people have become, and how much they depended on your kindness. You were a Godsend to them, Father, in a time of great need.

I am about to leave Geneva to join a hospital unit in France. I do not yet know its location. One is not given the details of the assignment until the very last minute.

My training has been completed. Still I feel clumsy and inept at times. They tell me that this will pass as I acquire more experience. Despite this insecurity, I am impatient to

315

get started.

I've enjoyed being in Switzerland. It has given me the opportunity to get to know my relatives here. I had not seen them since I was a child.

She ended by saying that she was unsure of her plans for the future and was seriously considering remaining in Europe after the war ended.

Philippe lay back on the bed, his head pounding more than ever. Turning over, he buried his face in the pillow. He felt his throat tighten and the sting of tears under his lids. He fought to keep from breaking down. Finally he fell asleep, with Dionne's letter still clutched in his hand.

* * *

A month passed before he heard from Paul again. His letter was more than just disappointing—it was a shock.

Deeming it to be in the best interest of the students, a consensus had agreed that Father LeClerc be kept on, to maintain the status quo until after graduation. Continued assistance to Father Tullie was requested of Philippe, until such time as he was otherwise notified.

It took all of Philippe's grit to go on as usual. To get through the summer months without going insane.

On most mornings, after singing the seven o'clock Mass, he rode his bicycle down to Boisvert and played ball with the boys at the orphanage there. Later in the day, he read or walked in the pine forest with Lago, who had remained steadfastly by his side despite the return of his former master.

* * *

On the first day of July, the nuns left Nicolet for their motherhouse in l'Ongueil.

The rectory was suffocating. The promise of an afternoon shower fizzled into a collection of clouds that released only enough moisture to splotch up the sidewalk.

Picking up his mail from the hall table, Philippe went outside and sat in a lawnchair close to the edge of the brook, hoping that any bit of air that might be stirring would waft his way.

Scanning the diocesan newsletter that arrived in the morning mail, Philippe's eyes were instantly drawn to an announcement printed on the second page:

Clergymen of all denominations are needed to join with the Canadian armed forces overseas. Any priest or minister who is available to serve as Chaplain will please let his wishes be known to the chancellery.

He ran the words around in his mind, then went on to read a letter from Melinda.

My Dearest,

I was saddened to hear that you won't be returning to Sherbrooke as you'd hoped. I don't question the wisdom of this decision, but I know how anxious you are to be settled again.

News from Le Baie is not good. Daniel has been ill most of the winter with a serious lung infection. Tante Marie-Élise had hoped that the warmer weather would bring some improvement, but so far it hasn't. He's been bedridden since March, and for the first time in memory the fields at Les Érables were not planted this spring. Dominique helps whenever she's able, but her baby is young and demanding of much attention. M-E didn't say so, but I know money is scarce and I suspect there is thought of selling the place. I have asked Father Jean to investigate, and if this is the case, I intend to purchase Les Érables myself. I cannot bear to have our home fall into the hands of strangers. There are generations to come who will claim this land for their own, and I want to be sure it is there for them.

Happily, the news from Boston is of a different sort. Marc and Catherine look forward to the birth of their first child in October. Since their marriage a year ago, it seems only good things have happened to them.

Earlier this week, Marc met here with Alex Friedman. Alex offered him a junior partnership in the firm and he's accepted. He and Catherine will be moving to Riverton as soon as Marc is able to find suitable housing. Need I tell you I'm thrilled that my first grandchild will be born in Riverton?

After rereading the letter, Philippe folded it and returned it to the envelope. Reaching down, he picked up the diocesan newsletter again and turned to the notice on the inside page.

How appalling to think that men were dying on the battlefield without benefit of the sacraments while he, a priest without a flock, was filling his days tending to menial chores more ably and appropriately done by a handyman. He felt the most useless of shepherds.

For a week Philippe pondered the pros and cons of his situation, ultimately concluding that he no longer belonged in this place. Thus he made his decision to enlist with the Canadian armed forces fighting in Europe.

* * *

Shocked to the core, Paul yelled, "Are you completely out of your mind!"

"No, Paul, I'm *not* out of my mind. I can be of real service overseas. These are desperate times, and I fail to see the difference between being a priest in Nicolet or being one on a battlefield."

"The difference is simple. You're not apt to catch a piece of shrapnel in your gut in Nicolet. Philippe, *think*, for heaven's sake! This isn't some kind of idyllic adventure you'll be committing to. It's war!! You'll be following infantrymen into the trenches! You'll crawl on your belly trying to reach dying men whose bodies have been blown to bits. Be realistic! It's like going to hell, Phil!" Paul's chest heaved and he pulled in a deep breath. "Promise me you won't do anything foolish."

"I promise."

Paul examined Philippe's face. He hoped he'd been able to reach him, but deep down he knew that he hadn't.

A month passed. At first the chancellery refused to give Philippe leave to enlist, stating that Father Tullie had not yet sufficiently recovered to carry on alone. When they did agree, he then found himself tangling with the Vatican bureaucracy. Special consent papers had to be filed before his enlistment could be accepted by the military.

His orders finally came through, and there ensued thirty days of grueling basic training at a remote camp somewhere in the Gaspée peninsula. In mid-September when he'd completed that, Philippe received his commission in the Canadian Army.

On October 8, 1914, Lieutenant Philippe Durand boarded a transport for England.

* * *

Their second day at sea found the North Atlantic at her most cruel, and the crossing became a nightmare—a voyage beyond describing.

Until now Philippe had known nothing of the wretchedness of seasickness. Below decks, bent over a wooden bucket, he vomited ceaselessly, until finally he lay beside his foulness simply retching. Ultimately he tasted the saltiness of blood on his lips. He felt for a time that he would die on that rolling, pitching vessel. But after the third day, the vertigo lessened and he walked the decks, sucking in the healing salt air.

For starters, Philippe was given dried toast to eat, and

later on, a simple broth to go with it. Soon he was able to tolerate rice and a small piece of lean meat. As he regained his strength he helped those who hadn't, by washing their faces and rinsing the stink from the buckets beside them. They too recovered in time and were able to eat and drink again and pass the time of day with the soldiers who occupied the hammocks around them.

In another few days, when the sea had quieted altogether, the western coast of Great Britain appeared on the far horizon.

* * *

Moisture-laden clouds hovered in the skies over Portsmouth while a rising ground vapor dimmed everything in sight.

In single file, the men followed each other's outlines down the narrow pier to a warehouse, where they stood waiting for further instructions.

Philippe wondered how many there were. Five thousand? Ten? One division? Two? They were lined up in front of him as far as the eye could see, and behind him as well. Many still so young, the smooth skin of adolescence still covered their faces.

Eventually—Philippe didn't know how long it took—they were herded into railroad cars, packed in like so many cattle. Philippe stood in the airless aisle, his calves cramping, the soles of his feet smarting. Elbowing his way to the rear, he found a space in a corner large enough to squat down on his duffle bag and relieve his aching arches.

Darkness fell soon after they arrived at Camp George Edrus-Elliott, three miles from the quaint village of Sherinden. Compared with the transport, their quarters appeared luxurious to Philippe. There were sheets on the cots as well as clean woolen blankets, and a lavatory at each end of the barracks.

At the very first opportunity, Philippe hurried in there. He bathed and brushed his teeth. He then changed into his new issue of clothing: soft, fresh-smelling undergarments that caressed his chafed, neglected skin.

In the officers' mess, the food was hot and satisfying, better than anything he'd eaten since leaving Nova Scotia. He gorged himself on roast lamb and mashed potatoes, and freshly baked bread seeded on top and twisted into a braid. Warm and with his belly filled to capacity, Philippe slept that first night as he'd not slept in a very long time.

Awakening early, Philippe hurried into the lavatory. He shaved again, rinsing off with water so hot it left tingles running through the pores of his face. He washed his hair three times. He couldn't get enough of soap and water, and no amount of brushing made his teeth feel clean.

Leaving the mess hall after breakfast, Philippe was met by an Anglican minister who showed him his way around.

"It isn't much," Reverend Fawcett allowed as they walked toward the tent where services were held. "But it does well enough for the men. You'll find the space fills up quickly. I usually leave the flap up so's those who choose to can hear from outside." Walking up to the makeshift altar, Reverend Fawcett looked back at Philippe. "A far cry from what you've been used to, I dare say?"

"Not as far as you might imagine, Reverend," Philippe replied. "I served in a small country parish. Nothing very grand, I assure you."

"Well, then, I fancy you'll manage."

Thereafter, Philippe heard confessions every morning at five. At six, he sang daily Mass.

Along with the Canadian infantrymen, Philippe underwent another period of training, this one more intense than anything he'd experienced before. As was true of the other soldiers, Philippe was ready to drop by four in the afternoon. But his duties as chaplain were far from over for the day.

Allowed the use of the tent for two hours each evening, Philippe heard confessions again, then counseled as many of the men as he was able to before falling onto his bunk like a dead man. Two months later, they were taken aboard another vessel.

No mention was made of their destination before embarking, but as soon as they were underway the captain made this announcement: "We sail today for the Port of Calais, on the coast of Flanders."

* * *

They joined the British forces in Belgium, at Ypres, where the Second Canadian Corps of the Second Army, led by General Plumer, was engaged in battle with the German forces.

Time became a fleeting, nebulous thing; By day, the fighting was fierce. By night, sporadic bursts of gunfire crackled through the darkness, the cry of an injured soldier oft times heard within seconds afterward.

Philippe slumped against the side of the trench, sleeping in snatches, awakening at dawn when the howitzers resumed their bombardment.

Saint Julien fell. Their platoon retreated to Neuve Chappelle. Soon after, it too was lost.

Death became his constant companion. Philippe loathed it with all his being, yet there were times when he welcomed the blessed peace it brought to those who suffered unendurable pain.

Each day was a mirror image of the one preceding it.

Inevitably, Philippe became hardened to the realities of the battlefield. No longer was he stricken mute at the sight of a young man, not yet fully bearded, lying with fixed pupils staring into nothingness. Nor did his limbs go to water upon hearing the groans of the mortally wounded, as life ebbed, then ended. He knelt beside their shattered bodies, anointing them. And when he could, he cradled them in his arms until death came.

Withdrawing behind the lines to a village outside Poelchappelle, Philippe's unit was given a respite from the fighting. Some were lodged at the inn, others in the church or

322

with a family willing to share their home. They received hot meals and a few days of rest away from the madness.

Letters from Paul, his mother, Marc, and Father Jean caught up with him. Other than survival, they were the most important thing in his life. He stashed them away in his pack until, finding a quiet, private place, he read and reread them. They were like unguent to a burn—or water to a man dying of thirst.

Your nephew, Joseph Dennis (better known to his family as Jody) sat up by himself today, Melinda wrote. *He's a sweet child and a vision to behold, with his father's eyes and his mother's auburn hair. Marc and Catherine are radiant with pride.*

I'm pleased that their coming to Riverton has turned out so well. Catherine seems very much at home here. As might have been expected, she and Caitlin are becoming staunch friends. She hasn't said so, but I rather think Caitlin fancies herself as much of a grandmother as I do.

When all is quiet in the night, I think of you, my dearest Philippe, and I sense that you are in terrible danger. I've read of the new machine guns being used by the Germans. It's said that they can kill a dozen men in the time it used to take to kill one. Why does war have to be? It never seems to solve anything. Sometimes I think the world has gone mad.

Altogether, I've received a half dozen of your letters, all from England. We live for word from you, my Philippe. Don't misunderstand, I'm not complaining. I know that you write when you are able to.

Philippe wrote home that afternoon on a two by three inch paper pad given to him by the concierge at the hotel, and with a stub of pencil he shared with two other men. Even the most rudimentary essentials were scarce and issued only to those who needed them most.

The Belgian campaign escalated. Advancing north of the Ardennes, the German left flank bore down on Liege. Then

Brussels and Antwerp became the focus of their attack. The French and Canadians held them off, at first losing ground, then regaining it.

The first attack of chlorine gas was let loose from the cylinders in the German trenches on April 22nd; the second attack on April 24th. At 4 A.M. a green cloud crept in on the morning wind, across the silent battlefield. It reached the Allied trenches, falling on the unsuspecting troops, most of whom slept and who had only handkerchiefs and linen bandoliers dipped in water to protect themselves from the poison. The casualties were horrendous. Philippe, who had gone to the rear with an ambulance of wounded, returned to find his platoon writhing in the trenches. He ministered first to those who convulsed, leaving the others whose need of him had passed, to the corpsmen who gently closed their eyes.

June, though mild, was rainy. July followed with a sweltering heat that caused Philippe's skin to itch and his body to smell fetid. Lice invaded his hair, and he dug at himself with his nails until he bled. At night his joints ached and he shivered despite the stifling heat inside his tent.

While marching along the Saint Julien-Poelchappelle Road on their way to join General Alderson's command further to the north, Philippe dropped to his knees. Reeling with dizziness, he attempted to stand, only to fall to the ground again. As he collapsed by the side of the road, unable to rise, a passing lorry stopped. It backed up to where he sat in the dirt.

"Get in, sir," a young corporal called to him.

With great effort, Philippe dragged himself to the back of the truck. Unable to hoist himself in, the corporal jumped out and assisted him. Once on the bed of the vehicle, Philippe fell into a semi-stupor.

Arriving at the medical station, his fever was raging upward.

A field physician examined the lesions on his body and made the dreaded diagnosis: "It's typhus! Get him the hell out of here!"

"Where shall I take him, sir?"

"We don't have any way of isolating him here. Take him to the Sisters at the abbey. Just get him away from the rest of these men or we'll be fighting an epidemic."

Philippe was promptly removed to the Solsetera Abbey on the outskirts of Saint Julien, where an order of decalced Carmelites had managed to remain intact in their convent. For the time being, the war had ended for Lieutenant Philippe Durand.

* * *

In a room on the topmost floor of the abbey, Philippe was placed in isolation. Except for his caregivers the Abess Mère Marie-Thérèse, and Mère Marie-Bernadette Soubirou, no one was allowed there. They too remained segregated from the rest of the community, lest they pass on this plague to their Sisters. Night and day a vigil was kept at Philippe's bedside; never for a moment was he left unattended.

For the most part Philippe lived in a world of garish hallucinations, hovering on the fringes of reality, only vaguely seeing the veiled figures who so devotedly stood at his bedside.

Water sucked into a rubber syringe was placed between his swollen lips and let out by droplets onto his tongue. Periodically, his hands were secured to the metal rails of his bedstead when, in his delirium, he tried to attack himself and his nurses.

Day after day the fever raged on. Mère Marie-Bernadette sponged him with alcohol and stood at his bedside fanning his body with a folded newspaper. She changed his urine-soaked bedding and when there was time, she knelt and prayed for his life. Leaving the room for her chamber and a few hours of rest, she often felt sure she wouldn't see him alive again.

* * *

In the early hours of the first day of August, Philippe awakened with a clear mind. His fever had broken and he lay staring at his surroundings. The wall sconces only dimly lit the austere room where for weeks he had been close to death. Wasted and weak as he was, his mind still not functioning at total capacity, he nonetheless realized that he had survived.

The patient was made to keep to his bed, but in his eagerness to regain his strength, Philippe forced the issue with the deaconess who had taken over his care.

"My judgment tells me this is unwise, Father," she advised him, "but ... if you insist, I'll permit you a moment of leg-dangling. Just a moment, mind you." Putting her arm around him, she helped him to sit upright.

Predictably, his head swam and the room whirled, and he would have fallen onto the floor had it not been for the responsive reflexes of this robust young woman.

Soon after this episode and much to the delight of the abbess and a number of Carmelites who watched from the grounds below, Philippe's bed was wheeled onto the long veranda outside his room. Bound to their vow of silence, the Sisters uttered no sound, but in concert broke into spontaneous applause.

Philippe's appetite returned, reluctantly at first, then all at once he was ravenous. He dreamt of eating succulent pork and poultry running with golden juices. Despite these cravings, he rigidly followed the urgings of the deaconess. Without complaint, he ate only the bland, easily digested foods she brought him. In time, fresh eggs were added to his diet, and fragrant breads still warm from the earthen ovens. His arms and legs began filling out, losing the gaunt, emaciated look of the deathly ill. His cravings for meat went unsatisfied, however. Only two laying hens cackled in the barnyard of the abbey, and the scarcities in town had forced the "charcuterie" to close its doors for the duration.

Mild exercise was added to Philippe's daily regimen, and the moment arrived—as everyone who had watched him mend knew it would—when he set out to test his strength.

He walked the two miles into Saint Julien and visited with the old men who sat reading newspapers in the shade outside the café.

Philippe Durand had regained his health. He was pronounced sound enough to leave this blessed place of refuge and return to the atrocities of war.

Chapter Thirty-Six

After reporting to the British commander at Poelchappelle, the Canadian chaplain was sent to the infirmary for a physical examination.

"Bloody awful, this typhus," the young British physician commented when he'd done with his probing. "Seems you're fit enough, though, Lieutenant. Raring for the front again, are you?" Philippe didn't know how to answer, and before he was able to say anything, the officer grinned. "I think that would be ill-advised, however. A bit of recuperative leave is in order before you throw yourself headlong into the fray."

Handing Philippe a written order, he said, "Check in with the quartermaster. He'll assign you a new uniform and anything else you're in need of. Enjoy yourself, Father, you've earned every minute of it. We'll process your papers in the meantime."

* * *

Bruges was an hour away by rail. Bruges—the historic old Flemish City of Bridges, canals, museums and towering Gothic cathedrals.

The former capital of Belgium looked amazingly serene as Philippe walked past the quaint little shops into the core of the city. Taking a room at a modest "pension" close to the center of things, he rested for a while before setting out to explore the nooks and crannies. He awakened feeling better than he'd felt in months.

Not a trace of war could be seen as he meandered through the narrow streets an hour later; at least not to the naked eye.

It was as though he'd dropped into a magical place where for centuries everything had remained untouched.

The Kunst-Museum was the first of Bruges' architectural masterpieces encountered by Philippe that memorable afternoon. Seeing it from a distance, its massive tiled roof soaring above the neighboring buildings, he headed toward it.

A few hundred feet from the entrance, Philippe stopped to appreciate the ornately gilded façade. The building suddenly reminded him of a palace he'd seen in a book of fairy tales he'd enjoyed as a child. He felt excited—stimulated—and a compulsion to enter took hold of him.

Echoes of his footsteps resounded from the richly veined marble floors, and a new wave of excitement went through him as he came to the portals of La Galerie d'Or. There upon its walls hung the works of Belgium's greatest painters.

A smattering of people quietly gazed, while in a hushed tone a man beside him leaned and whispered into his female companion's ear. Further along a group of uniformed schoolgirls, led by a pair of nuns, giggled with embarrassment as they passed Sir Peter Paul Rubens' voluptuous nudes. Light and airy, yet filled with vibrance and energy, Rubens' subjects' flesh seemed to quiver with life.

Philippe climbed the staircase to the second floor and found himself alone, except for one other person at the opposite end of the gallery.

Making his way along the wall, he stepped back every now and then to get a truer perspective. Never had he encountered so much beauty ... anywhere. It was hard to take it all in.

In this particular section, he came face to face with fifteenth century works by Memling, Van Eycks, and Van der Goes. It was impossible not to feel insignificant in a place like this.

Walking very slowly, Philippe allowed his eyes to caress the skin of a child, or the velvety texture of a tulip sunning itself on the edge of a windowsill. Stepping back to view a massive seascape, Philippe felt himself bump against someone.

Turning to apologize, he found himself unable to utter a sound. He felt as if he'd been struck a blow to the pit of his stomach as he stared into Dionne Caron's incredulous eyes.

Her hands flew to her face. "Father Durand! Is it *really* you?"

Somehow finding his voice again, Philippe gasped, "This must be delirium. I can't believe I'm looking at you, Dionne."

She laughed, and he knew then that it was truly she, for her laughter was like no other sound he'd ever heard.

"What are you doing in Bruges, Father?" A gauche question, she thought as soon as she'd asked it. Aware now of his uniform and the cross on his lapel, she answered the question herself. "A chaplain, of course ... how stupid of me."

"Not at all, Dionne. But tell me about you." He wanted to hear everything that had happened since the last time he'd seen her. Since that day in Montreal when they'd walked to the little bistro for a bowl of soup. "Are you stationed here in Bruges? From your letter, I'd expected you to be in France." His eyes clung to hers, and he held tightly onto both of her hands.

"I'm presently assigned to l'Hôtel-Dieu, right here in Bruges, but I'll be returning to the field hospital outside Antwerp soon. I've been on leave from the front for almost a month. They send us off to regain our wits when they see us beginning to pull apart at the seams." She laughed, and again it took his breath away.

"Dionne—can we go somewhere and talk for a while? There are so many things I want to ask you about."

"Of course, Father. There's a little place down the street. It's become a favorite of mine. I'm sure you'll like it there."

Leaving the museum, they dashed across the busy boulevard, Philippe still agog with wonder at the miracle that had brought them together halfway around the world. Stopping in front of a modest little café, Dionne looked up at him with her lovely pastel eyes. "Is this all right, Father?"

"It's perfect."

As they entered, the few patrons seated around small, intimate tables paid them little or no heed. The absence of the Roman collar had indeed reduced Philippe to the ranks of the ordinary.

The sound of a concertina reached their ears from across the room. A lovely sound, soft and sentimental, in tune with the way each of them felt at the moment.

From across the table, Dionne noticed the leaness of Philippe's face. His jaw seemed more angular, the cleft in his chin deeper.

"You've lost some weight, Father. You're well, I hope?"

"I've been ill with typhus, but yes, I'm well again."

"THYPHUS! PHILIPPE! You could've died!" Perhaps it was the uniform, or the news of his terrible illness that had shocked her, but she had forgotten to address him as "Father." "Please—forgive me, Father, I ..." She looked away, her face flushing.

"Don't apologize, Dionne. I'd like you to call me Philippe. This isn't Nicolet or Montreal. We aren't pastor and parishioner here." He wanted so much to reach for her hand. "We are Dionne and Philippe, and through some miracle we've come together amidst all this horror. There's so little time. Can't we forget what is past, and just think about this moment?"

"Yes, I want that too." Until this instant Dionne had not known that she wanted it more than anything else on earth.

"Will you dine with me this evening, mademoiselle?"

She smiled and the dimple at the corner of her mouth appeared. "I'd be delighted, Philippe." Somehow it didn't sound inappropriate anymore.

Laughter resumed and the awkwardness fled as they sat side by side on the streetcar that took them down Hans Memlincstrasse toward her lodgings at Gasthof des blauen Vogels.

Standing outside the door to her room, Philippe said, "I'll call for you at seven." Impulsively he took her hand into his and put it to his cheek. Turning his head slowly, he kissed her palm.

Each of them felt it was a dream. Still, there was an intense awareness of each moment ticking away, never to be lived again.

Together they visited the basilicas of Saint Sauveur and Notre Dame. They touched hands briefly as they gazed at DeCroyer's "Adoration of the Magi," and Michèlangelo's "Virgin and Child." They ambled through the marketplace, where Philippe chose a red lace scarf to adorn Dionne's hair. In the evening after dining, they listened to Vivaldi and Mozart performed in the intimacy of the old Concertplatz. There was a power ... something arced between them like lightning.

With each passing day, each hour, each minute, the end of Philippe's leave loomed larger on the horizon. A quiet melancholy began creeping into their hearts, replacing the joy and exhilaration.

On his final day of leave, they walked to the park where they shared a picnic under the Linden trees near one of the canals. Philippe was withdrawn and pensive as they watched the barges making their way out to Zeebrugge and on to the open sea.

"Don't think about it, Philippe, please."

"I'm sorry. You must find me a terrible bore."

"Would it help if you talked about how you feel?"

Removing his jacket, Philippe sat in the grass and turned his shirtsleeves back to the elbows.

Dionne did not see a priest sitting there; she saw a man. A man she loved, a man overburdened with feelings he was forbidden to express.

His eyes came to rest on her hair, long and sensual, undulating gently as a breeze played in its golden strands. He wanted to touch it, to put his hands into it and rub its silkiness between his palms. He wanted to pull her to him in a passionate embrace.

Did he have the courage to put what he felt into words? Could he ever say: *I love you, Dionne, and I think I was born loving you. But for most of my life I didn't know where you were. And when I found you, it was too late.*

He rose and walked to where she stood at the edge of the canal. "I'll try," he said, so softly she was barely able to hear him.

Their eyes met and his fingertips brushed her cheek.

"The strange part of all this is that inside, deep down where it really matters, I know what I feel for you is wrong."

"No, Philippe ... please."

"Let me go on, Dionne, or I may never be able to begin again. ... It's wrong because I swore to vows that make it so. But I've long since ceased caring about right or wrong. I care only about you. About loving you ... about wanting you. I've thought of nothing else since I saw you standing there in the museum. *God forgive me!* I can't help myself anymore."

It was a cry of anguish, like flesh tearing itself away from bone.

She reached out for him and held him tightly, her face next to his, her tears mingling with his. Philippe's arms went around her and she heard him whisper her name, over and over again.

His lips found hers and he touched them gently, but passion soon overcame all else.

"Not here, my love," she whispered, "not here."

* * *

It was hushed and shadowy inside her room at the Gasthof. Lifting her into his arms, Philippe lowered her gently onto the bed. They lay at last, united in each other's love. Nothing on earth mattered anymore.

Afterward he held her as she slept, her hair spread across his chest, her heart beating against his. He thought of deserting, of fleeing with her to some safe place where he could love her for the rest of his life. But when the first streaks of dawn touched onto the window shade, he rose and left.

Dionne awakened and even before she opened her eyes, she knew that he'd gone. There was an emptiness in the room, and she felt cold. She'd already begun to cry when she saw the note on the pillow next to hers.

Leaving you is the hardest thing I shall ever do in my life, but I must fulfill my commitment to the army.

Barring death on the battlefield, I will return to Bruges, to this room, as soon as I am able. And if for some reason you are not here, I shall wait until you come to me. I love you, Dionne, more than life itself! What we have shared will support me every moment that we are apart, and when this is finished, I will do whatever I must so that we may be together for always.

Philippe

* * *

Carrying on with his duties became almost impossible for Philippe. He felt himself the worst sort of hypocrite. There grew within his heart a deep sense of betrayal to these men who entrusted him with the most personal kind of information. So paralyzing was his guilt, there were times when he wanted to flee from them. But until he no longer called himself a priest, until his stole and chasuble were returned to the Church, he must carry on with the task that he was sent here to do.

January, 1916

The fighting in the Ardennes brought many casualties to the field hospital that Philippe was assigned to, and frostbite became their bitter enemy. Ears formed blisters that swelled to the size of hens' eggs, while gangrenous hands and feet had to be amputated. Philippe moved from one bed to the next, one cot to the other, hearing confessions and administering extreme unction. He had difficulty looking those who survived in the eye, when they thanked him for writing letters to their loved ones back home. By spring he felt hollow, with little left to offer anyone.

On quiet nights he'd lie on his bunk, memories of Bruges burning in his brain. He didn't want to sleep, to be cheated of the only time he had to think of Dionne, to re-read the letters that had finally come through from her.

Philippe lived one day at a time, going about his duties like an automaton, until spring brought news of important victories being won by the American forces fighting in France. War-weary infantrymen carried on with renewed dedication to the cause coursing through their veins. Things were turning around. The mighty Wilhelm was cowering, retreating with his tail between his legs.

In September, almost a year to the day when he'd last seen Dionne, Philippe Durand was given leave from the front. He returned to the City of Bridges.

* * *

Breathless with anticipation, Philippe jumped from the streetcar and hastened to the Inn of the Bluebird. Stopping in front of the building, he looked up at the window of the room where he and Dionne had spent their last night together.

Entering, he found the concierge's desk unattended. Darting past it, Philippe took the stairs two at a time. As he sped down the hallway, his mouth felt dry and his heart pounded madly.

Reaching the door, he knocked softly ... then more firmly. But no one responded. Hurrying down the stairs again, he hit the bell on the desk with the heel of his hand until the concierge emerged from his quarters.

"Aaah ... oui! Mademoiselle Caron ... la jeune garde-malade. Mais non, monsieur, elle n'est pas içi."

Philippe felt a shiver go through him as the man explained that he had not seen Dionne in a very long time.

"She returned here just once. I think it was during the summer. Or perhaps it was spring. I don't remember. I suggest that you ask at l'Hôtel Dieu. I'm sure they can tell you something." Apologizing, he went on to add that since the

335

bombardment, there'd been a lot of confusion everywhere.

Philippe had not heard that Bruges had been under siege. He wasted no time asking further questions. Taking to the street, he ran the two miles to l'Hôtel Dieu.

Entering the hospital, he looked around for someone ... anyone who might give him information. Midway down the corridor, sitting behind a counter, was a middle-aged woman sorting a large stack of papers.

Philippe approached her. "Excuse me, I was told you could tell me where I might find a Miss Dionne Caron? She's with Unit 112 of the International Red Cross."

"Dionne? Did you say Dionne Caron?" She looked at him suspiciously and before he could reply, she rose, saying: "One moment, please." She left her post, but in minutes she returned, followed by a man dressed in a long physician's coat.

He walked over to Philippe and held out his hand. "I'm Doctor Herve Laurier. May I ask who you are, please?"

"My name is Durand. Father Philippe Durand. I'm a friend of Dionne's ... and her family."

"I see. Please, sir, let's talk in my office."

Seating themselves, Doctor Laurier slowly inclined his head. "I'm afraid I have very bad news to give you, Father."

Doctor Laurier's voice suddenly sounded as if it was far away. Philippe heard words like airplanes ... explosions. ... Panic filled his entire being. He broke out in a sweat and his hands shook.

"I'm so sorry, Father. Three months ago, we lost our beautiful Dionne." The physician's voice trailed away to a whisper. Reaching inside his desk drawer, Laurier removed a packet of letters. "These belong to you, Father."

Philippe stared at them blankly. "Where is she? What did they do with her?"

"She's here in Bruges, in the Friedhof of the Holy Sepulcher."

It wasn't until the next day that the groundskeeper at the

336

cemetery found Philippe lying face down on Dionne's grave. At first he'd thought him to be dead, but on closer inspection realized he was still breathing. He then tried, without success, to get Philippe to speak. Calling out to one of his co-workers, the groundskeeper sent him to notify the authorities. Just before sunset, a Canadian army officer and an enlisted man came and took Philippe away.

Chapter Thirty-Seven

November, 1916

The hospital ship *Sanctuary* arrived in Halifax after a peaceful crossing—a blessing to the bewildered, broken men she carried.

The Reverend Paul Tremblay stood anxiously waiting on the crowded dock. He'd been standing there in the cold for almost two hours.

Having been notified by cable that Father Durand was being returned to Canada, the chancellery arranged for Paul to see to his transfer to Misericordia Hospital in Montreal. No mention was made as to the nature of Philippe's wounds. As a result, Paul was very tense; he had no idea what to expect. Philippe had written a number of times, but it had been months since he'd heard from him.

This had been a dismal year for Paul. In February, his father had died of an unsuspected heart ailment. Edgar Tremblay had left for his office one morning and never returned. Paul and his mother were still absorbing the shock of it when they received the news of Dionne's death.

Despite Paul's many attempts to do so, Monique and Leo Caron were not to be consoled. They were devastated ... totally incapable of accepting the tragic loss of their daughter. And now ... Philippe.

Paul walked alongside the huge transport searching for a vantage point from which he might see more clearly. Having no sooner found one, a macabre procession began passing before him.

A large number of wounded were being carried from the vessel on stretchers. Paul pushed his way closer, looking carefully at each litter as it passed, hoping that Philippe would not go by him unrecognized. Following the litter-bearers were the walking wounded—a grim collection of bandaged or otherwise altered bodies still capable of navigating under their own power. Philippe was among the first to descend.

Led by a corpsman who held onto his hand, he appeared to be sightless as he descended the gangplank. Paul suppressed an urge to cry out.

Gaunt, his parchment-like skin stretched tightly across his cheekbones, Philippe stared vacantly into the back of the man who led him. As he stepped onto Canadian soil, Paul called out to the corpsman.

"Yes sir?" the young man acknowledged immediately.

"I'm Father Tremblay. I've been sent by the chancellery in Montreal to accompany Father Durand to Misericordia Hospital. Can that be arranged?"

"Aye, Father, I'm sure that it can. Just follow me."

Paul put his arm around Philippe's shoulders. "Philippe ... Philippe ... it's Paul. Remember me, old buddy?"

Philippe's expression remained blank, his stare unfocused.

Paul turned to the corpsman. "He doesn't seem able to see or speak. What's wrong with him? Is he blind?"

"No sir, he isn't. I was told that it's shellshock. He hasn't spoken a word since they found him lying on a grave in a cemetery in Belgium. It sometimes happens that way. When it's just about over, their nerves give way."

During the hour or more that was needed to process the necessary papers, Philippe slumped in a corner of the customs building.

"If you'll sign here, Father, you can be on your way. There's transportation outside to take you to the railway."

Paul helped Philippe to his feet and led him out the door. They sat in the rear of an ambulance next to a man who'd lost a leg above the knee. He lay in a daze of laudanum.

As soon as they were underway, Philippe fell asleep. Paul held him in his arms like a child, protecting his head from bumping against the roof of the vehicle as they jostled through the rutted pavement into the city.

Arriving at the depot, Paul ushered Philippe onto the train. Although he didn't resist, Paul felt him stiffen as they mounted the steps.

"You're safe now, Phil. We're almost home, old buddy."

Chapter Thirty-Eight

The house felt warm and inviting as Melinda let herself in. Stooping, she picked up the mail from beneath the slot and laid it on the console next to the door. After removing her coat, she went into the kitchen to prepare a pot of tea.

Once it was steeping under the cozy, Melinda sat at the dining room table and sorted the mail. She dreaded going through it nowadays. Having had no word from Philippe in weeks, she lived in constant fear that something terrible had happened to him.

On top of the stack were several bills that she promptly set aside. Fingering through the others, she found a letter from her brother, Monsignor Bérard. Jean was so good at helping to keep her spirits up; so calm, so logical, all of the things that she wasn't. Beneath his was a letter posted from Montreal, bearing the seal of the chancellery. She opened it first ... it was from Father Tremblay.

Chère Madame,

Your son is once again safe on Canadian soil.

Melinda felt her body go limp, and her breath caught in her throat.

Despite his weakened condition, the doctors at Misericordia Hospital are satisfied that he is in reasonably sound health. Thank God we have that on our side.
It is with heavy heart, however, that I must tell you Philippe's mind has been tragically traumatized. So much so that

he has retreated inside himself, and so far no one has succeeded in reaching him.

Philippe is a strong man, and I am confident that with time, this condition will reverse itself.

After conferring at length with Doctor Canuel, the psychiatrist attending him, it was suggested that seeing his family might trigger a favorable response.

I will be more than happy to make any or all arrangements for your visit. My mother is alone at Terrebonne and would welcome having you stay with her for as long as you wish. We must together search out every avenue of help that is open to Philippe. I believe that with the aid of those who love him, he will eventually be himself again.

Anxiously awaiting your response, I am respectfully yours in Christ,

Paul Tremblay

* * *

The following morning as he walked through the factory toward his mother's office, Marc couldn't help noticing the dramatic changes that had been made at Miroff and Friedman. It'd been a long time since he'd last been here; since before his marriage to Catherine.

His mother's message to meet with her here had put him off considerably. She'd never sent for him before—ever. Something had to be wrong, probably having to do with his brother. But Marc wouldn't let himself think beyond that. He'd postponed everything on his calendar for this forenoon and rushed right over.

Finding no trace of Melinda in her office, he was about to search her out, when Sari Miroff came through the door.

Dammit! he thought. *She's the last person I wanted to run into this morning.* They'd not been in touch since he'd returned to Riverton, and their last encounter had left them both bitter.

A pair of hostile eyes looked up into his. "Well, if it isn't

342

little Marc Durand." Sari's voice was hard, flinty. "You're a little off course down here, aren't you? Your mother's office was moved upstairs over a year ago."

Marc considered thanking her and leaving, just letting it go at that. Instead, he grinned and said, "Good to see you, Sari."

"Liar."

"C'mon Sari, don't."

"Don't what?"

"Don't be so angry."

"Angry? That's hardly the word I'd use to describe the way I feel about you, Marc." Her eyes glowed like smoldering coals. "You know ... I still find it hard to believe you did that." She shook her head slowly from side to side. "I was stupid enough to think we meant something special to each other. If not love, then at least respect." She turned away, struggling to control her feelings.

Marc said softly, "Sari."

She whirled around and threw herself against him.

He held her close until she stopped crying.

"You bastard," she said as he released her. "Why didn't you tell me you were going to marry Catherine? *Why didn't you have the guts to tell me?* It would have hurt, but I could have handled that. You made me feel like a tramp, Marc."

When he answered, his voice was hushed with emotion. "I don't know, Sari. I was confused. I'd convinced myself that you didn't give a damn about me. God! Can you ever forgive me, Sari?" He put his arms around her again.

For a moment she couldn't answer. Then, pulling away from him, she admitted, "Yes, dammit, I can." She heard him sigh. Taking a handkerchief from her pocket, Sari dabbed at her eyes. "I'm glad this is over with. Maybe now I can give it a rest." Reaching out, she pulled Marc's head down and kissed his cheek. "She's a lucky girl. I'm so jealous of her I can't stand it." Her eyes filled again. "Be happy, baby. I really want that for you. Now, go already, before I make a fool of myself again."

Marc walked past the freight elevator and took the stairs up. He needed more time to gather himself before meeting with his mother. He stood outside her office for several minutes before going in.

The instant he entered, Melinda pushed back her chair and went to him.

"Thank you for coming so quickly, Marc."

She hadn't slept the entire night and her face reflected the stress that bore down on her like a dead weight.

"What is it, Mother? What's going on?"

"I think the best way to tell you is to let you read Father Tremblay's letter."

"PHILIPPE!" Marc cried out. Suddenly the worst of his fears was being realized.

Melinda reached for his hand. "Philippe is alive and uninjured, but there's something else we must deal with, dear. Please ... just read the letter."

Melinda walked to the window. A shaft of sunlight raised traces of gold in her silvering hair. Looking out, she could see the city hall and the giant hands of the clock pointing to the hour. Further down on Maincrossing Road, she saw Whitehead's green and white awning, its scalloped edges flapping in the wind. Why did it all look so normal when everything in her life was turning upside down?

Finishing, Marc laid the letter down on her desk.

"Will you go with me, Marc?"

"Of course, Mama."

"Thank you. What about Catherine and the baby? Will they be all right?"

"I'll ask Caitlin to stay with them while I'm gone. She loves visiting with Jody."

"When can we leave?"

"I'll need a day or two to rearrange my schedule at the office. ... Thursday. We can leave Thursday."

* * *

By noon, the train was north of Boston, approaching the

New Hampshire town of Walden. A dusting of snow covered the land and the roofs of the farmhouses they sped past. Melinda didn't see them, so preoccupied was she with thoughts of Philippe. Suddenly, she felt Marc's hand closing over hers.

"He'll be all right, Mama."

Melinda leaned against his shoulder and closed her eyes. She slept for the first time since receiving Paul's letter.

* * *

They arrived at the chancellery shortly after ten in the morning. Without wasting a minute, Paul took them to Misericordia Hospital.

Doctor Ramon Canuel was a short, swarthy man who spoke with a lisping Portuguese accent. His friendly, reassuring smile helped put them at ease immediately.

"Thank you for responding as you have. I realize that we've totally disrupted your lives. I'm sorry about that, but we do need your help."

Seating themselves on the well-worn sofa, Melinda and Marc nervously waited for him to begin.

"I'm sure I need not tell you that we are dealing with a very complex man. I've been told that for months, Father Durand has been on the front lines in Belgium ministering to severely wounded and dying soldiers. Think for a moment what the sight of this carnage could do to a sensitive person." He paused, allowing them time to do exactly that. "On an everyday basis, it might be enough to destroy even the most hardened among us." He coughed and cleared his throat. "I'm convinced, however, that this is not the only thing that propelled your son into the abyss of catatonia. I feel strongly that there is something more, something extremely personal that he's experienced, and is now repressing deep within his subconscious."

Getting up, Canuel walked around to the front of his desk and rested his body against the beveled edge. His eyes widened and he leaned toward them. "We must not allow him to

345

do that! We must uncover whatever it is he's hiding, and help him deal with it. He can never be well again until he does that. You understand what I'm saying?"

Marc and Melinda each nodded.

Marc said, "We'll do whatever it takes, Doctor. Just tell us how can we help."

Canuel returned to his chair. "You can help in a number of ways. First, we will attempt to talk with Father Durand. It's not probable, but seeing you might possibly shock him out of it. You can also help me to understand the more intricate facets of his personality. His childhood ..." he said, looking at Melinda, "important events that took place in his life. The milestones, so to speak. What shaped him and formed him into the person he is today. Perhaps there are letters ..."

Melinda rose from her seat. "I've saved all of Philippe's letters. Every word he's written home since leaving to study at l'Académie."

"Excellent, madame. Perhaps you will send them to me when you return home. Even the most insignificant note might turn up something that will help me to help him."

Melinda nodded. The color in her cheeks was returning.

Canuel noticed, and hurried to interject: "Please, madame, don't misunderstand me. There are no easy solutions to this case. Your son is a very sick man. It will take time for him to recover. And one thing more—sometimes we succeed, other times we fail."

Marc asked, "Can we see him?"

"Yes. But first I want to prepare you for the changes that have taken place in him. His appearance will not be as you remember it. He's very thin, and he's truly catatonic. He will not respond to you in any way. Don't expect that—and don't *force* anything. If we do, we risk pushing him further into himself. I suggest that you rest and return in an hour or so."

* * *

Smelling the onions in his omelet reminded Marc of how

346

little he'd eaten in the last two days. His mouth watered as he hurried to lift his fork to his mouth. Melinda picked at her plate listlessly, her thoughts still in Doctor Canuel's office.

"Try to eat something, Mama."

"I'm not hungry, dear."

"I know, but you need to keep up your strength."

Nodding, she began to eat a little of her salad. Then, looking at Marc again, she asked, "He will get well again, won't he, Marc?"

"We have to have faith, Mama."

"I know, but when I see what he's gone though—"

"Don't be afraid, Mama. Philippe will come back to us one day. I refuse to believe he was spared just to live like a caged animal."

Melinda stared at Marc. She hadn't realized until now how much she'd come to depend on his strength. He'd been there beside her when Joseph was hurt, and later when death took him without warning. So many times, he'd appeared out of nowhere when she was on the raw edge and anguish threatened to engulf her. Even as a child, he'd sensed her pain and wanted to share it with her. *Oh Marc, how can I tell you what this has meant to me?* her heart cried.

Chapter Thirty-Nine

Upon entering the chapel on the ground floor of the hospital, Melinda and Marc knelt for a moment of prayer. After a while, Marc left his mother and waited for her in the corridor.

Doctor Canuel found him there, leaning against the wall. "Still in the chapel, is she?" Canuel asked.

"Yes, I'll see what's keeping her."

"Let her be. There's no hurry."

Moments later Melinda appeared in the corridor with her shoulders squared and head held high. With Marc holding onto her hand, they went up to the second floor.

The door to Philippe's room was locked, but in the center of it was a narrow panel of glass at eye level.

Doctor Canuel looked through it, then moving aside, he asked, "Would you like your son to look first, madame?"

"No. No thank you." Without hesitating, Melinda walked up to the door and looked straight ahead into the room.

Philippe lay on his side, facing the wall. His hair hung down to his shoulders, and what little she could see of his face was covered with an unkempt beard.

"He's so thin."

"He's force-fed, Madame Durand. It's difficult to get any amount of food inside him."

"I see."

Philippe's bushy hair made his head look massive, yet at the same time he appeared meek and defenseless. He lay in a womb position, his knees pulled up toward his chest, his long, thin arms also drawn to the chest. His head fell forward slightly, and he looked as though he were sleeping. Had she not known it were Philippe, Melinda would never have recognized this man as her son.

"Mama?" Marc's voice returned her to the moment.

She withdrew.

Marc stepped up to the door and looked at his brother. Uttering an oath under his breath, he closed his eyes. When he opened them again, Philippe had turned over and was looking straight at him.

Back in Doctor Canuel's office, Melinda and Marc sat next to each other on the sofa. Melinda reached for Marc's hand. It felt cold as ice.

"I know this has been trying for both of you," Canuel began, his hands rearranging the stacks of paperwork that were piled all over his desk.

"I think 'shocking' would be a more appropriate word," Marc snapped.

Canuel turned to Melinda. "And you, madame, what word would you choose?"

"Hopeful. Philippe is alive. He's in God's hands, and yours."

The Durands remained at Terrebonne for two weeks, visiting with Philippe as often as they were permitted. Usually they found him much as they had the first time. Either he sat on his bed, his head cradled in his hands, or he lay facing the wall curled up like a fetus. However, on the day before their return to Riverton, they found him sitting on the floor in a corner of the room.

Melinda rushed over to him. "Philippe? Let me help you, dearest."

He looked like a terrified child. His eyes blinked frequently and they darted anxiously around the room.

Melinda sat on the floor next to him and folded him into her arms. She held him to her as she had when he was a baby, his head next to her shoulder, his hand resting on her arm. Rocking him back and forth, she hummed a lullaby, one that she'd sung to him a hundred times or more: "Un petit berceau d'or, pour mon joli garçon."

Philippe seemed not to see or hear her, but as she hummed, she felt the slightest bit of pressure coming from his hand. In a second it was gone, and she wondered if she had imagined it.

Melinda and Marc left Montreal. Paul attempted to comfort them with assurances that Philippe would always receive the best of care. He would see to it, and so would the order. Marc thanked him as he pressed Paul's hand tightly between his, thinking how blessed Philippe was to have such a man for a friend.

Philippe's failure to show improvement over December and January was not cause for Doctor Canuel to lose heart. To the contrary, he was encouraged that Philippe had not further regressed.

Melinda returned to Canada in mid-February, and Monsignor Jean-Philippe Bérard left his duties at Saint Charles Seminary in Sherbrooke to reunite with his sister at Terrebonne.

While they were there, word came of the death of Daniel, Marie-Élise's husband.

The next morning, a cold rain pelting down on them, they left for Baie de Saint-Jacques to bury their old friend.

Doctor Canuel regretted their leaving so soon, but if the truth be known, it was Paul Tremblay's steadfast loyalty that he had come to depend on.

Not a day passed that Paul didn't call at Misericordia to see Philippe. His visits were sometimes lengthy, other times lasting no more than five or ten minutes. Just long enough for him to put an arm around Philippe's shoulders and say "Good morning, old buddy."

Paul wouldn't give up, nor would he allow Philippe to be forgotten by anyone. Each week he wrote to Riverton and to Le Baie, giving Philippe's family the details of his treatment. A time-consuming task that he heaped atop his already burgeoning schedule.

Arriving at Misericordia late on a snowy March afternoon, Paul was surprised to find a beautiful young woman
sitting in the chair at Philippe's bedside, reading aloud from
a well-worn book of sonnets.

Her hair, dark and burnished, swept away from her face in
deep waves. Her elongated eyes, the color of polished mahogany, smiled at Paul as he entered.

Introducing himself, he asked who she was.

"I'm Dominique, Philippe's cousin," she explained.

"You're Marie-Élise's daughter."

"I am."

"I was saddened to hear of your father's death."

"Thank you. We felt it a blessing, really. He had lung and
stomach cancer and he suffered a great deal."

"How is your mother bearing up?"

"Very well. My mother is a strong woman. She never
questions Divine Providence. My husband and I have moved
in with her at Les Érables. Alain has agreed to take over the
farm."

"You're happy about that. I can hear it in your voice."

"Yes, I am. You see, Father, to me, Les Érables is a living, breathing thing. And thanks to my aunt, Philippe's
mother, Bérards will live there forever. My sons, and theirs,
will carry on long after we've gone from here. That is the
legacy Melinda Durand has granted us."

"How long has it been since you've seen Philippe?"

"Years. Not since he left Sherbrooke to go to Nicolet."

"Were you close?"

"Yes, very close. When we were children we spent a lot
of time together. Philippe was the first boy I ever fell in love
with."

* * *

Sundays were often Paul's busiest day. In the recent past,
many of them were spent at Terrebonne helping his mother
muddle her way through the reams of paperwork having to

351

do with his father's business. On this particular Sunday, however, he didn't go there. He went instead to Nicolet. François Caron had returned from Europe the previous week, and with him had come the body of his sister. On Monday morning, Dionne Caron would be buried in the cemetery behind Saint Basil's Church.

Agnes opened the door to Paul. "Père Tremblay, it's wonderful to see you."

"Thank you, Agnes."

"They're waiting for you in the sitting room, Father."

Paul was instantly aware of the sadness permeating every inch of this grief-stricken house; it unmistakably dropped like at leaden mantle over his shoulders.

Without greeting of any sort, François threw himself into Paul's arms. His shoulders shook as Paul held him in a moment so filled with love it was tangible.

Releasing him, Paul said, "Let me look at you. ... Let me feast my eyes." Paul walked in a circle around his friend, eyeing him up and down. "You look superb!"

"As do you, Father."

"Father? Since when have I been Father to you?"

"Since today—this moment. Do you mind, Father? I promise you, I won't let it interfere with our political discussions."

"Of course I don't mind. That is, unless you expect me to call you Major Caron."

Everyone laughed including Leo, who up until then had seemed extremely somber. While waiting for that rare moment of levity to subside, Paul kissed Monique's cheek and shook Leo's hand.

Crossing the room again, Paul stood beside François's chair and looked at each one in turn. "This is a very singular day ... for all of us. We gather to greet François with so much happiness in our hearts, yet we suffer the terrible loss of Dionne as well. Unless it's too distressing for anyone, I'd like to say a few words about that."

Slowly, deliberately, Leo's large leonine head nodded.

Monique's lips pulled into a wistful smile. She said, "Leo and I speak of her often, Father. We always shall. We cherish our memories of Dionne. They are all we have left of her. Please, say whatever you wish."

"Thank you. I was quite sure you'd feel that way." Paul thought for a minute, fixing firmly in his mind what he wanted to say. "I want you to know how pleased I am that Dionne's been returned to us. She belongs here in Nicolet. It was difficult for me to think of her lying in foreign soil. I'm sure it was for all of you as well."

"Very," Monique murmured.

François got out of his chair and walked to the hearth. He stared down into the fire. "I personally couldn't bear to think of my sister being buried in Bruges," he said, "unknown to anyone but her gravekeeper. I would have remained in Europe for as long as was necessary. I simply *couldn't* leave her behind." His voice dwindled to a whisper, and Monique went and put her arms around him.

"Dionne is home again, Father," she remarked as she stroked her son's back, "and yes, there is great sorrow that accompanies her coming. But there is also great comfort in knowing that she'll be nearby. She loved Nicolet. It's where she would have wanted to be."

Monique's words seemed to close a chapter. To put an end to the tragedy that was Dionne. And to bring forth instead her bright and shining spirit that would live on in each of their hearts. But Paul knew, as each of them did, that the loss of her had diminished their lives forever.

The next morning at the conclusion of the funeral service, Paul left the Caron family to their private farewells at the grave.

As he walked from the cemetery with Augustin Tullie, he looked up at the spire of Saint Basil's, which was wrapped in a cone-shaped blanket of snow. Philippe was never far from his thoughts, but here in this place he was haunted by him. The church, the rectory, the stone wall he'd built around the path to the graveyard. So much of him had been left behind.

Paul accepted a cup of coffee from Madame Boucher, but declined her invitation to stay for dinner at noon. He wanted to get back to the city in time for his visit with Philippe.

* * *

As Paul had come to expect, nothing had changed when he entered the room. Philippe lay on his bed, his eyes riveted to the wall, fixed in that vapid, trance-like state he'd been in since arriving from Halifax five months previous.

Removing his coat, Paul threw it over a chair. *Why is it always so hot in this room?* he wondered.

Reaching over, he touched Philippe's arm as he always did. "Hello Phil, it's Paul."

Dropping into the chair, Paul looked at the snowflakes collecting on the windowsill. He was tired, emotionally, and physically spent.

"I'm sorry I wasn't able to be here yesterday, Phil. I took the train to Nicolet. François Caron arrived home last week." Paul always spoke to Philippe as if he were able to understand him. "I haven't mentioned any of this before, but I'd like to talk about it now. ... Dionne Caron was killed in the war. She died in Bruges, in Belgium, in a bombardment of the city. François was allowed to bring her body back to Canada last week. They buried her this morning in the cemetery behind Saint Basil's."

Philippe sat bolt upright in his bed, his hands clawing his face. A tortured cry rose from deep within him. The sound of it made Paul's flesh crawl.

Panic-stricken, Paul rose and ran into the corridor, shouting to anyone within earshot.

A young intern left his patient and ran to investigate. "What's happened!" the intern shouted.

"It's Father Durand," Paul replied breathlessly. "He's sitting on his bed screaming. He hasn't so much as uttered a sound in months. Please go to him before he hurts himself. I'll try to find Doctor Canuel!"

* * *

After what seemed like an eternity, Canuel rejoined Paul, who was pacing the corridor.

"Relax, Father, he's quiet now. We've given him enough sedation to drop an elephant."

Paul sighed.

His blanched complexion gave the physician a moment of concern. "Are you all right, Father?"

"I think so."

"Just relax."

Paul nodded.

"Are you able to answer a few questions for me?"

Paul nodded again, his face still white as a sheet.

"Take it easy, Father," Canuel repeated. "This may just be the break we've been waiting for. Let's go into my office. I'll have someone bring us some coffee."

"I don't want any coffee," Paul answered as he walked down the stairs.

Paul poured himself a glass of water from the decanter on Canuel's desk. He took a couple of swallows, then drained the glass. "This has been one hell of a day," he said.

"Tell me about it."

"Right. Well ... I returned from Nicolet this afternoon. I went up there yesterday to attend the funeral of a friend. A very special friend, of mine and Philippe's. She was buried this morning. When I got back to Montreal this afternoon, I came directly here. Philippe was the same as he always is. Just lying there. I felt depressed, and I began talking about Dionne and the funeral."

Doctor Canuel looked surprised.

Paul hurried to set him straight. "I don't usually do that. I mostly just gab about everyday stuff, or I read him the newspapers. But today I talked about Dionne. I'm sorry. I guess I shouldn't have."

"Just what did you tell him? As closely as you can recall."

Paul's shoulders sagged and he let out a stream of pent-up breath. "I told him that she'd died in Belgium during the war. Was that wrong?"

"Nothing is right or wrong, Father. Just important or unimportant. Was he close to this woman?"

"He was her priest."

"Tell me exactly how she died."

"She was staying with a friend in Bruges. They were walking home from a café when they were caught in the bombardment and were both killed. I'm told the other woman was blown to bits."

"Did you tell him that? In those words?"

"Heavens no! I wouldn't do that!" Irritated, Paul glared at Canuel for several moments before continuing. "François Caron, Dionne's brother, brought her body home last week. I was telling Philippe about the funeral when it happened."

"Good God!" The doctor's voice was almost inaudible and his face was suddenly beaded with perspiration.

"What's the matter?" Paul asked sharply.

"I'm not sure, but there is one hell of a big connection here."

"What connection?"

"I guess you've forgotten, Father, but Philippe Durand was found lying face down on a grave in the city of Bruges."

Paul didn't sleep at all that night. As he'd left Misericordia, Canuel emphasized that it could have been merely coincidence, but Paul was sure that it wasn't. Vivid memories shot to the forefront of his mind. Memories of the day when Philippe had left the chancellery, livid with anger at Paul's suggestion that he cared too much about Dionne. For a moment Paul had felt Philippe might strike him. It was the only instance in all their years as friends that anything like that had ever happened. No, this was no mere coincidence. Whatever had happened to Philippe was connected to what had happened to Dionne. Paul was never more sure of anything in his life.

Rising, he dressed and ate something. He could no longer bear to lie abed and think. He left the chancellery and crossed Saint Catherine Street, over to Rue de la Charité.

The snow had stopped falling and a clear winter dawn

was breaking through the purple clouds.

Canuel was already sitting at the desk in his office. He'd been there most of the night, reading and re-reading Philippe's records, looking for something—anything—that would help unlock his patient's mind. He had never believed the shell shock business. This man was too strong to crack like that. Lighting a cigarette, he greeted Paul as he entered.

"Anything happening, Doctor?"

Looking up, his eyes puffy from lack of sleep, Canuel answered in a dull monotone. "Not so's you'd notice, Father. Listen, why don't you go back home and get some sleep. Father Durand isn't going to snap out of this just like that. We don't have miracles here," he added a bit abrasively, "just a lot of hard work." He stopped, instantly regretting the snide remark. "I'm sorry, I didn't mean that. ... No offense, Father. I could chew shoe leather this morning."

"Forget it. No changes at all, eh?"

"None. Not since the episode when you were here. He's been sleeping off the drugs ever since then. I've done a lot of thinking, though, and I have a plan that I think is worth exploring. It will take time and patience, and I'll need your help, Father."

"Anything."

"You know, I've never asked this, but you've given above and beyond the call for this man, Father Tremblay. Why?"

"I love him."

"Well, that's simple enough, isn't it? I'll try as much as possible to work within your schedule, but you're the most important bit of hope we have right now. Get some rest. You're going to need it."

Very early the following morning they climbed the stairs to the second floor. Doctor Canuel unlocked the door to Philippe's room and entered quietly. Philippe was turned, facing the wall, his eyes closed.

Doctor Canuel seated himself on a stool next to the door and with his hand, motioned Paul to approach the bed.

"Just talk to him," he whispered.

Pulling the chair up next to the bed, Paul sat for a minute, saying nothing. He didn't know how to begin. Finally he stopped thinking and just let the words flow. "Good morning, Phil. I'm sorry you weren't feeling well yesterday. I hope you're better this morning.

"Did I tell you that His Excellency is being retired at the end of this year? He's been battling his age for the last five years, and I guess it's caught up with him. He's done a great job in his tenure, but it's time they put the old guy out to pasture. His memory has failed a lot, and you can't be a shepherd when you don't know who the sheep are."

Paul took a deep breath and looked back at the doctor. Turning back to Philippe, he went on. "Do you remember what we were talking about yesterday? I don't think I finished telling you what happened to Dionne—"

Philippe began banging his head against the wall.

Doctor Canuel rushed to the bedside and took over. "Who is Dionne Caron, Father Durand? Why does the mention of her name upset you so much? Tell me, Father, tell me about Dionne."

Sobs began wracking Philippe's body, and his eyes stared wildly into space. It was as though he were seeing something he couldn't bear to look at. His lips twisted and pulled from one side to the other.

Leaning close to him, Canuel took the young priest's body into his arms. "It's all right, Philippe. Tell me about Dionne."

His voice raspy and almost unrecognizable, Philippe spoke his first harrowing words. "I killed her. ... I killed her." His body contorted and fell back onto the bed.

Doctor Canuel reached into his pocket and wiped the sweat from Philippe's face with his handkerchief. "No, Philippe, you didn't kill her. You were nowhere near Dionne Caron when she died."

Philippe's body slowly curled up. He turned and faced the wall. His eyes closed and he went limp. He seemed to sleep.

Paul stood against the wall in a daze, his face wet with

tears.

"Let's give it a rest for now. He's had enough." Canuel turned to leave. Seeing Paul's face the color of chalk, he walked over to him and gripped his shoulder firmly. "We've taken a giant step here today, Father."

Paul couldn't answer.

"Go home, my friend. I've a feeling our work has been cut out for us."

Each day another bit of Philippe's mind grasped reality. Each day he let go of a microcosm of pain. He began to trust again.

Canuel's approach was gentle. He pressed, but never too hard. Philippe still responded best to Paul, however. It seemed sometimes as though they were speaking in the privacy of a confessional.

It didn't always go well. There were entire weeks when Philippe once more retreated into the protective realm of silence, and Paul would fear that they'd lost him again. Other times, he would become agitated and violent. He'd strike out at Paul, his face contorted with rage.

Paul managed to protect himself most of the time, using his voice to calm and restrain Philippe. "It's all right. It's all right. Let me help you, Philippe."

"I don't want your help. Yours or that son-of-a-bitch who calls himself a doctor. Leave me alone!! Let me forget."

"You can't forget, Phil, you know that. Whatever it is that's made you sick won't simply go away. You have to face it, deal with it. If you don't, it will make you sick again. You can't run away, old buddy. The doctor's told you that over and over again."

April and May passed. Most often, they took one step forward and three steps back. Discouraged, Paul was sometimes tempted to give up the fight, to turn Philippe over entirely to the professionals.

But Canuel always talked him out of it. "Right now, you can do so much more for him than we can. He trusts you,

Father."

Now the calendar said June. One month had passed into the next and the next. It was so easy to lose track of time.

Entering Philippe's room on a morning that followed a long, difficult weekend, Paul realized immediately that something had changed.

Philippe stood looking out the window. "It's summer again, isn't it?" he asked as Paul came and stood next to him.

"Almost. It's the tenth of June."

Philippe smiled for the first time. "Tomorrow's my birthday," he said.

"That's right, it is. I hadn't remembered. You seem rested today. Did you sleep well last night?"

"I had a dream, Paul."

"Was it a good dream?"

"I dreamed about Dionne."

"Can you tell me about it?"

"I dreamed we were together again, in Bruges."

"I didn't know you were together in Belgium, Philippe."

"Yes, we were. I literally ran into her while I was on leave. I'd been sick for a long time, and I was on my way back to my regiment."

"I knew you'd been sick. You wrote me about it from Saint Julien, remember? Now, what was your dream about?"

"Dionne was so beautiful. I can't forget her eyes. Even when I close mine, I see them." Philippe pressed his lids together tightly. He continued talking, more to himself than to Paul. "I loved her so much."

"We all loved her, Phil."

"I don't mean that kind of love, Paul. I mean the love a man has for a woman. Passionate, physical love."

Paul felt a flutter of nerves break loose inside him. He tried to keep his voice calm. "You're a human being, Phil, even if you are a priest."

"I'm not a priest anymore. Not after what happened between Dionne and me."

Paul's hands curled into fists and his nails dug into the

flesh of his palms. "What happened, Phil? Were you and Dionne lovers?"

"Yes. We were."

For a time Paul couldn't speak. He felt so many conflicting emotions. Pity, anger, betrayal. Then he said, "Let me be clear about this, Phil. When you and Dionne were together in Europe, did you consummate that love?"

"Yes."

For an instant Paul was again stricken mute.

"Don't hate me, Paul, please!" Philippe begged.

"I could never hate you, Phil," Paul assured him, his voice hardly above a whisper. "When did all this happen? When did you know that you loved Dionne?"

"It was in Nicolet. The day we went on the sleigh ride, remember? The very first time I saw her ... I loved her." Philippe's voice ebbed away. He walked to the bed and sat on the edge. "When I returned to Saint Charles, I was depressed. I seriously thought about leaving the seminary. But I'd made a promise to the Lord, and I wanted to keep it. Crazy as it may sound, I loved religious life. I still do." Lifting his head, he appraised the impact his words had on Paul, then went on: "I prayed for guidance and the strength I knew it would take to put Dionne out of my thoughts. Eventually it went away, and stayed away for a long, long time."

Philippe's thoughts turned inward and Paul sensed that he was far away.

"On the day of my ordination, it returned again when she came to receive at my altar. I struggled for a while, but it was easier the second time, and I really believed I had it beaten once and for all. ... Until five years later when I went to Saint Basil's. Circumstances kept throwing us together there. But nothing ever happened in Nicolet, Paul. You have to believe that."

"I do, Phil, I do. Please go on."

"When we met in Bruges, it was as if it was meant to be. I couldn't fight it anymore, and neither could Dionne." Philippe cupped his hands and covered his face. "God took her from me, Paul. He punished me for loving her when I had no right to."

Paul heard rather than saw Philippe's torment. He approached him and pulled his hands from his face. "LISTEN TO ME!" he ordered angrily. "God doesn't punish us for loving each other. He took her—yes—but for some other reason. And we can't question that."

"I'd like to believe you, Paul. But inside my head I keep hearing 'Accipe Spiritum Sanctum.' I broke my vows."

Paul sat beside him on the bed and took Philippe's hand into his. "Yes, you broke your vows ... but we're all of us, sinners, Phil! God will forgive you, through me, and if not me, through some other confessor. Now for His sake, *try to forgive yourself!*"

Philippe raised his head slowly then leaning, he kissed the back of Paul's hand. "This will change everything between us, won't it?"

"It already has. We're closer than we've ever been. I love you, old buddy. Nothing you can do will ever change that. Priests are not perfect. We're just ordinary people like everyone else."

Philippe got up and walked to the window. "I'd like to see my family, Paul. And one thing more. Someday when I'm well again, I want to go to Nicolet. I want to say goodbye to Dionne."

* * *

When Melinda and Marc arrived, they were surprised to find that Philippe was no longer at Misericordia. Paul had taken him to Terrebonne to complete his recovery.

The sight of Philippe standing in the garden made Melinda and Marc all but weep with joy. His hair was cut and he was clean shaven. Gone were the vapid, unseeing eyes. Gone were the cowering demeanor, the guilt, and the need to retreat from the world.

There was a bonding such as they had never known. A rebirth of trust, a renewing of faith, and the complete coming together of a family, for the first time.

Chapter Forty

Readjusting to the hurly-burly world of a newborn and a two-year-old wasn't a problem for Marc. He stepped around the bassinette, over the toys, and pulled his wife into his arms. "God, it's good to be home," he confessed.

"You look tired, sweetheart," Catherine observed immediately. "We'll talk later, after you've rested. I'll call a taxi to take Caitlin home."

"No, I'll drive her. I want to fill her in on the trip."

In the automobile on the way to Sladesferry Landing, Marc told Caitlin all there was to tell, without revealing anything personal.

"It's over, Caitie. My brother is well again."

"Well, praise the good Lord for that, love. I was beginning to fear it would never be over for Philippe."

"If it weren't for Father Tremblay, I think that might have been the case. He always believed Philippe would recover. We owe him so much. I don't know how we can ever repay him."

"There's no need to repay things that are done out of love, darlin'."

Marc carried Caitlin's bag inside and helped her remove her coat.

"I'll fix us something to drink," she said, hurrying toward the kitchen.

"No thanks, Caitie," Marc said. "I'm tired and I want to get home." Walking into the bedroom, he set Caitlin's suitcase down next to her bed, and hung her coat in the closet.

He was putting her umbrella on the shelf above, when a metal strongbox tumbled to the floor, missing his head by mere inches. Stooping, Marc gathered up the contents that had scattered all over the place. He was replacing them in the strongbox when he recognized his own handwriting on one of the envelopes. On impulse, he slid the pages out from inside. It read:

Most kind and benevolent Sir:

Marc's heart began beating faster and faster. He looked through the rest of the envelopes. He found them. Here, packed together in this tin box, were all the letters he'd written to his benefactor while he was studying law in Boston.

Marc rose to his feet, still holding some of them in his hand. Hearing Caitlin's heavy tread approaching, he quickly replaced everything in the box and closed the closet door. He met her just as she entered the room.

She looked at him curiously. "What is it, love? Ye look as if ye'd seen a ghost."

"It's nothing, Cait, I'm just tired. I'll be on my way now. I want to run upstairs and check on Mama before going home. Thanks for staying with Catherine and the kids. I don't know what I'd do without you." He kissed her on the forehead.

"Psshaw, go on with ye now. Ye know they're the dearest things to me heart."

Marc dashed up the stairs, the adrenaline pumping, his pulses pounding. "Mama!—MAMA?"

Still holding onto a dress she was unpacking, Melinda ran from the bedroom. "I'm here, Marc, what is it? What's happened?"

For a few seconds he couldn't go on. He walked into the kitchen, and she followed him, her eyes filled with concern.

"Is it, Philippe?" she asked, her high-pitched tone betraying her anxiety.

"No—it isn't Philippe! This time it's me, Mama." Trying hard to control himself, Marc told her what he'd found in

Caitlin's closet. "What do you know about this?"

"I know nothing about it, Marc. Absolutely nothing! I swear to you on your father's grave."

She was speaking the truth. There was no doubt in his mind about that. "Do you know what this means, Mama?"

"Yes dear. It means Caitlin paid for your education."

"God! This is so bizarre!"

Melinda stood waiting for him to say something.

"You know, it's really quite absurd. For years I've racked my brain trying to figure out who this person was, and the answer's been right here under my nose." Marc went and sat in his father's chair. "I just don't get it."

"Please, Marc, try to calm down. You must know how dearly Caitlin loves you. You're like her very own flesh and blood. She struggled with me to bring you into the world. She blew breath into your lungs. There hasn't been a moment since then that she hasn't felt a part of you. She has all that money Charles Mulvaney left her, and nothing or no one to give it to. You and your family are her life, Marc." Melinda stopped, remembering now how angry Marc had been when he'd come into the house. "What did you say to her, dear?"

"Nothing. She doesn't know I found the letters."

"Are you going to tell her?"

"Not now. I will someday, when I can find a proper way to thank her." He rose and started toward the door. Then he recalled Caitlin saying *"There's no need to repay things that are done out of love, darlin'."*

Marc turned to his mother. "I'm sorry, Mama, I shouldn't have come barging in here like this."

"Don't apologize, Marc. I understand."

"Thank you. I love you, Mama." The words spilled from his lips without his having intended to say them.

Her arms reached out to him. "And I love you, Marc. Now go home to your family. They've missed you."

Chapter Forty-One

Marc lay awake next to his wife, his arms cradling her as she slept. He'd been home for over a week now and he still couldn't get enough of her. Pressing his face close to Catherine's shoulder, he drew in the smell of her skin. He wanted to make love again, but he didn't awaken her. With a new baby to take care of, she needed her rest.

From a distance he heard a wailing sound coming through the night. It went on for a long time. Moving carefully, he got out of bed and went to the window.

A streak of scarlet cut through the blackness of the sky. A fire raged somewhere in the city, and even as Marc stood watching, it seemed to worsen. He went down to the kitchen. Pulling out a saucepan, he heated some milk. He was sitting at the table drinking it when Catherine appeared at the door. She came and sat across from him.

"Don't you ever sleep?" she asked, stifling a yawn.

"I woke you, I'm sorry. Want some milk?"

"Unh, unh." She shook her head no.

"Then go back to bed. It's one o'clock in the morning."

"What's on your mind, Marc? Why can't you sleep?"

"It's nothing to be concerned about."

"It's that case you were telling me about this morning, isn't it?"

"I guess so."

"All lawyers lose cases once in a while, Marc. Even Alex the Great."

"I know, sweetheart, but Alex Friedman isn't planning on running for district attorney. I am."

"It'll all work out, darling, one way or the other." Catherine slid her feet back into her slippers and shuffled off.

Wishing that he'd been endowed with the ability to look at life the way his wife did, Marc swallowed what was left of his milk, and began to climb the stairs. Again the wail of sirens returned his attention to the fire.

"God damn, that's getting closer," he said, as he continued going up.

* * *

Marc must have been sleeping soundly because the telephone bell didn't awaken him.

Catherine nudged him with her elbow. "Marc, answer the telephone."

Half in a daze, Marc jumped out of bed and clambered downstairs to the kitchen. He lifted the receiver from the hook. "Marc Durand."

"Marc—it's Alex. I hate to wake you at this hour, but M and F Manufacturing is burning to the ground."

Getting into his clothes, Marc tried to answer Catherine's questions. "Honey, the plant is on fire. That's all Alex could tell me."

The clock on the bedside table read two forty-five.

"I'll be home when I can, Cath. You get some sleep." Marc kissed her cheek and left.

He cranked up the engine of his Ford and drove downtown. He parked on Rock Street, in front of the high school, then walked the rest of the way.

As soon as he made the turn onto Maincrossing Road, acrid smoke reached Marc's nostrils and stung his eyes. A half-block farther, he felt the heat of the flames. He ran, as others along the street were doing. He could see the fire raging ahead of him, and the sound of excited voices were all around. Marc pushed and shoved his way through the crowd to where a policeman stood holding people back. At times like this, panic was always a possibility.

Marc called to him, but the officer deliberately turned

away.

Everyone was pressing against the ropes that were strung across Central Avenue. Marc was about to push his way out again, when he spotted Sam Miroff standing about fifty feet away from him.

"Mr. Miroff! Mr. Miroff!' Marc shouted above the din.

Sam turned and waved his arm. In a few moments, Marc reached his side.

"Jesus Christ, Sam, this is awful! Does my mother know?"

Sam said nothing. He lifted his hand and pointed ahead of him. Melinda stood pressed against the barricade, her eyes locked onto the scene in front of her.

As dawn approached, the fire intensified. A wind blowing in from the bay blew sparks from one roof to the other, igniting more buildings, and by daylight half the center of Riverton was burning.

Pumpers from as far away as Taunton and New Bedford came to help, but it was only when the rain began falling that hope of controlling the blaze became a reality. In an hour, the danger to the rest of the city had passed.

Marc took Melinda by the arm. "Come on, Mama ... let's go home."

He led Melinda through the thinning crowd, and as they walked up to Maincrossing Road she turned several times to look over her shoulder at the devastation.

By the time Melinda and Marc reached the car it was pouring, soaking them through to the skin. Deciding she shouldn't be alone, Marc drove his mother to his house, where Catherine wrapped her in a warm robe.

"Your feet are icy, Mother Durand," Catherine declared as she rubbed them with a Turkish towel.

"I'm all right, dear. No need to fuss."

"You're sure you won't have something to eat?"

"I'm fine, Catherine. I'd just like to rest for a while."

"All right. But be sure to lock the guest room door so that the children don't disturb you."

Catherine spread their wet clothing over the radiators to

dry, then she rejoined Marc in the living room.

"I think she's asleep," she said, reaching down to massage his neck and shoulders. "Are you all right, Marc?"

"Sure, I'm fine."

"I'm glad you're home. I was worried about you."

"I'm sorry. There wasn't any time to get word to you."

"Is everything lost?"

"Everything."

"Oh God!"

* * *

It was midafternoon when Melinda awakened; she'd rested only an hour or so. She got out of bed and went to the window. Looking out, she saw the heavy cloud of smoke that still hovered over Riverton. So many questions ran through her mind. Questions she had no answers for.

Her thoughts veered to Sam. He was alone. ... Sari had left for Europe on Saturday. When Melinda and Marc had left to go home, Sam was still standing there in the rain, his collar up, his hands plunged into the pockets of his overcoat. He seemed to be waiting for something to happen.

Going into the hall, Melinda gathered her clothes together. "Sam shouldn't be alone at a time like this," she muttered as she went into the bathroom. Her stockings and underthings felt damp and uncomfortable against her skin. She was buttoning her blouse when she heard a knock at the door.

Marc stood in the hallway, frowning. "Mama! What are you doing?"

"Please, Marc, don't interfere. I have to find Sam. He needs someone ... he needs ME."

"At least let me drive you downtown."

"No, dear, I'll be fine. I'll get in touch with you as soon as I can."

* * *

For a long time Sam had stood with a handful of people watching a group of men clean up the debris from the street. Maincrossing Road was open to traffic now, but Central Avenue was still roped off. It looked like a bomb had fallen on it. Getting rid of so much destruction would be a monumental job.

Sam didn't know how long it had been since the night watchman had called him. It seemed like days. Still, he stood there looking around as sunrays managed to strain through the haze of heavy smoke. His gray face was practically hidden by his water-stained hat.

Melinda spoke his name softly, not wanting to startle him. "Sam?"

Turning to her, his eyes rimmed with red, the bags under them pulling them down a little, he said, "Tell me, Melinda—can you believe what's happened here? What kind of a bad dream is this I'm having?"

"Come, Sam, let me take you home."

He walked with her over to Bedfordgate. "Where's your car, Sam?"

He shrugged his shoulders. "It doesn't matter, we'll take the streetcar."

They rode in silence, and for the first time since Melinda had known him, Sam looked old ... used up. All of his vitality had perished in the fire. He slumped against the window of the streetcar, lost in thought.

Reaching their stop, Melinda pulled at Sam's sleeve, and he followed her into the street. They walked the three blocks to his driveway and up to the door where his housekeeper let them in.

"Mr. Miroff! Thank God! I was so—"

"Not now, Mrs. Acot." He walked past her into the library and sat in the big leather chair.

Melinda turned to her. "Bring us a pot of tea and some sandwiches, Mrs. Acot."

Sam leaned his head against the back of the chair and looked up at the ceiling.

"Take your coat off, Sam," Melinda said gently. "It's all

wet."

It was as if he didn't hear her. "You know, young lady, I feel a little like the day that I got off the ship in New York. It was my first day in a new world. I had nothing. Nothing but youth and dreams and my Natia. Come to think of it, that was a lot." He grinned, his expression at once nostalgic and bittersweet. "I have none of those things anymore."

"Don't, Sam."

"No more dreams, Melinda. I'm too old for dreams." He turned to the table beside his chair and picked up a silver frame. "How long is it since she's gone, my Natia. I can't even remember anymore. Too long for a man to be alone ... too long." Sam smiled again. "You know, it's a funny thing. So many times I wanted to say, 'Marry me, Melinda ... we're two lonely old friends, and I care for you so much.' But then I'd think: What does she want with an old Jew like me."

Melinda knelt beside his chair and tears streamed down her face. "I would have been honored to have been your wife, Sam."

"Thank you. You're a kind person to say that, but I know better."

He got out of the chair and stood in front of the fire, his hands gripping the mantle, his head lowered between them. "Go home, Melinda, get some rest."

Mrs. Acot entered the room with a tray that she laid on the library table in the center of the room.

Melinda poured Sam a cup of tea and took it to where he stood.

"Sit down, Sam. Eat something."

He waved her off with a twist of his hand. "I'm going upstairs." Walking from the room, he mounted the walnut staircase that curled to the second floor. A streak of sunshine darted through the mullioned window on the landing and rested for a moment on his dark hair. Sam seemed to hesitate briefly when it touched him, then he continued on his way up.

"He wouldn't eat, Mrs. Acot," Melinda explained. "Try

again later, after he's rested."

Mrs. Acot nodded, the worry wrinkles around her eyes and mouth deepening. "Call me if there's anything I can do for him," Melinda added.

Turning, Melinda walked into the foyer. As she opened the door to leave, her body froze at the sound of the gunshot.

She ran up the stairs followed by the housekeeper. Opening the bedroom door, they found Sam lying on the pale blue carpet, the blood gushing from his head wound staining the rug a deep crimson. The small gun he had put to his temple rested on the floor at their feet.

* * *

It was a simple service, held at Temple Brith Kodesh where Sam and Natia had chosen to worship when they'd first arrived in Riverton. Solly and Mila were there, as were their sons, along with many members of the Riverton business community. Honoring such a man was a privilege, and they knew it.

Alex Friedman, Sam's closest friend in life, sometimes wept openly as he gave the eulogy. He finished by saying: "Samuel Miroff was loved by many, and those who didn't love him, respected him. He was the epitome of the 'American dream'—the impossible success story. The lowly immigrant who'd stepped onto these shores with nothing, and made it big, one step at a time, with patience and integrity. We'll miss you, Sam. They don't make them like you very often."

* * *

The loss of Sam was something Melinda would never stop feeling. The moment she'd seen him lying dead on the floor, a vacuum had entered her life. An empty, hollow place that Sam had once tilled to overflowing, lay gaping inside her like a wound. To live in a world without Sam was a very difficult thing.

Sari returned from Europe. She and Melinda went together to Sam's resting place. Melinda hung back as Sari approached her father's grave and spoke to him in a loud, firm voice, "God, Sam! Why did you do such a terrible thing?"

Melinda backed farther away. She couldn't bear to listen to the pain.

Sari and she returned to the house on Sladesferry Landing and talked for a long time. Melinda told her everything. Every move Sam had made, every word he'd said, since the night of the fire.

Melinda shook her head in despair. "Why didn't I see the love, Sari? Why didn't I feel his loneliness?"

"Because he hid them from you. He didn't want you to know. I've never told you this, but in so many ways you've been like a mother to me. I grew up with you being held up as a model. So often Sam said: 'Try to be more of a lady, Sari. Try to be like Melinda.'"

She was talking too loud and too fast.

"Slow down, Sari, no need to hurry. No need to hurry anymore."

"Sam was right. You're one terrific lady. But I could never be like you. There's too much of Sam Miroff in me for that to ever happen."

After a long pause, Melinda asked, "What will you do now, dear?"

"When I was in Vienna last year, I met a man. His name is Erich Palmor. He's a flutist with the Vienna Symphony. When I saw him this last time, he asked me to marry him. When I get back to Vienna, I'm going to say 'yes.' There's nothing left for me here, Melinda."

"Do you love him, Sari?"

"Yes, I do. Not in the way I loved Marc. That was youth—passion and fire, and I wouldn't have missed it for anything. I love Erich in a less ardent, more comfortable way. A better love ... perhaps a more lasting love. Who knows?"

"Shouldn't you wait, dear? Give yourself more time to get

over this?"

"No, I don't think so. You see, I'd pretty much decided to do this anyway. It's taken a long time, but I think I finally know what I want out of life. I want a husband, a home, babies. All the things that I thought were so corny before. Dress designing is a great career and I'll go back to it someday, but it doesn't keep you warm in your old age, Melinda. Your children do."

Sari stood and picked up her purse. Starting to the door, she stopped and turned to Melinda. "Erich wants to teach. He's had an offer from Hebrew University in Jerusalem. More than anything, I want to go there with him." Sari walked back to the center of the room. "I'm sorry you won't be at my wedding, Melinda. I'll miss you. ... I'll miss you both."

Melinda rushed up and put her arms around her. She heard Sari whisper "I love you."

Then she was gone.

Chapter Forty-Two

Not having to get up in the morning was a luxury Melinda had never experienced, not even in childhood. Her body couldn't seem to accept the fact that rising before dawn was no longer a necessity. It was primed to activate at about 5:30 A.M. and continued to do so with annoying regularity.

Time lay heavily on Melinda's hands. She did the many things she'd never had time to do before, but still she didn't fill the hours in her day. She read the books she'd always wanted to read, and went back to doing needlework; she knitted for her grandchildren; she even went back into the kitchen. Costanza looked on with a jaundiced eye hoping that it was just a passing fancy.

Three weeks after Sam's funeral, Alex came by to discuss the insurance settlement and to inform her of the reading of Sam's will.

"Why do I have to be there, Alex?"

"You were a part of the business, Melinda. Don't worry about it, it's all pretty cut and dried."

* * *

Sam Miroff had amassed a fortune in the last twenty years. Even he didn't really know his own worth. Under Alex's guidance, he'd made solid investments and had reaped a bountiful harvest. But money wasn't the thing with Sam. The work was. Today it would be made known who would enjoy the fruits of Sam's success:

To my daughter Sarah, who's been a source of much pride to me in my lifetime, I bequeath half of my estate, with the hope that her generous but sometimes frivolous nature will not cause her to dissipate this gift in anything but a meaningful way.

To Alexander Friedman, I leave one fourth of the remaining half. Not because he needs it, by any stretch of the imagination, but as a reflection of my deep respect for him, and for the help that he gave to me in the beginning, when there was nothing.

The remainder of my estate I leave to Melinda Durand, who was with me almost from the very beginning: who sewed for me at night in her kitchen; and without whose enormous talents the business that became Miroff and Friedman Manufacturing, would never have been. I hope I can finally feel that she has been paid enough.

To the aforementioned in this document, I give my heartfelt thanks for a lifetime of faith in me, and for their loyalty to our company. Carry on!

Signed: Samuel Aaron Miroff, on this, the seventh day of January, in the year of our Lord, 1916.

Shalom!!

* * *

Holding on to Marc's arm, Melinda left the boardroom and took the elevator down to the street. The air was fresh after an early morning shower and everything around her seemed to have taken on a brand new look. She felt an energy inside her she had not felt since Sam's death.

Riding next to Marc in the car, Melinda looked around at the city. The war had given it stimulus and, as Sam always said, "Life goes on."

"Can we drive past the plant, Marc? I'd like to see what it looks like down there."

Marc turned down Bank Street and went left on Main-crossing Road. As soon as they reached Central Avenue, Melinda could see the ruins of their building amidst the wreckage around it. All that remained were half-collapsed walls looking for all the world like a misshapen vertebrate, its entrails twisted and charred into unrecognizable refuse.

Getting out of the car, Melinda paused momentarily before slowly walking through it.

Pieces of their machinery lay half buried under the piles of rubble.

Marc walked alongside her. "Be careful, Mama, the area is overrun with vermin."

Her eyes cast downward, Melinda chose her way carefully. Suddenly, out of the corner of her eye, she spotted something sticking up from under a heap of charred bricks. Stooping, she heaved some of them aside. Lying beneath was the sign that for all these years had hung over their door. She could only see a part of it, but miraculously, it seemed to be intact.

Melinda turned to her son. "I want that sign, Marc. Can you hire someone to bring it to me?"

"Of course, Mama. I'll do it tomorrow."

After looking around a few minutes longer, Melinda walked back to the car.

On the way home Melinda kept hearing the voice of the lawyer who'd read the will to them. "Carry on," he'd read in his resounding young baritone. Now—after finding the sign—Sam's final words seemed to take on a deeper meaning.

Again and again she heard the words, but it was Sam's voice she heard now, not the lawyer's. Could she? Did she have the energy and the fight to start all over again?

Seated in her parlor, Melinda drank a glass of sherry. Putting the glass down, she went to the telephone and gave the operator Alex Friedman's number.

"I need your help again, Alex."

"I'm here for you, always, you know that."

"Is tomorrow morning convenient?"

"Tomorrow is fine."

* * *

The cabbie honked his horn. Umbrella in hand, Melinda hurried from the house. Fifteen minutes later, Alex leaned back in his chair and looked at her from across the big desk.

"What's going on in that head of yours, Melinda?"

"Alex, I want you to help me open again. I want M and F to go on." She waited for some kind of reaction but got none. "What I need to know is whether or not the money Sam left me, plus my share of the insurance, is enough to get started again."

Alex lowered his head and grinned. "I think it's more than enough, Melinda, but I'd have to put things down on paper before I can tell you for certain. It would depend on a number of things."

"What things?"

"I'd have to have some idea of how big you wanted to be. There's also the question of product. What kind of quality you're after and so on. You can go in a lot of different directions nowadays."

"I want it to be as close to what we had as possible. Smaller if necessary, but no compromising on quality. Sam would have hated that. I'd also like to get Angelica back, and as many of our women as possible."

"What about your old partner? Do you want him back too?"

His question startled her—until she realized he wasn't talking about Sam.

"If you truly feel that you'd want to, Alex, I'd dearly love to have you."

He stood and extended his hand. "I think we're back in business, Melinda."

Knowing it would be a long time before the old property was cleared of debris and a new building could be constructed, Alex scoured the city for the best piece of available real estate he could find. Ironically, he found it on Bedfordgate, less that three blocks from where Sam had first started. It was a two-story building once used as a foundry, now up for sale since the former owners had moved into larger quarters. It had a new heating system, and room for offices on the second floor. After walking through it, Melinda agreed that it was ideal for their purpose.

Alex contacted Solly in New York, and together they came up with a deal on equipment.

Angelica, the best floor lady in the city, was lured away from her new employer, and she in turn got in touch with some of "the girls."

Harry Paulson, a young man from Providence who'd, coincidentally, known Sari at Amery, answered Melinda's ad in the *Journal*. After submitting his portfolio, he was hired to do their designing.

Melinda wrote to New York, Vienna and Rome, contacting Sari's connections and in less than a month, fabric samples began arriving at Melinda's home. Thirty years of working with Sam Miroff had paid off. He'd taught her everything she needed to know—and then some. Each day the dream came closer to becoming a reality. Each day Melinda's heart beat a little faster.

* * *

Two days preceding their opening, Melinda called on the craftsman who'd repaired their sign. She gave him the new address and asked him to deliver it there the following morning. She asked Alex to be there too.

It wasn't as nice a day as Melinda had hoped; it was cloudy and cold for early September. Rain threatened as she and Alex stood watching Mr. Smith drive in the last bolt that secured the sign to the building. It hung above the door, just where Sam would have wanted it. The new gold lettering gleamed against the black background. If anything, it was more handsome than it had been when Sam first had it made. When Mr. Smith had finished and gone, Melinda looked straight ahead at the sign.

Her voice was strong and steady when she asked, "Well, Sam, how do you like the new shop?" Melinda gripped Alex's hand tightly as she went on to say, "We'll try to run it as you would have, Sam. And you'll be with us, always, guiding our hands. Shalom, my friend ... until we meet again."

Alex and she walked into the building together, still holding onto each other's hand.

Chapter Forty-Three

Monsignor Bérard walked across the wide expanse of lawn toward the faculty quarters. He was still a straight, handsome man, his snow-white hair and sixty-five years notwithstanding.

Monsignor had not seen his nephew since he'd returned from a visit with his family in Riverton. Normally, the director of Saint Charles wouldn't seek out a member of his staff in this manner, but he couldn't wait another minute to hear the news.

He rapped at his nephew's door a touch more firmly than he'd intended.

Opening it, Philippe stood, rather wide-eyed, looking at his uncle. "Monsignor! Come in—please."

"Good afternoon, Father." Entering the room with a flourish, Monsignor greeted Philippe with a grin. "I thought that since the mountain hadn't come to Mohammed, Mohammed would come to the mountain." He walked across the room and seated himself on the studio sofa.

"I'm sorry, sir. I've been busy with a number of things since I got back yesterday. I had hoped to—"

"I know, I know. I'm overeager. Pay no attention at all." Leaning forward almost on the edge of his seat, Monsignor asked, "How did you find everyone? How is your mother, my boy?"

"She's very well, sir. Up to her ears in the new business. For a woman her age, she's outstanding."

"Age has nothing to do with it, my boy. She's a Bérard, and we're fighters." He paused, adding, "Aren't we?"

"Yes, sir, I guess we are."

Two months previous, Philippe had returned here from Montreal, to his former post at Saint Charles. Monsignor Bérard had greeted him on his arrival, elated in the knowledge that his nephew was fit as a fiddle again, but knowing as well that a part of the man who'd left here to go to Nicolet would never return again. That part of Philippe Durand had died on the blood-soaked battlefields of Flanders.

Although somewhat fragile, Philippe was nonetheless able to look ahead with some degree of confidence to the challenges of the future. He'd fought his battles and exorcized his demons, and was eager to get on with his life again.

After handing Monsignor a packet of photographs, Philippe seated himself next to his uncle. As the elderly gentleman looked at them, Philippe gave him a detailed account of his visit, enjoying the twinkle that appeared now and again in his eyes, as Philippe recounted the antics of his nephews.

"Catherine has her work cut out for her," Monsignor commented with a chuckle.

Philippe nodded. "She calls her boys the 'Katzenjammer Kids.'"

"Oh my! How delightful!" Monsignor chuckled again.

"They're a handful all right, but she obviously enjoys children. They're expecting another after the first of the year."

This time Monsignor made a poker face. "And you, my boy," he asked after hesitating a bit, "how are things with you?"

"Everything is going well, Monsignor. I'm anxious for the fall semester to begin."

"I was sure you would be," Monsignor agreed, his light-hearted mood ebbing away. His eyes searched Philippe's for a long moment. "I'm afraid I'm the bearer of sad tidings, Philippe. Augustin Tullie died while you were in Riverton."

Philippe felt something inside him lurch. "His heart?"

Monsignor nodded slowly. "It was quick, a good death."

Both reflected inwardly for a while.

"Saint Basil's needs a new pastor, Philippe. I wondered how you would feel about going up there?"

There followed a long hesitation. "I'll do whatever the diocese wishes me to do, Monsignor."

"I'm not concerned about what anyone wishes. There are others who can fill the bill. I simply wanted you to be the first to be offered Saint Basil's. It's yours—but only if you want it. Otherwise you can remain here and go on with your teaching."

Philippe looked at his uncle, not knowing how to answer.

"There's a little time," Monsignor assured him. "We have Father Vasconcellos up there now. Think about it for a few days before you decide."

Monsignor left soon thereafter. Walking to the window seat, Philippe picked up the letter from Paul he'd been reading when his uncle arrived. He started from the beginning again.

Rome,
July 27th, 1918

Dear Phil,

The Holy City is incredible! I love living here. I can hardly wait for you to visit; there's so much that I want to show you. The Catacombs. the Basilicas; the Via Appia; and of course, the Vatican itself. Everything tends to take one back to those who paved the way centuries ago. I feel as though I'm walking in the paths walked by Peter and Paul. I am inspired and awed at every turn in the road. There is no greater way to reaffirm one's faith than to be in the places where they have been. I understand now what you meant when you said 'big city' priests sometimes lose touch with what it's all about.

I was delighted to receive your letter from Sherbrooke. Saint Charles has always been a good place to be. I hope you are pleased with your assignment.

Can you believe that I'm working in the office of the Papal Nuncio? It's a revelation, I assure you. It's also a very exciting time for me. Five years here will give me a dimension that I otherwise would never have had.

If you get to Montreal, Phil, please look in on my mother. She's so fond of you. Since your long stay with her after leaving Misericordia, she thinks of you as another son. And don't be stingy with your letters. I truly need to hear from you— often.

Best wishes for the future,

Love,
Paul

Philippe turned his head and looked out the window. Paul—in Rome! The diocese was grooming him for big things. Philippe was sure of it.

So much had changed, yet here at Saint Charles everything was the same. The red tiled roofs, the church spires, the tree-shaded grounds all looked exactly as they had when Philippe had first come here. Time had stood still in this place; only the faces of the boys were different. Except for going to Saint Basil's and later, to war, Saint Charles had truly encompassed the whole of Philippe's life. He loved it here, with a deep, meaningful love. The way one but seldom cares about something.

It would be hard for him to leave it ... again.

Chapter Forty-Four

Stepping down from the train, Father Durand's eyes turned in the direction of the little station house. It had been repainted, but as usual it was deserted. Picking up his valise, Philippe began walking down the road toward the village. About halfway there he noticed something up ahead in the distance raising a cloud of dust. In a few moments he recognized the gelding. He stopped and waited for the buggy to reach him.

Coming to a halt at the side of the road, Pierre Boucher jumped down and came toward him, his crooked smile twisting his face, his hand reaching out. "Welcome home, Father," he said. "Let me take that suitcase for you."

"Pierre! This is a surprise! How good of you to take the time from your work."

"It's nothing, mon Père, things are slow at the mill nowadays."

"How is madame?"

"Bien, merçi—très bien. She's a memêre now, you know."

"That's wonderful news. A boy or a girl?"

"A boy, mon Père. A big, husky boy. My grandson will make a good lumberman one of these days."

Coming into the village, it was easy to see that nothing had changed here either: The low houses clustered together around the church like little children hugging their mothers' skirts. The roofs needed mending before the winter snows arrived and the barns went wanting for a coat of whitewash.

Stepping down from the carriage, a flash of black caught Philippe's eye. Lago, in a frenzy of joy, ran back and forth along the stone wall, his tail whipping about menacingly. Philippe whistled through his teeth. The animal rushed to him, his graying muzzle looking for all the world as if it were smiling.

"Good boy, Lago, good boy."

They walked up to the door, the dog pushing ahead, wanting to lead the way into the rectory. Philippe stood for a minute before going in, looking at the sign that was nailed to the house.

Presbytère: Philippe J. Durand, O.S.D., Pastor.

Turning to Pierre, Philippe smiled. "That was nice of you, Pierre, thank you."

"Pas du tout, mon Père, pas du tout."

Entering the rectory, Marguerite Boucher welcomed him with a hug. "I prayed dey would send you, mon Père. Father Vasconcellos, 'e's a nice man, but I can't understand a word dat 'e says."

Philippe grinned to himself as he followed her up the stairs. Reaching the top, he turned to the left in the direction of his former room.

"Dis way, Father," Madame Boucher reminded him, opening the door to the pastor's bedroom.

Philippe turned and walked inside.

"I made dese new curtains for you, mon Père, I 'ope you like dem."

"I do, madame, I do. They're very cheerful."

"Well, if dey is nothing more I can do for you, I'll go down and start de supper. I'm making de chicken you like so much." She closed the door quietly behind her.

Philippe opened his bag and carried some things over to the dresser. Suddenly a shiver passed through him. There on the top of it stood Dionne Caron's beloved figurine: the white and gold ballerina.

Alongside it was an envelope addressed in his name. He opened it.

Dear Father,

Needless to say, we are most happy to welcome you back to Nicolet. I was at Mass at Saint Basil's last Sunday when it was announced, and it warmed my heart to see how pleased the people were to hear that you were returning.

By now you've seen the figurine I brought to the rectory and no doubt you have questions. I'll try to answer them.

Dionne loved this piece above all others in her collection. She often took it from the shelf and held it to her. It had some sort of symbolism attached to it that I never understood but, as I said before, she cherished it. I want you to have it, Father.

When Dionne wrote me from Bruges, your name was often mentioned. I deduced that you and she shared something very special.

There are a number of things I would like to discuss with you, Father Durand, the most important of them being a trust fund that has been established for Saint Basil's in my daughter's memory. It is a large amount of money and I can't give you the details in this letter.

We are anxious to receive you whenever you are settled and able to spare us the time.

> *Sincerely and with affection,*
> *Monique Caron*

Philippe took the figurine into his hand. He held it to his chest for a long time. In a way, he felt that a part of Dionne had rejoined him. Even in death she was beside him, caring for Saint Basil's poor, lifting the burdens from his shoulders.

Replacing the figurine on the dresser, he reached for a sweater and pulled it over his head.

* * *

Passing the kitchen on his way out, Philippe called to Madame Boucher: "I'm going for a walk, madame. I'll be back shortly."

The dried leaves crackled as Philippe walked past the stone wall and down the slope to the cemetery. His step slowed, when for the first time, he saw the giant archangel that stood in front of Augustin Tullie's grave. Pausing, he offered a prayer, then he continued down toward the brook, where he could see the wrought iron enclosure surrounding the Caron's family plot.

Philippe stopped. He breathed deeply, then walked slowly up to where she lay. Kneeling, he touched the lamb at Dionne's feet. His eyes closed, but he did not weep. The time for weeping had passed. Rising, he looked down at the pink marble stone.

DIONNE

She Rests in Peace
Beyond the WinterWind.

Lago nuzzled his pant leg.

Leaning, Philippe scratched him on the head. "Race you home, old fella, race you home."

Published in loving memory of Louise Lajoie Kirby.
It was always her dream to share her stories with others.

1925-2002

Louise Adrienne Lajoie

Louise was born and raised in Fall River, Massachusetts, an old New England mill city. She learned French as her first language. Her primary education was taught in French by nuns from Le Puy, France. In Fall River, they sang "O Canada!" in the morning rather than recite the "Pledge of Allegiance."

Her father Philippe Lajoie was a prominent promoter of Franco-American relationships. He was Canadian born and the editor of the last French daily newspaper in the United States. Her grandmother never learned to speak English with comfort; French culture and language were the tradition at home.

Louise loved the culture and language of Quebec and France. She understood the immigrant experience through her family's history.